HEAVEN'S HELL

Heaven awoke abruptly, snatched from her quiet slumber. She felt her hair being yanked, and her head twisted painfully to one side. She looked up into the eyes of the Gnelf Master whose fist was tangled in her hair. He bent toward her, his leering face only a few inches from her own.

"'Lo, girly," he said through his grin. "Want me to rip you inside out?"

"No!"

"Want us to rip your momma inside out?"

"Nooooo!"

With his free hand he brought his sickle around and raked it across the pillow at Heaven's side. The fabric split open with a harsh, ripping sound and the tip of the blade plunged into the pillow. As he yanked the sickle upward, the pillow burst open, small feathers spraying into the air in a sudden white cloud.

"That could have been you," he said.

GNELFS

SIDNEY WILLIAMS

PINNACLE BOOKS
WINDSOR PUBLISHING CORP.

Also by Sidney Williams:
Azarius
Night Brothers
Blood Hunter

PINNACLE BOOKS

are published by

Windsor Publishing Corp.
475 Park Avenue South
New York, NY 10016

First printing: September, 1991

Printed in the United States of America

For Ann,
who rescued me from the slush pile.

Chapter 1

Heaven's scream pierced the night, cutting like a razor through Gabrielle's REM stage of sleep.

Throwing back the covers, Gabrielle jumped from bed and thundered down the hallway, moving as fast as she could toward the sound. A thousand horrible things flashed through her mind as the short corridor seemed to stretch on for an eternity. Her legs moved in slow motion, her feet bogging down in the thick pile of the carpet. It was impossible to lift them fast enough. She felt the beat of her heart in her throat, and another cry pierced the midnight darkness.

"Mommieeeeee."

Her nightgown fluttered around her as she ran, and she imagined its resistance was slowing her down, cutting away precious seconds that might mean the difference between her daughter's life and death.

Why had she let her sleep in her own room? There was no reason for that now. If Heaven had been only the space of a bed away instead of at the end of the hall there would be no need to run a gauntlet to rescue her.

If Gabrielle could provide a rescue. What if some child molester or other criminal had somehow found a way into the room? Gab had no weapon, no means of defense. She would have to throw herself on the attacker in an effort to drag him away from her baby.

With lungs heaving and heart accelerating like a racing car, she reached the bedroom doorway and shoved the door back hard, sending it crashing against the wall.

Her hand scratched up the Sheetrock, fumbling for the light switch. A sudden white blaze flooded the room as Gab dashed toward the small canopied bed.

The child sat at the head of it, huddling between the pillows and clutching the covers about her like a shield. Even her snow white teddy bear had been discarded in her fear. He lay at the edge of the bed, head precariously dipping over the side of the mattress.

Tears were streaming down the four-year-old's—five in another month—cheeks, and as Gabrielle embraced her, she felt the child's body tremble.

"What's wrong, honey?" She whispered gently, rocking slightly as she pressed Heaven's small body against her. "I'm here. Mommy's here. Are you hurt?"

"They wanted to get me, Mommy?"

"Who?" Gab's eyes turned quickly to the window, but it was closed and the latch was in place. A quick glance around the room revealed no signs of intrusion elsewhere either.

"The Gnelfs," Heaven sobbed. "Gnelf Master and his people. They had pitchforks and things."

Gabrielle cradled her daughter in her arms, gently touching her hair. She wanted to laugh as relief swept over her. Her heart slowed, her lungs relaxed, and the tingling fear that had danced through her entire body like an electrical charge subsided.

A dream, Heaven had had a bad dream, nothing more. No one had come to harm her, no intruder had threatened to take away her childhood or her innocence with twisted assaults.

"It's okay, baby," she soothed. "You had a nightmare. That's all. The Gnelfs are your friends."

The bedtime story, evidently the last thing on Heaven's mind, had mingled with the second helping of spaghetti she had demanded at supper, and had turned into a horror show.

The friendly nomadic band of the half-gnome/half-elf figures known as Gnelfs—soft *g* and silent as Gab kept pointing out to Heaven—had changed from beloved childhood figures to creatures of terror.

Having her afraid of them wouldn't be all bad, though, Gab thought. The merchandising connected with the popular cartoon was enough to give any single parent nightmares. Stuffed animals, toys, story books, cereals—the whole gamut of tempting items lurked on the store shelves. If Heaven was afraid of them, a fortune could be saved. Aware that it was a cruel thought, Gabrielle dismissed it as she continued to soothe her trembling child.

She couldn't be so selfish as to wish her baby to fear beloved heroes. They were part of childhood! Besides, the stories and cartoons soothed Heaven, and had helped in the last year, Gab hoped, to take her mind off the absence of her father.

In any case, if it wasn't Gnelfs, it would be something equally costly like Rainbow Brite or the Teenage Mutant Ninja . . . whatever they were.

Merchandised toys were just a part of childhood nowadays, and Gab wanted Heaven to have as normal a young life as possible.

When Heaven was at last asleep again, Gabrielle headed back to her own room with the *Gnelfland Bedtime Storybook* tucked under her arm so that her daughter wouldn't wake up and see the cover. She'd expected to let the child sleep with her the rest of the night; but moving Heaven would only wake her up again, better to let her rest alone than risk not getting her back to sleep.

After smoothing the covers over the child, she had also stashed the stuffed Gnelfs behind the other animals on the toy shelf so the child wouldn't roll over and find them glaring at her through the shadows. With luck, the last few hours of the night would be peaceful.

She looked at the book as she walked along the hallway. It wasn't inconceivable that the figures could be frightening to a child. They were green with pointed features and sharp eyebrows. The eyebrows were enough.

Mr. Spock had been frightening to her back in 1965, even though he was the good guy. Some of the artwork in the book was rather dark in nature, also. The Gnelfs wandered through ancient lands and visited odd kingdoms. Their images didn't compare with those of Maurice Sendak—they were more commercialized than that—but they did reflect the newer trends Gab was noticing in children's literature. But hadn't things always been that way? When had they made *Fantasia*?

Well, if the images continued to be a problem, they'd just have to find something else for entertainment. It wouldn't be too hard to find a copy of *Rebecca of Sunnybrook Farm*. She walked into her own room and put the storybook aside.

The bed looked soft and comfortable, but the fear of her daughter being in peril had rattled her so badly she knew she wouldn't be able to sleep again for a while. She turned on the light on her dressing table, then sat down in front of the mirror to brush her hair.

She didn't want to bother doing that in the morning while trying to get Heaven ready and then make it to the office on time.

Once she had taken great care with her dark brown hair, curling it just right with the hot irons. Now she allowed a more unkempt style. She figured there was an outside chance it was attractive that way. By neglect, she had achieved the look teenagers worked so hard for.

As she pulled at the tangles, she went through her regular ritual of checking for wrinkles. She was twenty-nine, still slender, except for a little poundage around the hips that couldn't be helped. Her breasts also were a bit heavier than she would have liked, although some would argue that was no flaw.

Things like those faint lines beside her eyes made her aware of how rapidly years passed. And Heaven was no longer a baby.

It seemed to have taken Gabrielle no time to become a mother, then a divorcee and career woman.

Yet not so long ago she had been in college, falling in love with Dave.

It had all passed faster than a television commercial break, including the experience with Martin last spring, something she had chalked up to her vulnerability.

Dave had not been a bad man, and he had not been a bad husband, but after a time they had realized they were not right for each other. Their interests, their ways of approaching things, even their ways of thinking were different. While many marriages survived such problems, they had decided to move on. He had not wanted to let go, not even when he had realized it was over, but finally he had accepted reality with limited bitterness.

His work had recently taken him out to the West Coast to a better job. He wrote infrequently and sent Heaven cards, but he didn't seem terribly disturbed about the distance. In a way it was almost as if he had never existed, yet Heaven had his blond hair and blue eyes as reminders.

It had been hard the first few months, not just recovering from the feeling of amputation divorce created but getting on her feet again. Finding a decent house to rent at a reasonable cost had seemed impossible. She'd also had to switch jobs. While she was married she had worked for a small commercial art company, but the pay wasn't enough to get by on, not on her own. No alimony was part of the agreement, and the child support Dave did contribute came erratically, so she couldn't continue earning something akin to minimum wage just because she enjoyed what she was doing.

In addition to working in the shop, she'd been doing

the bookkeeping, putting her college business classes to work, so it hadn't been that hard to make the move over to an accounting firm.

Working with payrolls and doing audits didn't have a great deal of appeal for her. She'd wanted to major in English, but her father had warned her about the impracticality of such a degree and she'd wound up in business, struggling through endless hours of economics and management classes.

She'd applied herself and learned the material well, and now, at least from a food-on-the-table standpoint, it was proving useful.

Even if she couldn't say she loved her work, it did allow her to keep Heaven in nice clothes and faddish lunchboxes. What more could she ask?

Maybe there was supposed to be more in life, but she wasn't sure. Love and romance hadn't worked out, yet she had been rewarded for the attempt with Heaven. She could not imagine life without her little girl.

Heaven had been like a little doll at first, something she could dress up and plan for, a tiny little creature for her to nurture. Watching her daughter grow, watching her learn, had been fabulous.

Heaven was always surprising Gabrielle. Her impressions of things, her ideas, her knowledge always seemed to exceed what Gab expected. Television was responsible for some of it, and Heaven had picked up a great deal in play school as well.

She could already recite the alphabet, and would probably rival some first graders in comprehension. Kindergarten should be no problem for her when she started in the fall.

Not intellectually at least. She had a few problems on the social level. That blond hair and those blue eyes were already drawing catty remarks from the other little girls. Gabrielle had never known such things started so early.

She hadn't been beautiful as a child and had never given much thought to beauty being a problem, but apparently it could be.

Perhaps the pressures exerted by the other children were related to the nightmare. The band of Gnelfs might represent Heaven's anxiety about classmates who supposedly were friends but who exhibited contradictory behavior.

She put her brush down. *Thank you, Mrs. Jung.* If the nightmares continued she might have to look into a checkup for Heaven, but that would wait. There was always the possibility things would get better on their own. They usually didn't, but one could always hope.

By morning, all seemed well again. Sunlight streamed in the windows, bringing the bright glow of April, and the day began with the typical routine of a Wednesday morning.

The alarm buzzed at six, and Gab dragged herself from beneath the covers and padded down the hall to rouse a reluctant Heaven, who had apparently dozed soundly for the remainder of the night.

Rubbing her eyes, Heaven moved from her room and into the small bathroom at the end of the hall, making no mention of Gnelfs or anything else.

Good enough, Gab decided. Trusting the child to take care of the basic preparations for school, she moved into the kitchen and began breakfast.

Neither of them had a stomach for much in the morning, but she always insisted Heaven have something to carry her through the day. Chex cereal was the compromise.

Gab always managed to put down her frequent demand for the highly advertised cereals, those with high sugar and marshmallow content. Once in a while she allowed Frosted Flakes, but most of the time that box was kept hidden in the pantry.

Again no mention was made of the Gnelfs when Heaven came to the table. Gab watched her carefully, and asked her a few questions. The child's responses were routine.

The small portable television Dave had bought for Heaven sat on the kitchen counter. Most mornings she asked that it be turned on, but not today. Gab didn't remind her of it. Gnelfs were available on early morning TV, as were other creatures such as talking dinosaurs. Gab had no way of determining what was frightening to children.

She tried to protect Heaven from Freddy Kruger ads, but her daughter seemed to know about werewolves and their ilk. Somehow kids learned about those things, though so far Heaven hadn't been traumatized by them. No, she was being scared to death by benevolent imps.

Of course it was never the things you worried about that scared a child. It was the little things out of left field. One of Gab's friends had a son in grade school. He'd been frightened to death that he was going to be shipped off to a mental hospital because he'd seen some public service ad that warned bad behavior might be an early sign of some disorder. Having recently been punished for misbehaving, he'd believed a mental hospital was the next step.

Mental health commercials or cartoon favorites, the milkman or Uncle Earl; with children, you never knew who your enemy was.

She watched Heaven eating, using her fingers to arrange the cereal squares on her spoon before shoveling them into her mouth. It seemed such an innocent move, and she thought of how much she loved her, how much she wanted to protect her and spare her from pain.

The world is not an easy place for children these days.

The ride to school was also uneventful. Heaven made no mention of Gnelfs, even though she was carrying her official Gnelfs lunch box. When Gab dropped her off, she saw her quickly fall in line with her friend Terry Guillory, who began to chatter and laugh. He was a slightly overweight kid and had whatever type of crush five-year-olds develop on the opposite sex. They were a good pair, really. Heaven thought of him as a friend. While she was quiet and introspective, Terry was quick to expound on his thoughts. Slightly pudgy, with short brown hair and glasses, he was something of an outcast, but he towered over Heaven like a protective giant. Perhaps they are friends because they are both ostracized, Gab thought. Terry was the weird kid, and Heaven was too beautiful. Remarkable how socialization worked.

She patted the dashboard, urging the aging compact station wagon to move onward.

Around noon Gabrielle went to lunch with Katrina Johnson, the receptionist. Katrina was vibrant and witty, and her outspoken opinions always made the meal hour more interesting. And she had two children of her own; Gab wanted to check her thoughts on Heaven.

Although Katrina, the daughter of a local civil-rights attorney, made an effort to seem down-to-earth, she was a keen observer of humanity and the best authority Gab had on what was normal about children's behavior.

"You think the same things scare black babies as scare white babies?" Katrina asked as they sat down at a table in Foster House, an elegant little restaurant with windows overlooking a courtyard. She was exaggerating her accent as she frequently did when she was with Gab. With clients her tone was sleek and precise, just like her appearance. She was unquestionably beautiful with high cheekbones and a cream and coffee complexion. She worked out to keep her lean figure under control, and her hair was always pulled back in a sleek bun.

"Our kids seem to be a lot alike," Gab said, sipping the iced tea the waitress had delivered.

"Maybe so, but I wouldn't worry 'bout Gnelfs or other such hoodoo," Katrina said. "Kids are kids. Stuff scares them."

"I guess I'm just feeling guilty because she was so frightened."

"Like it's your fault she doesn't have a father? You know it's not your fault Dave went to California."

"I know. It's just that it's got to be hard on Heaven, and I'm trying to be sensitive to her problems."

Katrina raised her Diet Coke to her lips, shaking her head as she drank. Her bright red lipstick rubbed off on the straw. "You don't want to treat her too delicate. She'll start expectin' it."

"Maybe you're right."

"Girl, my little monsters are always up to something. I'm always right where kids are concerned."

"I hope so, and I'm not overlooking some deep hidden stress syndrome in her or something."

"Gab, the kid's not even five years old. She's interested in dolls and playing. There're just too many damn books full of ideas that make you worry these days. If we just let babies be babies it'll be all right. If she's scared of those green monstrosities the kids all like, get her some of those books about that French elephant or something." She sipped some more of her drink. "You think you got problems you ought to try to find a black doll in this town. I ought to go to the ordering clerk at Toy World and let him explain to my little girl why she doesn't have a baby doll with skin the same color as hers."

Eventually their sandwiches arrived. The special of the day was turkey on rye bread, and it came with purple cabbage and a sliced dill, creating a beautiful-looking dish if nothing else.

They were finishing the last bites when a silver-haired woman strolled into the room and, noticing Katrina, extended a hand to wave.

"Barbara Richardson," Katrina said. "Dr. Richardson's wife."

"Friends?"
"Clients."
The woman now stood by their table, a broad smile on her face. "How are you doing today, Katrina?"
"Wonderful." The precise tone had arrived, and Gabrielle knew Katrina's forced smile when she saw it.
"I'm glad I ran into you," Mrs. Richardson said. "I wanted to invite you to a function my writing club is sponsoring."
"How nice," Katrina said.
"It's on Saturday morning, at eleven, and you just have to come."
"Well . . ."
"Oh, you'll love it. We have Jake Tanner lined up to read from his new book."
Katrina frowned. "Tanner? Tanner? Where do I know that name?"
"He's the mystery writer that lives in town. He wrote *The Spanish Moss Killings, Tuesday's Alligators* and all those. They aren't best sellers, but they are fairly popular."
"I don't think I'll have time Saturday—"
Mrs. Richardson turned to Gabrielle. "And who's your friend?"
"This is Gabrielle Davis. She works with me."
"Well, that's wonderful. Why don't you come along, dear?"
Gab gave her a nervous smile. "Actually it sounds interesting. I've always liked books."
"Have you read any of Mr. Tanner's?"
"I'm afraid not. I haven't even heard of them."
"That's no problem. You can pick one up at the Book Palace. I'm sure he'd be glad to autograph it for you. He's a wonderful young man."
"I see," Gab said.
"We meet at the library. Just join us."
She turned and fluttered from the room.

"Social butterfly strikes again," Katrina said, returning to her other tone.

"She seemed nice enough," Gab said.

"She is, really," Katrina conceded. "I just tend to get tired hearing about her writing. She wants to do romances, but she's not really very good. That poor writer is probably going to wind up reading some thousand-page epic she's working on."

"I think I'd like to go," Gab said. "I didn't know we had a writers' club—or any writers around here."

"I forgot. You're the paperback queen."

Gab usually had a book in her purse, and that qualified her as an avid reader in Katrina's eyes. Katrina read Danielle Steel almost exclusively.

Most of Gab's books came from used shops of late since books were low on the necessity list, but she had always harbored something of a desire to write.

Maybe slipping out to the meeting would be good for her. She had been somewhat reclusive since the divorce, pleading Heaven as an alibi when she was invited to parties or other activities.

Finding a place for Heaven to spend a little time on Saturday shouldn't be a big problem. If Katrina didn't want to go she'd take care of her. Provided Heaven wasn't showing any more signs of being upset.

Heaven sat with Terry on the bench at the edge of the playroom, a broad space akin to a gymnasium. Black electrical tape had been stretched out on the floor to designate various play areas, and several different games were going on. But as usual Terry and Heaven had been excluded.

Some bright orange blocks were around them, but they didn't do much with them. Heaven had been quiet all morning, and Terry had not protested. He was always tolerant of Heaven's moods, even when she withdrew almost totally.

She was his only real friend. The boys teased him about being friends with a girl, but they teased him anyway so he ignored the taunts. He had perceived that all of them thought Heaven was pretty, and it seemed that by paying attention to him, she afforded him what little respect he got from the others.

Halfheartedly he placed one block on top of the other while Heaven cradled her doll, silently rocking it.

Before long they would have lunch, then a nap, and that would kill some of the time until he could go home and get back to his coloring books.

"Terry," Heaven said unexpectedly.

He looked up, surprised she was speaking. "What?"

A slight frown marred her brow, and she continued to sway the doll back and forth in her arms. "Do you think the Gnelfs would hurt anybody?"

He laughed. "Of course not. The Gnelfs are good guys. Didn't you see the one where the dragon had the teddy bears trapped in a cave, and they uncorked the waterfall and put out his fire breath?" He extended his hands, making broad gestures as his excitement grew.

He went on for several seconds before he realized Heaven wasn't paying much attention to his synopsis. She was lost in her own thoughts again.

His mother kept telling him he shouldn't get carried away and tell people about shows, but sometimes his enthusiasm overwhelmed his judgment.

"I had a dream about the Gnelfs," she said after he had hushed.

"Really?" His face brightened, eyebrows shooting up and cheeks curling to form dimples.

"It was bad," Heaven said.

"How could it be bad if it was about the Gnelfs?"

"They were mean."

"Ah-uh. Not the Gnelfs." He shook his head.

"They looked like the Gnelfs, and they laughed at me, just like the kids did when I tripped on the pencil."

"Gnelfs wouldn't do that," Terry said defensively.

"Well, they did it," Heaven said. "And they said bad things about Mommy."

"They were green?"

"I guess. Gnelf Master was there, and he had a big pitchfork. He said I was a bad girl and that he ought to use it on me. Then he said I was bad because Mommy was bad and I was her daughter. He even called Mommy a bad word I think."

"What was that?" The thought of a forbidden profanity struck him as exciting.

Heaven sniffled, combatting a sob. "He said . . . he said she was a bitch." A single tear trickled from the corner of her eye before she got herself under control.

"That is a bad word. They said it on a show on HBO and Mama turned it off," Terry said.

"What's it mean?"

"A bad woman."

"That's scary," Heaven said, tears flowing now. "In the dream, Gnelf Master said 'bitches must suffer.'"

Chapter 2

Heaven reported no nightmares the rest of the week, and although she seemed a bit quiet and introverted, Gabrielle considered her behavior normal for a four-year-old. Children couldn't be happy all the time, and Heaven was probably still confused about the divorce.

By Saturday, the child's spirits had brightened. Since the tension had died down, Gabrielle decided it was safe for an outing. Besides, Heaven seemed to like the idea of dropping by and playing with Katrina's children for a little while. Gab dressed her, or helped her dress herself, in lavender slacks and a striped, pullover blouse with long sleeves. It was spring, but there was still a chill in the air. With the Velcro straps on her shoes sealed into place, Heaven bounced about the house as they prepared to leave, more energetic than she had been in days. Her hair fluttered about her head as she twisted and twirled her arms.

They took no Gnelf icons along.

Gab buckled her daughter into the front seat and drove over to Katrina's while engaging Heaven in a sing-along to keep her from resisting the seat belt too much. Only a recent graduate of car seats, Heaven had at first rejoiced at the opportunity to be more grown-up, but she was known to complain of discomfort and attempt to subvert the belt by loosening it until there was enough slack to provide freedom of movement. That freedom might also send her crashing through the window if a sudden stop was necessary, Gab frequently reminded herself.

Today Heaven was content as they rattled off tunes from the album they'd ordered from the ad on "Nickelodeon." The day was bright and clear with golden sunshine, and for the first time in several months Gabrielle allowed herself to wonder about happiness. Maybe she really was getting things back together. She was going out, doing something that interested her, which was a change from the way things had been lately. She'd devoted most of her attention to her job and to Heaven with little thought to other activities.

Her devotion to Heaven was complete and without question, but it couldn't be good for either of them to hibernate together. She didn't want Heaven growing up a recluse.

Katrina lived in a quiet residential section which consisted mostly of small brick houses with neatly trimmed lawns.

Once upon a time it might have been a neighborhood which would not have welcomed blacks, but at least in this part of town that sort of thing was not a problem.

No FOR SALE signs had sprung up when they'd moved in, Katrina had observed. Her husband had a job with the city and wore business suits most of the time. She sometimes speculated that that and their quiet habits kept many of their neighbors content. "Maybe we'll have a domestic argument and throw a few pots and pans just so they won't be disappointed," she said once. "Then they can say, 'Well, it's colored folk.'"

Harris, her husband, was working in the front yard when Gab pulled into the driveway. He had traded in his suit for jeans and a polo shirt that morning, but she felt there was no concealing the fact that he was an accountant.

"So you're going to hear the mystery writer speak?" he said as Gab helped Heaven from the car and they pulled some of her toys from the front seat.

"That's right."

"We'll take good care of Heaven," he said. "It's such a pretty day we thought we'd grill hot dogs outside." He squatted in front of the little girl so that he could look into her face. "Does that sound good?"

"Yes," she said, smiling and chewing on the finger tucked in the corner of her mouth.

"Say hello to Mr. Johnson," Gabrielle urged.

"Hello."

They walked to the front steps and Harris opened the door for them to enter.

The children were in the living room, watching television. Carl Matthew, who was six, and a miniature version of his father *sans* beard, sat on the floor with an assortment of toys spread around him. Seeing the visitors, he got up and stood slightly behind his father, peering around Harris's legs curiously. He recognized the visitors, but he was uncomfortable, a bit shy it seemed.

Matissa, the baby, was smearing crayons across the pages of a coloring book. She looked up proudly from her work, her smile revealing gums through which teeth were just beginning to make their way.

Katrina walked into the room, drying her hands on a dish towel, and also offered Heaven a bright smile.

"Hi, honey."

"Hi, Miss K'tina," Heaven said, still chewing on the finger. She was a bit flustered by the attention, and she rarely said Katrina's name successfully.

"We're gonna have a good time today," Katrina said. "It's Saturday. We can watch cartoons and play. Does that sound like fun?"

"Uh-huh."

"Yes, ma'am," Gabrielle reminded her.

"I'm sorry."

Katrina winked at Heaven. "It's okay."

Gab handed over the toys they'd brought along. "You have the number at the library, where I'll be?"

"By the phone," Katrina said. "It's all going to be fine. You go have as much fun as you can, listening to a literary reading."

Gabrielle smiled. "I'm just trying to get out a little."

"Be good for you. Hustle or you gonna be late."

Pausing only to bend and give Heaven a final kiss and warn her to behave, Gabrielle headed for the door.

"I'll be back by one at the latest."

"Fine, go," Katrina admonished. "Now."

Gab grinned. "Got you."

As she departed, the kids settled down in the living room to watch "Scooby Doo." Leaving them occupied with that, Katrina went back to her work in the kitchen, while Harris settled down to look over some forms he'd brought home from the office.

For a half-hour, things were quiet. Then Carl Matthew's voice peaked out at the highest decibel a six-year-old's vocal cords could muster.

"But we always watch 'Gnelfs' on Channel 7 after 'Scooby Doo' goes off," he insisted.

"Don't wanna watch 'Gnelfs,'" Heaven protested, doing a fair job of amplification herself.

"I'm not gonna change it," Carl Matthew stated.

Katrina pushed through the swinging door to see them standing toe to toe in the center of the room.

Harris, engrossed in his reading, had managed to shut out the racket in the way only a man could.

Matissa also was ignoring the fracas. She was still busy defacing the pages of her coloring book.

"What's going on here?" Katrina demanded.

"She won't watch 'Gnelfs,'" Carl Matthew protested.

With her face turned downward, Heaven continued to shake her head, her brow wrinkled defiantly, her hair swaying back and forth.

Katrina decided to try a diplomatic approach. "Honey,

Heaven had a bad dream about the 'Gnelfs' this week. We don't want to make her watch them if they upset her, do we?"

"You said dreams couldn't hurt anybody," Carl Matthew protested.

"They can be frightening. Why don't we watch something else? There *are* other shows you can watch; we get a hundred channels."

"That's old stuff."

"Carl Matthew, you aren't but six. How can anything be old to you?"

"I want to see 'Gnelfs.' Everybody watches it."

"It's on all the time. On Saturday morning there are other cartoons you can watch."

Shaking her head, Heaven turned from the two of them and ran through the swinging door, into the kitchen.

Harris had finally roused from his work. He followed Katrina after her, and they found her in the center of the kitchen.

She was sobbing, and tiny teardrops already trailed down her cheeks. "I don't wanna watch that show," she cried. "The Gnelfs are mean."

Katrina knelt in front of her and hugged her. "It's all right, baby. We aren't going to watch it."

Heaven gripped Katrina's shoulders and held tight. The child's small body was wracked with trembling.

Lifting her into her arms, Katrina carried her over to the kitchen table where she eased her onto a chair.

"It's going to be okay," she whispered.

Easing back in the chair, Heaven wiped her eyes with the sleeves of her blouse. She was pale.

"Is she doing all right?" Harris asked.

"Oh, she's fine," Katrina said. "Aren't you, big girl? I'd bet you'd like some Kool-Aid."

Heaven wiped her nose softly and nodded. She was still shaken up, but the prospect of Kool-Aid worked wonders in calming her.

Harris followed his wife to the cabinet as she got a glass.

"You think anything's wrong?"

"Not really. Just nervousness. She's in a strange house, with us, her daddy's left her, and she had a bad dream this week. Even rehashing it was scary for her."

"You said Gabrielle was worried about her."

"She's watching every little thing because she's so worried about the scars of divorce," Katrina whispered. "Maybe we'd better keep what's happened between us. It's passed, and I'm afraid Gab would worry herself to death over it just when she's about to get her feet back on the ground."

"You don't think she should know?"

"Maybe I'll mention it later. Let's let her have a good day. She needs one."

"Whatever you think."

She moved past him to the refrigerator and took out a freshly made pitcher of "berryblue" flavored Kool-Aid. She poured a glassful and took it to the table.

Seizing the glass, Heaven quickly swallowed a big gulp.

"See, she's better already," Katrina said.

The meeting room at the library had been recently remodeled in dark paneling that gave it the air of an intimate den. The lighting leaned toward dim, and the carpeting on the floor was thick and soft. Bookshelves lined the walls, filled with volumes being held on request or those awaiting return to other libraries.

Gabrielle wandered in, feeling a bit uncomfortable. She had slipped on her wire-rimmed glasses to drive, and she kept adjusting them as she looked around at the sporadic clusters of people talking and sipping coffee from paper cups.

They all seemed to know each other, but she recognized no one. The woman they had talked to at the restaurant, Mrs. Richardson, was nowhere in sight. She found herself wishing Katrina had come along, wondering if she would have been better off staying at home. More comfortable certainly, safer. She could have slept a little later if Heaven allowed it and then curled up with a book after fixing some breakfast and turning Heaven loose with the cartoons.

She had a stack of romance novels which had been passed on by a friend at the office. She could have spent the day working through them, reading stories about people whose love lives worked out.

She lingered around the door as the chatter from various conversations mingled into a hubbub. She had never been good at breaking ice. If she hadn't been pretty enough to draw some attention in high school, her shyness might have kept her a wallflower.

Even Dave, back in college, had had to be persistent. They'd met while studying in the school library, but he'd had to stalk her through the rows of metal bookshelves for almost an hour before making contact.

She began looking at the faces of the people in the crowd, hoping to sight the Richardson woman so she could approach her and say she was Katrina's friend.

She felt awkward standing around by herself, as if people were noticing her from the corners of their eyes and wondering who she was and why she had invaded their activity.

She was half considering making her way back to her car, thinking of poking around the mall for a while before picking up Heaven. Except she'd confess to Katrina who would give her a lecture. Gab didn't want to hear warnings about hibernation and stagnation.

"Excuse me."

Turning her head, she found herself looking into the face of a young man with sandy hair and blue eyes. He was tall and attractive in his way, with a squared chin.

"I'm looking for Mrs. Webster. Do you know which one she is?"

"I'm afraid I'm lost too," Gabrielle said. She realized her tone was cool. Her protective mechanism had kicked in, sealing her emotions inside her.

He looked past her at the crowd. "I don't know what she looks like," he said. "I've only spoken with her on the phone."

He adjusted some books he was carrying under one arm and checked his watch. He certainly is tall, Gab thought, and his dress is a little more casual than that of the others.

He wore jeans, tennis shoes, and a leather jacket that hung open to reveal a stylish shirt buttoned to the collar.

"I'm on time," he said. "I guess she's late."

Realization began to sink into Gabrielle's brain. "You're the writer?"

"Uh, yeah. I'm Jake."

"Jake Tanner."

He's just a writer, she reminded herself. No big deal. That is just what he does for a living. He's human, just like anybody at the office or the grocery store. It's not every day you met a writer, though. Books are found in stores or libraries, but the people who write them live far away somewhere. You don't meet them.

"So you're reading this morning," she said, almost wincing at the inadequacy of the statement.

One corner of his mouth twitched, and it was a bit of a relief to realize he was nervous too. "Yeah. I don't know what the people here are going to think of it. I've always thought they were geared more toward literary things."

He held up a copy of *Ellery Queen's Mystery Magazine.* "I guess I'll give them a try," he said. "I finally sold something to EQMM, so maybe it's worthy."

"I'm sorry I haven't read your books yet. But I've heard they're very clever."

"They sell well here since I'm local," he said. "And I guess they move in other places. I'm getting ready to start a series."

"Really."

"My agent has an editor interested. I've been doing paperbacks, but these will be hardbacks."

"That's wonderful." She was trying not to seem phony in her admiration. He couldn't be more than thirty. He must be very determined.

"Uh, I don't, uh, know your name," he said.

She was about to answer him when someone rushed past her.

"There he is. There's our author."

The woman was heavy, and her wavy hairdo would have been at home on a sixteen-year-old's head. On hers it looked out of place. Though past forty, she did some clever things with makeup that were almost effective.

"Mr. Tanner, I'm Delilah Webster."

"My strength is in my hair," he said.

She guffawed and took his arm. "Come this way."

He cast a fleeting glance at Gabrielle before he was dragged into the crowd. People quickly converged around him.

It happens every time, Gab thought. Just when they're breaking ground. Feeling defeated, she took a seat near the back of the room. At least she'd hear him read. That was what she'd come for anyway, not to make any connections. Besides, she'd probably misinterpreted his interest. If she hadn't been rescued she might have embarrassed herself.

There it was again, that feeling of inferiority. No matter how many times she was assured she was pretty, she couldn't shake her insecurities.

Nervously, she smoothed her skirt, wondering if its cut made her look overweight.

After a few more minutes of milling around, they introduced Tanner, and he took his place at the podium. He seemed more at ease at the speaker's stand than he had in conversation. Though she would have died at being in front of a group, for him it seemed natural.

He made a few brief remarks that drew laughs before launching into the story. It was more involved than she had expected, not a straightforward mystery at all. It was told in the first person, that being a young man who encounters a friend and slowly finds out the friend has just murdered his lover.

The ending was chilling, and she found herself literally on the edge of her seat, leaning forward as he read the final words in a quivering voice. The emotion of the story was catching him too.

He closed the cover of the small magazine softly and bowed his head slightly as people in the room began to clap. A slight smile crossed his face now, a sign of the nervousness returning. He was unsure of how to accept the crowd's reaction.

After a few moments, he began to answer questions, queries about publishing, the writing process and the plotting of mystery stories.

These he fielded without discomfort, walking around the side of the podium to lean against it.

Finally the session drew to a close, and a few people tugged out paperback copies of his novels for him to sign.

Gabrielle slipped from her chair and eased out the back door of the meeting room, feeling lost as the crowd formed again.

She was about to climb into her car when she heard his voice again. He was calling out to her.

"I still didn't get your name."

Her palms tingled, and a nervous lump formed in her stomach. Why were these things so difficult?

He walked toward her nervously, his tennis shoes squeaking as they struck the surface of the parking lot.

She introduced herself. "I thought you did a very good job in there," she said.

"They seemed to like it. Maybe I'll sell a few books. At least it gives me a chance to get out a bit. Writers spend a lot of time hovering over their computer terminals. It's a bit monastic."

"The way accountants hover over their ledgers?"

"I guess. You're an accountant?"

She nodded.

"Does your time budget include lunch today?"

The clever approach made her cautious. "I would've thought you'd want to linger in there awhile, basking in admiration."

He laughed. "Not really. They have other business to discuss."

Should she tell him about Heaven? That might immediately scare him off. Which was actually better, she decided. Let him run now if he had a problem.

"I was supposed to pick up my daughter. I guess I could call my friend who's keeping her and let her stay a little longer."

He grinned. "You aren't married, are you? Did I just walk out on another limb?"

"Do authors have problems with lunching with married women?"

"I write stories about murder. I don't want some jealous husband coming after me with a gun."

"My husband's in California, and he's an ex." Gabrielle held up her left hand and wiggled the appropriate finger. "You were right when you checked it."

He grinned, flustered a bit at being caught. Still, she figured it couldn't hurt to let him know she could be clever too.

"There's a phone in the foyer," he said.

"I'll be right back."

He was waiting in his car, an old blue Cutlass convertible. Since the sun was high he'd rolled the top back.

She tossed her purse onto the seat and climbed in beside him, maintaining her tough act for the time being. No need to let all of her secrets be known.

They could lower their shields over lunch. For the moment the war was still on. He was a man after all, and she was a woman. They were natural enemies.

She found herself quivering inside at the thought of

even casual involvement. I should have run to my car, she thought. I could have avoided this.

Things were stable in her life right now. Except for the attention Heaven required, and the occasional anxiety over Heaven's well-being—*was she selfish in that?*—she was comfortable and reluctant to jeopardize her peace by introducing another variable.

Yet as Tanner backed the convertible from the parking slot and pulled onto the street, she made no effort to escape. She'd already proven to herself that men could not control her or destroy her.

Heaven consumed her hot dog without showing any signs of mental confusion or fear. In fact, she performed the task of eating, with single-minded determination. The food disappeared into her mouth in almost magical fashion.

"It was just a remnant of the dream," Harris said. He was standing by Katrina in the kitchen, looking through the opening over the stove. It was a good vantage for observing the children at the dining table.

"Sure hasn't affected her appetite," Katrina agreed.

She walked back to the sink to finish washing the dishes. "Guess that settles it. Gab is having lunch with a nice gentleman, which is the first sign of life she's shown in a while. We definitely don't tell her about the tantrum."

"Agreed," Harris said. "Heaven will probably figure out soon enough that the Gnelfs are harmless."

Chapter 3

Gabrielle enjoyed lunch, which turned out to be pizza, but was reluctant to accept Tanner's offer of a movie that evening. He was pleasant and clever, but there were other things to consider.

For one, she didn't feel right asking Katrina to keep Heaven all day, even though Katrina would be quick to insist on doing so. Also she didn't want Heaven to feel deserted.

One of the things she'd read about the children of divorced parents was that they developed a fear of being left by the remaining parent. She tried not to stay away from Heaven for too long a time in an attempt to alleviate some of that fear, even if it was subconscious, despite Katrina's telling her that she read too many books and magazine articles about psychology.

"Why don't you bring her along with us?" Tanner suggested in a too-good-to-be-true offer that made her entertain for a moment the notion that he might be a pedophile. She knew from her reading that such men often preyed on women who had young children.

That was just one of the ironies to contend with in dating. If you found someone who didn't get scared off by your little one, you had to worry over whether he was interested in her instead of you.

She dismissed that notion, for Tanner had approached

her before knowing she had children.

"What could we do?" she asked. "Movies are pretty much out for a five-year-old."

"She's five?"

"Almost."

"Does she like Chinese food?"

"I don't think she's had it enough times to form an opinion."

"Well, why don't I fix some tonight, and she can decide."

"You cook Chinese food?"

"My mother gave me an electric wok for Christmas, and I'm learning."

"I don't know. Heaven is going to be tired. We usually stay in on Saturdays. Coming to your reading was an extravagance."

"Look, I'll rent some tapes for her. I have a friend at the video store, and I'll ask her to make sure I'm getting something that won't be objectionable."

The car turned into the library lot, and he eased the Cutlass in beside her heap. He didn't kill the motor.

"What do you think?" he asked.

"Persistent, aren't you?"

"Writing is the loneliest profession. When something gets me out into the world I have to make the most of it on a social level."

"Is that a line?"

"No. You're the prettiest girl who ever came to hear me read. That's a line."

"That might work if you keep it up. What time?"

"Seven-thirty?"

"That'll do. Heaven will have time for a nap. Where do you live?"

He gave her a few brief directions, mentioning landmarks, and she nodded. "Seven-thirty, then," she said. "I'll see you."

"I'll have the stir-fry sizzling," he returned.

She slid from his car and was already in the driver's

seat of her own vehicle as he pulled away. Sitting with her hands on the steering wheel, she couldn't keep a smile from her face. If he was a mover, he was a sly one.

But she didn't think he was a mover. There was a chance, perhaps ever so remote, that by some fluke she'd found a nice guy.

At least he was cute and close to her age. If nothing else, he'd made it more than a typical Saturday.

"I send you out to get a little culture, and you come back lookin' like a schoolgirl," Katrina said.

She'd been waiting in ambush when Gab had hit the front door. The questions which had been building since Gab had called to say she'd be a little late all flowed out.

While Harris played with the kids in the back yard, Katrina sat Gab down at the kitchen table for coffee and began to pelt her with questions.

"What's he like?"

"Cute. Pleasant."

"Cute?"

"Yes, cute." She wrinkled her brow. "I guess he's safe."

"Don't go worryin'. I've heard about him around town. If word was out he was an ax murderer or anything I woulda known it. Just 'cause he writes about murderers doesn't mean he is one."

"I just don't know if I want a man in my life right now," Gabrielle confessed. "In some ways I do, but, my God, relationships are complicated these days. I mean I wonder is he going to be nice or is he going to take me for granted? Is he going to be considerate, or is he going to be possessive like Martin?"

"Martin was older, and he had fifties' attitudes about women. This guy is young. He's a sensitive artist."

"That's another thing. Aren't writers strange?"

"How would I know? I live with Arnold the Accountant. Harris can be so normal it's annoying. Look at us, we're more middle-class white bread than some yuppies I know."

Gab smiled. She knew how hard Harris had worked to bring himself out of near poverty, and she knew Katrina respected him for that. She wondered if she would ever find something like what they had.

For some reason, romance had always eluded her. She always wound up with the wrong people, from high school onward. Maybe it was the passive nature she had toward dating. She'd never been given to pursuing men the way her friends had.

Sometimes it became frustrating, seeing relationships that seemed to work for other people.

"Scared aren't you?" Katrina guessed.

"As always."

"It'll work out. Just give him a chance."

"Oh, I will. I always do that. And they always cause me pain."

Rows and rows of brightly colored boxes lined the shelves in the family section of the video store. It was set off from the rest of the shop in a separate room decorated with mobiles and posters of the latest releases.

Tanner browsed over them carefully as Jamie Hyatt stood over his shoulder.

"It's easier helping you pick out *film noir* titles," she said. "Sure you don't want something with Bogart?"

"Not tonight." He picked up a tape entitled *Gnelf Voyages*. The artwork depicted a crew of little green Gnelfs tying off lines on a sailing ship. "Is this good?"

"That's the newest one, where they go sailing to everywhere and encounter pirates and sea monsters."

"Scary?"

"In a kid sort of way. Everybody's renting these things, so I guess they're not too bad."

"Okay. I'll take this one. What else is good?"

"You're in luck. *Noble Gnelfs* is back in. And there's

Journey with the Gnelfs."

He studied the artwork on the covers. In each the little creatures with their scrolls and swords wandered about.

"Gnelfs travel a lot I take it."

"They're nomads."

"Why are these things so popular?"

Jamie shook her head. "They're like *The Hobbit* and everything I guess. They're just in right now. In two months it'll be something else."

"Guess you're right. Wrap these up. I don't want to eat them here."

After debating what to wear, Gabrielle finally opted for jeans and a simple blue blouse with a sweater and scarf. Tanner had been dressed casually for his reading, so he would probably not be overdressed for a quiet evening at home.

Heaven had napped after returning from Katrina's, but her clothing was still fresh so Gab didn't make her change.

After a few brief reminders about behavior, they piled into the car and drove over to Tanner's.

He lived in a rustic-looking house made of redwood lumber. It was situated at the end of a street, tucked back behind some thick old pine trees. With a front porch and shutters, it resembled a mountain cabin, but its appearance seemed to thrill Heaven.

Gab pulled into the driveway and killed the engine before the child had much opportunity to struggle against her safety seat.

The smell of frying vegetables hung in the air when Tanner answered the door. Smiling, he ushered them into his front sitting room.

"This must be Heaven," he said.

"Um-hum."

"Yes, sir," Gabrielle prompted.

"Yes, sir," Heaven echoed.

Her eyes were scanning the room. The interior of the house was a bit rustic also, with dark paneling and various antique lamps and items of furniture.

"This looks like the stuff we saw at the dirty store," Heaven said.

Gabrielle rolled her eyes and tried to keep from blushing. "She's talking about the antique shop," Gabrielle explained. "Sometimes we go to a place I call a junk shop, and she forgets and calls it a dirty store."

"No problem," Tanner said. "I've got something I'll bet you'll like Heaven."

He walked over to the television, which sat against one wall and held up three videotapes.

"They told me at the store these are popular with little girls. Do you like cartoons?"

"Um, er, yessir."

After glancing at her mother to make sure it was all right, she moved across the room to Tanner.

"I got the three newest Gnelf tapes. How does that sound?"

Heaven's mood suddenly became more subdued, but she nodded. "Gnelfs are okay," she whispered.

"Does she not like them?" Tanner asked, looking back at Gab.

"She's really a big fan. She just had a little nightmare about them earlier in the week."

"Oh, I can pick 'em, can't I?"

"It's all right," Heaven said, remembering her mother's admonition to be polite.

"Maybe we'll watch a little later," Gab suggested.

"Maybe," Heaven agreed.

"Well, you can both watch me cook, if you want," Tanner suggested.

"Should be fun," Gab said. "You don't see men engaged in that activity very often."

"It was that or starve."

"It smells good."

"It's the only thing I know how to fix."

They moved through an opening into his kitchen, and he pulled up a chair for Heaven before returning to his efforts at making dinner.

"You really are reasonably proficient at that," Gab said, leaning against the counter.

"I'm better at mystery writing, but I do my best at cooking."

He dumped something onto the wok, sending a spray of smoke toward the ceiling.

"So what's next for you, mysterywise?"

"My series character is going to be a Cajun private eye who works in New Orleans. His name is Gaston, and he was raised in the swamp country before he went to study at Loyola."

"You doing much research?"

"A lot of it I'm drawing from Cajun people I've known. I've been making trips to New Orleans now and then to absorb local color."

"I love New Orleans. The French Quarter is so beautiful."

"It really is."

He finished cooking, and set the food on plates rather than setting the table. Then they moved back into the living room for the meal.

Heaven warmed to Tanner quickly, and she began to laugh when he teased her. Gabrielle found herself beginning to relax too. This was just a preliminary outing, and it was too early to tell overall, but he seemed decent enough.

The fact that he'd been willing to have her bring Heaven along won him points in a couple of areas. First of all it meant he didn't hold the child against her, and secondly it meant he hadn't approached her just to get her into bed. At least she hoped he didn't plan to try that while Heaven was occupied with the videos.

That would make her seriously question his character.

Eventually they did offer Heaven the video opportunity again. She thought it over and seemed a bit reluctant, but she finally nodded. "I guess it'd be good," she said. He had managed to rent tapes she'd been wanting to see for a long time, and that seemed to outweigh her fear.

Gab noticed that she seemed a little pale, but thought perhaps it was best to let her get back on the horse, so to speak. Heaven had loved the Gnelfs so much, Gab hated to see one nightmare alienate her from them.

They fixed her a seat in front of the television, and Tanner put on the *Gnelf Voyages* tape. It flickered on with a bright musical tune as the *Good Ship Gnelfgalley* rolled across the sea. The animation was good, and at the sight of the happy Gnelf crew, Heaven seemed to forget her fears.

Gab helped Tanner carry the plates into the kitchen, and she fell right into the routine of helping him clean up.

"So what are you after from me, Tanner?" she asked.

He grinned and looked over at her from his place at the sink, one eyebrow cocked slightly. "Straightforward, aren't you?"

"I'm just very tired of life," she said. "Games and lines, you know. My marriage didn't work out and I followed that with a bad relationship, so I'm scared these days."

He ran a sponge across one of the plates as water poured down on it from the faucet.

"I didn't really have a major agenda," he confessed. "I just thought you were nice, and it seemed you liked me a little."

"Maybe I did. But I'm nosey as hell. How come you haven't married?"

"Haven't met the right girl. The thing is I'm basically boring once you get to know me. Writing looks glamorous and all that, but it isn't really. The girls I fall in love with always seem to be going somewhere else. Besides, I'm shy."

"You didn't seem that shy with me."

"You were nice to me. Sometimes women look at me,

and it feels like they've got ice in their souls."

She smiled. "Sometimes I think men are the same way."

"No wonder it's so hard for people to get together. They've always got their signals crossed."

They studied each other's eyes for a long stretch of seconds, but they did not move to each other. She didn't want to make the first step—she'd just met him that morning—and she wasn't sure she wanted him to move either. Kissing, petting, Heaven in the next room. She didn't particularly want to be pawed.

Finally she broke eye contact. "It's getting late," she said. "I'd better get Heaven home."

"Wait before you go."

He disappeared for a few moments and returned with one of his books, which he quickly signed: To Gabrielle, best wishes to the girl I met at my reading.

"That's sweet," she said. She closed the cover and moved over to the couch on which Heaven had fallen asleep. Apparently Heaven hadn't been watching the video. She'd probably only allowed it to be put on to be polite. Following orders to make Mommy happy, Gab thought. At least she was trying to give her a fighting chance.

The next sign of trouble didn't come until Sunday evening.

In the early part of the day, Gabrielle had to report to Katrina, who called after returning home from church. She demanded answers and seemed disappointed when the truth proved to be boring.

"I thought this was going to be exciting," she said.

"Maybe next time," Gabrielle said. "The last thing I need to do is rush into something."

After the conversation, she hung up the phone and realized a knot of anxiety had formed in her stomach. She really didn't want to rush into anything, but now she was afraid he might not call again.

"Screwed-up world," she muttered.

She was in the kitchen fixing supper when she heard Heaven scream. The pot she was holding slipped from her fingers, clanging into the sink as she wheeled around and rushed through the swinging door and into the living room.

Heaven was huddled on the couch, her eyes staring into nothingness as she clutched a pillow against her chest, her arms wrapped tightly around it.

She was shivering. Sweat dappled her forehead and had moistened her bangs, pasting them to her scalp. Her face had gone pale, and tremors ran through her small body, making her shudder as if she were having a seizure. And her breathing was too fast, much too fast.

Gabrielle moved toward her, trying to embrace her, but Heaven began to shake her head in a brisk, jerking motion.

"Baby!"

Heaven pulled away from her, scrambling backward across the couch. She was so frightened, she was in shock and didn't recognize Gab.

Reaching forward, Gab grabbed her daughter and pulled her against her own body. The child twisted and fought violently, displaying a strength Gab had never dreamed she possessed. She was so small, yet she was like an animal, wild and struggling for survival.

"Heaven," Gab shouted, almost screaming due to her own hysteria. "It's all right, honey. It's Mommy. It's all right."

Muffled squeaks escaped Heaven's lips as her struggles continued. With her tiny fists, she swung at Gab's back and continued to twist about. Gabrielle was forced to grip her more tightly to keep her from slipping away. She feared Heaven would hurt herself, bump into the hard edge of the coffee table or even charge into the wall.

"Heaven, it's Mommy," she repeated.

"They're after me," Heaven screamed. She drew air

deep into her lungs. "They want to hurt me. They want to kill me."

Gabrielle held her tightly. She could feel Heaven's thundering heartbeat, and hot slashes of breath bounced off Gab's neck.

"Nothing is here," Gabrielle shouted. "Nothing is here."

"The Gnelfs are after me."

"Honey, it must have been another dream. You must have had another nightmare. You dozed off on the couch."

"They want to hurt me. They want to hurt you, Mommy."

Gab felt her fear subside slightly. At least she was calling her Mommy now. Heaven knew who she was. She'd regained some sense of reality.

"Get hold of yourself," Gab said. "There's nothing to be afraid of, baby. Please."

"The Gnelfs. They're after me."

"No, baby." Gab's hands went to Heaven's face. Holding the child's head still, she looked into her eyes. "Listen to me, baby. There's nothing here. You fell asleep and had a bad dream again. The Gnelfs aren't going to hurt you."

Heaven's eyes, like marbles now, were standing out in their sockets. She drew quick gasps of air in through her lips, unwilling to accept her mother's words.

Gabrielle hugged her, pressing her cheek against Heaven's and trying to let the shelter of her arms bring comfort. Heaven clung to her, still trembling, still crying, but slowly she began to calm.

Gab spoke soothing words, assuring her all was well. With her hands, she touched Heaven's hair and caressed her face. For warmth, she pressed her body against the child's, praying things would settle down as she felt her daughter's tiny, rapid heartbeat.

After fixing Heaven some warm milk and getting her into her pajamas and tucked into bed, Gab called Katrina.

"She had another nightmare," Gabrielle said as soon as Katrina was on the line.

"'bout what?"

"Gnelfs again."

"Didn't you say she watched them at what's 'is name's?"

"Yes. She seemed fine over there. Then tonight she blew up. She's gone to sleep again, but I gave her milk. Maybe that will keep her settled."

"She didn't want to watch the Gnelfs when she was over here," Katrina said. "I figured it was because of the dream, and I didn't tell you because I didn't want to worry you."

"So she was still upset about them early Saturday?"

"Evidently."

"That means it's not just that she's feeling threatened by me seeing Jake Tanner. I mean, it crossed my mind that that could be a factor."

"I don't know. Could be she saw the attention she got from you when she had a bad dream, got worried about this guy, and played on it. Kids can be sneaky, even if they don't know they are."

"What about at your house?"

"Don't get angry, but it could have been for attention there too. I mean later she watched the shows because she didn't want you getting aggravated. Now, she's thinking, Mommy has a new man, will she forget about me? Then she dozes off or whatever, and maybe her subconscious reminds her you paid her a lot of mind when she had a nightmare. So she has another one."

"But, Katrina, she was scared to death."

"The fear is real . . . maybe. She could be scared of losing your love. Hell, I'm not a child psychiatrist. Could be we're way off base. Could be something she ate again if she watched them last night without any problems and the dreams kicked in again today."

"What should I do?"

Katrina paused a moment. "Do you have a pastor?"

"No. We were married in the Episcopal church, but we haven't been participating members."

"Let me call my pastor. He can probably recommend somebody you can take her to see. That kind of referral is easiest."

"A psychologist?"

"Possibly. No big deal. But it'll give you peace of mind, won't it?"

"It just feels funny to think about taking her to see a shrink. It's like admitting your child is crazy."

"Not crazy," Katrina said. "Her world has been shaken up. That's a strain. There are things going on in her head she probably isn't even fully aware of. Maybe it's best to have someone help sort them out."

Gabrielle ran a hand back through her hair, pulling locks of it over her ear. "I guess one visit can't hurt. They'll give me time off at the office for that, won't they?"

"They'd better," Katrina said. She was accustomed to standing up for her rights against bosses.

"I guess I'll give it a try," Gab said finally. "Maybe it'll head off trouble."

Although she was wrong, the statement gave her a feeling of optimism.

Chapter 4

The coins fell like raindrops, a shower of glistening metal that tumbled through the darkness in a steady stream. They twirled and turned, end over end, and jangled as they touched, finally clattering down into the palms of two outstretched hands.

The hands quivered with anticipation and were pressed together tightly so that none of the coins would escape.

Coins pooled in them, cold and hard, the smell of metal mingling with the perspiration on the palms to create a sick, stagnant smell.

He sat up abruptly, hands at his sides, supporting him. For a moment he stared forward at the gray wall in front of him, confused and disoriented.

Then, slowly, he stopped shaking, and with one hand he reached up to his face to wipe the sweat from the portions of his cheeks not covered by his thick red beard.

The sheet over him was damp from the sweat that always covered him when he awoke from the dreams. He threw it aside and climbed from the bed, walking naked over to the window.

With a tug of the cord, he opened the slats of the blind slightly so he might look out on the city. It was raining, and the clouds had smeared a grimy gray haze across the sky.

Like tears, raindrops spattered against the glass and

trickled along its cold surface in erratic networks which cast shadows back onto his face and chest. Against his skin they appeared black. Shadows of black teardrops, he thought.

He looked down toward the street, at the rainbow of umbrellas which bobbed along, the people in raincoats. Some of those below attempted to cover their heads with newspapers, which quickly became soaked and looked like wet leaves.

He would not miss the city. Turning, he walked back across the creaking floor of the hotel room and sat down on the mattress. The springs protested his weight as he settled himself and sipped from the water glass that sat on the night table.

The water was room temperature and had a stale taste, but it soothed some of the rot off his tongue. Placing the glass back on the tabletop, he picked up the folded, brittle pages that also rested there.

They had found him again, now that they needed him. He never knew how. Not how they found him or how they knew where or when he should go. It didn't really matter. He was ready.

He would not argue. He looked down at the carefully lettered address on the envelope. It was almost like calligraphy, his name being the single word above the general delivery instruction: DANUBE.

How long had that served as his term of recognition? His name? Names didn't matter anymore. Danube was enough, and it carried as much meaning as a name. The Danube wandered, twisting through many lands. His path had done the same, carrying him around the world so many times. Too many to count, but enough, more than enough.

He was a vagabond. It was a role he had accepted, a role he could not have refused even if he had wanted to do so. He thought often of destiny, of the unfairness of it all, but he did not complain. It could serve no purpose if he did.

Rising from the bed, he walked across the room and into the dingy bathroom, where he showered and performed his toilet in a quick, efficient fashion.

Then he threw his few belongings into the battered black suitcase, saving only the clothes he would wear before throwing the catches into place.

He slipped on the black pants and shirt quickly, took only a moment to dust off the jacket before sliding it over his shoulders. The raincoat crinkled as he put it on, but the wrinkles quickly fell off of it. Last of all, he walked to the mirror and slipped the Roman collar into place.

The minister's office was small with dark carpeting and a Van Gogh reproduction on one wall. A narrow leather couch stretched beneath it.

Some plaques and civic honors decorated the wall behind the metal desk with the imitation wood-grain top.

Behind his desk, the Reverend Richard Marley seemed a bit uncomfortable. In his late thirties he might have looked better in a sweat shirt and jeans than he did in the plaid sports shirt and blazer he wore along with a tie.

Was it in Updike or Cheever Gabrielle had read of a staid old minister who would have looked like he was wearing a tight collar and suit even in his undershirt? She couldn't recall, but Marley was the opposite.

His brown hair was neatly trimmed yet tousled in a boyish fashion, and his eyes were clear blue and piercing. He seemed charming, although Katrina had warned he could go a little toward the deep end if you let him start talking about spiritual matters. He wasn't a fundamentalist, but he tended to take a lot of things literally. On the positive side, however, he had a way of pinpointing kids' problems. That had led to the recommendation by Katrina's pastor.

"So you've been having trouble with Gnelfs?" he asked.

"They keep scaring me," Heaven said meekly, a little

intimidated. Here was another new man being introduced into her life to add to the confusion. Gab was wondering if this was such a good idea.

Marley smiled. "A big girl like you, afraid?"

Heaven nodded. Although Gabrielle had dressed her in pale blue slacks and a brightly colored blouse, her mood remained somber. "They say bad things," the child explained. "They want to hurt me."

The minister remained jovial. "Now, Heaven, you know they can't hurt you."

"They come in my dreams." She went on to tell him how they had marched through her thoughts carrying pitchforks and other weapons.

"Why do you think the Gnelfs would want to hurt you?" Marley asked.

"They're mad at Mommy for some reason, and they know how much Mommy loves me."

Marley chewed on the inside of his lip, thinking that over. "They think it would upset Mommy if they bother you?"

Heaven nodded in the affirmative. "Yes, sir," she said, remembering her mother was beside her.

Marley frowned. "How do you know that, Heaven?"

"They said so. Some of them. Others made fun of me. Like the kids at school sort of. Only meaner."

"They make fun of you at school?"

Gab started to answer, but Marley cocked an eyebrow to silence her. He wanted Heaven's answer.

"Sometimes. They pick on me and stuff."

"Does that bother you?"

"Yes. Yes, sir."

"Do any of the Gnelfs look like the kids at school?"

"No."

With his eyes, Marley indicated to Gabrielle he thought he'd found something but that the line of questioning hadn't paid off.

"Did the Gnelfs say why they're mad at Mommy?"

"No."

"You haven't been mad at Mommy, have you?"

"No!"
"Are you sure?"
"Never mad at Mommy."
"Not even deep down?"
Heaven twisted her head from side to side.
"All right. Do they mention your daddy?"
Again she shook her head, then: "No, sir."
Marley leaned back in his chair. "Are you a good girl?"
"Yes, sir. Always."
"You haven't done anything wrong that you want to tell us about?"
"No. I'm good."
He folded his arms across his chest. "All right then, Heaven. Let me tell you. The Good Lord looks after his children, and I know he's not going to let the Gnelfs hurt you. You just trust in that. I don't want you to be afraid anymore."
Bowing her head slightly, almost sullenly, Heaven nodded. "Okay."
"Good girl. Now why don't you sit outside with Mrs. Simmons while I talk to your mommy?"
"Yes, sir."
"I've never thought the show was frightening or anything," Gabrielle said, once the door had closed. "I am careful about what I let her watch."
The pastor laced his fingers together and considered the dilemma silently. "It's hard to say what will scare kids," he said. "Their imaginations are quite active, and they haven't developed the ability to distinguish between the real and the imagined as you and I have. When I was little I remember being scared by the witch in *Snow White and the Seven Dwarfs* or was it *Sleeping Beauty?* What was her name?"
Gabrielle smiled. "For me it was a movie called *Two on a Guillotine.* Dean Jones was the hero, to give you an idea of how really scary it was."
"I remember it. Cesar Romero is a magician."
"And they bury him in a glass coffin." Gab mocked a

shiver. "Oooo, it got to me."

They laughed. "I don't think such things are really damaging," Marley said.

"Have you ever dealt with any similar problems?"

"People are always concerned about children's programs. They do tend to inject them with New Age philosophies these days, and that concerns some people. Once in a while the ideas reflect concepts from Eastern religions. Symbols turn up that are rather esoteric." He shook his head. "You can never tell what someone is going to protest. I'm very cautious, myself. In spiritual matters it's never good to jump the gun."

"I was just afraid this might be a symptom of something caused by the divorce," Gabrielle confessed.

"Maybe it is," Marley said, shaking his head again. "I can't really get at anything, but I'm not a child psychologist. Give it a couple of days, and I can recommend a counselor who is pretty good with kids if it keeps up. I would say wait a little while to see if it is just a temporary thing. No need to put her through a lot of trauma needlessly."

"I suppose you're right. I appreciate your help."

"Sure. Let me know if there's any further trouble."

"I hope there won't be," she said.

"You're welcome to visit us on Sunday morning."

Gab smiled and nodded, making her way to the door as politely as possible. She collected Heaven in the outer office and took her home.

After dinner they sat in the living room, and Gabrielle read some of *Anne of Green Gables* to Heaven. She'd found it in a box in the storage room, a dog-eared copy she'd had for years. It was something of a compromise. She hoped it wouldn't have elements that proved disturbing. She'd expected it to generate protest, but Heaven was listening without showing discontent or boredom. L. M. Montgomery's story of an orphan held her interest as well as any of the less imaginative modern stories that came her way.

Around seven-thirty, Gab said it was bedtime, and Heaven was bathed and in her pajamas by eight. Gab was sitting in the living room reading the latest Dean R. Koontz novel, which she'd borrowed from Katrina, when the phone rang.

It was Tanner.

"What's going on?" he asked.

A simple enough question, so why did it send that little bolt of fear through her?

Thoughts piled up in a split second. The reasons were multiple. That inbred schoolgirl fear was there. After all, he was a man who interested her. What should she say? What should she do? Then there were the more complex underlying reasons. His call was a threat to her routine. He was change. He was moving her back into a realm from which she had shut herself away. It was easy not to have to worry about a relationship, easy to get through day-to-day living without tension. It could be boring, but it was also comfortable.

Also, there was the matter of being worried about Heaven. What if something serious was developing with her? If so, she would require time and attention. It might be hard to devote time to dating. And letting Tanner into her life might further aggravate Heaven's problems if they were related to the divorce.

After this contemplation, she answered: "Nothing much." As an afterthought, she added, "What about you?"

"I had a productive day I guess. Almost finished a chapter, and I got a letter from *Mystery Scene* magazine. They want me to do a column on my next book. They have a new books' section where authors talk about how they came to write their books."

"Um, that sounds interesting." She'd never heard of *Mystery Scene.*

A brief lull in the conversation followed, one of those long silences that come frequently in phone conversations between people who don't know each other well.

Gab felt the awkwardness of the moment, but she could think of nothing to say. She suspected Tanner was having the same problem on the other end. She was reminded again of schoolgirl feelings, and decided he seemed to be like a shy little boy. Maybe this was a sign that they were well suited for each other.

"How's Heaven doing?" he asked, as if the question had come in a burst of inspiration to end the silence.

"Fine." She was leery of talking about Heaven too much to a man for fear of boring him or scaring him away, but the question gave her something to talk about. For now, just getting past the tension was her goal. Wit and eloquence could come later. "She's having some bad dreams, but she'll get over that. You know kids."

"Yeah. I can remember a few sleepless nights when I was a kid. In fact the ideas for some of my books have come from dreams."

"Really?" He was talking about himself, his work; that was good. Give and take, that was what conversation was supposed to be.

"Dreaming people were trying to kill me, things like that," he explained. "Dreams give you the 'what if,' and you plot from there."

"Heaven's got it in her head that the Gnelfs are after her." She bit her lip. She shouldn't have told him that. Now she'd have to admit—

"I hope the tapes I showed her didn't cause problems."

"She'd seen Gnelfs plenty of times before. I'm sure it wasn't triggered by seeing them at your house. I don't know what has her upset. She'll be all right as soon as they advertise some new Gnelf toy that costs thirty dollars."

"I just picked those up because they said so many kids watch them. The people that produce them apparently put a lot of care into the designs and everything."

She didn't want him to feel that he'd caused any problem. She thought it best to change the subject. What could she talk about? "Are you on schedule with your book?"

"Kind of. Every now and then I have off days. That happens. Sometimes I hit a wall, kind of like a runner."

"I guess writing a novel is like running a marathon."

"It can be."

"It must take discipline."

"I guess you'd call it that. It's just a matter of sitting in the chair every day."

The conversation droned on, nothing spectacular. He was no Oscar Wilde, but he was trying. She felt some of the ice melting.

For a few moments, she let herself entertain a brief fantasy. Heaven's problem would turn out to be minor, and something exciting and romantic would develop with Tanner.

She liked the idea of it even though she knew the little dramas played out in the mind seldom came true. Not the pleasant ones anyway. She'd learned that from experience.

Chapter 5

Katrina expected a report on Heaven when the coffee break rolled around the next morning, and when she learned Tanner had called she demanded an update on that as well.

"What's happenin' here, girl? It sounds like things are looking up."

"Hard to tell."

They sat at one of the four tables in the small shop, sipping from paper cups.

"He's obviously interested," Katrina said.

"I don't know."

"He called, didn't he? Why do people always get so paranoid? Why would he call if he wasn't interested?"

"Maybe he was just being nice. I've got Heaven to think about right now, anyway."

"That's an excuse, and you know it," Katrina said, dumping creamer into her cup. "Heaven is gonna be fine."

"Well, she slept okay last night. No screams in the dark. I thought about putting her in bed with me, if she gets frightened again."

"Don't let her get dependent on that," Katrina warned.

"I guess it would establish a life of fear for her."

"She'd never want to let go of you."

"I never thought I'd be creating so much trouble for

her when I decided it was time to end things with Dave."
"Children are delicate creatures. They don't make it very easy to be selfish."
"I know she's confused. Her daddy's gone. To her it looks like I sent him away, I guess. She's never said much about the thing with Martin, but I guess that bothered her some. He didn't relate well to her. He didn't particularly like children. He was very nice, cordial, but you could tell he thought of her as extra baggage."
"He was too old for you, anyway."
Gabrielle lifted her cup and sipped the coffee, careful not to let it burn her tongue. "He seemed so mature compared to David. A little gray at the temples, tailored suits. I was silly, but he was good to me. Sent flowers."
"I saw them. Remember?"
"Just thinking out loud. I don't know if I want to be involved with anybody right now."
"Tanner sounds nice."
"He's very nice. Soft spoken."
"Go after him. He's running toward you. It couldn't be that hard to meet him halfway."
"You have us running through a meadow or something. I don't own any white lace gowns."
Katrina picked up one of the small plastic stirring sticks and tapped the edge of the table with it playfully as her lips curled into a grin. "It's never that simple. Never just a matter of you and him. There are always other concerns, but somewhere amid the worries about Heaven and the worries of this sweatshop and whatever idiosyncracies he has—and there are plenty of them, I'm sure—you have to try to find something. That's the only way. Sometimes I want to put mine out the door, but then I think about it, and I don't want to be without him. Or my babies. You can't go through life alone."
"Sometimes it seems like it would be nice if there were no men in the world."

* * *

After work, she picked Heaven up at school, watching her carefully for signs of disorder. Nothing was evident. Heaven climbed into the car and sat in her seat, the newest Dr. Seuss book, *Oh, the Places You'll Go,* on her lap.

She was in one of her introverted moods and didn't have much to say, a phenomenon Gabrielle had learned long ago not to interpret as a problem. If Heaven didn't have anything she felt like talking about, she didn't speak at all.

Gab drove slowly, the way she always did when she had Heaven in the car. She was phobic about causing an accident which would somehow harm her daughter.

"How was school today?" Gab asked.

"Not bad."

"Did you learn a lot."

"We talked about the alphabet some more."

There was no trace of anxiety or dismay in her voice. She talked a little bit about the songs and the games of the day, and didn't seem bothered by anything. She made no mention of friends, but she didn't say any new atrocities had been committed by the other kids. Perhaps that in itself was a victory.

When another call came from Tanner that evening, Gabrielle allowed herself to be convinced he was interested. The conversation came a little easier, with fewer pauses, less awkwardness. They both seemed able to find things to say.

She laughed a few times at jokes he made, and that seemed to put him more at ease. She realized it was true for her also. When he was calm, she could be calm.

Jesus, did it ever get any easier than high school? She found her fingers tangling in the phone cord, twisting about the coils, and she watched them snap immediately back into place upon release. That was the same thing she'd done when she was talking to boys in eleventh grade, hoping they would be able to work up the courage to ask her out even as they stumbled over dutiful reports about football practice or the debate club. Everybody is scared and nervous, but breaking through the barriers of fear seems so impossible, she thought. She and Dave had never torn down all their walls. Perhaps that had been their downfall.

Could she reveal herself to Tanner? And could he open up? Weren't detective writers tough guys? Not sensitive artist types. She'd read interviews with Mickey Spillane even though she'd never bothered to check up on the adventures of Mike Hammer.

Tanner seemed nice enough, average in fact. He didn't have many pretensions, and he was polite, nicer than most men she knew. Maybe it was time to edge out on the limb a little, not too far but far enough to see how her weight affected the branch.

"Okay, Tanner," she said. "You fixed a meal for me. You wanna let me cook for you some night?"

"That would be nice," he said. She could have written his next line for him. "I wouldn't want you to go to any trouble."

She was prepared. "No trouble. I cook dinner almost every night after work anyway. Can you tear yourself away from your word processor tomorrow around eight?" Good line, she thought, pleased with herself.

"I guess I could manage that," Tanner said. "Should I bring anything?"

"Not really. Don't expect anything too fancy."

"Whatever you come up with will be fine."

Endearing, but not his best work, she decided. He couldn't be expected to be at his peak all the time. The main thing was that he was coming.

The fear of asking was over, and the risk had paid off. She'd known he would accept, still it was scary to make an offer. Rejection always seemed to loom on the horizon. People always said you had nothing to lose and everything to gain, but that wasn't true. A negative answer could be devastating. Not as bad as worrying about a negative answer—but bad nonetheless.

They began to work their way toward a conclusion of the conversation. She gave him directions to the house and said finally: "I guess I'll see you tomorrow."

He promised to be there, and she hung up, a feeling of warmth settling over her. It soon became a burst of enthusiasm and excitement, a tingling joy that made not grinning impossible.

She went back into the living room and found Heaven playing with her toys in the center of the floor.

"Who was on the phone?" she asked without looking up.

"Mr. Tanner." Gab sat down beside her daughter on the floor and rested an arm around Heaven's shoulders.

Heaven continued fussing over her dolls. Her expression was intent. She took great care with the dolls.

"Do you like Mr. Tanner?" Gabrielle asked.

"He's okay."

"He doesn't frighten you?"

Heaven shook her head. "No, ma'am."

"You're sure it won't upset you if he comes to visit?"

"It won't." Heaven put her dolls down and hugged Gab's neck. "He can come over."

Gab embraced her and stroked her hair. "Good, baby. Mommie wants you to be happy. You know that?"

"Yes, Mommy. I know. I am happy. Here with you. Really."

Gab closed her eyes and rested her cheek against the top of her daughter's head. How much she loved this little one, more than anything in the world.

He sat in one of the padded chairs near the plate-glass window which overlooked the runway. It was night. Various lights cut through the black scene with spots of red or blue or green. And it was raining. Drops streaked the glass.

Danube had spent nights in airports before. Flights were often canceled or screwed up. Storms did their share. No matter. His travels had taught him patience if nothing else.

Reaching beneath his raincoat, he took out another cigarette and lit it, puffing smoke into the air. A discarded newspaper lay at his side, ignored. It was the only thing that made the airport different from a thousand others. Like motel rooms, airports were interchangeable. The newspaper was the *Atlanta Journal Constitution*, but it might as well have been the *Los Angeles Times* or the *St. Louis Post-Dispatch*.

Just as the woman down the row from him, struggling with her restless children, could have come from anywhere and be headed anywhere. He had seen her in other places with those same restless children, in bus stations as well as airports, or at least people so like this group they seemed no different. He sighed and drew in another lungful of smoke. Nothing was different. Nothing changed. Not in a lifetime. Not in several lifetimes.

No matter. He had become immune to boredom, just as he had become immune to anxiety. He did not worry about the present or the future. The past he could not escape, but he did not fear it either. Not while he was awake.

That was why he didn't mind staying in the airport, waiting for the connection the following morning. That would be soon enough. It would take him to New Orleans. With luck, in the interim he would not doze, and he would not dream.

Once Gabrielle had put Heaven to bed, she picked up the book she had borrowed from a friend at work, one of Tanner's. In scanning the first couple of pages, she found it was a little more complex than she'd expected. This was no simple Perry Mason tale.

It opened in New Orleans, where a young man had

gone to search for an estranged lover. Told in the first person, the narrative revealed pieces of the lead character's soul even as the plot began to unfold.

She found herself wondering how much of Tanner's own inner feelings were reflected in the story. She knew it wasn't appropriate to assume a writer was his own main character, but the hero of the novel reminded her of Tanner, at least a little bit.

They came out of the darkness, their forms emerging at first only as outlines in the mist that curled up from the ground. They were short, walking four abreast, and their breath seemed to be grunted up from their throats.

Their green skin was marked with pocks and lesions, and their pointed features were twisted into hideous grins that peeled their lips back over sharp, yellowed teeth.

The brightly colored sashes tied about their heads were sweat stained, and the weapons they carried were crusted with dried blood and bits of torn flesh.

Gnelf Master, a much more hideous and bestial Gnelf Master than the one immortalized in the storybooks and cartoons, led the band, a huge pitchfork grasped in his thick green fists.

Their feet crunched on the gravel path as they followed it into the city. They skulked along beside the roadways, avoiding headlights and dodging away from detection until they were at the edge of the neighborhood they sought.

There they darted across lawns, over fences, and through backyards until they reached Heaven's window. She had known they were coming, and she sat at the head of her bed, pillows bunched around her and the covers pulled up to her chin as if for protection.

She could not move when the window opened and they struggled in, exerting themselves to squeeze their stout bodies through the opening.

When they were assembled on the carpet at the foot of her bed, Gnelf Master began to laugh. As he did, his breath seeped out in wisps of smoke, and something harsh and brutal rattled in his chest.

"Tryin' ta sleep?" he asked. His voice came from deep in his throat and his speech had a thick, slow pattern. "There is no sleep for little bitches," he said.

Heaven bit her lower lip. Her chin was trembling and tears came to her eyes as Master pointed his pitchfork at her and wiggled it, the tines pricking the sheet in front of Heaven.

"Your mama took you to see the holy man. Did he do any good? Did he keep us away?"

The other creatures grunted and laughed, urging him to continue the harassment. They were like little, deformed apes, their eyes dull and their faces almost seeming limp except when they growled and grinned.

"Sometimes we eat little girls," Master said. His squinting eyes seemed to gleam as he spoke the words, and the grin broadened on his lips. Then he clicked his teeth together as if taking two quick bites.

Heaven pulled the covers closer about her, bringing forth a laugh from the leader. He tilted his head back, and the noise roared up from his mouth.

"No one can hear us," he said. "We're in your dream. Only *you* know we're here. Poor little thing," he added with mock sympathy.

Heaven whimpered, but it was the only sound she could manage, a frightened little moan.

"Oh, you can't scream either," the Master said. "You're too scared. Try it."

Heaven's voice seemed tangled in her throat. It was true. She could not call out for help, and that made the shudders running through her intensify. She almost wet herself, and sweat covered her.

Moving around the edge of the bed, Master tilted his head to one side, his wrinkled face taking on a false look of concern. "Poor little one." He extended his hand, one finger outstretched, to caress her cheek.

"Not your fault you are born of a whore, but your blood is tainted. Your mother is a slut."

"Mommy isn't bad."

"If only you knew." He caressed her cheek and then suddenly grabbed a handful of her hair, jerking her head sideways.

"Maybe we should cut her into little pieces, eh, boys?" He looked over his shoulder at his minions who grunted and guffawed in approval.

His yellow-green eyes turned back to Heaven. They were filled with anger and hatred. "That bitch would scream then, seeing pieces of her little one strewn all across the living-room rug."

"No," Heaven pleaded.

"Or if we eat her, it'd just be the bones. Right boys?"

Again a round of approving grunts came in answer to his question, and the Gnelfs hoisted their weapons over their heads, waving them about in near-frenzied excitement.

"Don't hurt me or Mommy," Heaven begged. "We've never done anything to you. I used to like you."

"Oh, the poor little thing is scared." The Master let go of her hair and cupped her chin, gently for a second, but then his grip tightened. "You should be scared. This is nowhere near over, and your mother's friends ain't gonna be able to help. No one will help you. Not until we've finished with you."

He let go of her with a rough twist of his hand, then stepped back from the bed to join the others in his band. "We'll be back," he said. "Soon. But you won't know when. Neither will your mommy. But don't tell her. Not unless you want us to cut her into little pieces instead."

They all began to laugh again before they formed a single file and began to squirm out the window.

Master paused before his exit, his face splitting into another broad grin. "Take care," he said. Then he was gone.

Heaven awoke, tangled in her covers, her pillows bunched around her. She set up quickly, her eyes bulging from their sockets. But her room was empty, and the window was closed.

She lay there, shivering from the cold sweat that covered her. Wrapping herself in the sheet didn't seem to help. The fear was too intense. She thought for a few moments she couldn't breathe until the grip of fear relaxed enough to let her lungs function again.

She didn't try to scream now. That would only disturb Mommy again, and she didn't want her to worry. She also didn't want the Gnelfs to hurt Mommy the way they had said they would.

She didn't know what she could do, but for now she would have to keep things a secret. She would have no more outbursts like the one at Miss K'ina's. She had overcome that at Mr. Tanner's. Those tapes had not been expected. This time she knew what she had to do. She would hide things. For Mommy's sake she would have to.

Chapter 6

It was raining in New Orleans as the sleek silver Greyhound pulled out of the bus station, but the downpour could not ground a bus as it could planes. The storm seemed to be following Danube, washing spring down the gutter.

As the bus began its journey north, he watched the clouds forming on the horizon ahead of the vehicle. It could be a natural phenomenon, but he found himself wondering if his presence had been detected by other forces, those of the supernatural kind.

Nothing was to be ruled out. Not in war, and he had been a warrior for a long time now. Unwilling though he might be, he had learned to do what was necessary.

As he let his head fall back on the headrest, he found himself wondering again what he would find in Aimsley. He had heard mention of the area before. Bad things happened there, things that men could not explain in simple, tangible terms.

He tried to think back to when the world had seemed simple to him, but his thoughts could not grasp that time now. Too much had transpired. There had been too many pains, too many agonies.

He had traveled too many miles and seen too many nightmares. He knew what lay beyond reality and, worse still, what humans could do to each other. He had witnessed it all, and he had no escape from it.

The bus made its way onto the interstate, then onto the endless stretch of the bridge. He looked out across the water. The rain continued to slash down from the heavens, and the sky turned to a drab gray.

For a while he fought the drowziness that tried to overtake him. He did not want the dreams that would come with rest, yet he realized he would have to sleep soon. He could not face what was ahead in a state of exhaustion. Weak, he could be dragged into a fate worse than his present one.

After picking up Heaven at school, Gabrielle made a stop by Benson's Super Foods, putting forth an extra effort for her dinner with Tanner. He would hear that it was just something she'd thrown together, a simple meal. Letting him know she'd slaved would be akin to tipping her hand, letting him know she was interested. That was against the rules. If he thought he was doing the chasing he would continue the pursuit. If the situation was reversed, he might run away.

She selected a shopping cart and shoved it along the broad tiled aisles, her daughter strolling casually along behind her, in no real hurry to keep up. Heaven had no concept of being in a rush. She was busy scanning the shelves for things she might beseech her mother to purchase.

Keeping her in peripheral sight, Gab made the best time she could selecting fresh-looking vegetables and seasonings she usually passed over for the store brands. Then she hovered over the meat display for a while, gazing across the lines of roasts, small reddish brown lumps sealed in cellophane and stacked in neat rows. Dave had always claimed there was an art to making the selection.

She always aimed for picking one that was not spoiled. She knew the older cuts were kept on top, so she shoved a few aside to make her choice. Lifting a packaged cut, she winced at the cost per pound. Tanner had better be worth it. She'd probably have to water Heaven's milk to afford this.

Bad joke. She knew she would never skimp on anything for her daughter. She felt guilty over even joking with herself about that.

As she got back behind the cart and seized the handle, she realized Heaven had wandered off. Time was a major factor if she was going to pull this dinner off, and her daughter was doing a disappearing act. She gritted her teeth as she shoved the cart forward along the rear aisle. With luck, she'd locate Heaven at the toy rack.

The hunch paid off. She rounded the end of the aisle where the cheap novelty items were displayed beside the hardware rack. Sure enough, Heaven was standing there peering up at the display.

"We need to get a move on, Hev," Gab said as she wheeled the cart forward.

Heaven didn't move. At first Gab thought her child was being stubborn, but as she drew closer she realized Heaven was mesmerized by something on the rack.

Stepping from behind the cart, she walked to her daughter's side. Heaven didn't respond. She just kept on staring intently at the rack. Gab turned and traced her daughter's line of vision to the plastic bag of toy Gnelfs dangling from one of the metal hooks.

There were about a half-dozen figures including Gnelf Master and his buddies. Holding hoes and spades, they were molded into gardening poses, and the brightly painted card that sealed the bag shut showed them working in a garden full of brightly colored vegetables.

"Heaven, let's go. These won't hurt you."

Heaven continued to stare at them, her eyes wide. Reaching down, Gab took her shoulder and shook her lightly.

"Heaven." She looked around to make sure no one was looking on. "Honey, come on. They're just toys. The

Gnelfs won't hurt you."

Heaven drew a tense breath, and a shudder seemed to course through her small body. There was no indication that she'd heard Gab speak to her. She seemed mesmerized.

Gab cast a quick glance around to make sure no one would see and misunderstand. The aisle was clear, so she shook Heaven again, trying to get through to her. She could feel the vibrations of fear that emanated from the child.

Heaven did not seem to want to budge. She was cemented in her tracks, as if the tiny plastic figures held some control over her.

Reaching up to the rack, Gabrielle snatched the bag down and tucked it behind some other items, out of Heaven's sight. That seemed to break the trance. Heaven blinked and came back into the real world, shivering, perspiration breaking out on her brow. She recognized Gabrielle and hugged her.

"Mommy."

"What is it, honey?" Gab grabbed her and held her close. "Are you all right, baby?"

"Fine, Mommy."

Gab released her and gripped her shoulders. "Are you sure?"

She seemed a little disoriented and the shivers continued, but she nodded. "I think I'm okay. I guess I was just daydreaming or something."

"You were lost to the world, Heaven. What happened? You were staring at the Gnelfs."

"Toys?"

Gab nodded. "Did they scare you?"

Heaven's eyes widened again, and for a moment she seemed about to reveal something. Then she shook her head. "I don't think so."

A small, elderly woman rounded the end of the row, and started to push her cart toward them. Moving Heaven out of the way, Gab let the woman pass. Then she carefully headed her own cart up the aisle, Heaven at her side.

The checkout seemed endless, but finally they cleared the register and made their way to the car.

Strapped into place, Heaven seemed to quietly slip back to normal. Gab kept looking over at her, but she could spot no other sign of a problem. She'd never heard of a child experiencing anything quite like what she'd just seen. Her daughter had been in an almost catatonic state.

"Heaven?"

"Yes."

"Would you like me to ask Mr. Tanner not to come tonight? Is that why you were upset? I could call him and tell him you're not feeling well."

"No, Mommy. I like Mr. Tanner. You can have him over."

"Honey, you're sure Mr. Tanner doesn't frighten you or upset you?"

"No, Mommy. He's fine." She settled down in her seat and folded her arms. Her chin tucked in against her chest, but she wasn't pouting. She seemed to be contemplating something. If five-year-olds contemplated.

A call to Katrina was in order, no question about it. Gabrielle pressed the gas pedal a little harder, eager to get home. On arrival, she hauled the groceries in quickly and, leaving the bags on the kitchen table, snatched the wall phone from its hook.

Katrina answered on the third ring, and Gabrielle blurted out what had happened. "Have you ever seen that happen?" she asked.

"Not to that extent," Katrina said. "Kids can be moody, I can tell you that."

"It wasn't like she was pouting. She was staring at these things."

"I can't understand her fixation," Katrina said. "What is it about these little green bastards? My kids love 'em. Did her daddy ever buy some for her?"

"I think I bought her first Gnelfs. I don't know what it is about them. They are sort of ugly."

"Sort of like bad elves or something if you think about it. Could be she's looked at some traditional children's stories where the green, pointy ears are bad and it seems creatures with these have infiltrated her home. Maybe subconsciously she thinks they're just pretending to be friends."

"And that could be because her father left. She may think he betrayed her, so these friends will too. But hell, we could speculate all night. I guess it's time to get Marley to find somebody for her to see. We might as well get this all out now so she won't have to spend years in therapy later."

"Tomorrow we'll figure something out," Katrina said. "For now you'd better get your dinner cookin'."

"I guess it's too late to tell Jake not to come. She says he doesn't upset her."

"It may do her good to have him there, especially if she's missing her daddy."

"I hope you're right," Gab said. "And I hope he's understanding. I'm not going to have much time to bother with dating if Heaven's going to need attention. She's got to come first."

"If he's worth a damn he'll stick it out," Katrina said. "Now cook a good dinner."

"I guess I'll try," Gab said. She'd lost her will to be a gourmet.

Tanner, naturally, was prompt. And dinner, naturally, was not. Gab had him sit in the living room where Heaven was playing while she rushed into the kitchen. Everything was almost ready, but there was no way to rush the cooking. She briefly checked the roast to make sure it wasn't burning.

She'd already changed into a dark blue denim jumpsuit which bridged the gap between elegant and casual. It allowed some comfort for kitchen work and, she hoped, still looked just a little sexy.

After allowing herself a moment to smooth her hair, Gab pushed through the swinging door into the living room, where Tanner was making an effort to converse with Heaven. Apparently he knew the importance of hitting it off with someone's kid, but he wasn't having much success. Heaven was doing little talking. He obviously thought it was because she didn't like him.

"Sometimes Hev keeps her thoughts to herself," Gab said, sweeping past her and trying to sound upbeat. Just let them have a good evening, then she could break the news to him quietly and hope he was understanding.

She sat near him on the couch, one leg tucked under her in an effort to appear relaxed, knowing he could probably detect her apprehension anyway. He probably studied people so he could work their behavior into his fiction.

"Did you do a lot of writing today?" she asked. Let him talk about himself for a while. She'd have plenty to say later.

"It went a little slow today," he admitted. "Sometimes I plot myself into a corner. It's hard to do the playing fair business and not actually give everything away to the reader at the same time. You have to reveal things without letting people see what you're telling them."

"Sounds a little like Zen."

"Ah, is that one of your interests?"

"I read some of it in college. Enough to skim the surface, not enough to help me stay calm in adverse circumstances or anything."

"I've always found it a little confusing, but I guess you're right. Novels are a little like Zen."

"Is any of this new one set around Aimsley, or is it all in New Orleans?"

"More down in Avoyelles. I have a murder on the levee down there, and Gaston has to deal with all of the Cajuns who don't like to talk about things."

"Is there much action?"

"Quite a lot of it in the end. There'll be a manhunt through the swamps and that sort of thing. They have to take the crawfish boats out."

They talked for a while longer about his novel and other books, the conversation drifting to authors they liked and genres other than mystery. Tanner had recently developed an interest in Arna Bontemps, a black author from Alexandria, a town a short distance away from Aimsley. Although the writer had died in 1973, efforts were underway to preserve his legacy and that had sparked Tanner's interest in his work. He'd been reading Bontemps's novel *God Sends Sunday*.

"Katrina would probably like that," Gab said. "I'll have to tell her about it. Of course she may have read it."

The oven timer sounded, its harsh buzz filtering through from the kitchen. "I think it's about time to eat," Gab said.

She slipped off the couch and rescued the meat from the rack, quickly spinning on her heels and putting it on a serving platter already set out. Then, clearing the swinging doors, she placed the platter on a hot pad on the table.

Tanner offered to help her bring the other things out, but she insisted he just take a seat. In one more trip she had the vegetables on the table, and gave a quick sigh of relief. French bread, butter, and salad were already on the table.

Tanner had helped Heaven into her standard seat atop an old Sears catalog, so Gabrielle settled herself across from him, picked up a cloth napkin, and quickly spread it across her lap. Then she put both hands flat on the table in an exaggerated gesture of readiness and smiled. "Well," she said, "let's eat."

He picked up the carving knife and with care sliced the roast, serving a piece first to Heaven, then to Gab, and lastly to himself.

They took turns serving Heaven vegetables, and Gab

noticed Tanner seemed to handle that well. He was a little awkward, obviously not used to children, but dealing with Heaven seemed to come naturally to him. Heaven remained silent, but she didn't display any open hostility toward him, not even when he cut up her meat.

Finally Tanner sampled the roast, pursing his lips for a moment as if he were a wine connoisseur.

"Delicious," he said, his tone almost coy.

"Glad you like it," Gab said. "It's something I just threw together." Her smile this time was to let him know she was being coy as well.

They laughed, because they could both sense the tension, that frightening magnetic feeling that drifted between them, making itself apparent, making it clear that they were drawn to each other.

There was something positive clicking, that indefinable connection that somehow converts easily into love. Gab had felt it only a couple of times in her life. It had been there with Dave but it had not lasted.

Maybe this time that would not happen. Maybe this time it was real. The conversation flowed, and they kept talking long after the meal was finished. Then they sat, grazing across the table at each other, occasionally locking on each other's eyes.

Heaven soon excused herself and retired to the living room and her toys. Her play was quiet and became a soft background of sound as she hummed and spoke softly to her dolls. Tanner reached across the table, placing his hand atop Gabrielle's.

She let it stay, enjoyed the warmth of his touch and the stirring it evoked. It was such a simple gesture, yet it jarred her deep inside.

"Are you a romantic, Tanner?"

"Deep down."

"How come you don't write love stories?"

"Mysteries have love stories in them."

"I thought detectives bedded every girl they set eyes on. That's not exactly a love story."

"Gaston is different. He's something of a romantic himself. Tough as nails but soft inside."

"Is that you?"

"I'm not tough at all. I guess Gaston has a lot of me in him, but he's not really supposed to be an extrapolation of me."

"Right."

"Honestly. I am not my own hero. I'm just an average guy who makes his living at a typewriter or keyboard."

"Ah, a man of letters caught in his own mystique."

He grinned and absently touched his forehead with an index finger. "Touché."

She thought he might be blushing a little, but it was hard to tell. She had to discuss the matter of Heaven with him, but the playful banter could continue for a while. Their exchange would make it easier when she had to make explanations. If he was feeling what she was feeling there should be something they could latch on to, something that could weather this little storm.

She began to steer the conversation toward Heaven, first mentioning her schoolwork and her difficulty in adjusting.

"It's tough to be a kid," Tanner agreed. "I was always bookish. Wound up being picked on."

Maybe, Gabrielle thought, that background will help him understand. She was hesitating, about to say something, and trying to find the proper words when Heaven's scream shattered the silence.

Her head and Tanner's jerked in the child's direction as the shriek continued.

Heaven was now standing at the center of the living room, arms held in front of her, tiny fists clenched under her chin in a defensive pose.

Her head was twisting from side to side, and her eyes were full of fear. She seemed to be looking at something, some*things* perhaps. Yet there was nothing to be seen.

"Don't hurt me," she pleaded.

Tanner rose from his seat, ready to move toward her,

but he was confused. "What's wrong?" he asked.

Gab was hurrying to embrace Heaven, as she had when the other incidents occurred, but before she could reach her, something slashed through the air, and as if an unseen knife was striking, a tear appeared in one leg of Heaven's slacks.

"Mommieee!"

Gab didn't know what to do.

Heaven could see them. They were surrounding her, a half-dozen Gnelfs. Shirtless, their dull green skin glistened with perspiration, and patchworks of old scars lined their flesh.

Lips peeled back over their yellow fangs in sick, grinning twists, they waved their weapons about as evil seemed to emanate from their tiny, cruel eyes.

Gnelf Master stood directly in front of her. He looked like a pirate with the cloth tied around his head and the tarnished ring dangling from the lobe of one pointed ear. It was the sweep of his scythe which had made the slit in her pantleg. Now he chuckled. "Mommy can't see us," he said. "She doesn't know what's the matter."

Then he brought the scythe forward again, sweeping it sideways as he would have used it to cut wheat.

The second gash tore the cloth over Heaven's left calf and cut into her skin. Blood quickly began to stain the cloth around the wound. Gab screamed and rushed forward, toward Heaven who was now turning about.

Before Gabrielle could reach her child, another tear appeared in her sleeve, another cut on her flesh. This time in her upper arm.

The other Gnelfs were joining the Master in making harassing slashes. Some of them carried needlelike stilettos which they jabbed at Heaven, while others swung at her with swords and scimitars. They laughed and poked at her, the foul smell of their breath almost choking her when they moved in on her and slashed before darting back to their circle.

With Tanner at her side, Gab rushed toward Heaven, sweeping her into her arms. The child's blouse was already in tatters, and her back was sticky with blood. Narrow scratches had touched her cheeks also, and spots of red were in her golden hair.

She wept, heavily, more from fear than pain as Gabrielle gripped her closely.

Tanner was there at her side, flexing his fingers nervously as if he could think of nothing else to do.

"What the hell is happening?" Gabrielle cried, tears, to her surprise, spilling from her own eyes.

"I don't know," Tanner said. "I've never seen anything like it. We'd better get her to the hospital."

Gab stood, holding Heaven in her arms, and nodded. "Let's go."

From the hall closet, she grabbed a sweater and wrapped it around Heaven as she followed Tanner out to his car. The top was down on the Cutlass, and she told him not to bother putting it up even though the night air was chill. She didn't want to waste time. The wounds seemed superficial, but the bleeding scared her. Heaven seemed covered with blood, and she was so small. How much could she afford to lose?

They jumped into the front seat, and Tanner left a strip of rubber along the pavement in front of her house as he pulled away from the curb. The damp night air quickly began to slip down over the windshield to slap Gab in the face, but she tried to ignore its chill.

In her lap, Heaven was trembling and sobbing, tears mingling with the blood on her face.

"I don't understand what happened," Tanner said, his hands so tight on the wheel he looked like he was trying to squeeze it apart. He was more frightened by this than she had realized, but that was understandable. Nothing else was, but fear made sense in this situation.

"She's been disturbed lately, having nightmares," Gabrielle said.

"That still doesn't explain what happened. I've read about people's minds doing things, even making them bleed, but this is not like stigmata or anything. If this was just from her mind, how could her clothes get cut?"

"I don't know," Gab said. "It's like ghosts or something did it."

"Gnelfs? You said her dreams were about Gnelfs."

"Yes."

"What could that mean?"

"It doesn't explain anything."

The car screeched around a corner, and Tanner ran a redlight at the next intersection. He drew honks from other motorists, but he avoided a collision by a few inches.

Another block down he turned onto a cross street. It had buckled in several places, but he managed to hold the car steady as he roared along it, cutting almost a mile off the trip.

He swerved around a couple of cars and some pedestrians as the Cutlass entered the Riverland Parish Hospital grounds. A security guard making rounds looked up at him as he passed, but Tanner ignored the man and pulled into a parking slot near the door of the emergency room.

Gab was out of the car before the engine died. At a jog, she hurried through the automatic doors and across the waiting room to the small computer desk where the admitting clerk was typing in information on an elderly man with a bandaged wrist.

A kid in his mid twenties, a bad bruise on his left cheek,

seemed to be next in line. He was pressing an ice pack to an eye which was about to swell shut. Gab pressed past him.

"I need help quick," she shouted.

Coming out of her chair, the white-coated clerk stuck her head through the narrow doorway behind her and called out, "Incoming child, stat."

Seconds later, a blond nurse with a stethoscope draped over her shoulder appeared. The gummed soles of her shoes squeaked on the see-yourself waxed tile as she rushed over to Gab and began a quick examination of Heaven.

The doors buzzed open again, and Tanner joined them.

"Let's get her into an examining room," the nurse said. The name Cruse was on the tab pinned to her pocket. "Were you in an accident?"

A white-uniformed man with short brown hair and a mustache appeared a few seconds later with a stretcher, and Heaven was transferred from Gab's arms to the clean white sheets.

"Mommy." Her voice sounded weak.

"It's okay, sweetheart. They'll take good care of you. Mommy will be right here." She silently cursed the tyranny of procedure.

"If you want to go on in with her your husband can handle the—"

"Uh, he's—"

"I'm a friend," Tanner explained.

"Oh." A look of suspicion crossed her features. "Okay. Well, I'll take care of the necessary information as quickly as possible and let you join her. She's frightened I'm sure."

Gab sat in the chair the elderly man had vacated. She was conscious of the blood on her clothing and hands as she answered a battery of questions about insurance, allergies, and the like, her responses to all of them being typed into the computer. Then, an eternity later, after leaving Tanner in the waiting room to call Katrina, she was led through the doorway toward the examining room.

A gray-haired doctor with a beard that still had a few reddish streaks was already at Heaven's side, shining a penlight into her eyes. His wire-rimmed glasses had skied down to the very tip of his nose and seemed about to plummet over.

Heaven now wore a hospital gown, and a nurse was dabbing at some of her wounds.

The doctor straightened and looked at Gabrielle as he returned the light to the pocket of the lab coat that covered the pale green scrub suit he wore.

"I'm Dr. Edwards," he said. "How do you do?"

"Gabrielle Davis."

"She's going to be fine," he said. "Just some scratches. What the hell happened to her?"

"She was playing," Gab said. "All of a sudden she screamed, there were cuts . . . I don't know." She suddenly realized how bad that sounded. She was almost incoherent. Her panic hadn't subsided that much, but she realized her explanation made it sound as though Heaven got the cuts because she was clumsy, always falling down or something.

That was the typical excuse of the parent of a battered child. On top of everything else, she thought, someone might try to take my daughter away from me.

"Well these are only minor lacerations," Edwards said. "We'll get her fixed up. There won't be a need for stitches." He stroked the hair at his chin. Do all the men in this hospital have facial hair? Gab wondered. "Has anything like this happened before?"

"No. She's been a little strange—upset—this week, but no, nothing like this happened."

He nodded grimly, then turned to the nurse and gave her brief instructions about handling the wounds.

"We'll want to keep her overnight for observation,"

he said. "She is small, and she's lost blood. I'm not going to order an IV—AIDS, you know—but we will give her a tetanus shot."

He didn't ask any more questions, but he obviously had a few in mind.

Gab watched him walk toward the door, expecting him to look back over his shoulder, give her a final accusatory stare. He didn't.

She stayed with Heaven, holding her hand while the nurse continued cleaning and bandaging the wounds. Then, when that was done, Heaven was put in a fresh hospital gown and an orderly lifted her and swung her into a wheelchair for transfer to a room.

Heaven giggled as she was wheeled around, the thrill of the ride momentarily displacing the trauma of the attack she had undergone.

Katrina and Tanner had found each other and were in the waiting room whe Gab and Heaven emerged through the swinging doors. The orderly paused at Gab's request.

"She's all right," she assured Katrina, whose frown threatened to crumple her face.

"I still can't understand what happened? I mean you two were talking and all of a sudden—"

"It just happened," Gab said. "I can't explain it. They're probably reporting me to Child Protection right now."

"Don't worry too much about that at the moment," Katrina said. "There's no real evidence you did anything, and they have enough instances of real abuse to deal with. If there's much said, my cousin Isaac works in the D.A.'s office. I'll talk to him for you."

"Thanks. They're taking her up to a room for the night. Observation."

"We'll talk with you, make sure you're settled," Katrina said.

Tanner nodded. He had his hands in the hip pockets of his jeans and seemed uncertain as to what to do. He had no defined role here, and it made him awkward.

"Thank you both for being here," Gab said.

The room was small and narrow, with a bed and a chair that folded back to become a cot. At least it isn't a ward, Gab thought. Once Heaven had been tucked into bed, she dropped onto a seat, her hands trembling badly.

"I don't know what to make of all this," she said.

"I'm all right, Mommy." Heaven's expression was solemn.

She's worried about me, Gab thought. She made a conscious effort to seem chipper. "I know, baby. You just rest."

Before long the medication had Heaven dozing. Gab prayed she wouldn't have another nightmare.

"I can't explain what happened, and I saw it with my own eyes," Tanner said. "It was very strange."

"You're saying her clothes tore and these welts just appeared?" Katrina asked.

"That's it," Gab said.

Katrina's eyes flicked to Tanner for confirmation. He nodded.

"Something very unusual is happening here," Katrina said. "These nightmares and now this."

"What the hell can it be?" Gab asked. "It can't be, I mean, you know, supernatural. That's crazy."

"I feel like we're in a Time-Life Books ad," Katrina said.

"Things like this don't happen," Gabrielle declared. "My God, what if it happens again?"

"Look, we'll talk to Marley tomorrow," Katrina said. "This is his department."

"It's like the first part of *The Exorcist* or something," Gab said.

"Come on, she can't be possessed or anything like that," Katrina said. "Don't be ridiculous." She looked at

Tanner. "You're a mystery writer. Isn't everything supposed to have a logical explanation."

"If there is one for this I'm hard put to say what it is," he replied.

Gab rubbed her eyes. "Well, it's late. Maybe some answers will turn up when daylight comes."

Katrina nodded. "They'll bring you pillows and a blanket. You want me to stay."

"No, I'm fine. I'm going to have to call in sick, tomorrow. I hate to ask this, but could you stop by my house on your way to work and pick up something for Heaven to wear home. I don't want to take her out of here in a gown."

"I'll get some clothes for her and you."

"I'm sorry to have to ask you."

"Don't worry about it a bit. It won't take me five minutes."

"Would you like me to hang around?" Tanner asked. "I could stay in the waiting room."

"Jake, I can't ask you to do that."

"You don't have a car here," he reminded her, trying his best to be helpful in some way.

She put a palm against her forehead. "That's right."

"I could come back and give you a lift in the morning."

He was trying to help and to be near her as well. It was imposing, but what the heck. He was offering. "I guess around eight," she said.

"I'll see you then."

Gab couldn't sleep as she lay on the makeshift bed. The night light on the wall created odd shadows, and the events of the evening kept replaying in her brain. Heaven, standing there, cuts coming from nowhere.

Each pop and hum in the hospital made her jump, as if the whole scary business was about to start over again. She didn't know what had happened. Worse still, she didn't know how to keep it from happening again.

Chapter 7

Tanner was standing in the hallway outside Heaven's door while Gab was dressing her daughter when the priest approached.

Tanner had been feeling awkward, had been wondering if Gabrielle was going to tell him to get lost when the priest attracted his attention. A big man with broad shoulders, and with his long black coat fluttering around him, the priest looked as though he'd be more at home holding a longshoreman's hook than a chalice. Jake watched him move, noting the power in his walk.

Still, the man appeared weary. His bearded face looked haggard, and the skin beneath his eyes was discolored. He didn't seem like a traditional chaplain, but he was in command of things as he scanned the room numbers.

He finally stopped at Heaven's door and knocked. Tanner continued to watch him. Perhaps he was the family pastor. The other inference, in light of the previous night's events, was too weird and frightening to consider. Besides, this man didn't look like Max von Sydow.

"Come in," Gab called from within.

The priest shoved the door inward and strolled into the room, his hands tucked casually into the pockets of his raincoat.

Jake wondered if he should follow.

* * *

Gab was startled at seeing the big, red-haired man in the doorway. She'd been expecting Tanner to walk back in, impatient from loitering in the hall. Instead she was facing this imposing man with a slight scowl.

"Can I help you?" she asked.

"My name is Danube," he said. She couldn't place the accent. It was an odd mixture of tones, as if it had developed from constant use of several languages, yet he didn't stumble with English.

"Did Katrina ask you to come?" she asked. The man frightened her a bit. He was eerie in some way, not like a kindly parish priest at all.

"I came because I am needed," he said.

"What do you mean?" Her voice faltered.

His voice was firm, impatient. "Your daughter has been experiencing some trouble."

"She has, but I haven't talked to anyone about it yet." If he hadn't been wearing a Roman collar she would have been inclined to add an indignant complaint, but she refrained.

Cautiously, behind the priest, Tanner eased into the room, apparently uncertain if he should continue to wait outside or not. Gab motioned him to come all the way in. She was unsure of this priest, and she appreciated Jake's presence.

"You've been experiencing some difficulties," Danube said.

"I'm not exactly sure what happened," Gabrielle said.

"Something evil," the priest stated. "Pretending it did not is no solution."

"What do you know?" She hoped he could detect the suspicion in her voice.

"Little at this point. I will need to talk to you."

"Why?"

"To determine the precise nature of the evil, so that it can be dealt with."

Gab swallowed. He was like someone out of a comic book—The Phantom Stranger—except he was serious.

She could read it in his dark, piercing eyes. His gaze was relentless.

She turned her head, looking at Heaven to see if he was frightening her, but her daughter seemed more concerned with the Velcro straps of her tennis shoes. The gauze bandages on her arms and legs didn't seem to be bothering her.

"I have to get my daughter home," Gab said. "My friend is driving me, and I don't want to inconvenience him. If you'll excuse me . . ."

Danube still didn't take his gaze away from her. He peered at her for a long, lingering moment, then gave Tanner a glance and shook his head before walking from the room.

"How could he have heard?" Tanner asked as Gab helped Heaven off the bed.

"I don't know. He's probably some weirdo who found out there was a little girl in here. He can't be the regular chaplain. I'm not Catholic, but he's not like any priest I ever saw. He looks seedy."

"There is something strange about him," Tanner agreed.

Gabrielle shook her head. "You're probably getting a lot of story ideas from hanging around me." She turned her attention to helping Heaven finish with her shoes. The child was sore, but she didn't seem to mind movement.

After the checkout process, they went down to Tanner's car, and he drove them home at a far more relaxed pace than he had set the night before. Heaven aimlessly dialed the radio past blips of static intermingled with sounds she didn't linger on long enough to identify.

Gab didn't correct her because Heaven had been through so much. She would worry about social etiquette again once the trauma her child was experiencing had been dealt with. She was going to have to talk to Marley again, and hopefully he would be able to provide some answers. What kind of answers, though? Something she didn't want to hear, something mystical and dark.

Thinking of Marley made her uncomfortable. She was afraid he'd tell her things were possible, things she didn't want to acknowledge. She'd seen what had happened. Tanner had too. How could it be explained? Who could cough up a logical clarification of something like that? She wanted one, one that had nothing to do with unexplained phenomena or ghosts or devils. But she also wanted to hear that there was nothing wrong with Heaven's mind, that her child wasn't traumatized by the divorce. Who wanted to deal with the fact that they were raising a child out of a Stephen King novel? That was why she hadn't named her daughter Carrie.

When they reached the house, Tanner pulled in behind Gabrielle's car. She found herself glad he climbed out to help her with Heaven's things. She didn't want to walk into the house alone.

When they entered nothing seemed out of place. She left Heaven in the kitchen with Tanner while she checked her daughter's room for Gnelf toys and tapes and books, and when she had collected them she stuffed them all in the closet of her own room. Then she returned and broke in on the chat Tanner was having with Heaven.

"I'm going to put her to bed," she said. "She's still exhausted, I know."

"I'm not tired," Heaven said, but her eyes and the lack of conviction in her voice overruled the statement.

She didn't protest much as Gab picked her up. It was difficult because Heaven was getting heavy, but Gab managed.

"Would you like me to fix some coffee?" Tanner asked as she carried Heaven from the room.

"That would be great," she said.

He had it ready when she made it back to the kitchen a few minutes later.

"Asleep before she hit the pillow," Gab said.

"She's been through a lot."

"Too much." Gab sat down at the kitchen table. "You

found everything all right?"

"I'm a mystery writer. It's my job."

She laughed. It felt good, easing her weariness a bit. "What do you take in it?"

"Black for now."

He poured it in a mug with a "The Far Side" cartoon on it and then placed it in front of her.

"Didn't know you were walking into a family in crisis did you?" Gab asked as he sat down across from her, his own cup in hand.

"Life, like art, has its little unexpected twists," he admitted.

"You're probably thinking 'Why did I bother with this woman?' "

"No." He turned his face away from her, embarrassed.

She laughed again, slightly. "Jake, I know we hardly know each other, and with Heaven's situation I'll understand if you want to just back away."

He hesitated, still not looking at her directly. "You don't need the entanglement right now?"

"Heaven's going to need me while we try to work out whatever this is. It scares the hell out of me. I just don't know if I'll have time for any life of my own for a while."

He got up from his chair and walked over to the kitchen window, stared out. His hands slipped into his hip pockets, and he rocked on the balls of his feet.

"We've only seen each other twice," he said. "I can't say there's some major connection there that we can't let go of, but I don't know. It just seemed like there was something, you know?" He turned back and looked at her.

"I don't feel it's fair to you to ask you to stand by."

His brow wrinkled as he turned to her, searching for words, and his left hand came out of his pocket to slide through his hair, ruffling it over his forehead.

"I don't know. I'll be around, you know. This is not an easy town for meeting people, and meeting people you have a dime's worth of things in common with is even rarer." It was his turn for a slight laugh.

"I kind of know what you're talking about," she said. "It's hard to meet a man who's not scared away by your five-year-old."

"And me, hell, I'm not that exciting as people go. Once you get past that notion that I do something a little different for a living, I'm worse than average."

Gabrielle lifted her fingers to her temples. "Ah, life is so confusing. For the record, I like you, Tanner."

"I like you too," he said doing a bad Nicholson impression followed by a broad grin and raised eyebrows.

"You just met me."

"I'm a sensitive artist."

She felt the tension inside her tighten. She didn't know what to do, didn't know what to say to him or what to ask him.

He threw up his hands. "You've got enough to worry about without dealing with my emotions," he said. "I'll get out of your way. Uh, but if you need me you can call, or if you want somebody to talk to, you know. I'm around. Maybe when it's leveled off we can talk again."

"Let's stay in touch. I want to see you again. It's not that I don't. I hope you understand. I can't ask you to wait like I said, but—"

"I will stay in touch. And if you feel you have time to see me, just let me know. Maybe I can come by some."

"Soon. Really."

He walked over to her and softly kissed her forehead before showing himself out. She stayed at the table for several minutes, her eyes closed, trying to sort things out. She had much to do, but for a while she just let the emotions range about inside her.

After a minute or two, she got up, worry about Heaven winning out. She went to the small desk in the spare bedroom where she did her paperwork and dug Dave's number out of a cubbyhole. She didn't get an answer when she tried his house, and she had no work number for him. She counted the time zones in her head, realized it was still early morning in California and found herself wondering where he must be. Sleeping with someone? Add some jealousy into the mix. Why not?

Hanging up as the receiver still purred, she walked down the hall to the bathroom. She was just beginning to realize how tired she was, and viewing her face in the mirror crystallized the fatigue. Her eyes were red rimmed, her cheeks puffy. She wondered why Tanner had even hesitated to walk out.

The fact that he had lingered was a sign he was interested. It might not last, though. Not when he had time to think. Circumstances were not going to be propitious for romance, and she wasn't going to have much opportunity to give him the little ego boosts men needed. She found herself worrying that he wouldn't call and that she'd be faced with picking up the phone herself, something she wasn't inclined to do. Girls didn't call boys. Her mother had taught her that.

She felt guilty for letting her thoughts drift back to Tanner. He had wedged himself in between her and her worry about Heaven, but a flicker of anxiety cracked the dam and brought all of the fears back into her head.

There was no way she could make sense out of this mess. It was as unexplainable as a ghost story. She pulled her hair back into a pony tail in preparation for a bath. That would calm her some. She had to rest before she started trying to find an exorcist.

She had turned the water on and was testing its temperature with her fingertips when the doorbell rang. Cursing under her breath, she told herself to be thankful she was not undressed and in the tub.

Hurrying through the house, she paused to look through the narrow window beside the facing of the door before releasing the lock, and fear again manifested itself when she saw the priest on the doorstep. He stood at the edge of the stoop, looking back across the neighborhood while he waited for an answer. His hands were still plunged into the pockets of the black raincoat.

She held her breath as she looked out at him. His face was weathered, and his dark eyes were weary, shrouded with a squint that conformed to deeply etched wrinkles. The morning wind tossed the tangles of his red hair about, but he seemed oblivious to it, like a sailor on the bow of a ship. The sky was turning gray, and he was watching a formation of storm clouds.

Making sure the chain was in place, Gab eased the door open only a crack, ready to slam it if the priest caused any trouble.

"What do you want?" she asked. "I thought this business was finished at the hospital."

He walked the short distance from the edge of the stoop to the door and looked through the narrow crack she was allowing. "It's far from finished," he said. "It's only begun."

"What's going on? Who are you?"

"I'm Danube. You need me. I have come to try to help you."

"Come from where?"

"I've made a long journey."

"How do I know you're not trying to hurt my daughter? And me too for that matter?"

"I mean no harm. Something strange has happened to you. Am I right?"

"How do you know?"

"I have to know. Knowledge is survival."

"Of what?"

He offered no answer.

"Why don't you just leave me alone?"

His eyes grew even more intense than they had at the hospital. He did not turn for several seconds, but finally he nodded. "So be it." He bowed his head slightly; his eyes still looked at her. "I wish you well."

She closed the door without speaking again and realized she was sweating through her blouse. Her skin felt hot, but perspiration around her collar had chilled, making her neck feel as if she were being touched by ice.

"Fuck you," she muttered under her breath as she leaned back against the door. Poltergeists in the living room and weirdos at the door.

She looked out through the window again. No sign of the priest remained. She whispered prayerful thanks for that, then rechecked the doors to make sure they were secure.

Another call to Dave's number drew no answer. After letting it ring and ring, she plopped the phone back on the hook and returned to her bath. The hot water cleansed her of the sweat and worked on her muscles, but it did nothing to relieve the stress.

She slept for a couple of hours before calling Marley. He showed up about midafternoon with Althea Rogers. She was somewhere in her forties, with neatly brushed blond hair perhaps a little long for her age. Gab was reminded of how her mother had always criticized Barbara Walters for maintaining a youthful hairdo as she grew older, but in this instance it was becoming.

The woman wasn't beautiful though she might have been once, and some would still find her attractive in a mature way. The set of her jaw was perhaps a bit too square, and early warnings of wrinkles were forming. She was still slender, however, and wore a simple white blouse and tan skirt with a matching jacket which complimented her form.

Gab found her likable as she showed her into the living room. As Althea settled herself on the couch, her dark eyes conveyed genuine interest. After slipping her jacket off, she leaned forward, elbows resting on her knees, as she listened to Gab's account of the incident.

Gabrielle tried to give as objective an account of it as possible, describing what had happened the night before and the nightmares and Heaven's reaction to the Gnelfs.

She felt the woman was analyzing her, but she was not intimidated.

As Gabrielle's story unfolded, Marley sat at Althea's side, nodding from time to time. He placed an index finger against his temple, pushing a fold of skin toward his scalpline as he took in the information.

They all sipped, without tasting, the coffee Gab had prepared, as if doing something calm and normal would keep things within the borders of reality with which they were comfortable.

"What can be wrong with her?" Gab asked. "I've never heard of anything like this."

"It's unusual," the woman said. "Some trauma following a divorce is understandable, yet it sounds as if you've got some odd phenomenon accompanying it."

"I realize that," Gab said. "Can a child's mind bring on that sort of thing?"

"There are things that go beyond explanation," Althea replied. "I've read of them in journals, been told of others by colleagues at conventions. Some things we can't always get a handle on. We work very hard to gather explanations."

"Are you saying my daughter can't be helped? You haven't even talked to her."

"I'm not making any judgments. I just want you to understand. Marley called me for a couple of reasons. One is that I've counseled people who have been through ill-advised exorcisms and that sort of thing. I've learned answers are elusive at times."

Her voice was matter-of-fact, but somewhere in her tone Gab detected a trace of cynicism. This woman didn't believe in answers.

At Althea's request, she got a copy of the Gnelf storybook. Accepting it, the psychologist thumbed quickly through the pages.

"Is there anything in it harmful? I hear so much about children's books these days," Gab said, "but I never thought until the last few days there would be anything bad in these."

"They appear to be typical cartoon characters," Althea said. "Not images that would normally frighten a child. Of course we can never tell what will trigger a child's fears. Darth Vader, the boogie man, bug bears, Satan Claus."

She closed the book and placed it on the coffee table, and Gab immediately picked it up and held it against her with the cover turned inward. It had to be put away so Heaven wouldn't see it.

"Do you want to talk to Heaven?"

"Yes," Althea said. "Let's bring her in." She turned to Marley. "It might be better if you wait in the kitchen. We don't want to intimidate her with a crowd, but I would like her mother here."

Marley paused a moment, as if reluctant. He turned his lips inward as he nodded. "I guess you're right."

Rising, he showed himself into the next room while Gab walked down the hall to find Heaven. A few moments later she returned with her daughter at her side, holding her hand. The child walked a bit unsteadily, still groggy from her ordeal.

"Hi there," Althea said when Heaven was seated beside her on the couch.

The reply was soft, barely audible.

"How are you feeling today?"

Another almost inaudible sound: "Fine." The child's head was bowed, her lower lip protruding in something like a pout.

Althea went on with the small talk for a while, asking Heaven about school and other incidental matters. The child admitted she didn't care much for school and that she didn't have many friends there, but otherwise she answered questions as concisely as possible, usually with a single word.

Slowly, almost gracefully, the psychologist guided the

conversation around to the events of the night before. Her voice softened and she leaned slightly toward the girl, careful to be comforting and not intimidating.

"You had quite a scare last night," she said.

"Yes."

"Can you tell me what happened?"

For a moment, Heaven remained quiet, sullen. Her hair hung down around her face like a veil protecting her from reality. "I don't remember," she whispered.

"Now, your mom wants me to talk to you because she's worried about what went on. She doesn't understand it either, and we want to figure it out. We need your help to do that. Do you understand?"

Heaven's head bobbed slightly, but she didn't speak anymore.

"Do you remember what happened at all?"

Again Heaven gave no answer. She sat on her hands. Her feet dangled above the floor, and her heels bounced against the couch.

"All right, we won't bother with it for now," Althea said. "But I was wondering about something else. Your mommy told me that you'd had some bad dreams about the Gnelfs."

Heaven breathed inward, a bit sharply. It was not a gasp, but her pout seemed to deepen. "Sometimes."

"Aren't they your friends?"

"They're just stories."

"Do you think the Gnelfs would hurt you?"

Silence except for breathing.

"Heaven, did the Gnelfs have anything to do with what happened last night?"

Without speaking, the child stared down at her shoes. Her wide blue eyes were almost glassy.

"I guess we'll stop for now," Althea said. She motioned for Gab to join her in the kitchen once Heaven was put back to bed. They found Marley sitting at the table, idly staring out the window.

"Any results?" he asked.

Althea shook her head as she leaned against the cabinet. "She's shutting it all out—or in."

"What do you mean?" Gab demanded.

"She's keeping something in. She doesn't want to lie. You've probably taught her that's bad, so she's not saying anything at all."

Gab felt blood pulsing in her temples. She was still fatigued from lack of rest, and on top of that, this revelation brought new confusion.

"Why would she be keeping it to herself?"

"She's frightened. Understandably. Something strange has taken place. It has left her disoriented."

"But there is some kind of explanation for all this? I mean this is reality, not 'the Ray Bradbury Television Theatre.'"

Althea looked over at Marley, and then her gaze fell back on Gabrielle. "There is an explanation," she said. "I'm just not sure what it is. There is much we don't understand about the mind. I'm afraid Reverend Marley and I don't always agree on this sort of thing."

Gab turned to Marley. "You're not implying there's something more? Some crazy priest came around this morning, acting like something mystical was taking place."

"I believe very much in a spiritual world," Marley said.

Gab felt her heart thundering in her chest. The pressure of tears was building behind her eyes. She didn't want to hear this from these people. They were supposed to be telling her everything would be all right. Her friend had introduced her to them. How could she have found a counselor who was now telling her something beyond reasonable explanation was taking place.

"Maybe I need some time to think this over." Gab ran a hand across her forehead. "It's all very difficult to understand, and I'm very tired."

Marley took a card from his pocket and placed it on the table. "You can reach me if you need me," he said.

Gab nodded, watching silently as they exited through the kitchen door. The last thing she needed was a would-be exorcist or a well-meaning psychologist who'd want to publish a paper on the phenomenon of her daughter.

He heard the crowd's jeers and laughter. They threw things, bits of wood and stone, and they spat on him as he struggled through their midst. He was trying to follow the dirt path to his home, but they would not let him pass. They had learned who he was. Someone always learned.

How many times had they thrown stones at him? How many times had he been hated? All of the assaults ran together now; all of the people who despised him had the same faces.

Danube rolled over, half-awake as the dream continued to swirl about in his head, vividly re-creating the past, the long-ago trek into the mountains.

With a single guide beside him, he had ridden a mule up the narrow, winding path. Pitted and pocked by erosion, the trail was brutal, and winter's harsh breath had seemed to urge him to turn back.

He remembered the gray sky and the clouds so thick and threatening. Snow had come halfway through the trip, blinding, almost a blizzard, and the guide had wanted to turn back. As wind whipped at their clothing and white flakes clung to their eyelashes, only the reminder that he was being well paid kept the guide from leaving.

The convent was perched high in the mountains, and the chilling wind remained relentless as their mounts climbed onward.

The nuns had been waiting, a circle of stern-faced women of various ages, dressed in severe black habits. They showed him and his guide into a broad sitting room, where a fire blazed in an ancient fireplace. The orange glow heated the huge stones and gave off a warmth that seeped through his chilled skin as he peeled off layers of sweaters and scarves.

The room had high ceilings and was decorated with icons of the Virgin and of Christ. As feeling returned to his face and limbs, he looked up at the paintings of the crucified figure and at another which showed him holding his heart in his hands. Then he turned away from them, looking back into the eyes of the sisters who stood in a line at the edge of the room, their arms crossed within the folds of their habits. They were seven in number, and each one gazed at him accusingly.

They knew who he was. He made no attempt at denial. He stood before them with his hands thrust deeply into the pockets of his slacks, staring back at them.

"I have come to seek atonement," he said. "I have been a vagabond for too long."

"You will still wander the lands of the Earth," said the Mother Superior. "That will not end."

"I understand. I do not seek a home, only a purpose. It has been meaningless for too many years."

"Your task will not be easy," said the old nun. Her face was rugged, lined as if she could match every year he had known. He knew that was not true. At seventy, she was much younger than he.

"Our order is small," the old woman said. "We spend most of our time in prayer. You will carry the support of those prayers when you investigate things which need our attention. We do not leave the convent. You will be our eyes and our agent. You will purify yourself, and you will remain as such."

"Understood." He'd had his share of fulfillments which had not touched his soul.

He sat up in bed, the memories of the old nun's face in the flickering firelight fading from his thoughts.

Had he found what he was looking for? After all these years had there been fulfillment in the quest for righteousness?

He had kept his vows, had done as instructed by the nuns on what seemed a thousand journeys around the globe. He had earned scars and tears, yet he had faced the things of evil without flinching, things that would have sent many men scurrying for safety.

Yet what difference had he made? The world got worse. Things changed, governments softened their power, but did people change?

He walked to the window, looking down on another street. He was staying in the Clairmont, a renovated downtown hotel in Aimsley, elegant and quiet. Unfortunately the accommodations offered no solace.

He watched the faint misty rain falling beyond the glass and wondered what it would take for Gabrielle to accept his help.

Chapter 8

Katrina called around seven P.M. to check on things. Heaven was resting, and Gabrielle had just finished making an effort to eat a frozen dinner.

"You still haven't figured out what's going on?" Katrina asked.

"Not yet. Reverend Marley and his friend were kind of spooky about it all. They made me nervous."

"Well it *is* kind of spooky," Katrina said. "Can you explain it?"

"No, but with the psychologist and that weird priest that came by, on top of all that's happened I don't know what to think. It's like you wake up one morning and find out the sky is green and the grass is blue."

"Heaven still hasn't said anything?"

"Nothing tangible. If she knows what happened, she's keeping it to herself, and I still haven't been able to raise Dave on the phone to discuss it with him."

"Men are never there when you need them."

"I don't know what to make of Dave. I don't expect him to keep in touch with me, but you'd think he'd check on his daughter more."

"He's probably off pouting. Men do that. He'll get over it in time."

"Well, I haven't got time to worry about his immaturity. I've got Heaven to think about, work to worry about.

I'm going to eat up my sick leave quickly the way things are going. I have to stay with Heaven again tomorrow."

"They're usually pretty good about that kind of thing," Katrina said. "You're a single parent. They have to take that into account."

That statement stuck with Gabrielle when the phone was back in its cradle. She was a single parent. She'd never thought of herself as such, but it was true.

She had never planned on that. She had expected a perfect marriage, a normal family life. The world just didn't allow for that very much anymore. Everything was screwed up. Dave had been so immature and self-centered, the result of being spoiled and pampered by his parents.

Now Heaven was being affected by something. God, what kind of life would the child face when she was traumatized this early?

Gabrielle had always counted herself lucky that she had remained basically unscathed by life. Growing up, she'd had a fairly stable family, and she hadn't gone through the bad things some of her friends had faced. Until now. She had to find a way to protect Heaven—and to get her help.

Tomorrow she would contact a different psychologist, someone more traditional. Althea was skeptical about Marley's inclination, but she wasn't as quick to dismiss things as Gab would have liked. She shook her head, realizing she was upset because Althea hadn't told her what she wanted to hear, that nothing was wrong. Hoping for that wasn't going to do her daughter any good.

Tonight, Heaven was sleeping in her mother's bed. Stepping into her bedroom, Gabrielle sat down gently on the edge. The child seemed to be sleeping peacefully, covers tucked just below her chin. A teddy bear was embraced by her left arm.

Tomorrow, help. Tonight she would watch over her and pray.

* * *

Althea sat at the desk in her home office. If she'd been a man she might have called it her study, but as it was she had no pretentions about it. It was a small converted bedroom with a desk, a lamp, and room for her computer and the cheap photocopy machine she'd purchased about a year earlier.

Atop the clutter of paperwork rested the *Gnelfland Bedtime Storybook* she had bought. She drew it from the plastic sack in which it had been placed at the bookstore.

She'd stopped on the way home to pick it up. She tried to keep abreast of the latest items for children, but the Gnelfs had soared to popularity recently and she hadn't had a chance to look them over thoroughly yet.

Thumbing through the brightly colored pages of the book, she glanced at some of the simple phrases and studied the images. It was hard to imagine the comical figures being frightening even to a child.

The Gnelfs were bumbling, well-meaning nomads given to occasional altercations with dragons and the usual villains, nothing too vicious or violent.

Still there was no judging what it might be about the Gnelfs that frightened the child. Perhaps they aroused some anxiety, something related to separation from her father or to some other trauma in her life.

As to the event of the night before, Althea remained uncertain. There had to be some explanation for it, and though Heaven's mother didn't seem the type, abuse by Gabrielle couldn't be ruled out. She might be angry at the child, following the breakup of the marriage. She could view the child as responsible, or she could resent having custody of her, being tied down by her. The possibilities were really limitless. Althea had seen any number of such scenarios played out time and time again.

Abuse would be a more reasonable explanation than the bizarre supernatural occurrence Marley might favor to explain the cuts on the child's body. He meant well, and was quick to call her if necessary, but she was concerned about his willingness to accept an otherworldly cause as an answer. People were usually more threatening than ghosts. She knew that well, from cases she had dealt with and from her own experiences.

Opening the drawer at her side, Althea slipped out the package of Virginia Slims she kept hidden there. She smoked infrequently these days, but sometimes the need arose. She lit one and sighed as the smoke penetrated deep into her lungs, waiting for the soothing sensation. It wasn't as pleasant as she'd expected. The cigarettes were growing stale.

As she exhaled, she rose from her chair and walked across the room. She had no particular destination in mind. If the child was being abused, she'd need to look into it. The doctors who had treated Heaven had probably already passed word on to the Child Protection Agency, but suspicions wouldn't give the agency much to go on. Besides, Althea knew that organization was already overworked and understaffed due to recent state budget cuts.

She thought about giving Marley another call, but dismissed the idea. She didn't want to hear him postulating potential explanations. He was young, and his zeal became frustrating at times.

They had met when he had contacted her about a year earlier seeking help for a child from his congregation who had been molested by her uncle. They'd been able to defuse a potentially harmful situation and get the child out of danger, and they had stayed in touch. Marley called on her if he encountered a situation beyond his experience as a counselor. They didn't always agree on things, but they had developed respect for each other's position.

Althea was aware that she might need him if this proved to be an abuse situation. If Gabrielle Davis was mistreating her daughter, they would have to find help for them both.

She was about to walk back toward the desk when she heard some sort of movement at the window. She had already slipped into her nightgown and was wearing a sheer matching robe over it. She pulled that closed in case the neighborhood children had discovered her window. She hadn't given much thought to Peeping Toms, but the office was at the back of the house. The protective cover of the shrubbery there might provide even more inducement to horny kids than the thought of glimpsing her body.

At the window, she looked out through the glass but could see nothing in the back yard. Reaching over to the desk lamp, she clicked it off and again looked outside. Moonlight offered enough illumination to give her a view, but she saw nothing moving in the shadows.

Perhaps it had been her imagination. She was about to draw the curtains when the sound was repeated. Now it came from across the room, or had it been inside her head? Could there be something wrong with her perception of reality?

She dealt with such problems so often it was hard not to be concerned about herself from time to time, especially when something odd cropped up.

She fumbld for the lamp switch as she peered through the darkness in the direction from which the sound had seemed to come.

Before she could turn on the lamp, however, it tumbled over the edge of the desk. The shade bounced aside, and the bulb shattered against the hardwood floor.

She froze. Barefooted, she knew any move could leave her with a fine sliver of glass in her foot. She had visions of thin and razor-sharp fragments on the floor.

Carefully, she began to calculate where she might place a foot safely, and was about to make a move when another sound, something like a grunt, came from across the desk.

She turned, keeping her feet in place to look in that direction. The slit in her gown opened with a whisper. She felt something like a breeze and realized the fabric had parted near the calf of her leg.

In her turn she must have snagged the cloth on the edge of the desk, she decided. That could be the only explanation. Her fingers slipped through the fabric and touched her skin, making sure there was no cut. When she was satisfied the flesh was not broken, she straightened again, peering through the darkness.

She could see no sign of movement in the thick shadows cast by the moonlight coming through the window. She told herself there was nothing to be afraid of. What had happened to the child could not be repeating itself with her. That would not be logical. It would be ridiculous to think something from a patient's psychosis could be manifesting itself within her.

She prepared again to take a step, but as she lifted her foot the lamp cord suddenly tangled around her ankle, and she was thrown off balance.

She tumbled backward, arms flailing as she struck the floor. The impact jolted through her shoulders and knocked the wind from her lungs. Shimmers of pain curled along her backbone.

She groaned and was about to sit up when she realized she was moving. The lamp cord was still tangled around her leg, and she was being tugged along, dragged by it.

She began to kick to free herself, but the cord, now forming a slip knot, was only made tighter by her movements. She tried to look downward to figure out what was pulling the cord, but she could see nothing in the darkness. Something told her there was nothing to be seen.

On her back it was difficult to find traction. She tried to dig her fingers into the floor, but the wood was hard and slick.

She skidded across it in a quick slide, past the desk and in the direction of the fallen lamp, toward the shattered glass. When she realized that, she began to struggle harder, and tears came to her eyes as she thought about the razor-sharp slivers. She hadn't wanted them in her feet, yet now they would . . .

She was dragged across the pool of slivers. She felt their jagged edges streak up her calves, making small slashes in her skin. Stinging sensations pulsed through her nerve endings, and she was aware of the warmth of the blood flowing from her. The backs of her thighs were ripped open as if small cat claws were being raked across her flesh.

The hem of her gown was pushed upward, exposing more of her flesh. Tiny glass slivers were soon embedded in her. She screamed as a large shard cut through her panties and gouged a chunk of meat from her buttocks.

She gritted her teeth, trying to prepare for the pain she knew would follow. The streaks up her back were quick, narrow, parallel lines that shot up to her shoulders. Pain hammered at her brain.

By the time her head reached the area where the glass had been, most of it had been absorbed by her body, so only a few tiny fragments remained to stick in her scalp.

She was drawn only a few inches farther before the movement stopped and she was left lying there, her own blood soaking her gown and running onto the slick floor. The cord went limp and dropped to the floor with a light tap.

For a few moments, Althea lay still, her heartbeat a scatter gun, her breathing coarse and labored. The pain was not acute, but terror was ablaze within her. She could make no sense of what had happened. Tears streamed down across her cheek as she rolled over onto her side and began to touch her back.

The worst gash was the one on her buttock. Otherwise she had only minor sliver punctures and scrapes. She touched the deep wound and found her hand covered in blood. It was going to require stitches, and that was going to be embarrassing at the emergency room. It was as if some cruel joke had been played, as if some twisted sense of humor had made her the brunt of a cruel prank.

She wept, because above all she felt violated.

Standing on the walk in front of Tanner's house, Danube paused to look in through the front window, the curtains not being drawn. He could see the writer at his desk. The computer screen cast a faint green glow across Tanner's features as he tapped away at the keyboard.

He appeared relaxed, dressed in faded jeans and a dark denim work shirt. His glasses sagged across the bridge of his nose, and a pencil was stuck behind one ear. The craft did not appear that glamorous from this point of view. Perhaps it would not be so bad to disturb him.

Slowly the black-clad man mounted the front steps and rapped on the door with his fist. A second ticked by before the porch light blazed to life. In another moment the door opened and Tanner looked out.

When he saw Danube, his mouth dropped open slightly. "What do you want?" he asked, his voice a bit harsh, suspicious.

"A word with you."

The writer remained in the doorway, blocking the entrance with his body and making no move to allow entry.

"What's this about? Why did you show up at the hospital? You upset the hell out of Gabrielle."

Danube's patience twitched. He looked down at the porch planks beneath his dark shoes rather than display anger. He was so tired of explaining things or trying to. When he looked back at Tanner he had squelched some of his frustration.

"If you'll let me talk with you for a little while . . ."

A wisp of a breeze swept down under the eave of the house, bringing a feeling of dampness and chill.

"Inside," Danube added. He'd spent enough hours under uncomfortable conditions.

Tanner hesitated, but Danube stared him down until he finally stepped back and allowed his unwelcome visitor to walk into the living room. They sat down in armchairs, facing and eyeing each other.

"Where the hell do you come from?" Tanner asked.

"Far away."

"So what do you want here?"

"Something unusual happened. Did it not?"

"How do you know that?"

"I have to know."

"Why are you so damned mysterious? Did you have something to do with this?"

Danube shook his head. "I've come to help," he said without inflection, as if bored with the prospect of convincing Tanner of his good intentions. It seemed to be something he'd done before, something he was weary of.

"It would be a little easier to believe you if you weren't so vague about everything," Tanner responded. "Where did you come from? Why are you here?"

"Something dark has come here, Mr. Tanner." The imperceptible accent flared in Danube's voice. "Who I am does not matter, and you probably would not believe my answer. What matters is this: what is happening has to be identified and dealt with."

Tanner rose from his chair, his tennis shoes squishing softly on the carpet as he paced about, made nervous by the dark-clad man's intensity as much as by the subject matter.

"She's upset, probably about her mother's divorce," he said. "That's all. Don't come at me with some kind of mumbo jumbo about dark spirits."

Danube rose too. "You were there. Did it appear to be something which could be explained within your usual perception of reality?"

"What the hell are you saying? I saw it happen, and no, I can't explain it, but that doesn't make it something supernatural."

"No. The forces behind it are what make it something beyond the normal realm. The child is under some form of spiritual attack. I would not have been sent here if some disturbance in the spiritual fabric had not been detected."

"Detected by whom?"

"The order I serve, The Order of St. Marius. A circle of nuns once sanctioned by the Vatican, now serving on their own, forgotten by most. Their existence is lost in some forgotten file, but they are still active."

"What do they do?"

"Struggle to keep the powers and principalities of darkness from interfering in the human realm. It is a difficult task, insurmountable. Is that what you wanted to hear? Does that make you feel better now that you know, or is it even more taxing on your sense of what is true?"

Tanner laughed. "You're a madman. What did you do, slip out of the mental institution in Penn's Ferry?"

With a sigh Danube dragged a hand across his brow, wiping back the lock of hair that had fallen across his forehead. "Your tact escapes you," he said. "But I have been called worse than madman, Mr. Tanner. A time far back might have had me exacting retribution. I'm too weary for that now. I need your help. Tell me what I must do to convince you. I have no stomach for games or trial and error."

Tanner stared at him. "You're sincere as hell aren't you."

"I am."

He dropped back into his chair, letting his weight go so that the cushion sighed under him. "This is unbelievable."

"You deal in mysteries, Mr. Tanner. You put together pieces of puzzles. This is the same. It is just that some of the pieces lie in corners where you might not otherwise look."

"What do you think is going on here, Danube?"

"Somehow, or in some way, something has come into contact with the child. Something from the other side, the spirit world."

"Ghosts?"

"I do not suspect the spirits of the dead."

"Then who or what?"

"There are many things out there. You people all seem to think they're benevolent. And honest. The reason for that escapes me. I cannot tell you what it might be. I need your help to try to find out, and I will need your help to establish contact with Mrs. Davis. She is resistant."

Tanner's eyes grew skeptical again. "How do I know you're not some kind of pedophile trying to get to her kid? Crazier schemes than this have been cooked up."

"I have lived a long time. There was a point when I indulged in vices, though they were far more conventional than you are implying. That is past. I have sworn an oath to the sisters. A vow to refrain from the carnal. If I were driven by lust I could find ways to indulge myself without concocting elaborate ruses to lead me to little girls."

Tanner's eyes were still filled with confusion and disbelief.

"I cannot blame you for not trusting me," Danube said. "I know this is quite unbelievable. We must talk for a while. Give me information. We will worry about convincing you of the other matters later."

"What motivates you?" Tanner persisted. "Why this commitment if you're not really a priest."

Again the breath sighed heavily from Danube's lungs. "My father once betrayed a friend. I've spent most of my existence trying to atone for that."

The silence followed, finally giving way to Tanner's voice: "I don't know what I can tell you that will be of value."

"What did you see when the child was attacked? Were there any unusual smells? Sounds?"

"How do you know I was there? How do you know everything?"

"I thought we were beyond that."

"Okay. I was there. Smells, sounds? Just her screams. We were talking I think. Gabrielle's daughter—Heaven—just started spinning around. There was nothing there, but her clothes tore. Cuts started appearing. I mean it was like something invisible was making swipes at her with a blade."

"Did you hear anything?"

"Just her screaming."

"Had she given any indication of anything else unusual?"

"I think she had some kind of nightmare after she was over here the other night. I had some cartoons on tape for her to watch. She fell asleep while they were on. Her mother said the Gnelfs had been preying on her mind."

Danube held up a hand to halt his speech. "Gnelfs? What are Gnelfs?"

"Cartoon characters. Ah, the story is that they're nomads, half-gnomes and half-elves. They're little green things. Glorified elves really. Not something you'd think a child would be frightened about."

"She has what? Seen these on television?"

"Yeah. They have books about them too."

"And before this incident she was frightened of the characters?"

"For some reason."

"Do you have something that shows these things?"

"I took the tapes back. Let me see if I have something." He got up and riffled through various stacks of magazines.

He had piles of them near a window and others under the television in a basket meant for *TV Guide.* He finally found an issue of *Time* that pictured the little characters in an upper-corner inset on a cover featuring Tom Cruise.

Inside a feature in the television section profiled the creators, a couple of young men in their twenties, who worked at a studio in Los Angeles, maintaining their individuality even as the popularity of their creations climbed.

Danube studied the various illustrations, his red eyebrows wrinkling as his blue eyes scanned the two-page spread.

"They certainly do not look frightening," he said.

"Does that give you any insight into what you need to know?"

"I need to talk to the mother and the child."

Tanner threw up his hands. "I don't know about that. I mean Gab and I haven't known each other that long. I kind of thought something had sparked there, but she wants to devote herself to getting the child well. She kind of pushed me out tonight."

"She cannot handle this crisis alone. She will need support. The people she turns to for help will not be prepared to deal with it."

"You're the only one that can help, right? But she doesn't trust you, and she doesn't know me that well. How do you expect me to get you in to talk to her?"

"You have to try," Danube said as he rubbed his beard, smoothing it down over his jaws. "If you don't it might be too late."

Chapter 9

Gabrielle stood in the doorway for a long time, peering over at Heaven's still form beneath the covers. The child seemed to be resting well now, at last. She did not toss or pitch under the covers, and her head was still on the pillow.

Finally satisfied that her child's rest would not be disturbed, Gabrielle walked back into the living room and sat down on the couch. Picking up the remote control for the television, she began to flip channels. With the volume turned down, the images flashing past did little to touch her thoughts. She felt almost brain dead. She was tired, almost exhausted, and so confused.

She watched newscasters flash past and romance 900 numbers and old movies and talk shows and fake talk shows on how to combat cellulite. None of it looked interesting.

She rested her head, wondering if she would be able to sleep if she tried. Her temples were throbbing, and her vision was blurring.

Standing, she clicked off the television. No way could she follow a plot even if she landed on something she wanted to see.

Yet somehow she knew if she lay down she would be wide awake again, worried and restless. Instead of walking back to the bedroom, she headed toward the kitchen. Perhaps warm milk would weave whatever magic it offered.

She opened the refrigerator, took the carton from the shelf, and filled a glass which went into the microwave.

Heaven awoke abruptly, snatched from quiet slumber. As she came awake she felt her hair being yanked, and her head twisted painfully to one side.

She looked up into the eyes of the Gnelf Master whose fist was tangled in her locks. He bent toward her, his leering face only a few inches from her own.

"'Lo, girly," he said through his grin. The foul reek of his breath seeped out through his yellow teeth. She wanted to turn her head as the smell gagged her, but he held on too tightly.

"Lot of people have been by to talk to you, haven't they?"

"You hurt me."

He pulled her hair tighter. "Oh? You were hurt? It could be worse, a lot worse, little bitch. A lot worse."

Her face showed him her fear, and he began to laugh, and behind him his followers joined in the laughter, a chorus of grunts and heaves of putrid breath, like pigs gagging.

"We hurt that whore that came in here asking questions. We could have hurt anybody we wanted. Your mommy if we'd chosen. It was just easier to get the other bitch. She was alone, like you are now. We can do anything we want to."

"No."

"Oh, yes. Yes." He tugged at her hair, bending her sideways over the edge of the bed so that the stitches ached in her wounds.

"Want me to rip you inside out?"

"No!"

"Want us to rip your momma inside out?"

"Nooooo!"

With his free hand he brought the sickle around and raked it across the pillow at Heaven's side. The fabric of the case split open with a harsh ripping sound, and the tip of the blade plunged down into the interior with a belch of escaping air.

It was an old feather pillow, and as he yanked the sickle upward it burst open, the small feathers spraying into the air in a sudden white cloud.

They fluttered upward then began to rain down, snowflakes. Tears filled Heaven's eyes as the Gnelfs standing around the bed began to laugh.

"That could have been you," the Gnelf Master said. "Except when you rip a little girl open it's all red and slimy. The skin splits open and the blood runs everywhere."

"No. Don't say that." She sobbed.

"The blade hooks on her intestines and they come up out of her like snakes—did you know you have snakes inside you?—and then it pokes at her liver and splits it open so that it spits out this ugly stuff that's green—"

"Stop it!" Heaven screamed.

He tilted his head back, his laughter a roar that pulsed up from his chest. "Yes, scream. Say it loud. Noooooo! Let mommy know you're afraid. Let her know."

Heaven could not contain the fear, and the scream was already curling through her lips.

It was as loud as she could make it. She let it flood out of her lungs, pushing the sound up through her parted lips.

Gabrielle felt the glass she had just pulled from the microwave slide through her fingers. It shattered on the floor at her feet, splattering warm milk up onto her ankles.

Ignoring the sting, she stepped cautiously with her bare feet over the ruined shards and rushed down the hallway. It was like the trip she had made that first night.

Moving Heaven to the master bedroom saved only a few paces, and once again images of possible harm assailed Gab. Could the madness be happening again, or perhaps that crazy priest had somehow gained entry and was molesting her. God help her.

She rushed through the living room, realizing a sliver of glass had made its way into her big toe in spite of her caution. She left bloodstains to mingle with those that had splattered from Heaven the night before. No matter. The room would have to be cleaned anyway.

At the edge of the hall she felt something push past her, something unseen. She was frightened. Refusing to let that deter her, she plowed through the door to her bedroom after fumbling with the knob, only to step into a snowstorm of feathers. Coughing when they touched her face and nose, she waved her hands to clear them away from her eyes and fought her way through the mess to the bed.

Heaven was there, her eyes wide with terror. She was clutching the covers against her as her lips and chin quivered. The tears on her face had caught some of the feathers which stuck to her skin.

Gabrielle wiped those away and clutched Heaven's head to her breast, hugging her tightly. "What's the matter, baby? What happened?"

Heaven only moaned.

"Oh, God. What is going on?" Gabrielle whispered. "What's wrong with you?"

She was still clutching Heaven against her when the doorbell rang. She twisted her head around, cursing under her breath. Who could be calling?

Lifting Heaven into her arms, Gab moved down the hallway and through the living room. When she looked out she saw Tanner on the front porch. He hadn't heeded her wishes. She was glad.

Pulling back the chain with one hand, she yanked the door inward. "Jake, it happened again. She hasn't been hurt, but something tore up the pillow in the bed."

Tanner moved forward, trying to speak but stammering, and she saw Danube standing behind him. Instinctively, she pulled back, holding Heaven protectively although the child's weight was already making her muscles throb.

"What is *he* doing here?"

"He wants to talk to you," Tanner said. "I was leery, but I thought maybe you should hear him out."

"What the hell does he want, Jake? He convinced you to bring him here?"

"I'll take him away. I can't guarantee it, but he seems sincere."

Gabrielle made sure that Jake was between her and the red-bearded man. Heaven was still trembling, and she had to shift the child's weight to keep from losing her.

"What happened?" Danube asked. He had removed the white tab from his collar, and in its absence, clad all in black, he seemed even more sinister than before.

"Why do you keep coming here? What do you want?"

"I have come to help you. Something strange is happening. We have to find out what it is so that I can fight it."

She hesitated. "Why would I trust you?"

"Is anyone else going to this much trouble to offer assistance?"

She had no retort for that. She started to speak, then nodded at Tanner instead. "Let him in," she said. "For now."

They moved into the living area where she eased Heaven's weight down onto the couch.

"She's pale," Danube said.

Gabrielle ran a hand across the child's forehead, brushing her bangs away and noting the pallor of her skin. "She's been frightened."

"What happened?"

"She screamed. I ran into the bedroom, I guess I shouldn't have left her alone, but she seemed to be resting. When I got to her she was scared to death and the pillow had been ripped apart. I don't know if she had a nightmare and tore it in her sleep, or if . . . if something happened like last night."

"Let me see the pillow," Danube said.

"I don't want to leave Heaven. Jake, it's in the next room."

Jake went with Danube into Gab's bedroom. Some of the feathers were still floating in the air. The two men moved through them to the edge of the bed.

Danube leaned over and looked at the ruined pillow. "It's been cut," he said. "A child didn't do this with her hands."

"A blade?"

He held up the edge of the pillowcase to show Tanner the smooth edges of the cut. "Straight. It would have to have been a blade."

"But how?" Tanner moved to the window and checked it. "Locked," he said.

"Further evidence that we are dealing with something other than a conventional intruder," Danube said.

"This is too damned weird," Tanner said. "What the hell was it? The same thing as last night? What's going on?"

"I don't know yet," Danube said. "I would guess your little green men. As for ascertaining what they really are, that may take time."

They moved back into the living room to find Gab gently touching her daughter's skin. "She's cold," she whispered.

"Get a blanket," Danube instructed Tanner. Then he walked over to stand beside Gab. "Did you see anything? Any visible signs of anything?"

"Nothing. Just her scream and the results."

"Anything else that you remember. Any of it could be important, vastly important."

Gab blinked. "Something in the hall. I felt something brush past me maybe."

"You saw nothing."

"Just felt it. May have been my imagination."
"Not yours. Hers."
"What?"
"Mr. Tanner told me about the Gnelfs. It could be something is using those images in her imagination to manifest itself."
"A spirit of some kind is appearing to her as the Gnelfs?"
"Based on what I know of the universe, that's what it appears to be. If you felt it too, it could be growing stronger."
She stared at him, disbelieving. Instinctively she cradled Heaven protectively, more as a shield against Danube than any unseen spirits.
"You can't expect me to believe this," she said.
"You know that what has happened to her does not have an explanation."
"I talked to a psychologist this afternoon."
"And did you get an answer?"
She had to shake her head. "She only spoke to Heaven for a little while."
"Long enough to know she did not have an answer?"
Gab continued to stare at him. "Maybe," she said.
"She didn't offer you any explanation."
Gab's hand covered her eyes, and she shook her head. "No. She didn't."
"I would like to see something of these Gnelfs," Danube said. "It may give me a better idea of what might be happening."
"I don't want Heaven to see the book. It's been put away."
"Understood," Danube said.
"It's in a drawer in the kitchen. The one by the stove, Jake."
Tanner nodded and led the way through the swinging doors. Danube was on his heels.
The book was wrapped in a towel and concealed under some knives. Tanner slipped it out and passed it over to

Danube who took a seat at the kitchen table.

Opening the book, he began to turn the pages slowly and deliberately. His eyes scanned the words and studied the artwork, his gaze sharp and unwavering.

"They look harmless enough," Tanner said, standing beside him.

"That can be misleading as you no doubt have been told all your life."

"You're trying to tell me something is evil about these little guys?"

He turned the book around to show a double-page spread of Gnelf Master and some of his cohorts setting up a bridal cottage for a couple of newlywed Gnelfs. Master was sketching some kind of protective symbol over the doorway. The caption read "Gnelf Master drew the good-luck sign over the door."

"Gnelf magic," Tanner said.

"That symbol is not a good-luck sign," Danube said. "It's an ancient Sumerian character, one of the symbols of the gates which separate this world from the beyond."

"What? You sound like you're talking about something out of H. P. Lovecraft."

"It goes back further than pulp magazines, Mr. Tanner. Mr. Lovecraft created his mythos based on ancient wisdom. Some have speculated he was a student of Aleister Crowley. The Sumerian symbols are just a part of what I find in this book. Hebrew signs are here also . . . the mark here"—he held up another page which showed a symbol carved into the trunk of a tree the Gnelfs were walking past—"is the sign of Shomer Dappim. He is a demon, the guardian of books and pages. He would exact vengeance on someone who left a holy book open."

"What you're telling me is that there are hex signs in this book?"

"Various symbols, not hex signs. The point is these markings incorporated into the artwork are based upon actual symbols and are not just random creations of the artists."

"Somebody is throwing real occult symbols into children's books?" Tanner said. "You know a couple of years ago they caught Mighty Mouse snorting coke."

"These are not imaginings or false fears," Danube said. "I have heard about subliminal messages. No this is real, Mr. Tanner. I do not know why these images are here, but they are real."

"And these markings are what's affecting Heaven? Call Geraldo."

"No, the symbols are not, in and of themselves. If they worked that way, every child who had one of these books would be subject to something similar."

"Then what are you getting at?"

"Somehow these images are being used. Heaven is a target. Why is the question."

"A child her age can't have any enemies, no preschool witches."

"Then I guess we had better talk to Mrs. Davis about who might be angry at her."

They returned to the living room, presenting the book to Gabrielle so that she could examine the markings. Danube briefly explained to her what he had told Tanner.

"Someone is putting curses into children's books?"

"Not curses. Symbols. That can be used to make curses."

Gab shook her head. "This is unbelievable. You wander in here looking like someone out of a bad horror movie and tell me some unseen person is putting a curse on my daughter. Hell, there must be some other explanation. Couldn't this be something like the stigmata?"

"It could be, but it is not," Danube said stoically. "Now will you consider who might be angry at you? Who might want to harm you by hurting your daughter."

"I can't think of anyone." Her eyes closed, and she shook her head. "Except David."

Tanner frowned. "Your ex-husband?"

"I can't believe he would try to hurt Heaven," she said.

"Was he angry about the divorce? Your leaving?"

"He ran away. He went out to California."

Danube looked at Tanner. "This material, it is produced in California?"

The writer nodded. "At Gnelf Inc."

"Have you been in contact with your husband since this began?" Danube asked.

"I've tried to call," Gab said. "He hasn't answered the phone."

Danube ran a hand across his beard. "You have an address for him?"

"Yes. If he's still there."

"Perhaps I should pay him a visit."

"You won't hurt him."

"I will only talk to him."

"Don't expect me to cover your expenses."

"That is taken care of. And while I am in California, I can pay a visit to the creators of the Gnelfs as well."

"You think you can just walk into a cartoon studio?"

"I will make the contacts," Danube said.

"In the meantime, are we safe?" Gab asked. "Or should I expect more of these attacks."

"The symbols are in her mind. Those symbols can be used as gateways to channel many things. It could get worse."

"What can be done?"

"Let me pray a blessing over her. It will help some."

Gab looked to Tanner for approval. He nodded cautiously, so they carried Heaven into the bedroom.

While the child slept, Danube knelt beside her, whispering a soft prayer. Then he spoke a few words in Latin and touched her forehead, gently forming a cross before getting back to his feet.

"Will that ward off the demons?" Gab asked.

"It will help some. You would do well to pray if something more occurs. It should help, if you can summon faith."

"I can try."

She wrote Dave's address down for Danube and followed him and Tanner to the front door. She caught Jake's arm before he exited. He stayed with her in the doorway as Danube stepped outside.

"Do you trust him?" she asked.

"I don't know."

"He won't hurt Dave?"

"I don't think so."

"This is so crazy. It can't be real."

"Can't it? What's happened is beyond imagination."

"But to think Dave might have hooked up with some guru or something that could cause harm to Heaven."

"It doesn't sound rational to me either. I deal with stories where all the ends tie up neatly and there's a resolution that makes sense. Still, I guess I have learned in putting twists and turns in my stories that the unexpected has to be figured into the equation."

"And the unexplained?"

"That too."

She kissed him softly. "Thank you, I think, but be careful of him."

"I will."

He walked out the door and met Danube at the edge of the stoop.

"She is not consoled?" Danube asked.

"She doesn't know whether to believe you or not. She doesn't trust anyone about now."

"Unfortunate. I may be the only one who can offer help. If I can gather enough knowledge."

"Is there anything I can do?"

"Yes. Find someone able to interpret more of those symbols."

"You mean a priest or a minister."

"Or a rabbi."

They climbed into the car and Tanner began to coax the engine to life.

"A rabbi?"

"Some of those marks are very ancient."

"Don't you have sources you can draw on? From those who sent you?"

"There is much knowledge housed at the convent. But there is much that is not known. Often I have to draw on sources I can find close at hand. Someone familiar with the ancient teachings might be able to help. Some of this goes far back beyond the coming of the Nazarene."

"How far back?"

"The beginning of time. Some of those marks come from *The Book of Raziel.*"

"What is that?"

"An ancient book of wisdom. It was supposedly plunged into the depths of the ocean. Over the centuries, fragments of what it contained have surfaced. Whoever put those marks in that artwork was probably exposed to one of the fragments. But there is a chance whoever is using the markings has somehow acquired a true copy of the work."

"So what would that do?"

"It was created by God to do good, yet the knowledge it was reported to contain could be turned around. In the wrong hands it could destroy the universe."

Jake put the car in reverse and eased back onto the street, turning at the corner at Danube's request to take him back to his hotel.

The tip of the long *baculum* came down on the sidewalk across the street from Gabrielle's house. As long as a shepherd's staff, it bore intricate carvings which covered its dark surface. Narrow at the tip and thick at the top, it might have served its wielder as a club.

The man who held it stared after the car for a long

time, watching its red taillights disappear into the darkness.

His long blond hair was pulled back into a pony tail, so tightly it seemed his flesh was stretched across the bones of his face, while his gray eyes were masked with a scowl which made his pointed features seem hawklike.

He was dressed all in gray, a pale gray suit and stylish coat that reached to his ankles, a striped shirt and gray tie.

On his hand was a large gold ring with an arcane symbol etched into its texture. That ring now twitched as he adjusted his grip on the witch's staff, and he let his breath escape slowly through clenched teeth.

His name was Simon.

Chapter 10

Tanner awoke just as the morning sun began to send slivers of light in through the crack between the curtains. He had not slept well, and the intrusion of the light pierced his consciousness with ease.

The sweat from his nightmares had dried to a sticky coating on his body, and his eyes felt swollen and watery. He took a quick shower before dressing, letting the hot needles of water wash away the sticky feeling. But they couldn't take away his apprehension.

He was a bit excited about doing something tangible to help Gabrielle and Heaven, however. The legwork also represented a chance to break the monotony of his work routine.

He'd held many different jobs while hammering away at his novels until gradually he began to make a living from just the books. Once he'd achieved his goal of writing full-time he had discovered how lonely it could be. He spent his days in his home, tapping at the keys and breaking the tedium with television and paperbacks.

Sometimes the realization of a dream is not all it is cracked up to be. He'd always expected something different if he was lucky enough to publish. He had expected it to be relaxing and liberating—and it was, but liberty could be quite boring.

He talked occasionally to his editor and sometimes to

his agent, made occasional trips to the book stores to chat with the clerks and see how sales of his books were going, and performed the necessities of life with a mechanical precision.

Groceries were purchased on Tuesdays, laundry was done on Wednesday, and house cleaning was spread out over Thursday, Friday, and Saturday between chapters. He wrote every day, struggling through intricate plots he outlined on legal pads and note cards.

Sometimes he went over to the lounge at the Clairmont, where the reporters from the *Clarion* gathered. On occasion, if he needed to do research, he hit the police hangouts. He did that less and less frequently now because many of the cops did not like the way policemen were portrayed in his books.

He let himself think about Gabrielle as he fixed a quick breakfast. There was something between them; that was evident even at this point. The intangible attraction that drew people together, the feeling that transcended common interest or simple emotion.

He had not been in love in a long time. He had seen women, had spent months in relationships, believing that his emotions had numbed and that he would not feel intensely again. When those relationships ended, he did not mourn them for long, but he sometimes wondered if he was destined to spend his life that way.

Now he wondered if some mechanism of fate had connected him with Gabrielle at this strange moment in her life. She needed his help, and perhaps that would ultimately mean something. Perhaps they would build something out of all this pain, and perhaps in some way fate or maybe even God was calling him to help her.

He had the time because he was ahead of schedule on his book, and he had experience in research, so perhaps it would all come together.

After breakfast, he drove by a book shop near his house and picked up a copy of the Gnelfland Bedtime Storybook which was on a CHILDREN'S BESTSELLER shelf.

He took the book with him over to the B'nai Israel temple. The secretary there was a tall, dark-haired woman with a beehive hairdo and a thick Southern accent.

She led him through a maze of hallways to the rear of the building, an auditorium where the rabbi was testing sound equipment.

The rabbi was a thin man whose dark hair was thick and curly, and he wore wire-rimmed glasses which gave him a boyish look even though he was around forty. He had slipped off the coat of his dark suit and had rolled up the sleeves of his white shirt.

"Rabbi Benjamin Estleberg, I'm not sure if you've heard of Jake Tanner," the secretary said.

He put down the microphone and nodded with a smfile. "I have heard of your work," he said. "You're the mystery writer. What can I do for you?"

"I'm sorry to drop in unannounced," Tanner said. "I'm doing a little research." He left it at that, no need to lie to the man.

"I've got time for a few questions," the rabbi said. "I'm just trying to get things ready for a temple-youth program."

He sat down on the edge of the stage and invited Tanner to sit beside him. "What I'm looking into deals with symbols," Tanner said, slowly easing the book out of its plastic bag. "It may look silly, but a friend pointed out to me that this children's book has some genuine symbols in it. I find that kind of interesting."

"Let me see."

Tanner handed the book over, and Estleberg carefully flipped through the pages. He spotted a couple of the symbols himself and nodded when Tanner pointed out a few others which were more obscure.

"Interesting indeed," the rabbi said. "These are very old, not something you'd find in the Talmud or the Torah. In fact they're something to which I've had limited exposure. Have you ever heard of the Kabbalah?

Sometimes it's spelled with a *C* and sometimes with a *K*."

"It's been mentioned to me."

"It isn't ancient itself, but it deals with old concepts. Some of these markings are quite odd. Some I've never seen. I wonder if the creators were Jewish? You know the 'live long and prosper' sign in Star Trek is Jewish, Mr. Tanner."

"Really?"

"Oh, yes. You'll see it on the front of the Torah, the scrolls, here at the Temple. It means shalom, and I believe it was Nimoy, who is Jewish, who contributed the salute. It could be that something similar has taken place here. The artists wanted their symbols to look realistic, so they drew on things they had seen somewhere or other."

"Possibly so. But do you have any way of tracing the meanings of these things?"

"Good question. I might be able to help you with some of them."

They walked back through the hallways to the rabbi's office, a spacious room lined with bookshelves.

He pulled out a few scholarly volumes and began to look through the browning pages of one. The smell of old paper touched Tanner's nostrils as the rabbi adjusted his glasses and peered down at a page.

"Many of these things deal with evil of one sort or another," Estleberg said. "The Kabbalah was devoted in part to speculation about evil. It speaks of the sitra ahra or the world beyond, the evil realm. I'm simplifying a great deal, but you may find some commonality with your own background. You are what? A Protestant, a Catholic?"

"Protestant."

"You have had some introduction to the notion that the devil, created by God, was cast out of heaven then?"

"Yes."

"In the Kabbalah there is also teaching about the destruction of the realms God created which concentrated on judgment without mercy. They were done away with, but the remainder of those worlds is now supposedly a basis for evil. Some writers attributed personification to that evil, hence the development of discussion about demons and devils."

"I'm not sure I follow you."

"You're talking about a broad realm of writing encompassing more than a thousand years. It is mysticism and speculation, much of it compiled in the dark ages. It discusses demons of many sorts who plague man. Many of these symbols, which are not particularly part of the Kabbalah, no doubt make an effort to keep the demons on their side of the wall, so to speak."

Tanner nodded. It coincided with what Danube had said.

"Walls or gates?"

"Gates, I guess. Yes."

"So there could be keys?"

"Indeed there could."

"Keys to be found in some other book?"

"Perhaps, yes."

The rabbi closed the volume. "Many of these markings are not familiar to me."

"Keys would be forbidden markings. Symbols used to open the way for evil."

"Indeed."

"So some of these could be that?"

"Perhaps so."

"Have you ever heard of *The Book of Raziel?*"

"Oh, yes. You're speaking about something even further back in mythology. Supposedly it was taken away from man and plunged into the depths of the ocean."

"I've heard that. Why was it taken away?"

"I don't know."

"Perhaps because its contents included keys, and someone misused those."

"Perhaps, yes."

"Theoretically these markings could be keys?"

"Yes. If someone had somehow found the book."

"The keys, then, could be used."

"To unleash the powers from the other realm, Mr. Tanner? You have a very good imagination. You must be working on a supernatural suspense tale."

"Just trying to make sure I understand it all."

"You would have to study a long time to grasp everything. Scholars have devoted ages to all of this material."

"I think some things are falling into place for me," Tanner said. Though the rabbi had mainly served to confirm Danube's speculation, Tanner did have a better understanding. But he was looking for something more.

"How much of this is real?"

"It's not something that we deal with regularly, Mr. Tanner. Just as Christians don't do exorcisms that often. This teaching goes far back into history, and there are many modern concerns we have to be about. Who is to say what was real to our ancestors? We don't deal much in mysticism these days."

"But someone taking it seriously, someone seeking to unlock the gates could conceivably be dangerous."

"I would think someone trying to perform magic would be a bit questionable, yes."

Especially if he succeeded, Tanner thought.

Marley was sipping his morning coffee and thinking about his sermon for Sunday when Althea arrived at his office. He stood up and smiled, offering her coffee from the urn which sat on a table in the corner of the office. She declined the coffee and his offer to sit on the chair facing his desk.

"I think I'd rather stand," she said. She sounded a bit nervous, and she did not appear to have slept well. Although her makeup was applied with the precision she always exercised, her eyes looked tired and swollen.

"What's wrong?" he asked.

"Have you talked to Mrs. Davis again yet?"
"Not this morning."
"Something strange happened to me," she said. "There's something very unusual about all this. It may be in your field."
He smiled and lifted his coffee cup. "Is the celebrated agnostic and skeptic acknowledging there's something she doesn't understand?"
"It's not funny, Marley. Something happened to me last night. It was like things were out of control. Like, well, like someone playing a cruel prank. Except there was no one there."
"I don't follow you," the minister said. His voice was still bright with amusement.
"Something I couldn't see, a force or something, dragged me through a pile of shattered glass. I say it was like a prank or joke because my ass took the worst of it."
"What?"
"It was a broken light bulb, and it snagged my left cheek if you know what I mean, Reverend. I had to go get stitches, and that was embarrassing. The techs at the emergency room kept snickering, and it hurt."
"Are you sure you didn't just stumble and sit down on the bulb?"
"I wish that was what happened. Are you turning skeptic now? I'm telling you, Marley, something dragged me. You're always talking spiritual warfare, give me answers."
Her tone of voice and the seriousness of her expression convinced him she wasn't in the mood for their usual banter.. He set down his coffee cup and leaned forward.
His own expression had sobered. Until now there had been only supposition mingled with suspicion. He had continued to entertain the question of whether Mrs. Davis might have abused her child and concocted the strange story to cover it. Now, if Althea—always the

questioning one—was frightened, then something odd must certainly be taking place. Perhaps demonic activity was really at hand.

He swallowed, a feeling of excitement tingling just at the outer edge of the fear he felt. He had read about this phenomenon, had debunked false reports and had counseled a few kids who had reported involvement in self-styled satanic activity, but he'd never been faced with the possibility of actual spirits or of war with powers and principalities. His heartbeat quickened.

"We must go back and talk to them," he said. "She could be in danger, and the child could be harmed even further."

"What can we do?" Althea asked.

"Demons can be rebuked," Marley said. "Men have authority over them."

"I didn't feel too authoritative last night," Althea retorted.

Marley nodded, realizing he was not as confident as his words made him sound. Jesus had cast out demons, but while he himself strived for true faith, he wondered if he would have the courage to face assaulting spirits. He knew Althea's lack of belief left her unprotected, but he also knew people who faced demons had to be spiritually strong and unwavering. And good people were subject to attack too.

He knew priests went through extensive preparation for true exorcisms. Even then, things got tough for them sometimes. He'd read of exorcisms that took days. The people performing them were put through ordeals.

"We'll go see the Davises," he said. "We can't turn our backs on this."

"I know we can't. It's following us."

Gabrielle spoke briefly with her boss, explaining the situation in abbreviated terms and receiving more understanding than she'd expected. After hanging up, she tried Dave's number again without getting an answer.

As she returned the phone to its cradle, she found herself shaking her head. She remembered the warm moments at the beginning of their marriage. How could Dave have become involved in something so strange?

She cursed him under her breath, just in case he had launched some effort to harm Heaven. She recalled an old Ray Bradbury story her brother had read to her when they'd been in junior high. What was it? "The October Game," about a father using his daughter to exact vengeance on his wife. She closed her eyes as the shiver touched her. How horrible. It was unimaginable that Dave could do something like that, even more unimaginable than this very real nightmare that was taking place.

She checked on Heaven to make sure the child was still sleeping and then headed for the bathroom, where she removed her robe and hung it on the hook on the door. The thick terrycloth didn't hold well on the hook, but as long as the door was not jostled it would not fall. Gab didn't pause to study her reflection as she passed the mirror. She knew what her flaws and imperfections were without searching for them in a reflected image.

Leaning over the tub, she turned on the faucet and waited for the water to warm before she stepped behind the curtain and let the spray from the showerhead course over her.

Her eyelids sagged as the warm spray caressed her flesh, and absently she picked up the soap and began to lather it across her abdomen.

Steam began to rise around her in white puffs as she moved her hands across her breasts, refusing to let her fingertips linger on her nipples. When David had moved away, she had resolved she would not allow herself that sensation. Self-gratification was not a solution to loneliness or a refuge from the problems at hand.

Tilting her head back, she let the water touch her hair

and spray through to the roots. It seemed to melt some of the fatigue from her brain, she thought, enjoying the feeling.

She let her head roll back, let her mouth open slightly, let her thoughts clear. She ought to call her mother, talk to her without revealing the full extent of the situation. No need to worry her or paint a picture so gloomy her mother would want to rush to them, but she needed her support.

After a few more minutes, she reached forward and turned off the water, shaking her hair about as the swirl of water began to gurgle down the drain. Yanking the curtain back, she reached for the handtowel hanging by the sink to wipe her eyes. Then she seized a larger towel on a wall rack.

She was rubbing water away when she stepped from the tub and walked in front of the mirror. Steam had clouded the glass, but in an instant her eyes focused on the letters which had been streaked across it as if by someone's finger.

YOUR DAUGHTER WILL SUFFER, BITCH. Beneath this was an arcane symbol much like one of those in the Gnelf book.

She looked toward the door, but it was still closed and her robe was undisturbed. No one could have walked in, yet somehow something had found access to the glass. She had heard nothing over the spray of the water, but she knew no one could have entered without attracting her attention.

Grabbing her robe, Gab wrapped it around herself and tied the belt tightly in place at her waist. Then she hurried through the house to check on Heaven.

When she reached the bedroom, the child was still sleeping, undisturbed.

She did not rush to her for fear of waking her, but she watched her for a long time, praying for her safety. Somehow she would fight. She would protect Heaven from whatever assaults were launched against her.

Whoever was after her child, Gnelfs or whatever, they would not destroy Heaven. She wouldn't allow it. Not unless they took her life first.

—

Tanner came by around lunchtime and she tried drawing the symbol from the mirror for him after explaining what she had read. The condensation had dried before she had found any way of preserving what she had seen. She had a Polaroid, but she hadn't bought film for it in a long time.

"It's a little different than the others," he said. He briefly outlined what the rabbi had told him. "Maybe they used this as some kind of gate or whatever to get here."

"Or maybe they're taunting me. Letting me know how close they are. Letting me know they're getting closer. And stronger."

Chapter 11

Danube had swapped his black shirt for a loose-fitting white one with an open collar, which he wore beneath a floral vest, and when he reached LAX the sunlight let him know he would not be needing the raincoat he now carried over his arm.

The girl at the Hertz counter had long red hair, and sunlight had darkened the freckles that dappled her cheeks so that she looked like a schoolgirl except for the noticeable swell of breasts beneath her uniform blouse.

She smiled sweetly as Danube made his request, and when she spoke he detected a thick Southern drawl. She'd probably come up from Alabama or Georgia for the movie business. No doubt, she had a few small-town beauty-contest wins behind her and hoped to parlay that into modeling and acting.

At least she'd found work here and not in one of the darker places where so many aspiring actresses wound up.

"Have you learned your way around the city?" Danube asked, softening the usual harshness of his voice.

"Mostly. There's a lot of city here. I always thought Birmingham was big enough. This place is spread out everywhere."

"You are from Alabama. I thought we might be related."

She touched her hair. "You mean 'cause of this?"

"Common descendents, Ms. . . . ?"

As she returned his credit card, his fingertips brushed against the back of her hand, and something deep in her eyes seemed to click.

"Devon, Devon Rogers. Maybe we are related," she said. "Way back."

"Way back," Danube said, locking his gaze on her blue eyes. "Back far in history, perhaps my ancestors and yours were close."

She nodded, her eyes focusing on something unseen.

"I could use a guide," he said. "I haven't been in the city in a while."

She stared at him, frowning for a moment as if she wondered why she was nodding in agreement. "It's my friend Rosemary's day off. I could call her. Then I could be out of here in about an hour. We cover for each other here, in case we have auditions or somethin'."

"That would be fine."

An hour and fifteen minutes later, she had changed into civilian clothes, faded jeans and a bright yellow blouse that matched the ribbon she had used to pull her hair back into a pony tail. She sat behind the wheel of the rental car, guiding it through the twisting maze that carried them away from the airport. She'd been handling L.A. traffic for two years, so it wasn't hard to find a place in the flow.

She was not dazed, but her eyes were rather blank, and she found it hard to focus her thoughts. Danube had given her an address across town. The freeway would get them there quickly enough, and she was happy to take him, but she wasn't sure why. He was nice, but he was a stranger.

She shouldn't be taking him on a drive, leaving her job for him. Except that she felt compelled to help him, linked to him in some way. With his accent there was no way he could be closely related to her family back in Alabama, but some sort of tie, some deeper connection seemed evident. Maybe they did share common ancestry, although it seemed spooky, as if he had some kind of magical power over her.

Without thinking further, she swept the car up onto an entrance ramp and swirled it around onto the freeway, jockeying into the lane she sought. She'd learned to fight the automobile battles quickly after coming here.

Gradually she increased the speed of the dark sedan. It was bigger than her Datsun, but it handled well enough, taking them in and out of the mass of traffic.

The apartment was in a little brick and wood building at the end of a narrow street. It wasn't yet a bad neighborhood, but given time it would continue to decay. The building had probably gone up in the late sixties from the look of it, and the rustic ranch style had weathered badly so that the once-darkened surface was now faded to a brownish gray.

Danube got out of the car, rolling up his sleeves when the late-afternoon heat caught him away from the air conditioning.

"You want me to go with you?" the girl asked.

"Maybe you should wait here," he said.

He moved on up the walkway and rang the bell on the door numbered for Dave's house. When he got no answer he looked cautiously around and then used the same credit card which had paid for the car to open the lock.

The apartment had the stale smell of a place that had not been used in some time. The air was dry and hot and seemed to lie across the room like an oppressive blanket.

The curtains were drawn, so only narrow rays of sunlight crept into the room, splaying across the couch and the coffee table littered with forgotten mail and other debris.

A few bills and circulars were among the envelopes, but Danube found nothing that might indicate where Dave might be.

Moving on into the bedroom he found clothes piled on the floor and covers twisted about at the center of the mattress as if they had been left so when someone had climbed from the bed.

The nightstand drawer held a torn box of condoms. Several of the individual packages were gone. Closing the drawer, he moved on to the closet. Only a few shirts and pairs of pants hung there, and the dresser was also somewhat barren; still no sign of where David Davis might have gone.

Behind the dresser he found a letter that had slipped down to the floor and was trapped against the wall. It was from Gabrielle, and had been torn open. A snapshot of Heaven had been enclosed, but David Davis had not bothered to display it.

Finding nothing in the bathroom, Danube let himself back out the front door and then found Devon talking with an emaciated woman in a faded bathrobe. The woman's blond hair had been permed by someone with no knowledge of hairdressing, and she wore eye makeup that was not to her credit. It was orange.

"This is the manager," Devon said.

Danube masked his impatience with a smile.

"You looking for Mr. Davis?"

"Yes. He's a relative."

"He's probably still off with that girl."

"Girl?"

"Kinissa."

"Oh?"

"Little Oriental girl."

Danube nodded. "Do you know where she lives?"

"He gave me an address in case someone was looking for him."

She turned and headed back toward her office. Danube followed with Devon at his heels, the puzzled expression on her face indicating this endeavor was doing nothing to clear up her own questions about why she was there.

The woman riffled through a stack of papers and

finally produced a torn scrap with a barely legible inscription on it.

"Do you know how to get there?" Danube asked once the hieroglyphic had been deciphered.

Devon nodded. "I believe I can find it."

Danube took her arm and guided her back toward the car.

After a lengthy nap, Heaven crawled out of bed and found her way to the bathroom. Her bladder felt as if it were about to pop open, and the grogginess from the drugs made it seem like her head was floating. She didn't like the sensation. It was worse than the feeling that came when you hung upside down on the monkey bars for too long and then straightened up.

After flushing, she wandered back down the hallway and found Mommy asleep on the couch. Mommy had dozed off, and now her head lay back at an odd angle and she had a twisted expression on her face. It was late afternoon, and Mommy still wore her robe. Everything felt funny. Sick days were always like that. The time passed differently, just sort of oozed by, and the day was gone without anything happening in it.

Heaven hated that. As bad as school was, it had its good parts, and she always felt awake for it, alive. Everything felt sort of dingy now. The house seemed gray, icky.

She missed Terry even if she didn't miss the other kids, and she missed the story reading and some of the games. Why did all of this have to happen? Why did Daddy leave? Didn't he love her anymore? And why had the Gnelfs started bothering her? They had always been so much fun before. So sweet and happy on television. But now they were coming after her, slobbering, threatening, wanting to hurt Mommy.

She realized her head was hurting. It throbbed around her temples and across her forehead. Were the Gnelfs doing that too?

She crossed the living room and shook Gab's arm, wanting to awaken her. At feeling the tug, Gab sat up, disoriented. Her eyes quickly focused on Heaven. "Sweetheart, are you all right?"

"Tired, Mommy. My head hurts some."

Gab hugged her. "Maybe you're hungry."

Heaven's stomach felt a little queasy, but she nodded. Maybe some food would be good. She followed Mommy into the kitchen.

"What do you want?"

"Cereal."

"Good enough for now." Gab took down a box of Frosted Flakes and shook some into a bowl.

Heaven sat at the table, watching the flakes fall. The Gnelfs wanted to hurt Mommy. They had warned her about telling, but maybe she should so Mommy could be on the lookout for them too.

"Mommy?" she said as the bowl was placed in front of her.

"What, dear?"

"Why would the Gnelfs be mad at you?"

Gab was silent, and her face showed concern. "Why do you ask?"

"Just wondered."

"Sweetheart, they've been attacking you."

"But you would be upset to see me hurt."

"Yes."

"Who's mad at you, Mommy? Could it be Daddy that told them to come?"

Gab put her hand to her face, covering her expression as her eyes closed. For a moment she chewed her lower lip. "Baby, Daddy is far away because of his job."

"Doesn't he ever want to see me again?" Heaven's voice was soft and earnest.

"Of course he does," Gab said. "He'll come to visit. Soon."

Heaven began to eat her cereal, fighting the tears that wanted to flow. She wouldn't cry. Mommy was too worried already. Mommy still loved her, and she didn't want her upset. If Mommy got upset she might go away too.

When Althea and Marley arrived shortly after six P.M., Gabrielle greeted them at the door and showed them into the living room. Althea carefully lowered herself onto a seat, but neither she nor Marley seemed able to sit still. The pastor folded his hands in his lap, wringing them like a funeral director.

"I've put Heaven to bed again," Gabrielle said. "She's kind of upset."

"Has anything else happened?" Althea asked.

"Another incident last night. Not quite as bad as before. Nothing happened to her physically this time." She told them about the slashed pillow and about the message on the mirror. Then she repeated what Danube had related to her.

"It's hard to accept something this strange, but I know weird things are happening. Danube flew out to L.A. this morning. He's trying to check on my ex-husband. I'm worried because Heaven seems to have come up with that same idea on her own, that her father might be responsible."

"Children often puzzle over why their parents break up and why one goes away," Althea said. "They blame themselves either consciously or subconsciously."

"She may have overheard something too, I'm not sure. I'm praying to God this is not something Dave has cooked up to hurt his own daughter."

"What do you know about this Danube?" Marley asked.

"He's some kind of priest, not the traditional type. He works for an order of nuns."

"That's odd," Marley said, "but maybe it's fortunate that he showed up. Last night, Althea had an encounter of some kind. I think it may have been a spiritual attack."

Reflexively, Gab turned to Althea to get her opinion of what had happened, and the psychologist confirmed her suspicions with a nod. "Yesterday I would have scoffed. I'm not saying the parson is right, but I will tell you it's like nothing I've ever experienced before. I wanted to come back here because I was concerned about Heaven's well-being."

"She's been all right today. Danube performed some kind of blessing. There was the mirror warning, but that was directed at me. I can hardly believe it. I was hoping tonight would be different. Jake Tanner is going to drop by in a while. He talked to a rabbi this morning. The rabbi sort of confirmed what Danube said."

"Seems I'm a little behind in mystical matters," Marley confessed. "I guess I need to learn more about all of this. I've studied it quite a bit, but I guess I've only scratched the surface."

"I don't know what in the world is happening here or why it's happening to me," Gabrielle said.

Marley leaned toward her. "I don't have experience with this sort of thing. I've read about it, but I've never dealt with it firsthand. I will try to help you, though."

"Thank you. Let's hope you don't have to."

The address they'd been given for Dave was in an even more unpleasant part of town. The sidewalk which led up to the door of the bungalow was cracked, clumps of grass clawing through the gaps. The front porch was sagging, and exterior paint was beginning to peel away in dry, crumbling flakes.

Devon parked the car at the curb and looked nervously at the house across the street where motorcycles were parked. "You want me to wait here?"

Danube traced her gaze. "Maybe you should come with me," he suggested. He didn't mention that Dave might be as dangerous as a group of bikers if he was dabbling in the dark arts, not wanting to alarm her. She was all the help he had, so he didn't want to scare her off.

Together they got out of the car and made their way up to the front door, where Danube pressed the small button embedded into the facing.

The girl who showed up a few seconds later was blond, dressed in a short denim skirt and a tight blue T-shirt. Her hair fell to her shoulders in a limp, oily wave of tangles, and the tan on her cheeks made her look as if she needed to wash. She didn't look Oriental.

"Can I help you?"

"I'm Danube," he said. "I'm looking for Dave. Would you get him please?" His tone and the look in his eyes made it clear he would accept no excuses.

"Uh, sure," she said. "Just a minute."

Since the woman had seemed unafraid Devon decided to wait in the car, and as she stepped off the porch, Dave appeared, wearing white shorts and a pale blue T-shirt. He hadn't shaved in a while, and his hair was a tangle of curls.

"Do I know you?"

"I'm a friend of Gabrielle's. She's been trying to find you."

"She said she didn't want any alimony or anything." His face was suddenly hard. He began chewing the inside of his lip as he looked away from Danube. "What does she want? Child support? I haven't got any fuckin' money. I lost my job."

One of Danube's red eyebrows cocked upward. "So you are selling drugs?"

"What the fuck . . . ? Shit man you're not some kind of cop."

"He's got an accent, Davy," the girl said. "He's probably from INTERPOL or something."

"I haven't smuggled shit," Dave said. "Really."

"I am not interested in your activities in that sphere," Danube said. "I came to talk to you about other matters. Such as sorcery."

"What the hell do you mean?"

"Your daughter has been having nightmares. What do you know about the Gnelfs?"

"What, man? Fuckin' green men?"

Danube grasped his collar and shoved him back through the doorway into the darkened living area. It was a match for the front of the house, a seedy square with lumpy furniture.

"You seem to have assimilated the vernacular of this region," Danube said. "I'm wondering if you might have encountered someone in the spiritual marketplace. Perhaps someone willing to help you exact some sort of revenge on your wife."

"I don't know what you're talking about."

Danube seized Dave's wrist and twisted it, forcing Dave to spin around in pain. With his thumb, Danube then touched a pressure point, and a cry of agony shot from Dave's lips.

"Let him go," the girl demanded. "He's not hurtin' nobody."

Danube spoke through clenched teeth. "Now then," he said. "We were talking about Gnelfs."

"All right. My little girl had some books about them or something. That's all I know. I told Gabrielle I didn't want anything to do with her anymore. She wanted to leave, fine."

"You've lost your love for your daughter?"

"Hey, Gab wanted to take her. I can do without the responsibility."

"Your wife's leaving devastated you this badly?" Danube shoved him onto the couch across the room. Dave thudded against the ruined springs poking up against the cloth covering.

"The Gnelf books contain markings which could be utilized to harm the child. You know nothing about that?"

"What! Are you crazy? I've never heard of such shit. They're cartoons. That's all."

Danube looked at the man, thinking of how he must

have been when married to Gabrielle. "Oh, how the mighty have fallen," he whispered.

"What?"

Danube shook his head. "Nothing."

He walked toward Dave, slowly. Panicking, the blond man started to scramble off the couch, but something in Danube's eyes froze him and he sat and waited while Danube moved forward.

Kneeling in front of Dave, Danube placed his hands on the man's shoulders and stared into his eyes. Unblinking, Dave stared back, mesmerized by the intensity of Danube's gaze.

"Open your thoughts," Danube commanded.

Still staring straight ahead, Dave submitted to the probe by Danube's mind. He felt something moving inside his brain, darting in and out.

Sweat began to form on Danube's forehead, popping out in beads that looked like tiny pearls. Still he would not relinquish his contact. On Dave's shoulders his hands began to tremble, but he did not waver. He let his thoughts search, weaving their way through the brain patterns of the man before him.

It was not magic exactly, just an exercise, a process he had learned long ago. He used it infrequently, but today he had no desire for delay and the struggle of hours of questioning. He needed truth quickly.

After a few more moments Dave began to tremble and a thin trickle of saliva slipped over his lower lip. His eyes began to roll back in his head, and only Danube's hands kept him upright, prevented him from tumbling over.

Releasing his grip, Danube watched the man slump over onto his side. He had sensed no presence of magic here, and he doubted this man was capable of what would be required to perform the acts which had touched Heaven's life.

The girl rushed over to him, crying as she looked down at the slumped form on the couch. "What did you do to him?"

"He will be all right," Danube said, tilting his own head back and massaging his temples with his fingertips.

"He's dead."

"He will be fine. Let him rest."

"You bastard. What did you do?"

"I cleared his thoughts. The process was taxing for him." He turned his back on her and walked out the front door, almost stumbling as he exited.

Devon was resting her head against the steering wheel. She lifted it when she heard the door on his side close.

"Two thousand miles to dine on a dish of red herring," he said.

"Where to now?"

"I want to go to the place where they make the Gnelfs," Danube stated firmly.

She laughed. "Why?"

"I want to talk to their creators."

"Whatever you like." She wanted to argue, to get rid of him, but she couldn't.

Tanner saved the work he had just done on a floppy disk and turned off his computer. He wanted to get over to Gabrielle's. A feeling of concern had found its way through the storm of his imagination to nestle in his brain. Normally when he was writing he was able to shut out other notions and feelings even in the worst of times, but today he could not. He kept thinking of the things he had witnessed and of the eerie warnings Danube had conveyed.

The old adage of naming a fear to make it go away came to his mind. But this fear could not truly be named, or if it could be given a name, like Gnelfs, still it could not be understood, and that was at the heart of the saying. If a fear could be understood it could be conquered, but how could one understand some esoteric and forgotten myth that threatened to tear away reality and unleash nightmare visions of the unreal?

He pulled a light jacket from his closet, a white windbreaker. In one of his novels the hero would also select the proper handgun to tuck into his belt for security. He had no such option. No weapon. If something happened at Gab's he had no idea of how he would deal with it or if he could offer her any help at all.

On the drive over to her house, he listened to music, but that did little to soothe his nerves. He had formulated no answers to the phenomena when he knocked on the front door, and it was a relief to see other people present when Gabrielle showed him into the living room.

He shook hands with Marley and Althea, and then helped himself to a cup of coffee from the service on the coffee table. Casually, Gabrielle sat down on the floor in front of his chair and rested one arm against his leg.

Heaven was now curled up at the end of the couch, her head resting on Althea's lap. Her eyes were closed, and breath purred softly through her nostrils. She seemed so innocent and angelic—so at peace.

They all watched her for a while, their vigil silent except for the occasional sound an appliance made or the creak or groan of the house. Each noise made eyes narrow and muscles twitch. They were waiting for something bad to happen.

"Have you heard from Danube?" Tanner asked, to end some of the tension.

"No calls."

"I wonder about this man," Marley said. "He's a priest and he isn't a priest?"

"He's as mysterious as some of the other goings-on," Tanner replied. "I think I trust him, but I don't know what to make of him."

"I've studied the Bible and good and evil all my life. I've never thought anything like this could be possible, that it could manifest like this." Marley shook his head.

"Why did it have to choose me?" Gab wondered again. "A couple of days ago it looked like I might be getting my life in order. Now everything is screwed up again."

"I wish I could tell you how to resolve it all," Althea said. "That's my job, but I just don't know what to do in the light of all this. The parson and I spent the afternoon going through some of his books, and we didn't find anything pertinent."

Tanner related again what he had discussed with the rabbi. Marley nodded. Some of it he had heard before, and some of it was new to him. "We didn't delve very deeply into themes surrounding the Old Testament in seminary," he said.

"*The Book of Raziel* is apparently very powerful."

"I don't see how Dave could have laid his hands on that," Gab said.

"Ex-husbands can do a lot of things you'd never expect," Althea stated authoritatively. "You're married to them. You live with them. Then they're something totally different when it's over. They can do things you'd never believe the nice guy who used to send you roses would have pulled."

Gab looked skeptical. "I don't know. There's got to be some other explanation."

Before anyone could reply, the sound of the laughter filled the room.

Chapter 12

After a bit of discussion at the studio where the Gnelfs were merchandised, Danube was able to obtain the creators' office address. They preferred to work in the little studio in which they had started out, he learned.

Devon took the freeway again, and they reached their destination well before closing time.

Stepping into the air-conditioned reception room, Danube found a petite blond secretary behind a small mahogany desk. She was so short that her small body seemed a bit disproportionate to her head. Long hair hung down over one of her shoulders. If she let it fall straight down her back, Danube thought, she might trip over it.

"I need to speak to the creators of the Gnelfs," he said aloud.

"Do you have an appointment?" she asked brightly, in her voice a seemingly calculated Southern California inflection.

"It's very important that I speak with them," Danube said.

She smiled. "Sir, do you realize how many people say that? The Gnelfs are very popular. We have visitors frequently even though our office is not listed. If we accommodated every request for a personal visit we wouldn't be able to create more Gnelfs material. Now if you'd like to leave something to be autographed for your children . . ."

It was a memorized speech, designed to be polite but firm and to dispatch quickly any zealous Gnelfs' fans who appeared. Different versions of the same spiel were probably used to handle others. The secretary would have a lecture for children, one for would-be artists seeking help, and one for the generally curious.

"A child may die if I do not speak to them about the origins of their work."

"Sir, I hardly think this could be a matter of life or death."

"Ask them if they know anything about *The Book of Raziel.*"

"I'm not supposed to bother them. They're on deadline with a new project."

"Please."

Hesitantly she moved away from her desk and went through a door which led to the rear of the small building. She returned in a few moments, a puzzled expression on her face.

"That seemed to get their attention," she said. "Go right in."

The Gnelfs creators were laboring in a cluttered workroom in which a large drawing board faced a desk holding a typewriter and crumpled paper. The wall was decorated with framed cartoon cels of the various Gnelfs, and some of these were matched with background cels to re-create scenes from the program. The setup was simple considering the money their creations were bringing in.

The men were both in their early thirties. One was tanned and had smooth blond hair. He wore white slacks and a blue polo shirt. The other, who sat behind the drawing board, was heavier. He was dressed in jeans and a red T-shirt with Edgar Allan Poe's picture on it. He wore glasses and sported a beard, while a snap-brim hat covered his thinning hair. They both looked nervous.

"Can I help you?" the heavy one asked.

Danube stood in the doorway, looking from one man to the other, studying them quickly, spotting weaknesses and dangers with this hasty assessment. Softly, he spoke, introducing himself.

The heavy one shifted about on his stool. "What the hell do you want?"

Danube found a seat facing the men. "I want to talk to you about your creation," he said. "You are?"

"What?" the blond man asked.

"Your names."

"I'm Robert Eden," the blond man answered. "This is Allen Hyde."

"Eden and Hyde. Creators of Gnelfs and Gnelfland."

They nodded, intimidated by his presence. He kept his eyes glued on them so that they would make no move to summon security. He intended them no harm, but he wanted no interference.

His strength had been taxed by the encounter with Davis, the touch for Devon, and the effort to get past the receptionist. He wasn't up to the strain of battle or the further effort needed to extract information.

"The two of you do most of the artwork?"

"What is this about, man?" Hyde asked.

Danube closed his eyes, fighting to control impatience and building anger. "I need answers about your work," he said. "I do not have the time to go through the effort of creating a facade in order to talk with you, and I do not have the patience to try to make you believe who I am or why I am here. Now, you do the artwork?"

"I did the initial stuff," Hyde answered, still a bit indignant. "On the shows, hell, there's a whole staff of people. Inbetweeners, character—"

"The books," Danube said.

"Yeah, that's kinda how we got started."

"Why did you put the symbols in there?"

"What? What symbols."

The color began to drain from the blond man's face. In spite of his tan he seemed to go pale, snow white. "You're not from one of those coalitions or something, are you? You're not going to organize a boycott? We're not Satanists."

"I need to know why they are there—and where you found them," Danube said.

Eden glanced over at his associate. "Hyde put them in there."

Hyde smirked, and his eyes rolled upward in disgust. "They're nothing," he said. "Just like Procter and Gamble's man in the moon."

"They are a little more pertinent than that," Danube said. "They have an actual connection with ancient rites."

Hyde grimaced again. "We didn't know that, man. We just wanted something that looked authentic."

"Look, those are the earlier books anyway," Eden said. "When we signed the cartoon deal and the merchandising agreement, they made us quit using that stuff. They were afraid somebody would get the wrong idea."

"Someone did," Danube said. "Someone very powerful, I'm afraid. While those marks are harmless on their own, they can be utilized. They are marks for conjuring or binding, and once they are planted in a child's mind—"

"Come on," Hyde said. "They're bullshit. This is California; we picked up some stuff in some shops. It's nothing. It's like crystals or such."

Eden leaned across the table and touched Hyde's arm. "Remember? That night we were scared."

"We'd had a few beers. Who knows what happened. It could have been an earthquake."

"You were attacked?"

"We were fooling around, doing some sketches. We were doing a deal where the Gnelfs were opening up a cave of treasure, and it was sealed with this magic symbol. They couldn't enter. We were trying to figure out what the seal would look like, and Allen was doing some sketches. We were playing with some designs, inverting things, turning them around so we'd have a symbol of our own, not a duplication of those in the books we had."

"And what happened?"

"We heard something," Hyde said. "We turned and the door flew open. There was nothing there, but the room got cold. So cold we started shivering. It didn't make sense. It's always warm here, right?"

Eden remembered. "That's what I said then," he noted. "I was sitting here at the desk talking to Allen while he was drawing, so I got up to close the door. I figured I'd check the thermostat on the air conditioner too. We were trying to treat what had happened rationally.

"Before I made it to the door something picked me up, I mean right up in the air, and then I was pitched over the desk."

"I got up then and ran toward him," Hyde said. "And the drawing table turned over. I spun about and looked toward it, and all of these exacto knives started coming for me like darts. It was like a scene from one of those horror movies. You know, where they do it with butcher knives?"

Danube indicated he understood.

Before continuing, Hyde wiped a bead of perspiration from his forehead. Recalling the incident was reliving it.

"I don't guess those knives would have killed me," he said holding up one of the small instruments. It had a long silver handle and a small, razor-sharp blade. "But the lot of them would have cut me up pretty badly."

"You escaped?"

"I just dropped. They went over me, like a school of fish or something. That's where they wound up."

He pointed toward one of the framed cels on the wall. Eden turned to it and lifted the picture off its hook to reveal the slits in the wall where the blades had become embedded.

"There was no explaining that," Hyde said. "I stayed

on the floor for a while and asked Rob if he was all right. He was bruised, but he was okay."

"We started to get up then." Eden's expression was sober. "We didn't get far before the stuff on the drawing table started flying."

"Wind?"

"It was weirder than that," Eden said.

"The paper is kind of heavy." Hyde picked up one of the large rectangular cards he used for his work. Running a fingertip across the edge of it, he gave Danube an idea of its texture.

"It started kind of whipping through the air. Slashing toward us," Eden said. "We tried backing up a little. It followed us. I threw my arm up, and one of the sheets raked across it."

He held up his right forearm to reveal a thin white scar which streaked through his tan. "It felt like I'd been cut with a sword."

As their descriptions continued, Danube let his mind pick up the memories, re-creating the scene for himself as they told of how they had faced a swirling onslaught of paper. He saw it as if it were happening before him. . . .

The sheets began to spin en masse, twisting about in a uniform pattern that created a huge whirling column. As tall as a person, it came twisting through the air like a ballet dancer, ripping and slashing.

The blood from Eden's wound dripped down his arm, reminding them both that the force was not imagination. It was unexplained, but it was real.

Together they overturned the desk and huddled behind it, letting the paper slam into the desktop to disburse in another burst of wind.

Then, in an instant, it re-formed, taking a position on the other side of the desk and swirling after them again. Before they could move, it slashed forward, cutting Eden near his forehead and slicing through the loose shirt Hyde wore. They scrambled over the desk, and, fleeing the whirling cylinder, leaped over the drawing table.

Despite his weight, Hyde proved to be agile. Noticing a single piece of paper still resting on the table, Hyde had snatched it up.

It was the last drawing he had been working on, and it featured one of the symbols he had read about. He had been sketching a panel in which the Gnelfs open a chamber in a forgotten cavern. The symbol had something to do with openings in some ancient ritual, so he had used it.

As the column of paper moved up over the drawing board and hovered as if about to strike, he ripped the page to shreds.

When that happened, the column was no more. The now-limp paper showered to the floor as if it had been dropped from someone's hands. When it connected with tile, it was still and flat, offering no further sign of animation. As the two men knelt on the floor, looking at the paper, they heard the faint sound of—God almighty! —*laughter*.

"After that we stopped using the symbols," Hyde said.

"But countless editions of your books and episodes of the cartoon were already on the market."

"We couldn't pull all that shit back," Hyde exclaimed. "You know how much money that would cost the publishers? Hell, it'd make headlines too if we started talking about some weird experience like that. Everybody would think we're crazy. We'd never get work again."

"You realized the menace of the power those symbols controlled, and you did not attempt to do anything?"

"That was the only time anything happened. We didn't think it was real," Hyde said. "Hell, do you know what it was? Can you tell us?"

"Something you did acted as a summoning—through the symbol. You let something sealed in a realm beyond this world reach through, but you closed the opening before true harm could befall you. The creatures have no true form in this realm, so they manipulated what they could to torment you.

"What do you mean, no form?" Eden asked.

"They are not physical beings. They are spiritual, ethereal. They do not have a tangible presence, so they must either possess something or find some other way to form a physical presence. Fortunately your thoughts were not focused enough on the symbol or they could have utilized the image of it in your mind, and then there would have been no way to banish them. It is interesting the way they attacked you. The wounds you suffered were aggravating yet not life threatening. It was as if your tormentors were . . . playing pranks."

The laughter followed the wind through the living room, loud echoing laughter. Heaven sat up abruptly, clinging to her mother.

"It's them," she said. "The Gnelfs."

Gabrielle wrapped her arms protectively around the child and looked back to Tanner and Marley. She didn't have to speak. Both men were already on their feet, and Althea moved to her side, placing her body protectively over the child as well.

As the wind tore at his face and played with his hair, Marley stared into it defiantly until it subsided.

Tanner stood at his side, watching him, hoping the preacher knew what to do, but Marley seemed confused. His fists clenched and unclenched at his sides, and he kept wetting his lips with his tongue.

He was about to speak when something crashed down on the coffee table in front of them, shattering the sheet of glass that covered it and splintering the wood beneath. The table crumpled to the floor then, no more than a pile of fragments.

Marley's eyes widened, and he shouted. "Get the girl out of here."

Together, Althea and Gab rose from their places on the couch, and they carried Heaven, between them, as they moved across the floor to the end of the hallway. As they exited the room, a vibration began to stir the glass fragments and wood.

"I rebuke you," Marley shouted as the vibrations continued. He raised one hand and pointed toward the table. "I rebuke you in the name of the Holy One. I rebuke you and command you to go back to the pits from whence you came."

He looked at Tanner then, as if realizing he was being too melodramatic. The vibrations were continuing, and Tanner could feel shock waves in the floor beneath his feet even though the house was on a concrete slab.

When he looked back at the table he saw the glass blast upward, as if an explosive charge had been ignited beneath it. Shards were driving forward like buckshot, and he quickly pushed Marley down, snatching a chair cushion.

He swung it up just in time to deflect a spray of the glass. The shards padded into the thick upholstery like shrapnel, but they did not pass through the cloth and cushion.

Marley was shouting the Twenty-third Psalm now as he crawled behind the couch. Tanner dove after him as the sharp wooden slivers from the table sailed forward, small misshapen arrows.

Some struck the couch and others flew over it, sailing on across the room to become embedded in the wall or tangle in the curtains.

Marley rebuked the spirits again and shouted out assorted other prayers and blessings. He had begun a liturgy when the laughter returned, low guttural chuckles that mingled together.

Slowly, they began to subside. Tanner sighed as he collapsed back against the couch. Beside him, Marley continued to pray, his hands clasped together and his eyes closed tightly. He was asking God for protection for the house.

"I think they're gone." Tanner sighed with relief.

Cautiously, Marley got on his knees and peered over the couch. "I think so too," he said. "I think they left on their own. I wasn't very effective."

"You tried."

"But my faith wasn't strong enough," Marley declared.

"You can't blame yourself," Tanner said. "All hell was breaking loose."

Heaven was curled up between Althea and her mother on Mommy's bed. The three were huddled together like refugees from a storm, and though the child could feel the warmth of the women's bodies, she shivered.

Her face was pressed against her mother's shoulder, but even the familiar smell of the fabric softener in the clothing did not soothe her.

She wanted to weep, but Mommy was already upset. She didn't want to compound the distress so she kept the tears in check.

Until the words flickered through her thoughts. She shut her eyes tightly and tried to ignore the sound, but the guttural voice of Gnelf Master, that same Gnelf Master who had been talking to her the last few days, came back to her.

We could have killed them all if we'd wanted to, Bitch.

She grunted softly into Mommy's shoulder. She didn't want anybody hurt, not Mommy or Mommy's friends. These people were all here to help her.

We could have hurt them. We still could.

She didn't speak. Mommy would hear and be scared and worried. More scared and worried than she was now. No, she couldn't let that happen. That was what the Gnelfs wanted.

Tell your Mommy something for us. She held her breath and bit her lower lip, summoning defiance from somewhere within herself.

She'll need to know. We're going to get anybody that's in our way. We're going to fuck them good. Tell her that. Tell her her friends are fucked.

Heaven began to weep, unable to stop the tears any longer. She cried onto Mommy's shoulder even as Althea's hands touched her back in an effort to comfort her.

Why were they doing this? Why were they hurting people because of her? It didn't make sense to a four—almost five—year-old brain. They were going to "fuck" her mother's friends. She didn't know what that meant, but it had to be something horrible.

In the shadows which shrouded the night, Simon stood, his form almost invisible, near the oak tree on the corner. Slowly he lowered the *baculum* and nodded in approval. He was accomplishing his task. He would find what he wanted. He would gain what he needed. The door was opening for him, and the little girl would serve him even as he fulfilled the request for which he had been hired.

He had accepted the job not for money but for opportunity. It was the moment he had worked toward from the moment he had first picked up a book on sorcery. It was the moment of his destiny, the moment that would bring him the power he had always desired, the power of domination.

He had not been taken seriously, had been an outcast, the brunt of jokes, but that was past. Now he would be the one to be feared. He would rip open the world and reach into its guts and twist, and the universe would cringe and writhe in pain.

Tanner and Marley cleaned the remains of the glass and timber from the living room, plucked the embedded glass and wood from the walls and furniture, and carted the debris outside to the garbage can. They spoke little while they worked, each awed by what he had witnessed.

When they walked into the bedroom, they found Heaven dozing between Althea and Gabrielle.

The psychologist held a finger to her lips to keep them silent. Easing away from the child, she slid off the edge of the bed. She winced as her buttocks cleared the mattress but had regained composure when she reached the doorway.

"What happened?"

"The coffee table tried to kill us," Marley whispered.

"What did you do?"

"We ducked," Tanner said.

"This sounds like the bad trips my patients on drugs describe," Althea said. "I'm going to stay here with her. She's sleeping, and hopefully she won't have any dreams."

"I'll stay too," Tanner volunteered. Across the room he saw Gab's eyebrows rise. She couldn't protest verbally without waking Heaven.

He mouthed the word "couch," to her, then placed his palms together and rested his cheek against them to denote sleeping.

She shrugged.

"I suppose I should stay too," Marley said.

Althea shook her head. "You'd better go home to your family, Parson. If we all sleep in our clothes—uncomfortably—we'll all be exhausted."

"Well . . ."

"Really. Rest. You'll be needed again I'm sure. Besides, it wouldn't look right for a married preacher to spend the night in a single girl's house, especially when there's a hot babe like me on the premises."

He grinned, blushed a bit, and finally conceded. "Call me if anything goes wrong," he said.

"We will," Althea promised. "If we're able to call."

She ran a hand across her forehead. Her fingers were trembling despite her effort to appear composed.

She walked with Tanner and Marley to the front door,

where Marley reiterated his request to be called if anything went wrong. She promised again she would phone and then waved goodbye to him.

"What the hell is happening?" she asked as she walked back into the living room with Tanner.

"I wish I knew."

She found her purse and pulled out a package of cigarettes. After offering one to Tanner she lit another and tilted her head back in a classic smoker's pose. Her eyes closed as the smoke eased into her lungs.

"Guess I picked the wrong year to give up men and cigarettes?" she said as she exhaled.

"The devil made you do it, I guess."

"Don't even joke about it, Tanner. Forty-eight hours ago I would have told you the devil was the product of the human imagination, devised to explain evil. Now I'm rethinking that. It's all so real suddenly. Everything I've believed is being turned around."

"I've never been particularly theological," Tanner said. "I guess I'm not as shaken up in terms of my beliefs, but I can't remember being more afraid."

"This is a weird town," Althea said through another puff of smoke. "I've always heard talk of things going on. Remember the reporter who wrote that book about the girl who talked to angels?"

"That guy Gable Tyler? I heard about that book but never read it. I thought it was just another one of those Amityville-type things."

"It was strange. Then there were the animal attacks in eighty-eight in Bristol Springs. People said a witch was behind those. And in the south part of the parish they say all the answers never came out about that police conspiracy. There was talk of monsters. The Mormo. Now I'm wondering if maybe it's true. Maybe this whole area is cursed or something."

"Maybe evil is everywhere," Tanner said.

When she had finished smoking, they went back into

the bedroom and found Gabrielle talking to Heaven.

"She woke up," Gab said. "I guess she wasn't sleeping very soundly."

Heaven saw Althea and Tanner in the doorway and her eyes widened. "Where's the preacher?" she asked.

"The parson went home," Althea said. "He was tired, baby, and he wanted to see his children."

"He shouldn't have left," Heaven said. Her hands tightened on Gab's arm, and she looked into her mother's eyes. "He shouldn't have left."

"He just went home," Gab said. "We'll be fine."

"We will," Heaven said. "He may not."

Marley's home was in Penn's Ferry, a small town a few miles from Aimsley. Some called it a bedroom community. He supposed that was true. He liked living there. It was peaceful. Nothing ever happened in Penn's Ferry, and he was pleased with that.

He didn't have to worry about burglars ransacking his home, and he didn't have to worry about his children playing in the front yard. You had to be careful everywhere these days, but in Penn's Ferry he felt assaults on family, home, and nerves were far less likely.

As he guided his car along the black strip of highway toward home he listened to a sonata by Beethoven on the public broadcasting station. The music took the edge off the fear which had seized him at the onset of the attack.

Demons, no doubt about it. He would have to pray deeply and consult another pastor to find the answer to all of this. He didn't know whether he should trust the man Tanner had spoken about. If Danube was so mysterious, he might be connected with the spirits.

Tomorrow he would call Stephen Grant in Atlanta, his professor at the seminary. Grant would be able to put him in touch with someone experienced in these things, someone who could tell him how to fight the demons.

First, he would get home and rest. It was too late to

make the call that night. He rounded a curve and started up the last stretch into Penn's Ferry. The road ran along the lake on the outskirts of town and then past the mental institution before it led to the small subdivision where he lived.

He passed a set of oncoming lights and heard laughter over the sound of the radio. Nervously, he turned and looked into the passenger seat.

In the glow of the street lights he could see the outline of the figure seated there. He blinked, thinking some smudge on his glasses was creating the illusion, but he was mistaken.

There was a little creature the size of a dwarf next to him. Shirtless, its small torso was a mass of muscles. A thick mat of curly dark hair, spread across its shoulders, and it reeked of the foul smell of perspiration.

A broad grin wrinkled its hideous little face, and its eyes glowed, their pupils red vertical slits.

"You should have left us alone, fucker."

He looked back to the highway, making sure he was going straight. He realized his arms had tensed and his grip on the wheel was mashing the plastic into his skin.

The vision couldn't be real. He had been thinking too much about all that had happened and he was seeing what he had been thinking about.

He looked back to his side, a slight laugh building in his chest. He shouldn't be laughing, but it was ridiculous. He had an elf at his side, a rather disgusting and smelly elf but an elf indeed. It had sharp ears and a long pointed nose and chin. Beneath its lopsided cap, its greenish black hair was oily and fell down its back in a pony tail.

It wore grimy white pants and little shoes that turned up in points at the toes, and it was buckled safely into place with the seat belt.

"I'm real, fuckface," the little creature said. "See me in the books? Now I'm here. I'm what you're afraid I am."

Marley looked at him, then back at the road. "Then I

command you to leave."

"You could almost do that, except that you doubt yourself. Your faith is weak, and a little doubt is all I need."

Keeping his hands on the wheel, Marley edged toward the door on the driver's side, glancing at the road and then back at the creature. "I rebuke you," he said.

"Yeah, I know. But you believe in me, and you've looked at pictures of what I'm supposed to look like. It's your mind that's giving me form, shithead."

"Leave my car."

"Wish I could, but I have business here." The dwarf reached into the sash tied around his waist and pulled out a thin silver pike. Then, leaning over in the seat, he raised it in one hand and plunged it down into Marley's right thigh.

The blade burrowed into Marley's flesh, sinking in to the hilt. A cry escaped the pastor's lips, and he almost lost control of the car as he looked down in horror at the wound.

Laughing, the Gnelf pulled the weapon free and plunged it down again, driving it through muscle about an inch away from the first wound.

Warm blood began to soak into Marley's pantleg, and the pain of the cuts thundered up to his brain. He fought to keep the car on the road, swerving almost onto the shoulder before he righted his course.

"Does it hurt?" the Gnelf asked.

Tears filled Marley's eyes, and he could feel sweat breaking out on his flesh. "Yes."

Why was he talking to the little monster? He was being tormented by an evil little troll and then discussing the matter with the creature.

"Get out of my car," he demanded. "Leave me."

"Ah, ah. I'm with you now, Rev. Remember that class in seminary when they told you about all the fragments and strands that made up the Bible story? Made you wonder, didn't it? Was the J strand right? Or was it imagination, a good story. Should you take it literally or just as a piece of fiction?"

He shoved the blade into Marley's side, raking it down through his coat and shirt so the pike's point ripped open the flesh across the minister's ribs.

In the dim light, the stain spreading across Marley's shirt appeared black. The cut produced a stinging sensation followed by white-hot pain. Marley's arms wanted to relax, but he managed to keep his grip on the wheel. The car sped on along the highway, its headlights sweeping from side to side as his grasp faltered.

"We're not alone," said the Gnelf at his side, and suddenly an arm slipped around Marley's neck from the back seat. He gasped as the muscular small limb tightened across his larynx and the cold steel of a larger blade, a scythe, touched his flesh.

"I'll cut out your gizzard." It was a harsh, throaty voice. Marley felt hot breath against his ear, and he tried to scream.

The small bicep against his throat tightened, silencing him. He stared at the roadway through bulging eyes. The yellow line glowed in his headlight beams and seemed to be moving itself at a high speed. He tried to take his foot off the accelerator, but the creature beside him placed its foot over his, forcing the pedal to the floor.

"You don't want to slow down," said the Gnelf, gripping his throat. "You'll be late."

Marley croaked, an effort at posing a question.

As if in answer, the radio clicked to life, and the green digital numbers on the dial began to speed past channels wildly until the scan finally stopped on a call number Marley didn't recognize.

Then an unearthly voice began to pound through the car, a newscaster's voice, only slower, more like the voice of a dead man.

"And on a sad note, the Reverend Marley was killed last night when he apparently lost control of his car and drove into the lake."

Marley again attempted a scream, but the arm remained tight against his throat, and then the Gnelf in the passenger seat reached over and grabbed for the steering wheel.

Marley felt it slipping from his fingers against his will, and through the windshield he could see the headlights sweep across the oncoming lane.

A small embankment of gravel had formed on the left-hand shoulder of the road. When the front wheels hit that, the car's speed carried it upward. It became air-borne, sailing through the darkness.

A billboard extolling the virtues of milk was on display, a pair of spotlights illuminating the smile of a pretty blond girl with white teeth.

The car tore through the center of her face and continued forward, plunging down into the dark waters of the lake. For a moment it seemed the car would stay afloat, but then it began to falter, and water started to pour in under the dashboard.

Ripping free of the grip round his neck, Marley grabbed the window's hand crank. Clutching it he quickly wrenched it downward.

Water began to pour onto the seat, but the opening offered him a chance of escape. He knew the water pressure from outside would never allow the door to open, but if he could slither through the window opening he had a chance.

Kicking at the creature in the passenger seat, he forced his head through, then his shoulders. Water rushed into his nostrils, but he continued to struggle. Though he was underwater now, he could reach the surface. He knew it.

The water stung his wounds, but he forced his brain to shut out the pain.

His clothes were like lead weights, soaking up pounds of water as he tried to paddle with his feet and stroke with his arms. Quickly, he shrugged off his coat and kicked harder with his legs.

His lungs felt as if they were about to burst, and the

breath escaping his lips bubbled around his face. The chill of the water was jolting, almost paralyzing.

His wounds ached, but he ignored that, impelling himself upward with sheer will power. He thrashed his arms, kicked, pulled his body through the water with cupped hands. He had enjoyed swimming in his days in the seminary, had gone to the school's pool to relax between study sessions and research for papers. His muscles had not atrophied that much since, had not sagged.

As if by a miracle, his head broke the surface of the water, bobbed out into the air, and he began to cough and gasp for breath at the same time.

He gagged, but gained control of his breathing as he treaded water. He waited to feel tiny hands close around his ankles, but the grip did not come. Perhaps the water had affected them.

He floated on his back for a few moments, resting, and then began to make his way to shore. The crawl proved too difficult, exhausted as he was, and it caused the cut over his ribs to throb, so he did an incomplete backstroke.

Cold dark waves slapped him in the face, and he tasted the muddy water, but he fought onward. He was amazed at how far the car had sailed out over the lake, but the sandy bank was in sight now. Water stung his eyes and blurred his vision, however, he could see the dusk-to-dawn lights that blazed over the picnic area.

He made for them, keeping his mouth and nostrils clear of the water. Blood was flowing freely from his wounds, and he gritted his teeth against the pain of them.

He tried to look back over his shoulders to the area where the water's surface might still be disturbed by the automobile's descent, and saw no sign of the Gnelfs. Fine, let the water take them, let them stick in the muddy bottom forever. They'd leave the little girl alone there.

He no longer questioned the reality of their existence, and he did not attempt to explain it to himself. That would come later. He would discuss it with the professor, talk it over with Althea. Tomorrow. After he had dried out, after he had rested.

He tried touching bottom, but realized that still wasn't possible, not the way the bottom sloped. He would have to make it clear to the water's edge. Good enough. He kicked and half stroked harder, demanding that his muscles keep working.

He had children, a wife waiting to see him. He had a sermon to prepare. So many things to do. He made outlines in his head as he struggled on, using his responsibilities to drive him onward.

Water lapped at his face, and the night breeze wafted over him, more chilly than he had expected. He felt very cold. The water was icy.

For a moment, he just floated, letting his arms and legs rest. He even allowed his eyes to close as he sucked in air through his mouth.

Then he kicked hard and began to use his arms like oars again, stroking toward shore. He could hear his children's laughter now, could feel his wife's touch and smell the fragrance of her perfume. He thought about the way her hair smelled after she had washed it with herbal shampoo, and he remembered the softness of her touch. Last night? Had it been that recent? It seemed a decade had passed since he had seen her.

It seemed he'd been swimming that long too. He looked toward shore again. It still was a long way off.

He fought the numbness, concentrated on moving one arm, then the other; one leg, then the other. Stroke, kick. Stroke, kick.

He was still losing blood, and the ache in his muscles was growing worse. He wanted to scream but he couldn't waste the energy. His arms were getting weaker and weaker.

But he kept on. Kick, stroke, kick, stroke.

And then, unexpectedly, he was there, at the water's edge, reaching upward through the reeds to grasp the dock that shot out from shore.

He found a grip at the edge of a piling and began to pull himself upward. Then, in the light from the poles, he saw the outlines of tiny figures, a half-dozen of them, standing on the pier. How had they made it there from the car? It didn't make sense.

They laughed and cursed and spat down at him, and then he heard something, something like a rattle, yet it was not a rattle. It was a different sound, metallic. What was it?

Clink.

When the weight hit him, he knew what they were dropping.

Chains.

Chapter 13

The next morning in California, Devon helped Danube find his way through the crowded airport to his departure gate. She was dressed in her uniform, but she sat with him as he waited for his flight to be called. The conversations around them were casual as people drifted past, lugging suitcases of belongings toward their various destinations.

When the speaker blared Danube's flight number, he stood and slung his coat over his shoulder. Before he could leave, she took his arm, stopping him from walking toward the ticket taker.

"Who are you?"

Her brow was wrinkled with confusion. She was troubled by something she felt inside.

"You would not believe me."

"What do you know about me?"

"We are related. Far, far back our bloodlines have crossed. I have lived a long time, and I had some brothers and sisters."

"Brothers and sisters?"

"Your ancestors."

She almost laughed. "I thought I'd seen everything out here, but not a redheaded stranger. That's why you've been able to control me? You're not joking?"

"It is not control exactly, more suggestion, but yes."

She shook her hair out of her eyes and looked up into his face. "Will this—lineage, is that it?—will it affect me?"

He bowed his head. "It should not."

"You can tell whether I'm going to succeed or not. You can tell that somehow, I know it. You read it in me."

"You should not know the future," he said. "For better or for worse. If I had known my future long ago, I would never have been able to move forward. Now I know my destiny, and it is a very heavy burden."

"But—"

"Ask no more. You carry the blood of a man who had to exist, a man who played a great role in the shape of the universe, but he played his role as a betrayer. Forget that and move on. You cannot be held accountable for his sins. His guilt was his alone."

"And you?"

"I am not accountable, but I seek atonement—for myself. Not for him."

He turned and pulled his ticket from his vest pocket, quickly disappearing through the doorway to the boarding tunnel.

On the plane, he sat by a window looking out at the clouds. He had felt close to Devon in the brief time he had spent with her. If he hadn't had to leave he might have talked to her more, explained everything, and taken the time to know her. She was not quite a sister, not quite a daughter, but she could have been a friend.

But there had been no time. He was needed. He had followed an erratic strand of information. He had learned a little, but nothing of much value.

Dave had been ruled out as the man behind the conjurings, and the Gnelf creators had confirmed what he had suspected about the forces they had disturbed.

He had learned before that, despite the seeming chaos of the universe, things seldom happened without a reason. He feared that he had been directed or manipulated to follow this lead in order to be misdirected.

If that was true, he had to return to Louisiana as quickly as possible. Heaven and Gabrielle would be vulnerable. If someone had been wise enough to make the effort to get him out of the picture, and had succeeded in the attempt, then there could be real danger for the mother and child. He chose not to let his imagination play with the possibilities.

A crane borrowed from a nearby construction site was used to hoist the car out of the water once the Penn's Ferry police, working with hired divers, had managed to connect tow lines to it. With a creaking groan of metal and the whirring rattle of the machine's engine, the vehicle was hoisted into the morning air.

In the sunlight the water that poured out of it glistened like crystal as it showered downward. When people had begun to spot the huge hole in the billboard at daybreak, the cops had come out to look around and had found Marley's body, then his car.

Tanner watched from the bank, standing among the police officers and the onlookers milling around. The mayor, a heavyset man with a flat-top crew cut, stood with his hands in the pockets of his brown suit jacket, watching.

Tanner also had his hands in the pockets of his jacket, and he was thankful he was wearing it. The morning was brisk in spite of the season, and the dampness in the air, coupled with the nearness of the water, made it quite chilly.

"You were a friend?" asked Frank Ahern, the Penn's Ferry chief of police.

"Acquaintance," Tanner said. He couldn't decide how much to tell the policeman about the strange things that had been happening.

"How'd you hear about it?"

"Another friend of his, Althea Rogers, got a call from his wife. She told me about it."

Althea had gone directly to Mrs. Marley's side, and after Katrina had come over to join Gabrielle, Tanner had headed out to the accident's scene to see if he could figure out what had happened.

The police were still wondering about that, but he had an advantage. He knew there were demons involved. He could not question that any longer, even though he wished he could. The accident could be genuine, but he doubted it. Marley's body, which had floated to shore, was still lying beside the lake, but a sheet had been draped over it.

Tanner had made his way over to the chief after speaking to several other people. The chief had read his books and seemed talkative.

"It's a puzzler," Ahern said, taking off his blue cap and scratching his balding head. A thin, wiry man, he was wearing a brown plaid cowboy shirt and brown slacks held up by a thick brown belt that had his first name etched on it in back.

The design in the leather of the belt matched the design in the leather of his pointy-toed boots.

"Best we can figure he swerved off the road, hit that embankment, and went through the sign into the lake."

"Maybe something ran in front of him."

"Nope." Ahern shook his head. "He's got stab wounds. Several superficial ones and one pretty deep cut on his leg from what the coroner said. We're sending him to Bossier City for forensics, that's for sure, but I've seen stabs before. He'd been pricked like a pin cushion on his right side."

"You mean someone was in the car with him?"

"Looks like it. Like somebody was ridin' with him and started playin' a nasty prank, stickin' him. Only it went too far." The chief shook his head and plopped his cap back down on his head. "What I can't figure out is where the passenger went. He's not in the car."

"Maybe he made it to shore, got away."

"Maybe. If we find him we'll charge him with second-degree and it'll get bumped down to manslaughter or something."

"Did the stab wounds kill Marley?" Tanner asked.

"Oh, no. Not in my estimation, and I've seen my share of dead bodies. It's my guess he drowned."

Tanner thanked the policeman and headed back to his car. He pulled his jacket together in front and held it closed with one hand, but it didn't make him feel any warmer.

If Ahern found Marley's killer he'd be hard pressed to put him on trial. Unless he assembled some sort of tribunal of priests, Tanner thought.

He walked slowly down toward the edge of the water, past the sheet-covered body to a spot where the water lapped at cattails and licked at his shoes. A narrow, almost unnoticeable path had been made through the reeds. They had been pushed apart, evidently to allow passage.

He wanted Danube to come back. Things were getting out of hand, and despite his reservations about him, the red-bearded man seemed to represent the best chance of finding an answer to all of this and ending it.

Maybe it could be ended before anyone else suffered.

Gab sat with Katrina at the kitchen table, sipping her third cup of coffee. She had not slept well, and the caffeine gave her a temporary boost of energy on which to keep going. She had not cried, but remorse had seized her when word had come of the minister's death.

"It's not your fault," Katrina said, reading her thoughts through her expression. "You didn't do that to the man. If a bunch of spooks got him, you couldn't have prevented it."

"He was trying to help me, Kat. That wouldn't have happened to him if it weren't for me."

"You don't know that anything happened besides his runnin' off the road. That does happen. Doesn't mean ghost demons got him."

"Tanner went to check it out, but last night, after Reverend Marley had gone, Heaven woke up and was upset. She said he shouldn't have left here."

"Are you saying she had a premonition?"

"I think those things talk to her and she's afraid to tell me about it. You remember how upset she was at your house?"

"She was scared of seeing them on TV, but then she got over it for a while."

"She endured them when I was around because she didn't want to upset me. They must have told her something was going to happen to people trying to help me."

"Gab, you're tired. All of this bullshit is starting to get to you. This guy in the monkey suit has convinced you all this is real, and you're tired and you're believing it."

"Tanner and Althea are convinced, and if you'd seen what's gone on you'd believe it too."

"Right, right. Look, you need to get out of this house. You can come stay with me for a while, get your mind off this and regroup and get Heaven some help. You don't need to see this Danube character again if he comes back."

"He may be the only one that can help. You've got to understand, this is not something normal that's happening."

"Gab, you're not bein' rational. This is crazy."

"I've got to think of Heaven. Whatever it takes. If I have to bring a priest in to perform an exorcism, I'll do it."

"Listen to yourself. You need some rest. You've got to pull yourself together. There are no Gnelfs."

"Don't be so sure," Tanner said from the doorway.

Gab was out of her chair and moving toward him before Katrina could protest his intrusion. "What happened?" Gab demanded.

Tanner embraced her. "They found stab wounds on his body. It looks like somebody sat beside him and poked at him until he ran off the road."

"Oh, God." Gabrielle buried her face against his shoulder.

"She didn't need to hear that," Katrina said, giving Tanner a hard, cold look.

"It happened," he said.

"Is everybody going crazy?" Katrina asked.

"It's my fault," Gab said.

"No. It's the fault of whoever is causing this," Tanner said.

"Dave? Or whoever."

"Maybe Danube will know something when he gets back."

"You're trusting this guy." Katrina shrugged. "He's a nut. He just wanders in with some explanation about nuns in the Balkans and you guys buy it?"

"Katrina, we've seen unbelievable things happen," Gabrielle said. "We have to trust him. He's the only one with any answers."

"So he's snowed all of you. He must be some kind of cult leader. Don't drink any of his Flavor Aid. You think Dave is out in California summoning hobgoblins to aggravate Heaven and kill preachers? Maybe he's rubbing crystals together to do it."

"Somebody's doing something," Gab said calmly.

"I think it's getting worse," Tanner said. "Up until last night they were all pranks, even the assaults on Heaven weren't deadly. Now they're getting brutal, and they actually were able to do things to Marley physically. Before they were able to assault Heaven, but when they went after Althea they manipulated the things around her. Think about it. It was the same here with the table. They didn't directly assault us."

"They didn't kill Marley directly if they caused him to run off the road," Gab said.

"No, but they were able to affect his actions. It's like

they're gaining ground. Any one of us can serve as their channel—or whatever Danube was talking about. All of us have the gate symbols in our brains, and the more tangible the Gnelfs seem to us, the more they're able to do. I think they're using our thoughts to take physical form."

"You're all going crazy," Katrina said. "Gab, you shouldn't be hanging around with this guy. I might have known a writer would be weird."

Tanner grinned in spite of their grim situation. He could sense there was no malice in Katrina's words.

"What I'm saying," he continued, "is that these forces are gaining power over us. It's like they're using our thoughts, our images to make themselves real, tangible in the here and now."

Gab wrinkled her brow. "You mean, the more we conceptualize them—"

"The more that concept becomes real," Tanner finished.

"That's crazy," Katrina said. "Y'all's imaginations are coming to life?"

"No, our imaginations are being used by spirits without form to create forms for themselves. We're open to being used because we've seen the symbols of the gates in the children's books."

"Did you get all this from that rabbi?" Katrina asked.

"No. I'm a writer. I'm thinking it up as I go along," Tanner quipped sarcastically.

"It doesn't make sense to me," Katrina admitted.

"I'm following him," Gab said. "It makes sense. Heaven was susceptible first because she has the imagination of a child and no skepticism."

"That's why she was cut directly," Tanner said. "Marley had reached that point in his car. He wasn't doubting any longer."

"And they could strike any of us now," Gab said. "We know what they can do, but how do we stop them?"

"Maybe Danube will have the answer."

"Let's hope he gets back soon," Gab said. "Before something else bad happens."

A rainstorm kept planes on the ground in Denver. It was reportedly moving in a northeasterly direction, and the pilot had announced that takeoff would be delayed. Danube checked his watch and calculated in his head the effect of the delay. He would miss his connection in Houston. He might also be unable to catch a flight out of Houston for Aimsley that night.

Rising from his seat, he started up the aisle. A businessman in a starched white shirt and yellow-and-red tie was headed back along the aisle. Seeing Danube in his way, the man glared at him. He was unaccustomed to moving for people.

The stare that Danube turned on him spun him on his heels and sent him back up the aisle to make way for the red-haired man.

A stewardess met Danube at the curtain which closed off first class. She tried to explain that he could not leave the plane.

One corner of Danube's mouth turned up in a grim half-smile. "Madam, I am a psychic," he said calmly. "I have predicted that a failure in this plane's hydraulic system will create difficulties with the landing. You will let me off, or I will address my concerns to the other passengers."

"Sir, please be calm. You'll create a panic."

"You lost your virginity to a young man named Lewis Purdue in nineteen seventy-nine in the back seat of a Chrysler. It was blue I believe."

Her face looked as if it were about to slide off the front of her skull. Obediently she led Danube forward along the narrow aisle and opened the door for him.

"Will we be all right?" she asked.

"Probably," Danube said. He was in too big a hurry to tell her the hydraulic warning was a lie.

He turned and hurried up the walkway. Bursting forward into the terminal, he strode across the tiled floor to a bank of television screens which displayed departures and flight numbers.

A United flight to New Orleans was scheduled for departure in twenty minutes. Even if it was delayed, he would be taken directly to New Orleans, and he could drive up to Aimsley from there rather than being stranded in Houston.

He was in the Continental terminal, so he turned and set off at a light jog. A tall thin man with blond hair and a shorter fellow in a hat and sports coat were in front of him. Pushing between them, he increased his speed. He had to be back in Louisiana. He knew what any delay could mean.

Althea returned to Gab's place in midafternoon, tired and ready to collapse. She had not cried for Marley, but she'd felt tears forming in her eyes as she'd spoken with his wife, who had been crying. She knew holding her own tears back was not emotionally healthy, but she could not indulge the needs of her own pain. She had to be on hand for Gabrielle and Heaven. Marley had died for his calling, and she would not relinquish the commitment she had made long ago to help people. It had cost her a marriage, and it had cost her in other ways, but she couldn't run away from that responsibility now. She had once made a vow.

True, her involvement had been with psychology, learning, and catalogued theories. Still, confronted with a reality totally alien to her, she would face this evil in whatever form it chose to assume.

She had suffered as a child, trapped in the world of her mother and her mother's lovers. She remembered Theodore, the one who had moved in, the one who had wanted to be her "uncle."

At thirteen there was not much she had not seen, living under her mother's roof. She had watched men come and go, but Theodore, a thin, graying man with a professorial style, had seemed much more compassionate than the others. He read books quite a bit and stayed long hours in the living room, watching television while her mother scurried out for the night. He knew she was seeing other men, but it did not seem to disturb him.

He accepted her mother's style, drawing affection from her when it was available and doing without it when she did not offer it.

When he talked to Althea, he seemed to understand the agony of her age and the alienation she felt. He had always felt different as well, he told her, and they discussed their feelings of being misunderstood.

He won her confidence. Slowly, she accepted him as a friend, a confidant. She told him about her feelings, let him know which boys she was becoming interested in, what she hoped for in terms of dates.

When he began to question her about her physical awakenings, she had been glad to express her confusion over them. He listened intently, telling her the confusion was natural.

After a while she trusted him so totally that she did not think it strange or odd when he began to explain that young girls need the proper teachers in such matters. He talked about this earnestly in his soft-spoken, fatherly manner, dropping suggestions only occasionally during their evening talks.

At first she did not fully understand what he was saying. She believed he meant that instruction in conduct and proper behavior were important.

Slowly, even as she denied it to herself, she came to understand what he actually meant. She kept telling herself that could not be the case, but finally she could deny it no longer.

It happened while they were having one of their usual

conversations at the kitchen table. He sipped his coffee and put his hand atop hers as she spoke, gently caressing it.

Then he again began talking about her need for a teacher, someone who would be gentle, tender; someone who loved her.

She listened without committing herself in any way, pretending she did not suspect what he was about, but this time he was not dissuaded.

They moved from the kitchen to the den, where he began touching her while they were watching television, and then to her bedroom.

The events were blurred now, but she could recall the transformation that came over him. He turned from a docile professor into a grunting slobbering creature, placing his mouth all over her, touching her, and finally producing the hideous thing that he usually kept hidden away in his pants.

It had been large and brown, exaggerated in size if not in shape, and when he forced it into her she screamed and bled, but there had been no one to hear her. She'd had to endure it, all the agony and humiliation.

Sometimes she wondered now where he was. Her mother had eventually broken off with him, never knowing the truth.

Now Althea was left to think about it and deal with the scars that had not been erased even by therapy.

People could find so many ways to hurt each other and use each other. That had been his way. Now some entirely different method was being used to attack Heaven, but was it that different? It all wound up being the same thing—assault, violation that tore at the very soul. Someone out there had feelings perceived as needs, and whatever had to be done, whoever had to suffer, to fulfill those needs did not matter. Marley was dead, others were hurt and frightened.

She would find a way to put a stop to this. She would do

everything in her power to keep Heaven from suffering the trauma and the horrible nights she herself had known, and if possible she would help Gabrielle fight back.

Gab had fixed a fresh pot of coffee. As Althea sat by the coffee table, a cup was set in front of her in an attempt to bring her out of the trance she seemed to have slipped into.

"You're pretty tired," Gab said when the psychologist looked down at her cup.

Althea picked it up and sipped, wincing at the bitterness. "Just thinking," she said. "Where's Heaven?"

"Resting."

"Has there been any word from your friend Danube?"

"No. Tanner went home to rest, and Katrina went back to work. She wants to come back this evening, but I'm worried about her safety. I'm worried about everybody."

For the first time Althea noticed how deep and black the circles under Gab's eyes were. "None of this is your fault," she said.

"I wish I could believe that. I must have done something, something that's brought the wrath of hell down on my family."

Althea shook her head, remembering the guilt she had carried for so long. It had been years before she had spoken of it, not until she had begun to make breakthroughs, to achieve some understanding. Now she heard the feelings that had once plagued her coming from Gab's lips.

"You are being made a victim," Althea said softly. "Someone is using Heaven to bring guilt and pain to you. That is not your fault. It's the fault of whoever is behind this, Dave or whatever or whoever it is."

She could see the anguish in Gab's eyes, the same confusion she had held inside herself for so long. Softly she touched Gab's hair, wishing she could offer comfort, but all of her training and experience did not give her words to speak. There was nothing to say. This was a hell that had to be endured.

Danube watched through the cabin window as the jet climbed up through the blue-gray storm clouds. Tiny droplets of water formed on the glass outside, were quickly pressed flat and became small moist streaks like the tracks of tiny slugs.

Then they were above the clouds, and he was looking out across a blanket of damp gray cotton. Hadn't he experienced this just days ago? He seemed to be repeating his path, only this time traveling from a distant coast toward New Orleans.

And now it was more urgent that he reach his destination. He could sense the disturbances, spiritual disturbances, and he knew he had been drawn away by the investigation in California. It had been a mistake to leave Gabrielle and Heaven.

He had faced many dark forces during his time with the order. He had encountered creatures known as hell hounds that were conjured up by a madman, and he had felt the breath of demons. He had also seen their work and heard their cries, had watched people torn apart; but never had he been quite as disturbed as now.

Something or someone had seized some great power. He could sense that, could feel vibrations inside himself that he had never known even in the presence of almost pure evil.

The use of the gates was just the beginning. More and more power could be obtained, and if the proper doors were opened he could only begin to list the nightmares which might be released.

The drugged-out man he had left in Los Angeles could not be responsible, nor were the Gnelfs' creators aware of the full extent of the powers with which they had dabbled. What did that leave?

Some other lunatic who had been able to lay hands on

forbidden writings. He had known many sorcerers. All of them were maniacs driven by the hunger for power and the need to avenge some wrong, perhaps even a perceived wrong. They were dangerous men, always.

Before, he had known his opponents. Now he had no indication of who might be behind the assaults on Gabrielle Davis and her daughter. The faceless sorcerer seemed to loom over the clouds, a sinister outline of a man unknown.

There were only two things Danube could discern about his opponent at this time: he was evil, and he was powerful. Defeating him would be as great a task as Danube had ever undertaken.

He could sense that too, and he wondered how bad it would be if he lost. In losing, at least he might be set free. Free for the first time in almost an eternity.

A new scene fluttered into view, projected above the clouds from his memory. It was a dirt road, crowded on either side by people, hundreds of people, perhaps thousands. They shouted and jeered at the man walking down the road, Roman legionnaires behind him.

Danube had stood among the crowd, not jeering or throwing things or spitting. He was too young for that, too young to be swept up in the frenzy of the people and the anger of the moment.

He did not understand why they hated the man so. He could not explain the fury in their cries. The man—he had hardly known him—had seemed so gentle, so caring.

Many things were confusing. He could not understand why his father had been so withdrawn the night before, so despondent and sick.

Had he been upset because he knew his friend was to be punished?

Shimmers of heat danced across the brown dust, layering the ground, and he could smell the sweat and the blood which dripped and oozed from the man's mangled back as he passed.

Then as the man reached the spot where the boy stood,

he turned his face toward him. In his eyes was the same kindness that had always been there, but the pupils were clouded with agony.

He reached out then, touching the boy's cheek. The contact left blood and dirt on it as he was prodded on, and the lad's tiny hand reached up to feel that sticky residue.

The boy knew then that his father had betrayed the man. The realization seared into his brain as if he had been struck by a solid ray from the overhead sun. The man had trusted his father, had loved his father, and had been destroyed by his father.

At that moment he knew he would have to make amends for the man's betrayal, he would have to atone.

Now, so much later, he could still remember the look in the eyes, the touch, and the anguish he had felt.

Had any of it prepared him for what was coming now? Could any of his past experiences or his dedication since the moment the stranger's hand had touched his cheek prepare him for what awaited?

Perhaps he was facing the last battle, the battle that would release him from his commission and would let his soul go free to whatever reward or condemnation was to be bestowed upon it.

Chapter 14

Tanner slept for a while, showered, and tried to write. He was unsuccessful. His imagination was blocked by thoughts of Marley. He had known the man only a short time, yet he was shaken by his death.

He rose from his chair and walked toward the kitchen. The computer popped as it cooled, making him wheel and look back over his shoulder . . . at nothing. A smile of relief crossed his face, and he turned, heading again for the kitchen. He was not thirsty, but a glass of water, the act of running the tap and drinking, promised to bring solidarity. It was a normal act, a common act, an anchor in reality.

As he passed the windows, he noticed the sky was turning to charcoal, light ebbing from it. Evening was turning into night quicker than he'd expected. He realized he did not relish the approach of darkness and flipped on an overhead light.

Then he was at the sink, running the water, letting it cool, filling a glass, sipping. The metallic taste that always seemed to taint tap water touched his tongue, and he poured the remainder of the liquid down the drain.

It was time to head back to Gabrielle's. When darkness came, things happened, and he didn't want her to face such things alone.

He returned to the living room, switching off the

kitchen light in spite of his uneasiness about darkness. The humidity in the air seemed to indicate he would not need a jacket, but he decided to take one anyway in case the night turned chill.

He was on his way to the hall closet when he saw the man standing in the corner of the living room near the arm chair. There was no light on in the room, and with the fading light outside, it was mostly in shadow. This helped conceal the man, but Tanner's eyes adjusted, focusing on the blond-haired figure.

He wore an oversized black shirt and fashionable gray pants pleated so that they ballooned out at the thigh and tapered at the calf. They seemed to make the man's slight frame appear larger. There was a frailness about his pale features, and his hair, which seemed soft and delicate, was drawn back from his forehead.

He took a step toward Tanner, and at first it appeared that he was using the long stick in his right hand for support. Then Tanner realized he was holding it without letting the tip touch the floor.

"Dave?" he asked.

The man's smile was immediate. It folded back his thin lips, revealing gleaming, even rows of his teeth. "No. You're mistaken. I'm not David," he said. "Not her husband."

"Then who are you? Are you responsible for what's been going on?"

"You could say that I've made it . . . possible, I suppose."

"What do you want? What has Gab—or the kid—done to you?"

"You're quick with questions. Are you a brave man, Mr. Tanner? As brave as the heroes in your novels?"

Tanner held back his retort. He had not been frightened at first—he had been angered—but now he began to wonder about the confidence of the man in front of him. Could this man, in spite of his size, be dangerous? He seemed somehow sinister, evil. He stood at the edge of the room, completely calm. There was no sign that he sensed himself to be an intruder. Tanner wondered if he might have to find an escape route. The crosspieces securing the panes in his living-room window were metal, so he abandoned any thought of diving through the glass to safety.

"No, Mr. Tanner. You have no exit," the man said.

"Do I need one?"

"You should have stayed away from her."

"She needs me."

"You can offer her no protection, Mr. Tanner. You cannot even protect yourself."

Tanner started to edge to his left, hoping he could at least make the couch and dive over it before the man could attack him with the staff he carried. Perhaps the sofa cushions would serve as a shield once again.

As he glanced back at the intruder, he saw shadowy figures forming around him, small, greenish shadows, almost transparent yet real, their outlines matching drawings he had seen in storybooks and on videos. They swarmed around the man, huddling together and snarling. As Tanner peered at them they seemed to gain substance, until he was looking at solid little monsters with twisted faces and grime-covered flesh.

The smile on the intruder's face broadened as he stood there amid his charges. The image was like a parody of some photograph that might have appeared in a magazine. Tanner could recall shots of Jim Henson standing amid the Muppets or Walt Disney depicted with his creations. But this picture was hideous, frightening.

"You believe in them," the man said.

Tanner fought his own thoughts. Realizing the creatures were enabled to assume their forms due to his own imagination, he denied their reality, closed his eyes, and tried to think the creatures back onto the pages of a book.

He thought of them trapped in stories, seeking to erase them from his living room. If he could do that, if he could deny them, perhaps they could be removed.

When he opened his eyes again, they remained, but they were not as tangible as they had been a moment before. "They're not real," he said. "They are discorporate entities that you're seeking to make into Gnelfs."

"But I am real," said the man, "and I have the ability to control them whether they are Gnelfs or spirits."

He waved the staff, and the images deteriorated into wisps of green. Like snakes, they swirled through the air of the room, streaking away from the man and slithering along the walls and around the corners, dashing about in a frenzy before settling back to the floor and rematerializing.

"You didn't banish them," the man said.

Now they surrounded Tanner, grinning monsters brandishing pikes and scythes and laughing at him.

He looked from one to the other, searching for an opportunity to bolt. They left him no opening, and as if to prove it, two of the creatures broke off from the others and began to cartwheel across the floor, crisscrossing each other's paths like precision gymnasts. Their knives were clenched in their teeth, but they quickly slipped them back into their palms when they landed on the balls of their feet.

As they poised, one at Tanner's right and one slightly behind him and to the left, their backs to their companions, he realized they were about to rush him. Their small round eyes, dull but filled with evil, stared at him.

Then they rushed forward, blades slashing the air in front of them. Lifting himself onto the balls of his feet, Tanner jumped upward, clearing the one in front of him by only a few inches. If they hadn't been trying to kill him, it might have been comical.

When he came down, two more rushed toward him. He

dodged them and dove, launching himself with all the strength he could summon from his legs. Headlong he plunged over the back of the couch, hitting the cushions with a grunt.

Bouncing forward, he planted his feet on the living-room floor and tried to head toward the front door.

Behind him, the Gnelfs dematerialized again, and in an instant tiny green streaks shot along the walls and re-formed in front of him.

Their laughter now was a loud cackle, and one of the heavier creatures, stoop-shouldered and with a mis-shapen head, moved forward. Its gnarled hands were clutched around the shaft of a scythe. With its tongue sticking out one corner of its mouth in a parody of a determined face, it took aim and swept the gleaming silver blade downward.

The thin, honed edge raked Tanner's shoulder, then sliced his shirt and bit into thick flesh and muscle as it flayed open his upper chest.

Blood gushed from the wound. Instinctively, Tanner raised his hand to the cut, as if pressure would quell the flow, and when hot blood coursed through his fingers, he knew the wound was deep.

He staggered back, his vision clouding from pain. He felt as if his brain were adrift on some dark sea.

Still clutching his wound, he reached toward the wall with his other hand to steady himself, fingers stretching toward that stability. Before he could touch the paneling, the scythe came down, slicing away the digits at the second joint. As spurts of blood sprayed from the opened veins, Tanner looked down at the severed tips.

Numbed by the sight and by the loss of blood, he closed his eyes and let his body sway. The pike jabbed into his back with great force, but he could barely feel it. It was a sudden pressure. He was aware of the blade's presence in his muscle, but it did not immediately hurt.

He did not react when the foul breath of the Gnelf

behind him touched his neck and swirled around to his nostrils. His strength was gone as a green hand gripped his face, tilting his head backward so that his throat was exposed.

When his head toppled from his shoulders, all function ceased. Stories about the eyes and brain working after dismemberment did not prove true. He did not see. He did not hear. The satisfied laughter of his attackers and their summoner fell on dead ears.

The telephone's ring made both Gabrielle and Althea jump when it pierced the silence. When she answered, Gab had no idea who to expect on the other end. Dave? Tanner? Danube with bad news?

It was none of them. It was Terry's mother. Missing Heaven at school, her young friend had been hounding his mother to check on her.

Jill Guillory had the bright, soft voice of a suburban housewife, and she apologized for disturbing Gabrielle.

"I know you're probably trying to keep things quiet for Heaven. What is it, the flu? Terry's been climbing the walls at school without her to talk to."

"It's one of those things," Gab said. "We're not sure what it is. The doctor is with us now."

"Oh, did we call at a bad time? Terry was hoping he could talk to Heaven."

"It's not a bad time. The doctor is a friend."

"Do you think Terry could talk to her? He's about to pull my arm off."

"Sure. It'll probably make her feel better to hear from him."

Gab put the phone down and headed toward Heaven's room, saying to Althea, "I guess it's okay to let her talk to one of her friends."

"I don't see why not."

Heaven was lying on her bed, staring up at the ceiling.

She had no expression on her face.

"You've got a phone call, kiddo," Gab said. "Your buddy Terry. You feel like talking to him?"

Heaven sat up, and her expression became noticeably brighter. Swinging her legs off the mattress, she slid from the bed. "Is he on the phone now?"

"Sure is."

"I miss him."

Heaven hurried along the hallway, making it difficult for Gab to keep pace. She reached the telephone and almost snatched it up, pressing the receiver to her ear.

"Hi, Terry," she said.

"Hello. How are you?"

"Okay. Mommy makes me rest a lot."

"I miss you at school. It's boring without you. I just kind of hang around."

"It gets kind of boring here too. There's nothing to do."

"Can't you watch TV?"

"I don't want to."

"Why? Oh, the Gnelfs? Is it the Gnelfs?"

Heaven looked up at her mother, wondering if Gab could hear what Terry was saying. "Yes it is," she said softly.

"What'd they do?"

"Everything."

"Wow. They were mean?"

"Uh-huh."

"Why are they doing it?"

"I don't know."

"What are you going to do about it?"

"I don't know."

"When will you come back to school?"

"I don't know."

She swallowed as a long silence followed. She couldn't think of anything to say, and Terry didn't seem to have anything else to talk about either.

"Could I come see you?" he asked finally.

"Maybe when I'm better."

"You mean when the Gnelfs are gone?"

"Yes."

There was another silence, and Gabrielle leaned down. "Tell Terry goodbye," she whispered. Kids usually were not good at making conversation on the phone, so she saw no need to drag things out.

"Um, I guess I'd better go," Heaven said. "See you."

"Okay. I'll call again. Be careful."

"I will."

Gab reached down, took the phone, and replaced it in its cradle. Then she ran her hand through Heaven's hair, tousling her bangs. "Did that make you feel a little better?"

"I guess," Heaven said. "I feel funny mostly. This isn't supposed to happen, is it?"

"No," Althea said. "It's not, but it's not your fault."

Heaven eyed her solemnly. "Whose fault is it?"

"We don't know yet, but we will find out. I promise."

"Is anybody else going to be hurt?"

"We hope not," Althea said. "We're going to try to make sure nobody else is."

"How?" Heaven asked. "Is Terry safe?"

Althea and Gabrielle looked at each other, their expressions questioning. Althea turned back to the child. "I think so, sweetheart. I think Terry should be fine."

"Is something else going to happen tonight?" Heaven asked.

"Let's hope not," Althea said.

As soon as Terry was off the phone he began to pace around the living room, swinging his arms about anxiously and slapping his left fist into his open right palm. He got on his mother's nerves almost immediately.

While she sat at the kitchen counter waiting for the

timer to go off for the chicken she had in the oven, she sipped a cup of coffee and tried to ignore him. She thumbed through a month-old copy of *Ladies' Home Journal*—her sister had passed on to her—but she found it impossible to read.

Jill wasn't usually impatient with her son, not even when he launched into long rambles about television shows or comic books, but right now she was ready to strangle him. His father was away on a business trip, and without Don's stern presence to keep Terry in check, the child was more restless than ever.

Placing her coffee cup down hard on the counter to catch Terry's attention, Jill stared across the room at him. "I know you're worried about your friend, but you need to find something to do."

"Aw, Mom. I want to go see her."

"Her mother said she's been very sick. She probably shouldn't have visitors right now. Besides, you might catch what she's got. You don't want to have to stay in bed for three or four days do you?"

"She's not just sick, Mom. She's been havin' bad dreams too. She's afraid the Gnelfs are mad at her."

"She's probably had a fever, babe. I'm sure she's going to be fine, and you can see her in a day or two."

"But, Mom . . ."

"Sorry. That's my best offer."

He slammed his fist hard into his palm to convey his frustration and then beat it up to his room to avoid a lecture about his temper.

Terry's room was the cause of constant arguments between him and his father, who did not particularly care for the efforts his son made at decoration. Terry wasn't given money for posters, but he'd gotten some anyway. A Batman foldout was pinned to one wall. It had been stapled into an issue of *Detective Comics*, and Terry had snared it.

He also had a poster of *Shocker* which had turned up as

a foldout in a comic book his mother had bought for him in a used book store. He hadn't seen the movie, but the artwork was scary.

Another poster he'd found discarded at school. It showed a large gorilla, and the logo read: WHEN I WANT YOUR OPINION I'LL BEAT IT OUT OF YOU.

Terry plopped onto his bed and rolled over onto his stomach to reach underneath and pull out the flat box that held his newest comics. Stuffed under some *Archies* was a wrinkled copy of a horror comic. It had a SUGGESTED FOR MATURE READERS label, so his mom would have vetoed its purchase, but he'd put it in the middle of a stack of comics at the store and she had paid for his selections without noticing.

The comic scared him, and he didn't understand the words, but he liked the pictures anyway. He thumbed through it, and at the sight of the monsters he thought about Heaven.

Tossing the book back into the box, he went over to the window and looked out. It would still be daylight for a while, and his dad wasn't coming home that night. His mom would get mad if he slipped out, but at least he wouldn't have to deal with his father.

Heaven's house was only a couple of blocks over. He could probably go and come back before dark. It might even be possible to return before he was missed. Chicken usually took a while to cook, if he remembered correctly.

He looked over his shoulder at the closed door. Mom never came to check on him as long as he was quiet.

He considered the punishment she would inflict if he was caught. What the heck! He walked to the door, pressed his ear against the wood and listened. He didn't hear Mom's footsteps. A good sign. She'd stay at the counter with her magazine, waiting for the chicken to be done.

Tiptoeing back across the carpet, he flipped the latch on the window and grasped the frame to lift upward.

* * *

He could hear the coins falling, and somewhere far away he could also hear the child's screams. She called to him, begging for help, breathless, her voice wracked with pain.

He ran across clouds, black clouds, clouds filled with smoke, and he could not find her.

Then . . . laughter, deep and harsh. He wheeled around and saw his father there. Strands of fiber dangled from his neck, and his face was swollen and bloated, stained purple, yet he was jangling the coins in a small pouch. Slowly, he opened the pouch, and poured the silver into his palm, rattling the coins as they slipped through his fingers. Danube turned, and again the girl's cry pierced his consciousness. She was out there somewhere, out there in the smoke, and he had to reach her. He ran, his legs heavy, his feet weights which sank into the cloud floor beneath him. He was almost running in place.

Then he looked up at her and saw her, beckoning to him as she was dragged away by some unseen figure traveling across the sea of clouds.

He tried to follow, but when he stepped forward he sank into the clouds as if they were quicksand. They gripped him, sucking him downward.

And suddenly, from beneath him a bolt of lightning shot upward, clawing its way through the clouds, jagged and with many prongs like a silver oak with no leaves shooting from the earth in a burst of growth.

It ripped at him, lifting him from the cloud and hurling him high toward the black nothingness above.

The flash that bit through the blanket of dark clouds outside his window woke him, its bright flare touching his eyes and jolting him. The cabin lamp over his seat had been turned down, and his head was resting against the small pillow the stewardess had given him, his face turned toward the glass.

He bolted up in his seat, scaring the old man beside him, a thin gray-haired character in a plaid sports coat and cowboy hat. A tattered copy of a book called *Azarius* by Gable Tyler lay across the man's lap.

"Easy, son," he whispered. "It's just a little lightning."

Danube straightened in his seat, his eyes adjusting to remind him of where he was. He rubbed them, smoothed his beard, and took a deep breath. He was trembling.

"Bad dream, son?"

"The worst."

The old man lifted a glass of tomato juice to his lips. "I don't think the storm's going to get too bad," he said.

Danube looked back outside. The view resembled his dream. He did not fear he had had a premonition about the storm, however.

He feared the other images, the ones of the girl. If those were true, all of his anxieties would prove valid. If she was dragged away into some nothingness where he could not follow, he would fail, and the hope of atonement would be set back again. He would be forced to face another eternity of the nightmares and the laughter. He did not want to fail. For the girl's sake—and for his own.

As the shadows began to overtake the trees, Terry began to rethink the wisdom of his decision. He wouldn't be able to get home before dark after all. He was beginning to think he might not even make it to Heaven's before dark. It was farther to walk than he'd expected. It had never seemed that far when they drove by in the car.

The wind seemed to be picking up too, and he thought he heard thunder somewhere off in the distance. Maybe that would explain why it was getting dark early. Bad storms could come up at any time. He'd learned that from his mom who always tried to find a weather report when it got cloudy.

He was closer to Heaven's than to his own house now. Might as well head on that way, he decided. If Mom misses me I'll be in line for trouble anyway. I might as well make the most of it.

If it did start storming he could just stay at Heaven's house, and Mrs. Davis could call his mom so she wouldn't worry.

As a new clap of thunder echoed, a little closer, he ducked through a hedge and took a shortcut through Jack Steadman's back yard. He wanted to get to Heaven's before the storm broke.

Chapter 15

On the fifteenth ring Gabrielle replaced the telephone in its cradle and walked back to the window. The branches of the pines in the front yard were swaying like baseball fans doing the "wave."

"I guess Tanner's on his way over," she said. "I hope he beats the storm. I wanted to leave him out of this, but now I'm thinking it would be nice if he were here."

"He'll be along," Althea said. "If they're interested, men always come sniffing around. Doesn't matter what you do, intentionally or unintentionaly, to discourage them."

"Is that from your psychology training?" Gab asked, walking toward the couch on which Althea was sitting.

"No. My grandmother. She was smarter than the experts."

"Do you like Tanner?"

"As much as I like any man."

"That's not that much, I take it?"

Althea picked up her coffee cup, holding it between both hands. "Bad experiences," she said before taking a sip.

"I've had a few myself," Gab said. "I don't know if Dave meant to be—a bad experience, I mean."

"None of them mean to be. In his own mind each man is doing right, operating within his own code of ethics. He doesn't think he's doing bad things. To him, he's just looking out for his own needs. Men make up reasons for everything."

"Women can be bad too. I guess I've got a few notches in my belt."

"Feeling guilty?"

Gab laughed. "Sometimes I think about it. When I was a kid I hadn't been dating that long, but I was going steady with this guy named Jimmy Anderson. He was a really nice guy. He worked at McDonald's so he'd have a little cash for us to go to movies and stuff. And he liked me a lot. You know, sixteen-year-old crush, adolescent emotion, and all."

"Exactly," Althea said.

"Then another boy, Matt Greer, asked me to go to a football game in Penn's Ferry. Jimmy had to work the night shift on Fridays, but I always went by the store and waited for him to get off. Then we'd get chocolate shakes and go riding in his old Chevy. Well, Matt was so cute and cool with this Firebird he drove, I told him I'd go, and I told Jimmy I couldn't come by the restaurant because my friend Susie wanted me to spend the night at her house. He knew Susie, so he bought it.

"Well, I went to the football game, and I had a good time, and I figured everything would be fine. Jimmy would never know, and I'd had this boost to my self-esteem because of Matt's attention. He was eighteen, you know.

"Problem was he drove fast, and there was kind of a caravan of kids heading back from the game. Everybody started passing each other, weaving in and out of traffic, and Matt ran into a pickup truck.

"It wasn't that bad, but they called an ambulance to get us checked out, so the *Clarion* reported the accident in the next day's paper. Listed cars, drivers, and passengers. Jimmy never talked to me again after that. I can't say I blame him. Not when you consider how tender our feelings are at that age."

"Yeah. Some people never outgrow that age," Althea said.

"Textbook or personal observation?"

"Both. There are a lot of damned Peter Pans out there. Men are interesting specimens," Althea said. "They never cease to come up with ways to screw things up."

"Maybe human beings just aren't meant to be together," Gab said. "If we're all alone we can't hurt each other."

"I don't know what the answer is," Althea said. "I've been observing things for ages, and it just seems relationships get harder and harder."

"Will you ever get involved with anyone again, Althea?" Gab asked.

"Who knows? It's looking less and less like a good idea. I haven't met anyone interesting in a while." Her eyes peered into Gab's. "I guess it would have to be someone very special."

"Maybe when Heaven is safe and all this is over Tanner and I will have some time," Gab said.

"You haven't had much time to think about that, have you?"

"Not much," Gab conceded. She checked her watch again. "I guess he's been scared off."

"That's been known to happen too."

They both sighed. Conversation masked the anxiety of waiting, of wondering if something more was going to go wrong. The minutes were ticking past. It was getting to be that time.

Danube's flight touched down on time in New Orleans, but that left him with several hours to drive. He fought his way through the crowd of people who walked the carpeted floor, some hurrying, some setting a leisurely pace.

It took almost a half-hour to go through the process that placed him behind the wheel of a battered Chrysler.

It smelled of stale cigarettes, and the knob on the gear shift fit loosely on its shaft.

He quickly familiarized himself with the placement of essentials and then guided the car out of the parking lot. The stretch of road leading from the airport was narrow, and traffic was backed up on it. He had to creep along behind a van which blocked his vision and made it impossible to determine what was wrong ahead.

Finally they came upon the remains of the car wreck. One small vehicle was jacked up on a wrecker which was about to pull it away. Police cars and an ambulance sprayed the area with brightly colored lights, red and orange glistening off shattered fragments of windshield strewn on the ground. Finally a uniformed man waved Danube's car through the intersection.

He was on the way, but he had distance to cover. Once clear of the police, he swerved around the car in front of him and pressed the gas pedal downward.

Even as he watched the narrow orange needle on the speedometer creep past numbers, an uneasy knowledge gripped him, warning him that he would be too late.

The downpour began at about eight P.M. Gab joined Althea at the living-room window to look out at the darkness. Heavy rain slashed through the glows made by streetlights and the lamps at the front of the house on the opposite side of the street. The trees, their branches pitching about wildly, seemed to be taking part in some wild revel.

"This storm makes things worse," Gab said. "Like this is a horror movie."

Before their eyes the street became eerily light again in the flare of a lightning bolt. Then it was dark once more, and a clap of thunder that was almost deafening followed.

"That doesn't mean anything," Althea said. "It's just a storm."

"Who's to say what's tied to all this?" Gab asked. "What's natural and what's not? If it's real then it's part of the reality, but isn't everything linked?"

"Maybe nothing will happen tonight," Althea said. "It's past the time when things usually occur."

"That could mean it's going to be worse tonight," Gabrielle said.

The lightning came again, another bright flare, another burst of thunder. They moved back into the living room. "I can't believe it's gone away," Gab said. "Well, I'd better check on Heaven."

As rain beat upon the roof, she moved down the hallway and looked through the bedroom door. Heaven was sleeping and appeared peaceful. Her head lay against the pillow, and the covers were pulled up to her shoulders.

Gabrielle stepped softly across the carpet and touched her child's hair. It was so soft, and her skin was so smooth. Angelic. She hated anyone who could make Heaven suffer.

Touching her daughter's cheek gently, she decided it felt a tad warm, but the house was a little stuffy—the air conditioner hadn't come on in a while—and Heaven seemed to be sleeping well.

She found Althea in the kitchen, fixing some fresh coffee. "We're keeping Maxwell House in business," the psychologist said.

When the coffee was ready, Althea poured each of them a cup, and they were about to return to the living room to continue their vigil when the rattle came at the kitchen door.

They looked at each other with frightened eyes.

The door rattled again, and something pounded on it, jarring it in its frame.

"The things haven't come from outside," Althea reminded her.

Gab moved over to the window on the door and pulled

the curtain back to peer outside. She saw no sign of anything, but then the pounding came again.

She jumped back from the sound as if from an electrical shock. Turning to Althea, she gasped. "Jesus that scared me."

"What is it?"

Gab pulled the curtain back again and this time looked downward when she peered through the glass. Through the lower pane she could see Terry's soggy head. Grasping the knob and yanking the door open, she motioned him inside. "Come in out of that storm before you drown," she ordered.

Terry sloshed into the house, his soaked clothing clinging to his body. Water ran down off his hair, seeped into his shirt, and dripped from his pants.

"It's further from my house than I thought," he sputtered.

"Your mother must be worried sick. We'll have to call her and let her know you're all right."

"I snuck out. I wanted to see Heaven. Do you *have* to call my mom?" he begged.

"Unless you want her to worry herself sick," Gabrielle said.

"I guess not," he said reluctantly, although his tone suggested that might be preferable to her wrath.

Gab had just picked up the phone when Heaven began calling from the bedroom.

Danube pressed harder on the gas pedal as he passed through the small town of Krotz Springs. He saw a string of gas stations and quick stops, and ignored them. A few miles past the town was the turn which would take him up U.S. 71 toward Alexandria. The girl at the McDonald's outside Baton Rouge had told him that from there it was about two hours from Aimsley.

Before reaching Alexandria, he would veer off onto the

state highway which would carry him northwest into Riverland Parish. If he could keep the speed above sixty he might be able to shave off some time, and that would be essential.

As the car rushed forward, he came upon the taillights of another vehicle, its chrome bumper reflecting his own headlight beams back at him.

Swerving into the other lane, he urged his vehicle forward, cursing under his breath. His palms were tingling with the anticipation created by the sense of evil that was gnawing away at his nerve endings. When he thought of Heaven, vibrations almost shattered his mind, telling him something was awry.

Before he could return to the proper lane, he saw headlights bearing toward him. Truck headlights. He jerked the car back hard to the right, sliding into the lane on a diagonal that put him in front of the car he was passing by a fraction of an inch. By less than that fraction the truck sped past.

Ignoring the blare of horns, Danube sped onward along the black road. Thunder was rumbling, and he knew he would be heading into the same storm which had been plaguing him in one form or another since New York. That was to be accepted, part of the battle.

Dark forces were at play here, forces that would manipulate anything at their disposal to make his task more difficult, even impossible. He did not know yet what they were, not exactly. They were all different, had special powers, special tasks.

Some he had encountered before, some he had heard about, but others, those that lurked about now, those that were preparing their assault, were unknown to him. They could possess sinister powers like none he had ever seen, and if someone had succeeded in opening some ancient gate then the powers might be unknown to anyone.

The results of that were beyond speculation. The only

reality was his growing fear that something he could not combat, something he could not contain, might be waiting when he returned to Aimsley.

Far ahead of him, he spotted a running streak of lightning—heat lightning—which seared its way through the night clouds in a flaming flare of color.

He did not like the sight. It was odd, unusual, and again symbolic of all that he feared. It was different, strange, an omen. The forces of nature offering a warning.

His temples began to throb with the thoughts that assailed him. He was hit with memories, with anger. This trip was futile, hopeless. He would never reach the house in time. Perhaps they had known that all along, those who had ordered him to this task; perhaps in their mystical knowledge they had understood this was a battle too great for him and had dispatched him so that he could fail and meet the eternal condemnation that had followed him all his days.

Perhaps all the things he had done were only vain stabs at correcting the evils of his past. They had said his father's act had been necessary for the order of the universe; yet even so, it had not been done out of a pure motive, and thus it had become his greatest shame.

If his task was hopeless, he would resign himself to failure, but he would press on, do everything he could to reach the girl before whatever awaited could befall her. He would drive with all the speed the car would allow, and he would be prepared for confrontation upon arrival at the house. He would not look back. He would not surrender.

He would fail, but they would know that he had failed while fighting to succeed, still seeking redemption, still seeking to correct the impurity of his father's soul. He would seek to serve the angels, and if they offered him damnation he would bow down and accept it without complaint.

Forcing the gas pedal almost to the floor, Danube

leaned forward over the wheel, his eyes peering into the darkness.

Simon sat in the soft armchair across from the silver-haired man whose form was concealed by the shadows in the darkened room. The older man wore a dark gray suit and sat in a velvet-covered chair, his hands resting casually at his sides. Simon could see the ring he had provided sparkling on his right ring finger. It had a black stone in an ornate gold setting.

"You're sure you don't need to be there?"

Simon shook his head. "Not tonight. It would not be wise to be too close."

"These little bastards will do the trick?"

"They have been set free, they are gaining power. They will taunt and torment."

The man nodded, accepting Simon's prognosis. "We will be able to watch?"

"As I promised," Simon said, a bit impatiently. He did not expect his competence to be placed in question, not even offhandedly.

"How soon?"

Simon extracted a golden pocket watch from his dark blue suit, and flipped open the cover. "Shortly," he said.

He clicked the watch closed with a snap. "If you wish, we can proceed."

"Yes."

Simon rose from his chair, and together they walked to the opposite end of the room, where a spiral stairway led downward. The soles of their shoes echoed off the steps as they descended, the echoes preceding them into the darkened room beneath.

In the shadows, Simon had set up the cauldron, and in the open fireplace beneath it coals and embers glowed bright orange. Their glow offered the only illumination to the room which had once been a basement.

The shadows projected on the dark walls looked like the ghostly figures gathered for a coven sabbat or some other arcane ritual.

The older man kept glancing around, as if he were making sure they were alone as he walked up the steps of the platform which had been built of sturdy polished wood and iron to provide a working area over the makeshift fireplace. A huge black vent with a draw fan had been fashioned above it, but the room still reeked of smoke.

Simon carefully peered over the edge of the dark iron pot. The surface of the gleaming liquid he had prepared was smooth and still in spite of the heat, and for a moment he was looking at his own reflection in a dark mirror. As the man eased around beside him, however, he raised his thin white hand and moved his palm slowly across the opening of the pot.

From somewhere within its depth, the liquid began to glow, silver at first and then golden, a blazing yellow fire growing within the liquid.

For a moment the man turned his face away, but Simon continued to stare into the glowing light, ignoring the glare that seared into his retinas.

Softly he whispered the memorized words of the incantation, and the glow subsided slightly, flickering until images began to become visible.

The gray haze swirling inside the liquid began to part, revealing the scene at Heaven's bedside. Gabrielle knelt there, one hand holding her child's hand, the other on Heaven's forehead as if testing her temperature. Beside them, Althea looked on nervously.

"They don't know what's happening?" the man said.

One corner of Simon's mouth twitched up in a grim smile. "Our friends are trying something different tonight."

"What are they doing?"

He shook his head. "I'm uncertain. It's in their hands."

"You can't ask them?"

"Not at this point. They're doing some conjuring of their own." He swept a hand across the liquid's surface, eliciting small blue pulses which flickered through the clouds.

"Those are signs of their magic," he said.

"What if they're out of control? Can you rein them in?"

"They function on their own, but they are created beings, Martin. Their power is limited. They are kesilim and lezim, fooling spirits and jesters, mischievous spirits who have killed only at my request. They have no reason to harm the child."

"Unless it amuses them?"

"There's no need to worry. They're acting to bring about what we wanted. They're tormenting Gabrielle. Tonight they're just varying their routine. They know she's grown used to their regular assaults."

"What's wrong with the little girl? Have they made her sick?"

"We can only wait and see," the sorcerer said.

Althea carefully placed the thermometer under Heaven's tongue as Gabrielle whispered softly to the child, urging her to keep it in place.

"Hot," Heaven managed to mumble.

"I know you are, baby," Gab whispered. "We're trying to make it better." She gently placed a hand against Heaven's forehead, and found it so warm she was frightened. She couldn't remember her feeling this hot even when she'd had fever as a baby.

She recalled those moments now, the times with Dave, the fear, wondering if Heaven was seriously ill or just suffering from some childhood virus.

They'd been up long hours, taking turns monitoring her temperature and offering her doses of the medicine prescribed by the pediatrician they'd called for advice.

Where was Dave now? He couldn't be responsible for this crisis, not with his own memories of pulling Heaven through those early days. Nothing could make someone turn that cruel.

She patted Heaven's hand as Althea eased the thin thermometer from the child's lips and held it to the light.

"Hundred and two," she said, squinting at the mercury.

"We've got to get it down somehow."

"Let's try some aspirin first. She could just be reacting to the stress she's been through. There's been enough to upset her system."

"You think so?"

Althea bit her lower lip. "Let's hope that's what it is."

Gab went down the hall to the bathroom and found the small bottle of baby aspirin in the medicine cabinet. That brought memories too. Heaven, barely old enough to talk, taking the soft, sweet tablet between her lips and repeating the warnings which had been drilled into her by both parents. "Just take one," she'd said. "Make Heaven sick—sick—to take more."

God, I don't want to lose my child. Gab felt so helpless. What could she do if this was something more than a fever, in what way could she fight for her daughter? If Danube did not return soon, they would be facing things beyond comprehension—and with no notion of how to do battle.

When Gab returned to the bathroom, Althea was holding Heaven's hand and gently brushing hair out of her eyes. "She's sweating."

"What does that mean? The fever's breaking?"

Althea's face remained solemn, no sign of optimism in her expression. "I'm afraid it means it's not a fever at all," she said.

The headlights flashed off the glowing white and green

of the road sign. One corner of it was bent, and the surface was dappled with pits, the result of a random shotgun blast fired by a drunken redneck on a spree. Even through the rain Danube could make out the words: Petittville 5.

He was on the right path, would be able to follow this road through the small town which was at the edge of Riverland Parish.

He had not wanted to delay to make a phone call at the airport. Before that he had been too rushed, frantic, but now he knew he would have to try to make contact with Gabrielle. If he could get an idea of what was happening, he might be able to give advice which could allow her to survive until he arrived.

It was a slim hope, but it was his best. He blinked; the constant thump of the windshield wipers was lulling him as he fought his fatigue.

He passed the first spattering of signs, his headlights illuminating announcements of fresh peaches and vegetable stands ahead. He didn't expect to find anything open in the town, but with luck he would sight a service station with an outside pay phone.

He turned on the radio, letting the music assail him as the air-conditioning vents he opened sprayed icy air into his face. The blower made his eyes water, but the chill kept him alert.

The car rounded a curve, and the headlights blazed across the trees just off the road's shoulder, trees he would have slammed into if he'd let the wheel slip only slightly.

The radio preacher who filled his ears spoke of the evils of sin. If only he knew how many forms it has, Danube thought. Evil has so many faces. He had thought he had seen them all. The conjurings and sorceries he had faced had taken many shapes, but now his heartbeat thundered, telling him some new mode had been allowed entry.

On the roadway, the yellow center line seemed to

move, rushing toward him like a huge, bright flatworm. Finally he saw the flashing orange eye of a caution light which dangled like a medallion from a power line across the road. It marked the edge of town.

He passed under it, into a narrow stretch of asphalt that ran in front of a bank and two parallel rows of closed shops. He drove by a small dress shop, stiff mannequins looking through the plate-glass window at him. A photography shop, its front window ablaze, presented an array of family portraits and smiling graduates in cap and gown, caught forever with false joy on their faces.

Finally the headlights bounced off a Chevron sign. It was not lit, but the shiny red and blue surface reflected back his high beams. On the same post as the sign was a small square with a white on blue telephone handset outline.

Good enough, he turned into the lot and cruised up in front of the station, past the pumps. He rolled to a stop at the edge of the building, where the telephone was attached to the wall beside an ice machine.

The overhang of the arcade which covered the pumps did not quite stretch out over the phone, and a steady trickle of rain poured over the roof's edge. He had to stand in it as he dropped a quarter into the slot.

Drops ran down inside his collar as he dialed Gabrielle's number from memory, and as the purr of the receiver sounded in his ear, he heard the static created by the weather and the lightning.

He didn't count the rings. He let them persist, waiting. The rain soaked through his hair, plastering red curls across his forehead. He closed his eyes as water ran down over his eyebrows.

The ringing continued. Her phone must have rung more than ten times by now. An arc of lightning ripped down across the sky behind the store, and thunder followed.

He swatted water from his eyes, and finally he heard a

click on the other end of the line.

He could hear a quiver in Gab's voice as she said hello.

"Danube," he said. "What's happening?"

"She's very hot, but it's not a fever. Her temperature is climbing up and up, but she's sweating."

Danube turned, hunching his shoulders and trying to shut out the sensation of the pounding water.

"Have there been any other occurrences, any other signs of the unusual?"

"Not at this point."

"They're there, somewhere," he said.

"What? The Gnelfs?"

"They have great power. They are spirits, the symbols in the books give them a gateway."

"So why is she so hot? Are they hexing her?"

"I'm afraid they're conjuring. If they were able to enter this realm through the doors they may be trying to bring others."

"But why is she so hot?"

"There are many forms of demons. They could be summoning a fire demon."

"What?"

"A demon that manifests itself as an element."

"What can we do?"

"Keep her cool. Douse her with water, do whatever else you can, and I'll be there within the hour. They have a ritual to perform to open the gate for their brother. Perhaps it can be delayed long enough."

"How do we fight it if you're not here?"

"Pray for blessing," he said. "I'll be there soon."

"Danube . . ."

"Yes."

"Who's doing this?"

"Not your ex-husband. He's not capable of it."

"Then who?"

"We shall have to find out. Once we deal with the crisis at hand."

He hung up the phone and returned to the car, running a hand through his tangled hair to keep the water off his forehead before he coaxed the engine to life once again.

Althea brought towels from the bathroom, while Gab lugged a pan of ice water in from the kitchen. Dipping the towels into the water, they quickly spread them across Heaven's body, not worrying about her gown getting wet or the spillover onto the bed.

"What's happening, Mommy?" Heaven asked as Gab bathed her face with a washcloth. The child's cheeks were flushed bright red now.

"Just rest," Gab whispered.

"I feel hot from inside," Heaven complained.

"That would follow, in line with what Danube said," Gab said, looking across the bed at Althea.

Placing her hand on the child's forehead, Gab could almost feel the heat increasing. Gently, she pulled her fingers away and replaced them with another rag dipped in the ice water.

"Is she real sick?"

Terry had found his way to the door. He stood there, the towel he'd been using to dry his hair draped around his shoulders. His hands nervously clutched the cloth at each end, and he sawed it back and forth across the back of his neck.

Althea moved from the edge of the bed to put her hands on his shoulders. Gently she turned him and guided him back into the hallway. "Heaven is very sick, and we don't know what's wrong with her," Althea said. "We have to let her rest."

"Why is she so hot?"

"It's a bit like a fever."

"Is she gonna be all right?"

"We don't know. Now please, go back to the living room and wait."

She watched him walk dejectedly back down the hall, then slipped back through the doorway to Gab's side.

"I think she's getting hotter," Gab whispered as she squeezed water across the child's neck.

"We only have to hold out a little while," Althea said. "Danube will be here."

Gab's eyes drooped closed. "Please God, don't let my baby die here. Please."

Opening her eyes, she looked down on the child's tortured features, and from somewhere in the room heard the sound of laughter.

Chapter 16

When Danube pressed the pedal almost to the floor, the tires hydroplaned across the coating of rain on the roadway while the steering wheel vibrated in his hands. He did not decrease speed.

He was nearing Aimsley now. Shortly he would reach the edge of town, and it would not take long to make it from there to Gabrielle's home.

He had gained slight confidence from the phone call; at least he knew what he would face. He would have to deal with a conjuring, would have to counteract it if possible. But if the demons themselves were doing the conjuring, he wasn't sure he would be successful.

He had no doubt that the powers of light were stronger, but was it their hour to prevail? The demons' powers would be immense, and he knew that everyone of the world's dramas had to play out in its own way. They had played pranks, had harassed, and now they had moved on to greater efforts.

He wished he had time to make contact with the sisters, but that wasn't possible. He would have to go it alone, trusting in his own faith and ability.

In the darkened room, the man smiled as Gab frantically squeezed ice water onto her daughter's forehead. The liquid provided a picture so clear that he could see the lines of panic cutting across Gab's brow. It was better than watching a video monitor.

It was a grim smile that crossed the sorcerer's countenance. Success was being realized here. He had unleashed the forces, and now they were acting on their own, functioning to fulfill the goals he had set forth at his employer's request.

Stepping back from the cauldron, he walked down the steps of the platform. He had traveled a great distance since that day he had acquired his first *grimoire* in the old shop in London. He had searched and studied a long time, and had finally found the man, Joseph Hall-Patch, who could help him learn even more.

He had stayed with the old man in the cramped rooms over the shop, spending the days poring over musty books with brittle pages. Gradually, the old man had revealed things to him, things learned in secret meetings or gained from forbidden books. Hall-Patch had studied under many teachers, and he had much to offer Simon.

The most important of them was the book, ragged and faded, its leather binding dusty and cracked. The edges of the pages were ruffled and flecks of crumbling brown paper fluttered free whenever he plucked it from the wrappings which had been placed around it to protect it from further decay. It was a scrapbook of all the old man had gathered, reflecting all his journeys, all his contacts.

While his host continued to peer into the depths of the liquid, Simon knelt at the base of the platform and removed his book, holding it gently in his soft hands as if it were his child.

It was too fragile for casual handling, too important to be used frivolously, yet he loved the old book, cherished it, because it explained to him all of the things he must know to build the power he had desired all his life. And that knowledge would allow him to fulfill his feeling of uniqueness.

Gently, he peeled back pages of the book, scanning the

ornate lettering. He had known from the first moment his eyes fell upon the pages that he must possess it. Knowing it could become his only if he took it, he had worked diligently, studying, struggling with the spells and incantations; learning first the simple charms the old man suggested he master before moving on, practicing things in the dark hours after midnight on his own. He pored over the book, studying, memorizing and finally breaking through the barriers—or veils, as they were called—that separated the other realm from his reality.

He had looked into that world and invited its patrons to come into him. He had learned their ways then, growing more and more powerful.

The dark feelings that burned within him gave him meaning for the first time, meaning that substituted for the loneliness and emptiness he had known since the death of his parents. He had been placed in an orphanage where religious dogma had been hammered into him until he had nothing but contempt for it and its rules.

He laughed. The forces he gave himself over to represented the opposite of everything he had hated, abandon instead of restraint, anger instead of repressed rage, and indulgence instead of repentance.

The old man had gradually learned of what he was doing, and at last had confronted him.

"You know you are delving deeper than is wise or safe," Hall-Patch had said in his cracked voice.

"I am doing what I must," Simon had replied.

They were standing in the front room of the old shop, Hall-Patch behind the narrow counter, his wrinkled hands placed flat on the wooden surface.

"You are opening yourself to demonic control," Hall-Patch warned. "That is always a mistake."

"A mistake? Or is it just that none are brave enough to try? Mine is the way of finding all power."

"It is a path that will lead to your death," the old man stated, adjusting his wire-rimmed glasses on the bridge of his nose. His voice was weary, heavy with impatience. Its tone conveyed that he had seen this all too many times.

"I'm ready to go beyond what anyone has ever tried," Simon responded. "I'm ready to find all of the power. I can feel it. We're in touch with some, but there's so much more that can be drawn."

The old man turned from him then. "I thought you were a wonderful pupil, but you're a fool. I want no more to do with you, Simon. You're going to cause destruction."

"Am I the fool, old man? If I have to go, I want the *grimoire.*"

Hall-Patch laughed then. Simon had known he would laugh, had known he would think the notion so absurd that he would turn away. He had, in fact, counted on that.

The old man *did* turn his back on him then, so he bowed his head slowly, calling on the forbidden names, whispering the forbidden words he had committed to memory.

Then Simon clenched his teeth as Hall-Patch continued to laugh, and his eyes flared.

His face flushed with anger at the old man's contempt, he focused his thoughts on Hall-Patch, attempting something he had never tried, pushing his abilities to their limits.

The laughter stopped abruptly. Simon wasn't sure if it was because the old man was already feeling the effects of his anger or because he had turned back and seen the glow in his eyes.

He felt his own temperature rise. Sweat beaded on his brow, and his breath grew short. He had to gasp for air, yet he persisted, drilling his thoughts into the man.

Slowly, the old man's eyes filled with terror, bulging as if they might pop from their sockets.

Hall-Patch tried to scream, without success, and his eyes rolled back into his head until only white was visible. He was standing away from the counter now, and as he realized what was happening, his mouth fell open.

He wanted to run, but he was frozen in place as his body began to quiver. His face and hands became incredibly red, and his flesh was drenched with perspiration. He began to swat madly at the air, as if he were being attacked by something flying about.

Again he tried to scream, but only a choking sound gurgled in his throat.

It would have been a hideous sight to an onlooker, the sight of death in slow motion, but to Simon it was beauty, the actualization of his plan.

The old man's lungs filled with air, his chest cavity expanding and then deflating, the process being repeated several times in quick succession. His chest looked like the small plastic bag attached to a hospital breathing apparatus. He then tried to speak, perhaps to beg for mercy, but just as he could not scream, neither could he plead.

Feet planted firmly on the plank floor of the old shop, Simon raised his hands and shouted the remainder of his spell, calling on all that he had learned.

A tear escaped the corner of the old man's eye as the process continued. Even though his muscle and form were fixed in place, held there at the center of the room, inside his skeleton began to quiver. The stench when his bowels collapsed seared Simon's nostrils, but he only chuckled before he continued mouthing his words. His heart pounded; his erection, which had begun when the spell had been first cast, throbbed, its thunder hammering through his body, throbbing at every nerve ending. He wanted to cry out with ecstasy.

Wind from nowhere swept around him, swirled through the interior of the small shop.

Everything shifted, and then the old man's bones began to obey the orders they were receiving, First the toes twitched, rising upward. For a moment only bulges in his shoes were visible.

In the next instant the bones broke through the flesh that contained them and then the leather of the shoes.

Blood spewed through the ripping material, and the old man's eyes rolled farther back in his head.

Yet his bones were not still. The foot continued to rise, and the flesh of his shins began to separate. The leg, then the kneecap, broke free.

Simon watched, amazed even though he had anticipated the power of this spell for a long time. Slowly, the skeleton stepped forward, the hips pulling through the flesh that bound them, and the rib cage forcing its way through the muscles of the chest. As that ripped open, internal organs began to spill from within the chest cavity in a bloody, steaming mass. When the stench of them reached his nostrils, Simon almost vomited, yet he could not avert his eyes from the hideous scene.

The shoulders pulled away next, and then the skull forced its way through the face. Lips and cheeks tore open, and the face of the skull emerged, the exposed teeth and bone seeming to smile in satisfaction as the act was completed.

For a moment the skeleton stood there, the ruined meat of the body at its feet while blood and bile oozed and dripped over the bones. Then, teetering, it slowly toppled, falling apart like a pile of precariously balanced Tinker Toys.

With a deep breath, Simon let his thoughts soften, then stop. It was like letting go of a heavy burden. He staggered and had to brace himself against a table to keep from falling. His hair was now a mass of tangles about his head, and his muscles ached from the tension of the conjuring.

Breathing through his mouth, he allowed himself a few moments to regain composure.

Then he moved behind the counter, lifted the book from its hiding place, and rushed to the door, stepping onto the street quickly and hurrying away, He never did learn how the police explained what they found in the old shop when they went in to investigate the smell.

Now the book was a trophy in his hands, the recollection of the conjuring like a runner's recollection of a great race. But the book did more than bring back memories of past accomplishment. It offered so much more, secrets he was only beginning to unlock.

The little ones he had called from the beyond worked on their own in the child's world now. Their strength powered by the energy from the thoughts of those who believed in them, they performed magic to fulfill Martin's twisted desire to cause pain.

That allowed Simon time to do more. He was almost ready to take a new step, to unlock new doors and to discover things that had perhaps never been known or experienced before, even by the greatest of sorcerers.

He was ready to go on, to take the next step, and to find whatever awaited him, him and anyone he might need in the process.

"We're going to have to get her into some water," Althea said as the heat from Heaven's body could be felt in the air around her.

"Run some in the bathtub," Gab said. She slipped her arms under her daughter's body, ignoring the heat as she hoisted her from the mattress.

Preceding her down the hallway, Althea stepped into the narrow white porcelain bathroom, light blazing bright and pure off the tile as she moved to the edge of the tub and turned the COLD handle as far as it would go.

Water began to pool in the tub as she shoved the stopper into place, and she pushed herself back against the wall to make way for Gab, who was struggling with her child's weight.

Quickly Gab knelt at the tub's edge, lowering Heaven into the rising water. It almost began to sizzle as her form submerged.

"Better get more ice," Gab said. "Just bring all the trays of it."

In the living room, Terry looked up as Althea passed

him, but she moved on before he could ask more questions.

As she returned to the bathroom with the vat of ice cubes, she could feel heat emanating from the tub. It seemed as if she were approaching a small room in which a space heater had been left on for too long, and when she stepped inside she found the air thick and difficult to breath.

She rushed across the room, immediately dumping the ice cubes into the tub. Steam began to rise as Gab dipped her hand into the water and splashed it onto Heaven's face.

Althea began to help her, cradling the child's head just above the water with one hand as she tried to open the COLD faucet more.

Her own face was flushed, and beneath her blouse perspiration was showering through her pores. About to collapse from the heat, she pulled back, desperate for a breath of fresh air.

Gab's scream forced her to shake the confusion from her head and look up. *Spontaneous combustion—the shower curtain was on fire.*

"Can it be that hot in here?" Gab shouted.

Althea ripped the curtain down and stomped on it, but before it had stopped smoldering, fingers of flame had shot from it, licking up the slick tile to the painted plaster where they found fuel.

Blue and yellow sheets of flame blanketed the ceiling in an instant. Gab looked up to see Terry standing in the doorway.

"Run," she commanded. He didn't disobey, but he didn't get far either. Just as he was turning, he collided with Danube who now stood framed in the doorway behind him.

Gently setting the boy aside, he stepped across the room, kneeling beside the tub. He placed a thumb on Heaven's forehead and began to recite a blessing.

Steam continued to rise from the tub, and the flames

began to eat away at the ceiling above, but he was not swayed from his task as Althea and Gab moved back to give him room.

"Demon from the pit of hell, I order you back into the nightmare from which you have come!" he said. "You are being summoned by one force, but by the power of the Creator of all things I command you back."

Heaven sputtered, but her face remained flushed, and the flames continued.

Ignoring the rising heat, Danube gently submerged Heaven, continuing his prayer of blessing. Above him, bits of the covering for the ceiling began to peel and flutter down in snowflakes of flame that had burned to brittle black ash before touching the floor.

"We've got to get her out of here," Gab said.

"That will do no good," Danube shouted. "The flames are emanating from the demon that's being conjured. Taking her out of here won't take us away from the fire."

Reaching around his neck, he pulled a rosary free. For a moment the cross made him hesitate, think of his father, think of a thousand things. Then he quickly draped it around the girl's neck. It might help some, provide one more obstacle for the summoning.

He looked around then and saw them, a dozen of them. They were standing on the counter by the sink, atop the toilet, along the wall; snarling little monsters, laughing at him as their leader gently chanted.

He had not seen them when he had entered, and he knew Gab and Althea could not see them at all. They were amused by that, and some of them made gestures and lewd faces in front of Gab, celebrating her being unaware.

Shaking free of his raincoat, Danube wheeled around to face the leader, the one Heaven would have called Gnelf Master. He knew it to be the chief kesilim, the fooling spirit that led these others who had been charged by someone to torment this child.

"You'll kill her," Danube warned.

The kesilim only laughed, and continued its chant.

"Do you see it?" Gab screamed.

"I see the form it has here, the form it is using," Danube said. "It is a hideous version of the creatures in your child's book."

The being opened its mouth wide in a grin then, shaking a playful finger at Danube.

A piece of the ceiling sagged away from the beams, dangling from the corner of the room near the doorway, more sparks and fluttering bits of flame raining down from it.

Danube ignored them, ignored the smoke, ignored the heat as he faced the beings before him.

"Where are they?" Gabrielle asked.

"I can't see them," Althea said.

The water in the tub almost reached boiling point. Bubbles began to spew up over the edge, splattering hot droplets of liquid about the room while at the same time flames continued to eat away the ceiling.

"Let the girl go," Danube commanded. "You were sent here, not summoned. I command you to leave."

The Gnelfs laughed. "You command us?" the leader asked.

"In the name of God."

The Gnelf laughed. "You sought to kill God."

"Not I. I am sanctified now. There is no blood for which I am responsible."

"None at all." From out of the air, Gnelf Master snatched something, then held it in front of him. It was a small pouch, and the movement created the sounds of coins rattling.

"Does this not haunt your nightmares, oh sanctified one? Are you proud of your past, holy man?"

"Leave," Danube demanded.

"We've got to get Terry out of here," Althea said, while Gab clutched at Heaven who was still in the churning water in the tub.

"No," Danube instructed. "I need the boy."

Althea's eyes opened wide. "You can't harm a child."

"I won't harm him," Danube said. "I need him. He is a friend of the little girl?"

"Yes."

Danube pointed to Terry who stood in the doorway. "Come here."

Frightened, Terry drew a quick, uncertain breath. He had stayed in the same spot, watching everything, but he didn't want to walk into the flaming room.

"Now," Danube said.

Slowly the boy walked forward, stepping around some debris and holding one arm in front of his face to ward off the heat.

In the doorway, flames curled over the threshold and began to reach out to the rest of the house.

"The whole place is going to go up, and we won't be able to get out," Althea warned.

Danube did not acknowledge her words. He knelt in front of Terry and whispered a soft blessing. His thumb gently formed the sign of a cross on the boy's forehead.

"You love Heaven?"

"She's my friend," Terry said.

Danube placed his hands on Terry's shoulders and turned the boy so that he faced the band of Gnelfs. "Do you see them?"

He squinted, looking through the smoke.

"They see you, but they want *you* to think they're not there."

Terry nodded as his eyes found the shapes, the muscles and the scars. He was looking at a group of nightmarish little gnomes with leering eyes. He bit his lip and let the bearded man's words fill his ears.

"They want to harm Heaven," Danube said. "But you can stop them. You can tell them to be gone."

"Why me?"

"Why him?" Gnelf Master repeated.

"He is as pure as the other child. You came upon her unawares with your efforts to control her. He is her friend, and he stands ready to reject you."

"He has no effect on us."

"Ask them to leave, Terry."

Danube put a hand on the boy's shoulder and stood silently. After his eyes darted around for a moment, Terry nodded. "Leave. Go away. Leave Heaven."

"You cannot corrupt here," Danube said. "You are in the presence of love and caring. You are in the presence of friendship and mercy. You are of corruption and judgment. Leave us and stop your summoning."

"The demon has been called. He cannot be turned back."

"He cannot come here," Danube said. "He has no right or invitation."

"We are all invited. The child invited us into her mind. You invited."

"No, you invaded," Danube said. "You came here with lies and deceptions, masquerading as the friends of her imagination. That is not an invitation. If you have awakened some spirit that will expect an explanation, it is yours to deal with."

"This is not finished," the Gnelf warned.

"Cease the summons," Danube said. "And leave this place."

"You will pay, holy man," the little being said. "You will pay dearly." He muttered some other phrase, and the stubby figures vanished.

With a moan, Heaven relaxed in the tub, and the churning of the water ceased. Quickly Gab lifted her, hugging her soaked body. The heat was leaving her.

Heaven buried her face against Gab's shoulder, weeping.

"She's all right," Gab said.

"But the fire," Althea shouted. "We've got to get out of here."

Danube quickly ushered them into the hallway, where the smoke was already growing thick. Fire crawled along the walls of the corridor, devouring the paneling.

Taking Heaven from Gabrielle, Danube carried her.

They burst into the living room ahead of the flames. Here, the haze was not quite as thick, and Terry led the way to the front door, flinging it open. The knob crashed back against the wall, but there was no need to reprimand him. The dent wouldn't be there long.

Gab followed him out into the night. Rain still pelted down, but already fire trucks were pulling to a stop in front of the house. Their red lights blazed through the driving storm, reflecting off the drops, making the rain the color of blood.

Quickly the firemen came forward, some of them helping Gab and Althea, a tall black man relieving Danube of Heaven.

"You stopped them," Gab said, when she found Danube sitting on the rear bumper of one of the trucks. He was breathing deeply, ignoring the rain soaking his shirt.

"Only temporarily," he said.

"You drove them back."

"I ran a bluff," he said. "We have to figure out why they were summoned and what we must do to stop them."

As the firemen in their heavy black jackets and yellow helmets yanked hoses free and hurried toward the house, Gab accepted blankets and consolation from neighbors. In an instant, the house was engulfed.

Simon's eyes bulged from their sockets as the scene unfolded in the depths of the liquid. He had joined Martin again at the side of the cauldron when he had heard of Danube's arrival.

That had worried him. Now he was terrified. He screamed when the Gnelfs were banished, one hand flying out to grip Martin's forearm.

"What the hell's wrong?" Martin demanded, yanking his arm away.

"They were conjuring something. It had nowhere else

to go," Simon shouted.

"So?"

"We summoned the kesilim. They summoned it."

"You're saying . . ."

Before the last of his sentence escaped his lips a cylinder of flame shot up out of the cauldron. It was a swirling pillar of orange blaze, and it quickly blossomed into a cloud that burst through the air above the pot.

Simon dove beneath the platform, seizing the book and pressing it protectively against his body.

The man cursed as Simon pulled him down. The flame continued to waver, dancing, tendrils of it lashing out.

Hurriedly Simon peeled open the brittle pages of the *grimoire,* his long fingers running over the symbols and incantations.

"It's gonna burn the fucking place down," the man shouted.

"I will do something," Simon said.

He eased from beneath the platform, the book open in front of him. Raising the *baculum,* he traced a symbol in the air and murmured the soft syllables of a forgotten tongue.

For a moment the flame stabilized, shimmering as if it might be about to retreat back into the nothingness within the cauldron. Simon was guardedly prepared to let his shoulders sag with relief, but then, in a burst of force, the flame billowed anew, became a whole new cloud of orange, as if someone had thrown gasoline onto a Bunsen burner.

He wanted to vomit. Not only was he facing a power he might not be able to contain, he was letting his employer see him shudder and fumble around in an attempt to prevent the man's house from being burned to the ground.

Simon's initial glee at the Gnelfs' functioning on their own had begun to fade as he'd wondered what was going to happen. He had been almost thankful when Danube arrived to turn things around. The simple spells cast to obstruct his return had been overcome, and perhaps that was for the best.

Except that this blasted demon had to be dealt with. It deftly thrust an orange tentacle in Simon's direction.

Without moving, he voiced a quick protection spell which diverted the flame before it could consume him or damage the book. That worked, but he couldn't keep that up all night.

It would want something. If he couldn't provide something to appease it, the demon might take the house down—and destroy him and his employer in the process.

He gritted his teeth. Through most of his efforts, he had managed to avoid situations like this. He had provided small sacrifices and had taken great care to be in control of his summonings.

When your summonings started summoning, however, you got into trouble. As the flame shimmered again, prepared to lash out once more, he began to mumble a new spell, one hand slipping beneath the folds of his coat as he spoke.

Sweat poured from his brow, and he could feel it dripping from his armpits. Did the perspiration come from tension more than heat? He wasn't sure.

Carefully, he moved in a semicircle around the platform, mumbling protection spells.

The flame hesitated, still dancing, but in a smaller area, around the cauldron. It was waiting, wondering what he might do.

"Who are you?" he asked. If he were to receive a response, even a lie, that would indicate a willingness to bargain. Then, by Enki, lord of magicians, he might stand some chance to turn this around.

The words filled his mind even though no audible sound reached his ears.

I am Girra.

He had read the name in many ancient texts. Was that

truly this being's name or merely a name it was using, a name it knew he would recognize as the spirit of the flames?

If it was truly Girra, then it was willing to bargain. "What can I offer you?" he asked.

There was no reply, but an image of Heaven fluttered through his thoughts. He couldn't tell if it was an errant notion of his own, or something suggested by the spirit.

"I can't give you the girl right now," he said. "There are obstacles. Later maybe."

He waited, straining to pick up whatever message might be offered. When the awareness settled over him, he had to fight the feeling of panic.

He began to shake, and he had to swallow to keep from being completely seized by fear.

This was the kind of thing he'd always been so careful to avoid, but this had come out of something beyond his own doing.

He nodded, letting his hand slide slowly down into his inside coat pocket. He had picked up the ornamental dagger in a shop in Europe, rumor holding that it had once belonged to an Egyptian necromancer.

It was golden in color, though he'd never had it appraised for its true composition. He was also unsure of the true nature of the jewels in the handle. Perhaps they were real, or perhaps it was decorated and designed to look the way one would expect an authentic dagger to look.

Regardless, the blade was sharp and would serve his purpose. With fresh sweat pouring from his brow, he gripped the dagger handle in his right hand and held the left hand up, displaying it for the flame.

"What the hell are you doing?" Martin called from behind him.

"What I must," Simon whispered. "Be ready to help me if I need it."

He gritted his teeth and closed his eyes as he slipped the blade down the side of his pinkie, letting the cutting edge rest at the base of the finger.

Then, tensing his muscles, he forced it to the side, cutting through the fleshy web of skin and grinding the blade through muscle, then bone.

He felt his strength ebbing as the blood began to flow, and his brain began to spin. For a moment he thought he would faint, but he forced himself to remain standing, commanded his mind to peer through the black haze that was trying to settle over him.

As the finger tore free, he let the knife clatter to the floor and used the belt of his jacket as a tourniquet, wrapping it around his hand in an effort to stem the spurting blood.

Still staggering and shuddering with the shock that was sweeping over him, he held the bloody member over his head and hurled it forward into the flame.

That blazed brightly for a moment, roaring as if it might be ready to consume the entire house, but then it was gone, as if it were being sucked back into the cauldron.

Dropping back to the floor, Simon forced himself to hold onto the makeshift tourniquet. A moment later he felt his employer's hands at his back, supporting him.

"That was a demon?"

"Of sorts."

"It would have killed us?"

"Yes. I appeased it."

"Dammit, it could have screwed up everything. It could have killed the little girl."

"But it didn't. It served its purpose."

"These blasted kesilim of yours are out of control."

"No," said Simon. "They are merely gaining strength. All is well."

"The hell it is."

Simon's head rolled back against the man's sleeve. He was pale as death. "Martin, please. I'm very tired. Could we talk about this in the morning?"

Chapter 17

A neighbor found Jake Tanner's body early the next morning. Gabrielle learned about it when Katrina spoke to a friend at the newspaper. She almost broke down, but Katrina seated her at the kitchen table and put a cup of coffee into her hands.

She didn't cry, couldn't cry in the wake of everything that had happened, but remorse and guilt seized her.

"It's my fault," Gab said. "He only got involved in all of this because of me."

"It's not your fault," Katrina said. "No way. Besides, he was stabbed. The police are checking into the possibility that it could have been some crazy fan."

"It wasn't," Gabrielle said. "It was those same damned things that are attacking Heaven. They went after him so he wouldn't be able to help me."

She did cry, not sobbing but not fighting the tears. Katrina tore a paper towel from the roll by the refrigerator and gave it to her. The paper was rough, but it absorbed the moisture when Gab dabbed her cheeks.

"What am I going to do, Kat? They're driving me crazy. They're killing my daughter, and there's nothing I can do to prevent that. I can't call a cop and say 'Hey, officer, my daughter is under attack by demons.'"

"Kesilim and lezim," Danube said walking into the room. "Jokesters."

"That was no joke last night."

"To them it was," he said, pouring a cup of coffee for himself. He winced when he tasted it.

"Well, whatever they are, how do we stop them? They killed Jake. They'll kill us, won't they?"

Danube took a seat. "We have to figure out why they are after you. They are powerful, but somehow I suspect they did not come for your daughter without some impetus. She was not experimenting with a ouija or making any other effort to open herself to spiritual attack."

"No. She's not old enough to know about things like that, and you said yourself it couldn't be Dave."

"Who does that leave?"

"There's no one else."

Katrina put a hand on Gab's arm. "What about Martin? You said when you broke up with him he was possessive."

"That's why I broke up with him, but I don't think he's crazy enough to do something like this."

"You broke up. He was possessive, but he never called again, never tried to make up?"

Gabrielle had to nod in agreement.

"He's the only boyfriend you've had since Dave, except for Tanner and he's been effectively ruled out."

Gabrielle looked at Danube to see his reaction.

"I know nothing of him," he said.

"He's in his fifties. I did some bookkeeping for him. He took a fancy to me, and we went out for a while. But it was too soon after Dave, and he wanted to know every move I made. He bought me presents for a while, but he was always accusing me of slipping around, seeing someone else. I wasn't that interested in dating at that point, not in seeing more than one man, I mean. I got enough of it all pretty quickly and told him we should break off. He wasn't as polished as I'd first thought. The attraction of his being gallant and mature faded."

Danube took another swallow of the coffee, wincing

again. "His reaction?" he asked.

"He was mad. Not so mad as to hit me or anything, but angry at me for leaving him."

"Did he scream?"

"No. He internalized his rage. Was very gruff, but nothing more. I left and never saw him anymore."

"This was when?"

"A few months back."

"You did bookkeeping for him. He is older. Am I to assume he has money?"

"He was well off. He was in real estate, that sort of thing. He had investments."

"The kind of disposable income that would allow him to hire someone," Danube observed.

"That's absurd."

"Had he traveled?"

"He and his wife used to travel," Gabrielle said.

"In what we might call the East?"

"Some, I think."

"To places where he might be exposed to things which might make him a believer? Once a believer, such a man might be willing to take steps to achieve what he perceived as a source of power."

"I don't know," Gabrielle said.

She didn't want to think about Martin, yet she felt anger rising in her. She had asked him to get out of her life when it had become clear she would not fall in love with him. Perhaps he had loved her, but his kind of love was really a consuming desire to own, to possess; and she didn't want to belong to anyone.

He had no right to pry into her world, to terrorize her daughter through some bizarre game. She could not imagine Martin—he of the three-piece suits and shirts with button-down collars—donning a black robe and kneeling in a pentagram to conjure demons. Yet, if he was driven by some mad sense of revenge, driven to find some crazy way of sending demons after her daughter, she would kill him.

She recalled his kisses, his touch, and the memory of them made her shudder. She closed her eyes, wanting to spit in his face if he was responsible for all this—Heaven's torment, Jake's death, Rev. Marley's death—just because he didn't want to lose? It couldn't be that he loved her, his feeling was sick, twisted.

"Did you ever have any indication he had an interest in the occult?" Danube asked.

Gabrielle did not want to think about days with Martin, but she searched her memory, trying to think of what he had talked about, what interests he had mentioned. Usually caught up in his business dealings, he had only gone to movies because she had suggested them. And he'd never talked about books, music—only about his deals, his plans for developments, how he hired men to accomplish his plans.

"He's a contractor," she said. "A planner who hires other people to—"

"Execute his ideas," Danube finished. "For that at which he is not skilled, he finds someone who is."

"Exactly."

"He desires to strike at you, yet he cannot do that without being arrested. He searches for some method that will allow you to be tormented without his being implicated. Perhaps he speaks to someone. This person makes a suggestion, and it clicks for him. Using his contacts, he locates one who can fulfill his wishes."

"You mean he hired a wizard?"

"A wizard, mage, there are many names."

"A Satanist?"

"Not necessarily. But ultimately, based on what we have seen, he is summoning forces of evil. He or she."

"Can you stop him?"

"I don't know how powerful he is."

"The forces of good aren't stronger than those of evil?"

"It is not as simple as that. We live in a fallen world, a

world separated from its Creator by disobediences and corruption."

"My child is innocent. She has never harmed anyone. She's never hated anyone."

"But she lives in a realm where evil is at play, ready to use anyone and everyone as a pawn for the sheer thrill of it. The kesilim and lezim are seeking the excitement of existence. They have been banished into a realm of suffering. Being conjured here gives them a chance to run rampant. Last night's events are evidence of that. They were seeing how far they could go, and when I reminded them of their limitations they backed down. That may not happen every time."

"I just want this to be over," Gabrielle said, clenching her fists and closing her eyes tightly.

"It will have to end some way," Danube said. "I suggest we charge it head-on."

"How so?"

"I will seek out Martin, question him. Perhaps I will be able to learn how he is causing this—if he is the culprit."

"He has to be." Gab was shaking now. "I want to fight. I want to make them leave my daughter alone."

"We will fight, once I know what steps need to be taken."

She drew in a long breath, filling her lungs and then expelling air in an attempt to calm herself. She wouldn't tolerate this. It was senseless torture.

"I'll get the address of Martin's office," she said.

Danube waited at the table until she returned with the slip of paper from the yellow note pad Katrina had provided.

He folded it and put it into his pocket. "I will be back soon," he said.

Heaven sat up in bed, sipping the juice Katrina had poured for her. She was pale, and the dark circles under her eyes almost made her look like an old woman. Gabrielle had to reach deep inside herself to manage to smile.

"How are you feeling, sweetheart?" she asked, sitting on the edge of the bed.

"Okay," Heaven said. "I feel like I had a bad dream."

She had been sleeping since they had brought her to Katrina's. There had been no trace of fever during the night, and while she had tossed about some, she had not awakened, being too depleted to rouse.

"We had a rough time of it," Gab said. "It's going to be all right now."

"Why don't they go away and leave us alone?" Heaven asked.

"I don't know, baby." She wished she had a better answer.

Just days ago it had seemed things were finally getting on track. Now everything was in a shambles. Her home was gone, and there was no end in sight for the struggle. Not unless Danube could find some way to make Martin go away.

Somehow she couldn't picture it being that simple. Not if he'd gone to this much trouble to torment her. She couldn't understand that kind of obsession, couldn't understand how someone could want to punish her so badly he would want to hurt Heaven.

Martin was wealthy, attractive, and no doubt able to find other women. There was no reason for him to want to hold her except spite and a desire to manipulate and control everything around him.

There were so many things you could not tell about people. When you met them, they were on their best behavior, displaying smiles and their best manners.

She had first run into Martin at a dinner party thrown by one of the firm's clients. He had been wearing a charcoal gray suit and had seemed debonair.

In contrast to Dave, he had seemed striking. Dave's opposite, not an unsure youngster, he had seemed to have his own corner chiseled in the world. That had appealed to her because, in starting over, she didn't want to repeat what had occurred with Dave.

She had read that some people follow the same patterns, becoming involved in the same types of bad relationships over and over again. She had been trying to strike out in a different direction, but had still managed to find someone who was bad for her. What an uncanny knack she had.

Not only was it causing pain for her daughter, but it had cost Jake his life. His only crime had been caring for her, wanting to help. Leaving her daughter's bedside when the child fell asleep again, Gab went into the bathroom.

Her own eyes had even darker circles, and her hair was in tangles. Was she somehow cursed, destined to bring pain to those around her?

No, she wouldn't let herself think that way. She turned on the faucet, running some warm water to splash on her face. That was what Martin wanted. To tear her down, to make her feel this way. She would not give in to this torture.

He had done bad things, and they had caused pain. She could not accept the responsibility for someone else's evil.

Besides, she had other things to think about. Calling the landlord, explaining it all, as well as she could, anyway. The fire department was speculating about lightning. She wouldn't argue with their findings. It wasn't an act of God, but it was something beyond human control.

Althea settled into a tub of hot water. Her muscles ached now that the adrenaline had ebbed from them. She had been so tense during the previous night's events that she ached almost from head to toe, and she was reminded once again that her youth was passing.

Gently, she let her head sink beneath the water, the

warm suds soaking her hair and easing the throbbing in her skull. She was not completely comfortable, being alone, but she tried not to think about potential harm while she sought to relax. She hoped the forces of darkness were temporarily appeased.

Yet she knew that probably was not the case. She was living in a nightmare world, one in which people found new ways to hurt each other—or recycled old ways. This was all out of the dark ages. Someone with her training was not supposed to believe that devils caused madness, yet what else could explain what she had witnessed?

All of Freud's and Jung's theories, all of the techniques she had so carefully studied were futile now. A little girl's sanity, her mother's, and Althea's own all were being attacked by forces from a realm outside her understanding. The mysterious, mystical man who had wandered into this world seemed to be their only hope.

Danube did not represent reason, yet he was the only one who appeared able to make sense of the assaults. She had promised herself she would fight for Gabrielle and Heaven, but her training—her answers—were not enough.

It was frustrating to realize that, frustrating to think the fears and superstitions she had fought so hard to overcome over the years were the alternative. She wondered if this might not still prove to be some sort of delusion. But that thought did not tarry in her consciousness. She knew what they had experienced was real, all of it.

After soaking a while longer, she pulled herself from the tub, using a thick towel as a wrap. Then, taking a second towel from the cabinet beneath the sink, she tied it around her head. Standing at the mirror, she decided it looked like a turban. With the bright fluorescent light reflecting off the white cloth, she found the lines in her face more noticeable, mostly around her eyes. One more thing she couldn't control, aging.

Still clad in the towel, she walked from the bath into

her bedroom. The bed looked inviting. Rest would have been welcome, had she not felt she should get back to Heaven and Gabrielle. And she did not want to be alone.

That just didn't seem to be a good idea. Lately people died when they were alone. Having survived last night's nightmarish episode, she should feel invincible, but she did not.

Pulling open the louvered closet door, she selected a soft pants suit and carried it over to the bed. If she let her hair dry en route, she would look presentable if a little unkempt. That was the least of her worries. She wouldn't bother with makeup either, in spite of the wrinkles. This was a no-frills day. She had to get back to Gabrielle.

She was about to disentangle the towel, knotted between her breasts, when the arm slid around her neck. Before she could capture a breath to cry out, a hand, wrapped in gauze and reeking of the sickly sweet smell of dried blood, closed across her mouth.

Before her eyes another hand appeared, this one clasping a long golden dagger with a wavy blade. The blade glistened in the glow of the overhead light, its tip visibly sharp, honed to a point perfect for piercing flesh.

"Let's be very quiet." The hiss came from behind her, hot breath touching the back of her neck and making the hairs on it stand up in spite of their dampness.

With a twist, she felt herself being spun around, and then, just for an instant, she was facing the blond-haired man with the pointed features. Before she flew backward, bouncing onto the bed.

In the next instance, he was on top of her, his weight pressing down on her before she could think about struggling, and she closed her eyes, reliving the terror she had known as a child. Her flesh burned, as if aflame with fear of violation. She was about to be subjected to a different torture.

She felt the smooth skin on his face as his lips pressed gently against her ear. "I want you to be calm."

She opened her eyes, and found herself looking up into

cold eyes. A scowl was carved into his features, but she detected no sign of lust in his expression. She realized she was also feeling no indication of his manhood even though his loins were pressed close to hers.

She managed to swallow despite the dryness of her mouth. He was either going to do something more hideous than violate her or he had some other purpose.

Summoning calm as she had learned to do from years of practice, she forced herself to analyze the circumstances. He was not pawing her.

"What do you want?" she asked, containing the quiver in her voice.

He laughed softly. The bandaged hand was placed before her eyes, and he unfurled the gauze to show her the jagged stump where his finger should have been. She almost gagged as the smell of it hit her. Raw flesh shining slightly. It had not been stitched after the amputation, but it was sealed. It appeared to have been cauterized, badly, with an open flame.

"You're partly responsible for this," he said.

"How did I do that?" Althea asked. Could he be the victim of some former patient somehow blaming her? He was obviously disturbed. She would have to deal with him on those terms.

"You were with the woman and her girl. You helped them drive the demon back at me."

Her heart contracted. He was the one, the one who had conjured the demons, the sorcerer. With new fear, she looked into his cold, emotionless eyes. He might want something she couldn't offer.

Chapter 18

Danube rode the silent elevator up to the sixth floor, where Martin rented a suite of offices. As the doors hissed open, he stepped off into the carpeted lobby and found a slender woman in her mid thirties at a receptionist's desk. Behind her, the wall was adorned by a metal replica of the company's logo, a gold emblem on a clear plastic sheet.

She had thick eyebrows, brown like her short hair, and one of them arched upward in involuntary suspicion as he approached her. He did not have the look of a regular client.

"Can I help you?"

He asked for Martin.

"Do you have an appointment?" Her speech was affected by her protruding jaw, making her tone even more irritating.

"No."

"Your name?"

"Danube."

She picked up a telephone handset that was connected to a board of buttons. Her eyes remained locked suspiciously on Danube as she pressed one button down. "A Mr. Danube is here."

She listened a moment, then cupped her hand over the mouthpiece.

"He's very busy."
"It's in regard to Gabrielle Davis and her daughter, Heaven," he said. "You might call it a matter of life and death."
The receptionist's eyes widened at that remark, and she spoke softly into the mouthpiece, trying to keep her words from Danube's ears.
After a moment she nodded and hung up. "He'll see you briefly," she said.
Danube walked past her desk before she could speak further.
"I'll show you back," she offered.
"I can find it," Danube said.
He pushed through a doorway at the end of the hall and then moved on down the carpeted corridor, past the decorative plants to the last door in the row. Pushing it inward, he stepped slowly into the room.
Martin waited behind his desk. His sports coat buttoned in place, tie perfect, hair neat. He looked ready to meet the "60 Minutes" cameras.
"What do you want?" he asked. His voice was hard. He leaned forward in his chair. He was a man used to taking the offensive.
"Heaven Davis almost died last night," Danube said.
"I haven't seen Gab in months, let alone her kid, and I don't believe I know who you are."
"For now you can consider me her protector."
"Who are you, the 'Equalizer'?"
"I am Danube. I have seen magic. I can sense magic." He raised his hands, setting his fingers in a careful arrangement, aiming them toward Martin. "You have been in the presence of magic."
Martin began to shift about uncomfortably in his chair, although his eyebrows continued to dip down, forming a valley just over the bridge of his nose. Danube cocked his head slightly, studying him closely.
"You have been near magic without calling upon it

yourself," he said.

"What the hell are you talking about?" Martin stood up and walked around his desk. "Are you crazy? You come in here making accusations and talking about mumbo jumbo."

Danube moved closer to the edge of the desk, facing Martin, keeping his hand raised as his eyes scanned the air. His ears tucked back slightly, he was searching for vibrations while exaggerating the technique in order to make Martin squirm.

Only after several moments did Danube let his eyes wander back to Martin's face. "You have been in contact with someone who uses magic," he said. "You know what's been happening to the child."

"I don't know anything, and you can't prove what you say," Martin said. "Get the hell out of my office."

Danube made no move to leave. He had been deliberately testing Martin's reaction. He could sense lingering traces of magic, but he was now more interested in studying the businessman's eyes and demeanor. Martin's flare-up confirmed the suspicion he'd had contact with a magician.

Leaning against the desk, Danube offered the man a frozen stare. "You are dealing with very dangerous forces," he said. "You must call this off."

The businessman's face and neck had gone scarlet. He loosened his collar and glared at Danube. "I told you, I don't know what you're talking about."

"The fire could have destroyed you. In a way I am surprised it did not. You will regret what's happening. I can promise that. I have known many who turned to the darkness to fulfill their desires. The results are always horrendous."

"I'll call security."

Danube threw up his hand. "Unnecessary."

He walked slowly backward, eyes on Martin, fingertips still pointed toward him. The businessman continued to squirm as Danube found the knob behind him and eased the door open before stepping into the hall.

When the red-haired man had disappeared, Martin slumped back in his chair. It was a relief to have him gone. He had been like some mad Gypsy, but he had been right about one thing. Dabbling in magic was horrendous. Simon was strange, and now another strange man had shown up.

Martin wasn't sure what it was, but aside from inherent weirdness, he had sensed something else that was unsettling about Danube. The man was even odder than Simon, and that was a hard thing to be.

This had gone beyond what he'd expected. He'd wanted to lash out at Gabrielle in some way, make her suffer because he had suffered. He had everything, so much to offer, and she had walked out, giving him some cooked-up excuse about his being too possessive.

And nothing would change her mind, not all the money he had or all the power. He could snap his fingers and some other young girl would fall into line, but Gab wouldn't pay any attention to him, wouldn't think about looking back or giving him another chance.

He had suffered for a while. It had been hard to concentrate on his work because he believed he loved her. He had tried going out with other women, had dated a couple of really young girls his friend Harper had fixed him up with, then an older woman, one closer to his own age. All of them were poor substitutes for what he had felt for Gabrielle.

Slowly his feeling of loss over her walking out had turned to a simmering anger. Why hadn't she been willing to give him a chance to make things up? So many women wanted him, but she turned away. She had caused pain without allowing him any prospect of alleviating it.

He had begun to consider some way of giving that pain back, but he'd had no way to hurt her the way she had hurt him. She did not love him, and his pain was born of love.

Then he had thought of her daughter. She did love the child. At first it had been only a passing idea, a notion he had thought it impossible to act on. Kidnapping was too extreme. Yet the thought had festered in his mind. He could not actually do something to the child. The risk of prosecution was too great, but there were other ways.

Then he had spent some time in New Orleans, and a friend had taken him to some of the magic rituals performed there by voodoo priests. Martin had been impressed, and he had recalled that he'd heard of people who had suffered under curses, not those inflicted by voodoo but other bizarre magic rites.

He had returned to New Orleans and had sought out a dark priest, but the man had been unwilling to perform his task.

"Too much danger of angering the demons," he had said. "Powerful magic would be needed. Too risky."

But the priest knew of another man who practiced a different magic. This man feared nothing, they said. He was a powerful dark mage. He collected forbidden works and worked spells that others were too frightened to perform. He had come to New Orleans to look for the writings of the madman Matthew Laird and had stayed to study other rituals.

Finding Simon had not been easy, but finally Martin had located him in a musty old shop in the French Quarter. The mage had bargained hard, demanding front money for his bank account.

Only when that had been deposited did he agree to talk with Martin about what would be required. They had sat down in a dark little room decorated with Mardi Gras posters, two of its walls lined with shelves supporting jars of obscure substances and crumbling books.

There, with faint light creeping in through the curtains of the windows, Simon had interviewed him. Questioning him about Gabrielle's habits and then about the child, he had determined what was possible, had outlined a plan.

"She is an open vessel," he warned. He had then taken up a musty book and had shown Martin the symbols of darkness. "I have been waiting for a chance to try these," he had whispered.

It had seemed so easy, so simple back then when Martin had considered the effect on Gabrielle of watching her daughter suffer, of wondering why she could find no explanation for it. Now he felt like a fool, an old, twisted fool driven to some madman in order to get revenge. Now he needed no revenge. He had gotten beyond that, yet what was he to do? Could he make Simon leave?

Magic had been a perfect way of punishing Gab without being captured. Who would believe he was attacking her child with magic? They would think her the crazy one. Except it hadn't worked that way. Simon's magic had gone too far, and now Gab had found an ally, someone who believed her. Dammit that was not supposed to happen. Worse, somehow the man had figured out he was involved. There was no explanation for that because he had been careful to make no contact with Gabrielle.

He picked up a spindle and slammed its point down into the wood on the surface of his desk. The point dug into the finish, but the wood did not give in enough to allow the implement to stand. The spindle fell onto its side and rolled off onto the floor.

Martin snatched up the receiver, tapping out the phone number from memory. He had rented a small place for Simon, had provided the luxuries the magician had requested.

After several rings he slammed the handset down. He had expected the man to be resting, recovering from the night's disaster. If he was not at home, where could he be? Last night the child had come too close to death, and two others had died because of the magic. It was time for this to stop. He had to find Simon. Whatever the mage was doing, more suffering could be the only result.

Danube stood outside Martin's building for a while, looking through the rainy drizzle at the office window. He searched the morning air for vibrations of magic, but he could detect none. Whoever Martin's sorcerer was, the mage was not present at the moment.

That was fine if it meant the wizard was somewhere recovering from the exhaustion of conjuring. It was another matter if he—or she—was preparing for more evil.

There was a chance this morning's visit had frightened Martin, but Danube could not rely on that possibility.

If Martin was not frightened by dealing with the dark forces of evil, there was little that threats and sideshow performances could do to throw fear into him. He could not be afraid of prosecution. No laws that dealt with casting spells against another person were on the books. What recourse could Martin expect other than eternal judgment or the wrath of God?

No one could threaten him with those. Eternal judgment came only in the end, and Danube had learned the Almighty worked in His own time. While other forces might be manipulated by the will of men, He acted only when He chose.

Danube was left to wonder what action he should take. He knew the source of the conjuring now, but not how to attack it. If Martin had somehow located a powerful dark magician to fulfill his needs, the task of defeating such a person might be formidable.

He was torn between waiting there and trying to follow Martin to his contact or heading back to Katrina's to prepare Heaven and Gabrielle for further struggles.

He would have to be ready for whatever came next. Another assault like the one of the past night would kill the child if he had not prepared her with blessings and prayers.

He looked up at the bleak, gray sky. Was there a chance for blessings? He felt alone, lost and more isolated than ever.

The rain was still stinging his face a few moments later when he saw Martin come out the front door of the office building. He was wearing a raincoat and carrying an umbrella.

As he headed around to the parking lot at the building's side, Danube stepped from the doorway where he had been standing and slipped along the sidewalk to the corner.

A gray cab was parked there, a large black man in the driver's seat. His massive frame seemed wedged behind the wheel, and he wore wraparound sunshades in spite of the haze. He folded up his newspaper when Danube tapped on the glass.

"A car will be coming out of that lot in a few moments," Danube said. "I want to follow it."

The man gave a grim nod and put his paper aside. He was wearing a black muscle shirt which revealed his thick biceps, and a gold chain was stretched around his wrist. A Zulu medallion dangled from the rearview mirror.

"Whatever you say," he growled. "You wanna play James Bond, I can kick ass."

Danube settled into the back seat. "Try to be inconspicuous."

"Will do."

Just as the old car's engine was rattling to life, Martin's Lincoln eased out of the parking lot.

"That the one?"

"It is."

He yanked the gearshift down and slid onto the street, setting a slow pace that kept him a few car lengths behind the Lincoln.

"So, you a DEA agent or something?"

"Concerned citizen," Danube said. He was leaning over the seat, keeping his eyes focused ahead as the windshield wipers labored to push the rain away. He noticed the cabbie's license identified him as Joe Wilson.

"Last time I did a deal like this, it was a woman trying to catch her cheatin' husband. We got the motherfucker too."

"You did a good job?"

He tipped his hat. "Trailed him out to a cheap hotel. He never even knew we were on his bumper."

The car skirted out along Wagner Street, which connected with Quinn Extension. The traffic was heavy, so they spent a good deal of time sitting still, waiting for lights to change, then waiting for the cars in front of them to gradually begin moving.

"You picked a good time of day for this," Wilson muttered.

Finally the Lincoln pulled off Quinn and shot along a side street into a parking lot.

The lot bordered an apartment complex, two rows of units stretched back from the roadway, the galleries decorated with elaborate ironwork.

Wilson parked the cab on the street, letting the motor idle while they watched Martin climb from his car and hurry up the outside stairs of one row of apartments.

He stopped in front of 206 and banged on the door. When he didn't get an answer, he fished into his pocket and produced a ring of keys which he used to open the lock.

Danube leaned over the seat, peering out through the passenger window. He saw Martin disappear into the apartment. A moment later he exited, still moving in a rush. He bounded down the outside stairs and rushed back to his car.

"Want to keep followin'?" Wilson asked.

"No," Danube said. "I'm going to have a look upstairs. You can go on if you want."

"Hell, no. You need a lookout." Wilson pulled his glasses off and stared into Danube's eyes. "Remember, I'm inconspicuous."

"You don't even know what I'm up to," Danube said.

"Way you're acting, way that guy was acting, way your eyes are moving, I'd say you're after somethin' bad. Might get yourself hurt, ruin my reputation."

Danube handed him a fifty. "Cough if you spot trouble."

The big man shut the engine off and followed Danube up the stairs. They walked slowly along the upper corridor, carefully looking over their shoulders. No one seemed to be watching them as Danube stood in front of the door he sought.

It was locked, but blocking the door with his body, he worked on it only momentarily before the bolt was sprung.

As he stepped into the darkened living room, goose pimples rose on his flesh. Leaving Wilson outside to keep watch, he stepped across the floor.

The feeling of magic, bad magic, filled the air, but the place was almost barren. The living room was devoid of anything besides the furnishings that came with the place, and the kitchen was unused.

In the bedroom closet, Danube found some clothes, and the bed was rumpled from use. It was in the spare room, however, that he found interesting materials. The bed frame had been collapsed, and the mattress leaned against one wall.

In the center of the floor, chalk had been used to draw various symbols. Squatting, he studied them, recognizing the markings as gates, signs for summoning or for opening the veil of the beyond.

Some would have been easy to learn. Others would have been more difficult to obtain. He found nothing terribly complicated, but he was able to determine that some of the rudimentary conjuring had been performed here.

Straightening, he looked over at the closet. The door

was closed tightly, and as he approached it, he could feel strong vibrations of magic dancing around the frame. They were almost like an electrical field. A spell had been placed around the closet.

He paused. If a spell was necessary to protect it, he needed to know what was inside. Stepping back he bowed his head, praying for blessing. Then he stepped forward, gently touching the doorknob.

The force of the cold shot through his fingertips and jolted up his arm, knocking him back several steps. The hair on his arms stood on end, and his face throbbed. He steadied himself, shaking his head as waves of coldness continued to sweep over him.

He felt a bit nauseous, and the chill bit deep, coursing through his muscles. The sensation lasted almost a full minute, letting him know how powerful the spell must be since he had not firmly gripped the knob.

That much force would not have been contained in a simple incantation, which indicated the help of a demon must have been obtained.

Reaching into his coat pocket, Danube withdrew a crucifix. Holding it in front of him, he stepped toward the door. The knob began to glow as he held the icon close.

"In the name of the Lord God I command you to be gone," he whispered. "You have no right to this realm."

The glow continued, becoming brighter and brighter. He was forced to turn his eyes away as it flared, becoming almost a blinding white burn.

The explosion came in a rush of icy wind, the impact hitting him like a solid blow. He rolled with the force, going to the floor, using his shoulder to absorb the impact. Then he bounced back to his feet to face the image flickering before him.

The manifestation was a smoky white face covered with whiskers that seemed to be rimed with frost. Laughing, it seemed to draw a deep breath and spit at him.

He jerked the crucifix up in front of him just as the misty white cloud approached. As it touched the holy symbol, the cloud dispersed, splitting apart in a burst of molecules that headed in all directions.

"I rebuke you," Danube said. "I command you to leave this realm. You were summoned here, but your summoner is gone. Return to your home in the pit."

The being hesitated, and in the air was a sound like an unnatural growling. Danube straightened, keeping the crucifix leveled in front of him.

Flickering, the image before him slowly began to swirl. Then in a burst of noise almost like a small clap of thunder, it seemed to implode. The room reverberated for several seconds before it was still.

Danube paused for a moment, letting his heartbeat slow. It had quickened to a threatening pace, and for a while it continued to hammer in his chest, driving a rush of blood through his system. Finally, almost reluctantly, he stepped forward.

The door sagged open now, the latch shattered. He touched the wood this time, pulling it open. The chamber was almost empty, except for some books resting on the shelf above the hanger bar.

They were basic texts on sorcery, the spells within them not elaborate. Equivalent spells might be found in mainstream books on the occult that could be purchased at any bookstore. There should have been no need to risk the dangers of conjuring a demon if that was all the closet concealed.

Danube knelt, searching the floor carefully, and he noticed the carpet had been ripped up in one corner. Peeling it back, he found the crumbled edges of brittle, brown pages. Something had rested here in concealment until recently. He picked up a few fragments, studying the markings. Most of the pieces were too small to reveal anything, but one was a corner piece from a page. He held it to the light and noticed the glowing aura around it.

He could make out just a fragment of an image, the tail of a symbol. That fraction was enough, and he dropped the paper quickly, unwilling to hold it longer.

The forbidden symbols had been taught to him only for the sake of recognition. For a moment he could not believe what he was seeing, but there was no denying it. The vibrations of the magic which emanated from it were too strong. It was definitely evil magic, the most evil.

The symbol was one of the dark runes. It came from *The Red Book*, the book that long ago had been stolen.

Stolen from Satan himself.

Chapter 19

Slowly, Simon let Althea sit up on the bed. With his hand still at her throat, he looked into her eyes, his own gaze boring into her soul.

"Do you know who I am?"

"I have an idea?"

"I am the one who brought the demons. I am the one who controls the darkness. I could feed you to the demons right now if I chose."

Althea looked back at him without flinching, showing him she would not give in to his intimidation.

Her defiance only made a grim smile spread across his features. "You think you can stand against me?" He tilted his head slightly toward her. "What do you fear most?"

She didn't answer.

His continuing smile showed that he didn't need her reply. He loosened his grip, caressing her throat with his thumb.

"You fear violation."

She couldn't keep her eyes from betraying her.

His smile continued. "Your experiences, they were harsh. You never enjoyed the love of your husband." Realization spread through his eyes. "Each time he filled you, you recalled what happened to you. It was more agony than pleasure."

She shook her head.

"I can show you what it would be like in other worlds," the magician said. "Would you like that?"

"What the hell are you talking about?" she shouted.

"You've seen the Gnelfs. There are others that might also touch you, caress you, enjoy you."

"No." She felt hot tears flowing.

"Dark angels, the love of dark angels."

"You bastard."

"Imagine an eternity of it, or just an hour."

"Damn you."

"Prepare yourself. You can endure it for as long as you can, or you can help me."

Tears filled Althea's eyes now. She wanted to spit at him, to curse him more, but her fear was taking over. She couldn't face the abuse he was threatening. Not even the stamina she had built up over the years would allow her to stand up against worse tortures than she had endured before. She couldn't go through it.

She wept, trembling, her arms drawn up in front of her chest. "I won't help you," she said.

At a wave of his hand, the shadows in the corner of the room seemed to flicker, and slowly the small stooped figures of Gnelfs began to step forward.

Their mouths gaped open in grins that revealed yellowed teeth on which their tongues played, and their eyes were filled with lust as they looked at her.

Simon's laugh provided sick background music for their approach, and as one of the Gnelfs reached out for her, Althea relived the moments from her childhood, cowering from an unwanted touch, whimpering as it drew near her.

She felt the oily hand brush her arm, and then, without warning, her face was jerked to the side. Simon's hand had shot up to her jaw, closing over it, to sharply turn her head.

"Do you want them to go away?"

She nodded, swallowing, feeling her throat muscles

press against his palm.

He only seemed to blink, and the oily fingertips were gone.

"I can bring them back at any time," he warned. "Understand that?"

He shifted his weight off her and slid to his feet, roughly gripping Althea's arm and pulling her up as well.

"Get dressed," he demanded.

She hesitated, and his eyes almost seemed to glow. His anger was evident. She had worked with many people on the brink, and she sensed that he was dangerously close to losing control, to dipping over into total madness.

The cab driver cruised to a slow stop in front of Martin's house. It was a red brick with large columns in front and a driveway that wound across rolling green lawn to a hidden carport at the back.

"You want me to wait?" the cabbie asked.

"I suggest you cruise for a while," Danube said. "Circle back to see if I am waiting. Otherwise keep moving. A cab parked here would be too conspicuous."

"Especially with a big black man behind the wheel. Got ya," Wilson said. Danube watched the car pull away through the gray afternon haze before turning to walk across the damp rye grass.

Ignoring the front door, he went up the driveway and spotted the Lincoln parked under the carport beside a more extravagant MG roadster.

He eased past that car and crept to the back door. He could again sense the traces of magic in the air, but they were not as strong as he had expected. Martin's magician was not here. That was no surprise.

Gently, he pressed his ear against the door, listening. He could hear the faint sound of Martin's voice, apparently raised in anger although his words were not clear through the wood.

He tried the door and found it unlocked, so he eased it

open and stepped inside. In the next room Martin's voice still roared.

"Well, tell him if he shows up there I want him over at my house immediately. He has questions to answer."

The phone was slammed down. Danube stood on the tiled floor in what proved to be the kitchen, listening as Martin clomped around in the next room.

Only a few seconds passed before the businessman entered the kitchen, stopping fast when he saw Danube waiting for him.

"Have you lost your sorcerer?" Danube asked.

Martin's reaction went from surprise to anger, then outrage. He jabbed a finger at Danube and spoke through clenched teeth.

"I thought I told you to get the hell away from me. I don't know anything about any sorcerers. You must be deranged."

"That accusation might fall more appropriately on your shoulders," Danube said.

A nerve jumped involuntarily in Martin's cheek.

"A powerful man who resorts to magic over something so simple as a love affair gone wrong. Is revenge that important?"

"She shouldn't have left me. She didn't give me a chance."

"Was it worth what you have wrought?"

"Everything's all right."

"We do not know that at this point," Danube said. "You have no way of knowing what your magician is doing."

"He does what I tell him."

"Is that why you have been so frantic to find him this afternoon? He was doing experiments last night. He might still be."

"Why the hell did you follow me?"

"I thought he might come here. He has to be stopped."

"I'll stop him."

"He is not motivated by your cash. He is motivated by

power. You only granted him time and an opportunity to test his skills. He needs you no longer. Your support is past."

"How do you know all this?"

"I know the corruption magic brings. There is only one true source of dark magic of the nature he uses, and it exacts a powerful price."

The businessman shifted nervously in the doorway. His tie was already loosened, but his hand went up to tug at it as if it were strangling him.

"You can't prove anything against me."

"That is not my purpose. I seek to end this. Let me. He will come here. This has to be where his conjuring was done. I searched his apartment, and the markings and magic traces there were rudimentary."

"You're trying to trick me, make me reveal something. Are you wired? It'll never stand up in court."

"My interest is not in courts. Show me where he performed his sorcery. He is very, very dangerous, and there is little time." For the first time urgency was evident in Danube's voice.

"I think you should get out of my house before I call the police."

"What happened last night? Heaven almost died. What happened here?"

Martin's silence indicated the evening had not been uneventful.

"I need to see where he has been working. It might give me an idea of what he has planned. I don't know where he is right now, but he will have to come back here before he does anything else to prepare himself."

Martin still hesitated. Danube crossed the room to him before he could draw another breath. Gripping the lapels of his coat, Danube pulled Martin's face close to his own.

"Show me where he worked or we could all wind up dead."

He shoved Martin away but continued to stare at him. A lock of his red hair fell down across his forehead, making him appear wild, dangerous.

"It was in the basement," Martin said.

"Take me there."

Martin hesitated. Taking him there would be a final admission of what he had done. It would reveal the strange markings and the other paraphernalia down there.

"Now," Danube said.

Martin led him through the kitchen to the stairway that led to the room beneath the house. He flipped a switch on so that the lamps he'd had installed in the side walls flickered on. Their stark white light flooded through the room, creating eerie shadows from the platform and floor.

Danube walked past the raised stand to look at the markings on the floor. Some matched those in the Gnelfs storybook. Others were from *The Book of Raziel.* A few others he did not recognize. Those he found most frightening.

The ones he did not recognize immediately must have come from *The Red Book,* he decided. They resembled the markings he had read about, and the fragments he'd found as well. The potential they exuded was frightening.

He knelt beside one of the runes, running his hand slowly across the surface. It had been drawn with chalk, and the powdery substance stuck to his fingers. When he got back to his feet, he looked at the edge of the platform, where a brazier sat. He walked to it, looking down into the black ashes.

Though he picked through the residue, letting the gray crumbs slide through his fingers, they revealed no clue he could interpret. But the burning must have been conducted for a reason.

Near the edge of the platform, he noticed the brown, drying bloodstains. He turned back to Martin. "He cut himself?"

"Used his own finger to appease the fire demon you sent here."

"He's resourceful. That's bad."

"Why?"

"Because he's experimenting. He's trying to take magic and sorcery to new limits. What he might unleash in the effort could be devastating."

An ashen color spread across Martin's face, as if someone were stroking it on with an invisible paintbrush. "What do you mean?"

"Death for us. Destruction. Some of the great terrors of history were not created by nature alone. Earthquakes, famines, madness. They are the price frequently exacted."

Martin raised a hand to his brow, bowing his head slightly and blinking his eyes. "What have I caused?"

"So far, nothing that cannot be stopped," Danube said. "Help me. Has he spoken of anything to you?"

"He's just been promising that he could deliver what I wanted."

"He has given you no indication of what else he might have in mind?"

"No."

Danube ran a hand through his hair. He was frustrated, but had no outlet for his anger. He could not strike Martin, and he could do little to prepare for a confrontation with the magician.

"What is his name?" Danube asked.

"Simon. That's all he's ever told me."

"Not surprising. He considers himself the greatest of witches."

The greatest of witches sat silently in the passenger seat of Althea's car. He had stowed the dagger beneath his coat, but Althea could not bring herself to defy his will. In addition to his threats, she could feel some impelling force urging compliance. She suspected she must be touched by some spell in addition to his fear tactics.

She kept trying to force some way of resisting to develop in her imagination, but her thoughts would not serve her. Instead, images of the slobbering Gnelfs kept fighting their way to center stage, reenforcing her apprehension.

She didn't want to be violated by the little creatures, dammit. He'd found her weakness, her unwillingness to endure the tortures she'd known before.

Her hatred of what she had been put through deepened her desire to thwart his efforts to terrorize Heaven further, however. She thought about wrecking the car, but when the notion entered her brain, he turned to her with a wry smile, as if he knew everything she was thinking.

Some familiar was probably sitting on her shoulder, telling him every time her brain fired an electrical impulse. She wanted to drag her fingernails across the chalk-pale skin of the bastard's face, then spit in his eyes; but she knew she wouldn't move an inch before he knew what she was about to do.

The glimmer in his eyes as he continued to look at her confirmed the fact. Then, casually, he reached over and patted her leg.

"It will be all right," he said. "As long as you cooperate."

"What about Gab and Heaven?"

He was silent.

"What did they ever do to you, you bastard? Leave them alone."

"There are greater causes than the well-being of a few mortals," he said coolly. "I need them. It is as simple as that."

"And me? I'm a pawn too? Why should you be allowed to manipulate and hurt so many people?"

"The simple answer is because I can." He laughed, a cold, dry laugh. "The more complex answer is that I have suffered. I have always been construed as different. You're a psychologist. 'Alienation,' I believe, is the word you might apply."

"If you want my sympathy you must know you won't get it. If you are aware of the scars, you must realize you should have sought help instead of hurting other people."

"You know things are not as simple as that. I'm addicted to power. I'm not responsible for my actions."

She felt contempt for him, for his self-examination and for his willful acts that harmed others, but her professional orientation stirred her to ask, "What happened to you?"

"It started when I was very young. I was a small boy, thin. Some things carry over. I became bookish since my mother feared I would be harmed by playing with other children. I could read before I started school, and subsequently I had more knowledge than the average child."

He seemed to grow more pale as memory tightened its grip on him. "The class bully seemed to zero in on me from the beginning of first grade. But he was a goddamn clever bastard—the teacher's favorite." He smiled. "You know the type, Doctor. You'd have a word for that too. His name was Mal James. He had one of those flat-top haircuts. They weren't in then. He would do things, tell on me, pull various stunts to get me into trouble. The teacher always fell for them. I bumped into him once while a group of kids was playing. He went to the teacher and told her I had kicked him, and the fucking whore ranted and raved at me for five minutes. Five fucking minutes."

Althea gripped the steering wheel more tightly as the anger began to burn through him. She realized something was always simmering inside him, resentment, rage.

For a moment, just for a moment, she was almost touched even though she had seen the horrors he had caused.

"Another time, Mal grabbed me and choked me, held my throat until my face turned purple. It took me a while to catch my breath, but then I went to the teacher, expecting, since a kick on the playground had inspired such ire in her, the whore bitch would do something to him finally. I told her he had choked me, but she didn't look up from the papers she was grading. I repeated it, that he had choked me, and she ignored me.

"And Mal had other moments. The time he put a snake on me. The time he pulled my pants down. The bastard."

There were tears in Simon's eyes now, angry hurt tears, the tears of a little boy who didn't quite fit in, a little boy thrown into a situation he didn't quite understand because he had no reference point for the contempt of peers or the pettiness of some people in positions of authority.

She bit her lip. She couldn't let him make her feel sorry for him. He was too dangerous. Maybe under other circumstances she could have helped him, but for now she had to view him as an enemy. She had to think of Gabrielle and Heaven.

His fist slammed down on the dashboard, the vibration jarring the plastic. His pale cast was gone, replaced by a red, twisted mask.

Slowly a smile formed again, however, and he sat back in the seat, smugness settling over his features.

"It took me a while to find Mal after I had begun to learn to manipulate the forces that lurk around us," he said. "He was working in California, but he had a job that required him to travel. I began to watch him, studying his actions. He had numbers he could call when he stopped in cities. The calls would bring women to his door.

"One night he was visited by a particularly beautiful one, a woman with hair of flame and a sensuality he had never known. When he lay with her, he thought he had never known such pleasure."

Simon's eyes almost seemed to gleam now. He wasn't talking to Althea. He was reliving something he had watched, savoring the memory.

"She fulfilled his desires in every way. Performed the acts he dreamed about, and he cried out with pleasure. Then, when it was over, she lay over him, kissing him, letting her mouth move down across his chest and stomach."

He did turn to Althea now. A spray of perspiration dappled his brow, and one drop slid down from his temple, trailing along his cheek. "Can you imagine what happened?"

Althea was suddenly very cold, chilled from the inside. She could not imagine how fear had seized the man, but she knew it had been horrible. She tried to swallow and found her throat had closed.

"Well?" Simon asked.

She licked her lips, but was still unable to produce much moisture. "Emasculation, I suppose."

"Emasculation?" He whispered his confirmation: "Yes. She closed her lips over him, over his man-root if you choose, then she bit down.

"He screamed, oh so loudly," the magician said, his voice now gleeful. "Then he saw two things. He saw her yank her head back, his genitals dangling from her lips, and before his eyes, the image of my face was projected by magic. He looked at me and, with terror in his eyes, knew why it was happening to him. He wept. Wept the way I wept on days after school when I went home suffering from his humiliations.

"I had never wanted to harm anyone, had been content to leave other people alone, but he spearheaded the effort that made me what I am. It was fitting that he should serve as an experiment, for I was just beginning to test my skills in those days." He laughed now, deep and hard. "I was good, so good, and I laughed at him because I knew then, for certain, that I had the power. And his blood served as a sacrifice to the demons of the night, and they became my brothers then. My servants, because I had delivered for them. They descended, and while he was alive, they feasted on his sinful soul. He cried out to God, but he had no redemption that night."

Althea found it hard to steer the car. The horror of what had happened was almost paralyzing. She kept picturing the scene in her mind, hearing the screams.

For the first time it became apparent just how dangerous this madman could be. He had caused horrible deaths, but he was capable of much greater cruelty and brutality.

She thought she was going to be sick, but he placed a hand on her forearm, gripping it tightly. She felt pain as the muscle was squeezed. It was like a lightning bolt shooting up her arm. "You won't lose control," he said.

It was not a reassurance. It was just a warning that she would regret noncompliance.

She didn't want to submit to his control, didn't want to comply with any of his orders; but for now she would go along, waiting for an opportunity to resist.

Moving the brazier so that it would not topple off, Danube stooped beneath the platform. More fragments of brittle pages were there and also something silvery reflecting light.

He reached into the shadows and extracted it, a small bowl-like crafting of metal with symbols etched into its surface. He turned it over carefully, his fingertips tracing the markings he recognized as protective symbols. The discovery did nothing to ease the burning feelings that were gnawing away at him.

The holder of *The Red Book* would need a protective helm. Danube had heard it mentioned in legend, how the conjurer wore the metal guard to read the book.

"Did you ever see him wearing this?"

Martin looked down at the bowl. "Sometimes when he was studying his symbols. What is it?"

"A shield of sorts. it basically kept him from becoming a channel for the spirits before he was ready." He turned the cap around, displaying the markings for Martin. "These signs block things out and allow his thought powers to prevail."

Martin's mouth dropped open slightly.

"You did not realize the extent of all this," Danube said.

"No."

"Few people realize what they are opening the door to."

"I only wanted to scare her."

"She is scared," Danube said. "As am I."

Chapter 20

At Katrina's insistence, Gabrielle took a long shower. When she had finished she slipped on one of Katrina's nightgowns and lay down in the guest bedroom, where she managed to doze for a while.

Heaven was resting, and Gab knew she, too, needed rest. She would not be able to support her daughter if her own condition deteriorated. Her nerves were starting to remind her of old rope, unraveling in all directions, but her mind shut out her anxieties and allowed her to drift off.

She even managed not to dream. At least for a while. Until Tanner showed up. At first, in thoughts detached from the dream, she wondered if her brain was offering up a vision of solace, a collage of might-have-beens to distract her from pain and anguish over Heaven's dire situation.

She wondered if pastoral scenes were going to unfold, bringing bittersweet nonmemories of trips never taken and laughter never shared. Those were the kinds of things you woke up feeling both complacent and disturbed about, warmed by the pleasant feelings they provided, then tortured by the slap of reality, the reminder of how unreal the visions were.

When she saw the look on Tanner's face, she knew it was not that type of dream. He had not come to comfort her. He looked at her accusingly. Yes, this was to be a dream drenched in guilt, guilt trotted out from the Pandora's box of her subconscious.

She had come to know her psyche well in the months since the divorce. It had played many games with the skeletons buried in the boneyard of her brain. She had dreamed of what the separation would do to Heaven, had been tortured over whether she was acting for herself without concern for her daughter's needs.

Now she was about to suffer the blame for Tanner's death. Hadn't she caused it, after all? Wouldn't he be alive right now if she hadn't gone to hear him read? Perhaps she deserved whatever accusation his image offered.

Yet he did not point a finger and shout *J'accuse.*

He walked forward, a grim expression on the features she had thought so handsome. She waited for his mouth to open, for him to shout at her, curse her for costing him his life.

Instead, he spoke softly, even in the dream the words were almost lost as soon as they passed his lips. But Gabrielle heard them.

Continue to love.

Nothing ominous like *Beware the dark veil.* Just a simple suggestion of hope. She took comfort from the remark.

Gabrielle knew she was not in contact with Tanner, knew his presence was not with her, but she also realized that in the brief time she had known him he had imparted a message.

Her brain had captured that vibration and held on to it, interpreting it now to offer it back to her.

She woke up weeping.

Her head, against the pillow, felt heavy, and tears slid across her face in soft, tickling streaks. She let the moisture ooze from her eyes for a while before sitting up and wiping at it with the sleeve of her borrowed gown.

She found Katrina sitting beside Heaven's bed.

Katrina's husband had taken the kids out to keep the house quiet, and she was reading as Heaven dozed, apparently peacefully. She lifted her index finger to her lips as Gab eased the door farther open.

With exaggerated facial gestures and nods they communicated briefly, and Gab learned her daughter had been dozing for a while without any sign of disturbance. That was a relief. The child needed rest, for rest would help her recuperate or prepare for the next onslaught.

As Gab peered over at Heaven, she thought about the dream message. She would continue to love Heaven always, but was that what the dream had meant?

Perhaps it was a warning not to give in to hatred in spite of the anger simmering inside her. She had endured all of this for no reason other than some idiot's anger, yet she could not let hatred consume her. To give in to it was to be irrational, and she needed her wits, her courage.

Walking over, she knelt beside Katrina, squeezing her friend's forearm. Katrina smiled down and patted Gab's hand. Then, closing her eyes, she nodded in reassurance that things were going to be all right.

Gab prayed it was so.

At Simon's command, Althea turned her car into the driveway which wound around behind Martin's house. She recognized the neighborhood, and wondered what she might do to attract attention. A Lincoln was parked under the house's carport, and she thought about ramming it.

The sound would be minimal, as would the result, and might do no more than raise Simon's ire. She shoved the gearshift into PARK after braking to a stop.

"A wise decision," Simon said, letting her know he had detected her dilemma, either by clues from her movements or by reading her thoughts.

She kept looking straight ahead without responding. Laughing, Simon got out of the car and took his staff and a package from the back seat, where he had placed them earlier. Then he walked around to Althea's door and opened it with a gallant sweep of his arm.

She slid from behind the wheel without looking at him. Simon tucked the package under his arm and pressed the fingers of his free hand against the small of her back to usher her toward the house.

A chill seemed to emanate from his hand and course into her body. She wanted to shudder at his touch, but not wanting to allow him the satisfaction of feeling ripples of fear jar through her, she contained herself, preventing the discomfort from showing.

Without hesitating, Simon opened the house's rear door and showed her inside. Immediately the dwelling's smell touched Althea's nostrils, that distinctive, individual smell each home has for an outsider.

It was tinged with a hint of potpourri, evidently left behind by a conscientious maid, but somewhere within the scent she also detected something familiar. Danube's face flickered into her mind.

Smell triggers memory and mind pictures, she told herself. She must be picking up the scent of his clothing and his other scents. He had been through there, recently, because scents like that do not linger. She quickly turned her thoughts to something else so Simon's reading of her thoughts would not be valid.

Somewhere inside, however, she felt a shimmering flicker and realized that it was that dying pilot light of hope being rekindled.

They walked over to a narrow doorway which opened onto a stairway. She wondered how someone maintained a basement in Louisiana, with the water table and the lowlands, but she had no time to ask questions before he urged her downward.

Danube looked up when he heard the footsteps, and he saw Simon at about the same moment the magician set eyes on him. The magician smiled first.

"So you've found my playground," he said.

Danube didn't speak. He just stood where he was, near the platform, and nodded a brief greeting to Althea.

She nodded back even as Simon's fingers bit into her upper arm. He jerked it slightly and then guided her across the first landing and on down the steps.

"You almost burned this place up," Simon said when he reached the floor. "You bluffed the demon."

"It wasn't totally a bluff," Danube said.

"Who are you, man? What kind of spells do you use?"

"I am no sorcerer," Danube replied. "There is but one source of magic, and I have devoted my life to its opposition."

"So you aren't a white magician? That's what I thought at first. But you're a man with a mission. That's why you've been such a pain."

"Someone has to stop you. You are very dangerous, Simon."

"Very powerful," Simon corrected.

"The time has come to call a halt. You have toyed with enough lives, done enough damage."

"Don't try to get in my way. I'm not finished yet. A sorcerer must peer into the face of death to find true greatness. I will not quit. Not until I accomplish what I want."

"Everyone who has used *The Red Book* has died. Is that what you want? To kill yourself?"

A look of surprise crossed Simon's face. "So you know about the book."

"I have known others who tried to use it. It has left a path of pain and hardship everywhere it has been, throughout history."

"Because people didn't know which spells to try or how to deal with what they acquired. I'm always careful."

Danube held up the helm. "You think this is all you need?"

"I have taken other precautions. Now I have other matters to attend to." He released Althea's arm and took a step toward Danube to reclaim his helm.

Martin moved forward, stepping between Danube and Simon. He raised a hand to halt the dark magician's progress. "Your sorcery has gone far enough," he said. "It has served its purpose. I want you to stop."

A laugh burst from the magician's lips. "It may have served your purpose, but my work is not complete," he said.

"Dammit, people have suffered enough. I was crazy to let you go on with all this. It's over. The little girl has been through enough."

"I need her. The more impressionable a person is, the more open that one will be to sorcery."

"Forget it. Drop it."

Simon formed his next word carefully, his lips exaggerating the syllable: "No."

Martin clenched his hand into a fist which he used to pound the air. "Dammit, back off. It's finished. I brought you into this; now I'm telling you to stop. Collect your pay."

Again Simon laughed. "I don't want your money anymore, Martin. This is more important than money. It goes beyond your comprehension."

"Simon, I want it to stop. I'll give you money. You can get out of town. Play your games somewhere else."

"Sorry, Martin. I've come too far. Things are in motion. I've made promises. I've worked a lifetime to get to this point. It's ridiculous that you suggest I just stop." His eyes widened, and there was a faroff look in them, the look of madness.

He raised his hand in the air, snapping his fingers. "Snap, snap, and all my efforts are gone?"

He shook his head. "That won't do, Martin. Sorry."

He stepped forward, placing his slender right hand on the businessman's shoulder. For a moment, Martin glared at him, but then he jerked back, one hand rising to his chest as a shudder began to wrack him.

Danube began to move toward him, but before he could reach Martin, the businessman spun around. His face was a fiery red, his eyes were rolling back in his head, and his teeth were clenched so hard ripples went through his jaws.

Frozen in place, Danube watched as the flame shot up through Martin's scalp, as if a volcano were erupting inside his skull. The bright orange cylinder of fire extended above his head several inches, then seemed to peel apart and lick its way back down his body.

His screams were lost in the sudden roar of the flames that ate away at him, enveloping him, consuming him.

Danube raised an arm in front of his eyes to shut out the glare of the sudden, seering light. He felt the heat, and the smell of sizzling flesh burned his nostrils and throat.

Simon's laughter punctuated the event, echoing through the confined basement space. Slowly the flame dissipated, flickering around the charred ruin of Martin's body. In an instant all crumbled to ash, a small black pile on the concrete floor.

"You've heard of spontaneous human combustion?" Simon asked.

Danube looked down at the smoldering pile. Thin white wisps of smoke curled up from the black ashes, but the flame and the heat were gone.

"You are indeed powerful," Danube agreed. "What more do you want than this?"

"Do you have to wonder?"

"There is no absolute power. You cannot hope to achieve it."

"I can if the interference will stop. I can become a god."

"You deal with created beings, spirits that cannot bestow that power even though they promise it."

"You are rooted in theology. Weep with your gray-haired old God, but stand aside so I may reach the spirits who will grant me what I desire."

Danube was about to step toward him, but he was not fast enough. Simon raised a hand, and in an instant Danube could not move. Pain seized him, slicing through his muscles, sinking into his abdomen. He twisted about and crumpled to his knees, the helm slipping from his fingers to clatter to the hard stone floor. Involuntarily Danube wrapped his arms around himself, clutching at the ache which blasted through him. He felt as if his intestines were being ripped apart.

Then, while he doubled over toward the ground, he saw the tiny green feet approach. He felt something tangle in his hair, and his head was jerked up, forcing him to look into the snarling features of one of the Gnelfs.

"Greetingsss," the dwarflike creature hissed through a broad grin. Then he slammed his fist into Danube's face.

The red-haired man reeled as his head was jerked to one side. He heard Simon's footsteps approaching and, through his squinting eyes, saw the magician squat beside the helmet.

Realizing he was in Danube's line of vision, Simon smiled, then scooped up the metal hat and gave a curt nod. Danube felt small, coarse hands close on him while Simon's footsteps drew away.

Some lumber and a nail gun left over from the construction of the platform lay against one wall, and a couple of the little creatures scurried over and seized boards, dragging them back toward Danube.

He gritted his teeth against the pain even as he watched Simon fit the helmet over his head and take Althea's arm. Guiding her gently up the steps of the platform, the mage opened his book.

She looked down in horror at the scene before her, but she didn't resist Simon. She could not escape him.

As Simon softly began to mumble an incantation, the Gnelfs stuck two boards together and hammered a nail through the crosspiece, creating a makeshift crucifix.

Then, leaning the cross in an inverted position against

the platform, they nailed it into place. They had gained complete existence in the physical realm.

The pain in Danube's abdomen continued to eat away at him, making it impossible for him to resist. Simon had imbedded a spirit of pain in him, and it had snared his body with its fierce claws.

Pausing from his incantation, Simon looked over the rail of the platform. "Are you frightened, holy man?"

Danube gave no answer. He wanted to warn Althea to run, to urge her to fight at any cost, but he could not form words.

Then he felt the cord of the nail gun being wrapped around his ankles. His eyes were beginning to cloud over, but he did not lose consciousness as they hoisted him upward.

Above him, he could hear Simon's mutterings, and he knew the mage was casting a spell which would give him control of Althea. Unaware, she was waiting for the right moment to run. Danube wanted to warn her that she would not be able to resist at all if she did not try to do so now, but he could not speak.

The nail gun hung down beside him, dangling from the slack that remained in the line. Blood was rushing into his face, but he tried to grasp the tool. Before he could clench his fingers around its handle, however, his wrists were seized by the tiny Gnelfs. He could not summon enough strength to struggle against them as they pressed his hands into place.

Then, the greasy, snarling thing that seemed to be their leader picked up the gun and pressed it against Danube's left palm.

"Remind you of anything?" he asked, and, with a tittering laugh, he squeezed the trigger, driving sharp metal through Danube's palm with a single pop of the instrument.

A scream escaped the red-haired man's lips as the shaft forced through flesh, muscle, and tendons, partially protruding from his palm and from the board behind it.

A red wave seemed to seep down over his eyes, and while he was aware of some blood seeping out around the wound, he concentrated on shutting out the pain.

Tears formed in his eyes, but he squinched them shut. As he did he remembered the street on that day so long ago, the day the gentle man had walked that path, the rough-hewn board balanced painfully across his shoulders. He had been tortured with the whip, battered until his flesh was a pulpy mass. The crown had been forced down on his skull, ripping open his scalp so that trickles of blood trailed down through his hair, staining his face as he moved toward . . .

Golgotha.

They were stringing him up as a parody of it all, teasing him because they knew how long he had sought to reconcile his feelings about the innocent one's sacrifice.

He heard their laughter, knew it was meant for him. Then the warm spray of spit spattered onto his cheek.

He tried to shut it all out as they lifted his other hand, flattening it against the board.

He did not cry out as the next nail was driven into place. The pain inside him consumed almost all of his feeling, and the agony of failure echoed through his brain even as memories of jeers and shouts and the cursed jingle of silver ricocheted through his brain.

Althea wanted to scream as she realized what they were doing to Danube, but she forced the sound to stay inside her, biting her lips to prevent even a whimper from escaping.

While one hand encircled her forearm, Simon was not paying attention to her, not at the moment anyway. He had set a fresh fire in the brazier and was stirring the flame with a short poker while he continued to chant some bizarre words.

Then, without warning, his hand shot up to her face, twisting her chin so that she was looking into his eyes.

The flames flickered in his pupils, and before she could avert her gaze, she felt herself being mesmerized.

As Danube had suspected, she had intended to pull away from him and run when the opportunity arose. Now she knew it wasn't coming.

"Spirit of the flame, seal my bond to this woman," Simon whispered. "Engender her to do my will."

She heard the words, but they were far away, as if her consciousness had somehow been sealed deep inside her brain.

Her thoughts were tied into Simon's, and gradually her consciousness gave way to his. She could not resist, could not struggle against him any further.

He fell silent, and as the fire blazed, its brightness flickering across his features, he smiled grimly. "You will struggle no more?"

She shook her head.

"You will take me to the girl?"

She nodded.

"It will be easier. They'll let you in. I won't have to expend the energy of breaking in and handling their struggles against me."

Althea just stared at him blankly. He took her arm and guided her gently down the platform. The Gnelfs had disappeared again, leaving Danube's unconscious form dangling on the cross.

Chapter 21

After she had dressed in a pair of slacks and a lightweight sweater set off by a soft scarf, Gabrielle joined Katrina in the living room. The house seemed pleasant, quiet. It gave her a feeling of security. She wasn't sure why, but she felt isolated from the madness here, perhaps because it was a home. Katrina's marriage had worked out, and this house was like a fortress, not a rented, temporary place.

As she set across from Katrina, she used her hand to try to straighten her hair, which she knew was growing frizzy from lack of attention. Maybe there would be time soon to attempt to put herself back together. If Danube could succeed in shutting down the magical assaults, sanity would be restored.

The soft flutter of the rain against the windows was at last soothing instead of threatening. Gab sat in a chair by the window, pulling her legs up in front of her and hugging them with her arms.

When she had been a child, rain had been dreaded, depressing, a sign that she would be confined within the walls of the house. Today it was a bromide. She let her head fall against the back of the chair as she watched drops clinging to the glass.

A feeling akin to complacency settled over her. She felt relieved, even with her home burned down and all of her belongings gone. Heaven was resting, and they were both alive.

That might not be all that she could hope for the world to offer, but it was a starting point. They would put their lives back together. She would get things back on track at work.

She would have to let Althea work with Heaven. Healing the wounds and working away the scar tissue would take time, but the climb out of this would be possible.

The rustle in the hallway made her look up, and she saw Katrina entering the room. She had two mugs of coffee in hand.

"I thought you were keeping a vigil," Gab said.

"She's sleeping, and I figured I'd better check on my other patient."

Gab accepted her cup. "So I'm under your care also."

"Yep. I'm keeping an eye on you too."

"I've just been sitting here trying to think of what I want to do with my life. Maybe I should go somewhere else."

"Where would you go?"

"A tropical island maybe."

"You suppose a tropical island would be as romantic as you imagine, do you?"

"Probably not. I guess I've always fancied the notion of traveling to romantic places."

"I can't say as I blame you for thinking about escape just now."

"I guess you've spotted the psychological trigger for the fantasy. I'm worried about Heaven, so I want to go far away and start over."

"Not a bad idea."

"Maybe that's what I should have done, if not after Dave at least after Martin. Then I might have been out of range when he decided to play games with the universe. Maybe Heaven could have been spared all this."

"Don't start that, blaming yourself. It won't do any good. It won't change anything. It'll only make you start feeling bad, and that's what he wanted. No way could you have known some man was going to come up with this kind of craziness. Hell, I still hardly believe it. I keep thinkin' we're all gonna wake up."

"I wish I could."

Simon sat calmly in Althea's passenger seat as she guided the car through traffic. He no longer had to threaten or warn. She was headed, without hesitation, toward the house where Gabrielle and Heaven were sequestered.

Entry would be easy now. They would welcome Althea and her promise of guidance and healing, not knowing he was close behind.

He would offer guidance, but it would be his own form of guidance. He reached beneath the folds of his coat and extracted a small, thick crystal sliver. It was not powerful, but when he whispered a few soft words it began to glow somewhere within.

Like a burning diamond, it flared, reflecting a rainbow of light across his features as he peered into it. In the depths of the stone, bouncing around the edges he could see Gabrielle as she spoke about far away places.

He found the confirmation he was seeking. She was unsuspecting, believing that her situation was improving. She was trusting Danube to rid her world of magic, and she was not expecting any further disturbance. Danube had banished one demon, so foolishly she believed that the worst was over.

The sorcerer had to laugh. Let her believe that. It was almost ironic. She wanted to travel, and he was going to take her on a trip. She wanted exotic locales, well, there wasn't anyplace that could be much more exotic.

* * *

The image began to melt through the gray burlap that covered Danube's pain. It was an image of . . .

Suffering.

Pain.

Not his own. He'd felt the suffering from the beginning, from that day on the hillside.

It was hot, the dust swirling in the wind, and the smell that swept down from the tortured body was tainted with the sick smell of decay and infection. He saw the agony on that face, and suddenly the eyes looked down at him.

He still remembered. He had thought it was in accusation, a gaze of blame. Instead now, through his own pain, it was different. He saw something else in the eyes. It was a look not of anger or scorn. Though blurred by pain the eyes showed understanding.

The message that had been pumped into his subconscious was not condemnatory. He had not been charged with seeking redemption, because that had always been afforded him.

His charge was a special responsibility, and that had throbbed at the back of his being, tearing him apart when he had resisted, driving him when he had finally made his journey into the mountains.

Now he did not need redemption. Forgiveness, not for his father's sin, but for his own sins had always been there. As he looked up into those eyes now, he saw that it was not atonement that was expected from him.

Only that he fulfill his responsibility, the promise he had made to the sisters, the promise he had made to himself. He was to struggle against evils and injustice. To carry on.

Slowly, his consciousness began to re-form out of the grim haze that gripped him. He could not die here in this mockery of the other's suffering. He could not perish because he was still needed. The sorcerer could not be allowed to succeed. He was attempting to perform acts not meant to be achieved.

Satan was never to have allowed his book to fall into human hands; the magic and the conjurings Simon had managed were not to have been achieved. If the image was allowed to continue, he would unravel the fabric of existence prematurely. It was not yet time.

Danube was here because the culmination could not be allowed. He was in place to stand against the darkness.

If only he could manage to fulfill that plan.

He came to full consciousness now, the pain in his hands making him aware of reality. The nails had bitten deeply into the wood, the force of the mechanism driving them into place.

His hands were fastened against the boards with no leverage or leeway allowed them. It was difficult to move them in the slightest and that movement caused pain so acute it brought tears to his eyes and sent charges up his arms.

A long moan escaped his lips, and bile churned up his esophagus. How had this been endured? He had not been scourged, had not hauled his instrument of torture through jeering crowds; yet this was almost unbearable.

Surrender would be so easy. Surely now death could find him. Rest at last would come. If only he could relax. If only he could shut out the pain.

That was not allowed, however. He had to get free. Heaven and Gabrielle were vulnerable, and they were dependent on him. No one could face Simon alone. His magic was too powerful, and Danube had not yet discerned what he intended. He only knew it had to be horrible.

Clenching his teeth and shutting his eyes tightly, he forced himself to move his hands. As the agony quivered through his palms, he felt the slight movement.

It was the worst pain he had ever known—fire and ice blending—but he felt the nails wiggle in the wood. He was undermining their grip.

He cursed and cried out, but he did not stop. Pain

pounded into his brain, threatening to send him back into unconsciousness, but he willed his thoughts to work around it, to keep him alert.

Tears streaked out the corners of his eyes, and the pressure of the excess blood in his head, brought there by hanging upside down, made his arteries feel as if they were going to burst. He could sense that his temples were bulging.

And still he wiggled his hands. New trickles of blood escaped from his punctured palms and dripped down his thumbs, forming puddles on the concrete floor.

Sweat beaded on his forehead and soaked into his scalp, and he could feel it congealing on his chest beneath his clothing. His new raincoat held heat in, making his body temperature its own enemy.

He had to stop his efforts before the pain's intensity sent him into oblivion. He was breathing heavily, his lungs struggling for each difficult gasp. In his unusual position his muscles seemed confused and uncertain of how to function.

He tried to look at his torn hands, but he could not see them, not with his vision blurred by tears and his brain in confusion.

He told himself to concentrate on the wind trying to wear away a stone. Patience, he told himself. An eternity might pass, but he had to continue.

"Mommy thinks maybe it's about to be over," Gabrielle whispered.

"Our house burned up?" Heaven asked.

"It did, but we're all right. That's the main thing."

"Was it my fault?"

"No. Somebody did it to hurt Mommy. Mr. Danube has gone out to try to talk to the man so he'll leave us alone."

"Will that work?"

"Uh-hum. Mommy just didn't think about who might be angry at her before. Now that Mr. Danube knows who to talk to, everything will be fine. He'll make the Gnelfs go away."

"We'll have to get all new stuff."

Heaven seemed to brighten at that prospect. To her, new stuff was good. It wasn't yet real to her that you had to come up with the money for it."

"We'll go shopping soon," Gabrielle said.

"Can we buy new toys?"

"We'll get new toys," Gabrielle said, smiling. "Lots of new toys."

At least Heaven was now worrying about the things a five-year-old was supposed to worry about. A shaky, shimmering image of stability crept into Gabrielle's thoughts. She could see Heaven entering grade school, following through to junior high, high school.

She could see her dating boys and finding true love and marrying and having children, making her mother a grandmother. That was just fine. Aging didn't bother Gabrielle. She would grow old without protest, dammit, if her child would just be allowed to live peacefully again.

She stroked Heaven's hair and smiled softly. There was no need for words. The communion of silence was enough. Heaven knew how much she loved her. Love flowed through them both, manifesting itself in the invisible vibrations which passed between them.

Wrapping her arms around the child, she held her, pressing her cheek against Heaven's soft, golden hair and whispering gentle words that said nothing and everything.

The sound of a car pulling into the driveway broke the moment. Gab pulled back and placed her hands on Heaven's shoulders.

"Sounds like Althea's here."

"I'll go get her," Katrina said. "I'm sure she's ready to examine y'all's heads."

"Examine our heads?" Heaven asked, dimples forming as she smiled at the thought.

Katrina nodded, an exaggerated frown on her face, before slipping into the hallway.

The front room needs vacuuming, Katrina decided as she walked from the hallway on her way to the front door. She would undertake that while Althea was with Gabrielle and Heaven. The Kirby unit her husband had purchased from the door-to-door salesman was quiet enough to allow that, since they would be down the hall.

When the doorbell rang, she already had her hand on the knob. Turning it, she eased the door open. When she saw Althea on the doorstep, she said, "Hi." A moment passed before she realized the woman in front of her was not reaching for the hand she'd extended.

The stark, empty look in Althea's eyes issued a warning that something was wrong, but before Kat could react, the man was through the door. He had been standing just to Althea's side, out of sight, until his hand had shot forward, pushing the door farther open, and he'd slipped past the psychologist.

Katrina grabbed for his arm and missed it. He was moving toward her in an instant. His face seemed harsh, full of madness. She attempted to move backward, but stumbled, and he grabbed for her.

Her hands shot up, pushing his arms away. Her left hand managed to reach his face, and she dragged her fingernails down the pale flesh of his cheek, leaving red streaks in his skin.

She saw the blood before the realization that she had drawn it touched her, and then she moaned softly.

The man only grinned and pressed his hand against her forehead. Needles of sharp agony throbbed into her brain, and she felt her eyes closing against her will. She was being forced into unconsciousness.

She tried to protest, to struggle, but there was no time. Before she could offer any real opposition, she was headed for the floor.

The feeling that something was wrong hit Gabrielle while there was still silence in the front room. By the time she heard something heavy strike the floor, she had Heaven in her arms.

Rushing through the doorway, she headed along the hall. She would go out the back door and run until she found some place of refuge, perhaps a church or some other place where the evil might be kept at bay while they waited for Danube to find them and dispel the dark magic.

A few days ago, Mace would have been the first thing that came to Gabrielle's mind; she would have been thinking of warding off an attacker. When reality was ripped away, however, you altered your survival skills.

Heaven was already getting heavy when Gab reached the end of the hallway and raced past the den toward the playroom which opened onto the back yard. She realized her legs weren't as sturdy as they once had been. She hadn't played tennis in a while, and she was out of shape.

She had reached the door when she heard Althea's voice. She turned and found herself looking into the pale face of Simon. His arm was around Althea's neck, and he pointed a dagger toward Gabrielle.

"Don't move," he commanded.

She froze, clutching Heaven against her. "Who are you?"

He grinned, his eyebrows arching upward impishly. "Simon says be still," he warned.

"Damn you. Leave us alone. You've hurt us enough."

"I've made promises, Mrs. Davis. I don't have any choice but to keep them." He fumbled into his coat and found a metal skull cap, which he placed on his head.

"You can tell whoever you're working for to go to hell. I've had enough."

"The ones I work for are already in hell."

She turned, fumbling for the knob, but he shouted before she could get the door open. When she looked back at him the dagger was pressed against Althea's throat.

"She won't resist me," he said. "I could open her throat right now and she wouldn't struggle at all."

"Leave her alone!"

"I'd like to, but I must have your daughter." He held up his hand, showing a jagged nub where a finger should have been. "I made a down payment, but there are those expecting more."

She continued to look at him, but she reached back, trying to find the knob.

He realized what she was doing, and before the door opened, blood began to drip from Althea's eyes. The crimson tears streaked her cheeks, dripped down her jawline, and trickled from her chin.

Gab stopped moving, and in that same instant, the nightmare continued to blossom. With a quick movement of the dagger, Simon split the flesh at Althea's throat. It parted as if it were a mouth opening to belch out a red spray of spittle.

Gab closed her eyes, placing a hand across Heaven's face to protect the child from the sight as well.

Releasing Althea's body, Simon let it slump to the floor. "Don't be upset," he said. "There had to be a sacrifice to open the doorway."

"What do you mean?"

Suddenly he was flanked by the Gnelfs. The ugly little creatures huddled about him, wringing their green hands in anticipation. They were like mad brethren preparing for some dark communion.

"It is time my debts were paid," he said. "You see, it's almost as you desired earlier, Gabrielle."

She clutched Heaven to her chest, fear coursing through her like an electric shock.

Simon walked forward and placed his hands on Heaven, tugging her away, while the Gnelfs grabbed Gab and pulled her back before she could struggle.

"Mommy," Heaven shouted. "Don't let him take me."

She reached out to her mother, but the Gnelfs had pinned Gab against the door, their gnarled hands pressing her into place as guttural growls and hisses issued from their lips.

Standing over Althea's body, the blond man smiled. "Simon says, *we're* going to hell," he said. "Or at least to Hades."

Chapter 22

The nails were loosening in the boards. As pain assaulted his brain, Danube slid his hands along the shafts, clenching his teeth tightly as he strained his forearms, pressing forward.

The wounds in his hands had grown larger with the movement, and their throbbing was constant. The pressure against the nail heads stung the tattered openings in his palms, but he curled his fingers forward to avoid ripping his hands apart. The effort brought excruciating pain.

Tears were continuing to flow from his eyes, and his beard glistened with sweat. His internal organs felt as if they were trying to force their way up through his throat. Part of him had grown numb even though his palms were alive, and it would have been easy to lose consciousness again. The thought of it was tempting.

As he tugged at the nails, he fantasized about sinking into oblivion, letting his thoughts fold in on themselves. That would be simple enough. He would hang there, upside down, strangling without suffering, suffocating without protest.

To quit suffering, that would be wonderful. Wonderful to escape the pain, the heavy feeling in his head, and the fire in his body.

He might fall in his task, but he would be able to rest.

Let the other paths of the universe take their own course. He could die here.

Almost unexpectedly, the nail in his left hand pulled free from the crosspiece, jerking him back from the fading limbo of unreality. He opened his eyes wide.

His hand looked awful as he brought it in front of his face, even to his badly focused eyes. It was coated in blood, and a gleaming silver shaft shot through the jagged opening in his flesh.

With a grunt, he brought the back of his hand toward his lips. Closing his teeth around the nail head, gripping it tightly, he slid his hand off the spike. It seemed to move slowly along the cylindrical length of the shaft, the nail finally slipping from the wound, but when his hand came free the sensation was akin to ecstasy.

He spat the nail from his teeth, listening to it clatter to the concrete floor. It sounded like no more than a pin. How could it have caused such agony?

Without further speculation, he reached over and pulled out the nail in his right hand, tossing it to the floor as well. The delirium of relief, despite the jagged, raw pain still pounding at his nerve endings, came in a rush that brought forth as much of a sigh as his lungs could manage.

Blood was pounding in his head now, and his ears were roaring. As he tilted his head upward to see his feet tangled in the cord, a wave of dizziness swept through him. He lowered his head again after only a moment of studying the knots that encircled his ankles. They were not complex, but they were far away.

Simon did not vanish.

It was as if the air opened up, and he stepped into some invisible doorway. Gabrielle screamed as she heard Heaven's cries. They continued for a split second, and when they faded it seemed she was very far away.

Gabrielle's cry raked its way out of her throat,

resounding throughout the house. It lasted a long time, continuing even after it ceased being a conscious act. She sensed the dangerous edge of hysteria starting to slice into her.

Stumbling, she moved over to a chair, bending forward to allow her face to meet her hands. She breathed deeply, forcing herself to regain control. She had to think. Where could the sorcerer have gone? If her belief in his magic had ever wavered, now it was firm and complete. He could do everything Danube had warned about. Somehow he had opened a doorway and carried Heaven away with him.

Or perhaps it had been a trick, a stage maneuver. *They do it with mirrors.* Bouncing off the seat cushion and to her feet, she raced through the house, hoping that she might reach the front window and look out and see him running across the lawn.

At least then she could give chase. She might have to run until her lungs were bursting and her legs rubbery, but she would keep after him until neighbors began to pour out of their houses. When they saw he was trying to abduct a child they would help her.

She had no hesitancy, no fear of going after him. He had murdered Althea, but he had her child and he would have to kill her too if he was going to get away. If she didn't rip that dagger out of his hand and use it on him first.

Her hopes fragmented when she reached the front room and peered out onto an empty lawn. Althea's car was still parked in the driveway. He didn't need that kind of transportation for his escape. He had taken his own mode, escaping into some magical realm.

What would they do to Heaven there? The Gnelfs had terrorized her, but he had spoken of promises. Would they destroy her in some sacrificial rite?

With her heart still kettle-drumming in her chest, Gab spun around and saw Katrina awkwardly sitting up in the center of the floor, a hand resting against her forehead.

"Jesus, Lord, what did he hit me with?"

Gab knelt beside her, placing one arm around her shoulders. "I don't know. He killed Althea."

Katrina stared at her in horrified disbelief.

"Katrina, he took Heaven."

Blood drained from Katrina's face. "He left with her?"

"Disappeared into thin air. I don't know where he went. How do I follow him?" She was almost screaming again.

Katrina closed her eyes, struggling against the pain. "I don't understand."

"He vanished with my little girl. Into nowhere."

"Sorcery? It's impossible."

"It's real. What are we going to do?"

"It's gonna take that Danube character."

"I don't know where he went, or how to find him. He comes and goes. He could be anywhere. What if he never shows up again?"

Gradually, Katrina managed to get on her feet. Together they moved over to the couch and sat, side by side, supporting each other.

Gripping Katrina's hands, Gabrielle tried to find something inside herself that would give her control. She had to think. There had to be a way to locate Danube.

"Tell me what happened," Katrina said.

"He slit Althea's throat, and then he snatched Heaven away from me. The Gnelfs held me, and then he was just gone. He took a step and he and Heaven weren't there anymore."

"The Gnelfs went with him?"

"They were gone right after he was."

"Weird. Like all of this. Did Danube say anything about other dimensions? Like on 'Twilight Zone'?"

"I don't know."

Katrina closed her eyes again. "I'm gonna have to have something for my head. Can you get me a cold cloth?"

"Sure." Gab rushed into the bathroom, tearing open cabinets until she found a washcloth. Running cold water she soaked it, then took the Tylenol in the medicine cabinet and returned to the living room.

"Thanks," Katrina said. She placed the rag across her forehead. "Give me a second, then we'll try to figure out what to do."

Danube's stomach muscles felt as if they were going to rip out of his abdomen as he bent double, pulling himself upward by gripping his trousers and literally hauling his upper body up. It wasn't as high as Everest, but he had to struggle to reach the electrical cord binding his feet.

Twice he had it in his hands, and twice he lost it, the pain in his stomach proving too great, the blood making his hands slippery so that he flopped back down like a fisherman's catch.

Perspiration streamed from his brow now, dripping down through his hair, soaking it and splashing onto the floor to mingle with the blood.

His mouth was so dry now that his breath rasped in his throat as his lungs expanded, forcing themselves outward against the constriction of his muscles.

He had to get free. He had to go on. The temptation of giving up was still present, but he was not going to turn his back on his purpose. He would get free.

Straining upward once again, he began to clutch at his pants, dragging his way up until finally one wounded hand found the knots.

His weight held them fast, pulling the cord taut so that it was impossible to manipulate. He held tightly to them with his fingers. Now that he had it, he didn't want to let go. Gasps of desperation curled through his throat. He couldn't give up. He might not be able to make it up there again.

With a moan of defeat, he dropped down again, dangling, the waves of nausea rippling through his stomach and the throbbing returning to his face. He was going to have to try some other tactic.

For a moment, he let his gut rest, let the fluids inside him settle down and let his temperature settle slightly. His heartbeat did not slow, but he had no time to worry about that. He knew he had nothing to fear from cardiac arrest. The normal physical concerns had never been a bother.

Now he only had to worry about physically freeing himself. He had been in magic prisons and hemp bonds, in chains and dungeons, but none had held him. There had to be a way.

After another moment of resting, a new idea had struck him. Tensing his legs and then relaxing them, moving his body in a slow motion, he began to swing. If he could make himself a pendulum, perhaps he would sweep up to where he could grasp the platform, taking some of the tension from the cord, perhaps creating enough slack for him to get untangled.

Swatting the air with his arms, Danube began reaching out for the edge of the platform. He was not at a good angle to grab it, but he tried to close his fingers on the edge of the planks.

He almost gripped them once but lost his hold, the pain as well as the fact that his fingers were only at the board's edge contributing to the failure. Shortly he was again dangling in the position from which he had begun his efforts, the throbbing in his temples threatening to take away his consciousness. He began to think of the havoc Simon must be wreaking while he was held here.

It was a simple cord, not shielded by magic or curses, yet he could not find a way to escape it. He felt his eyes rolling up in his head, and the pressure of the blood in his cheeks continued to flush his features and numb his skin.

He knew his consciousness was waning. Weakened as he was, with the aches still alive in his palms, it was difficult to stay alert.

He fought, trying to avoid delirium, trying to keep himself aware. He couldn't sleep now, he couldn't lose consciousness. He did not fear dying in his sleep, but the blackness would waste time that could be spent struggling.

Still the blackness closed over him, seeping into his thoughts like the slow shadows of evening creeping across the world in the wake of a setting sun.

He bit his lip, opened his eyes wide, and stretched his face; but he knew his brain was closing down.

He had to find some way to keep it working. He began to recite poetry under his breath, latching on to his own words as he spoke memorized fragments of old verse.

His speech was garbled, slurred, but it gave him something to do, trying to remember words, trying to . . .

The click of the door opening jolted him. He tried to look to the stairs, but he could not turn as he wanted to.

He listened to the footfalls as they descended, then the clack of hard-soled shoes on the concrete. At least it didn't sound like Gnelfs approaching.

"Looks like you're in a spot of trouble." The cab driver seemed to have spat his words onto the floor.

"A little," Danube croaked.

"Reckon I ought to cut you down?"

"It would be appreciated," Danube managed.

"Watch your head," Joe Wilson warned.

A search of the back room, with careful steps around Althea's body, revealed no secret openings or escape methods of any traditional nature. Thin air was the only explanation.

"Where would he take her?" Katrina muttered. "I don't know enough about this magic crap to figure anything out."

"He said something about going to hell."

"All right. We're going to have to wait for Danube."

"What if he doesn't come? Or what if it's a long time? He'll just be getting farther and farther away with Heaven."

"Danube will have a way to find him. He must. He's

been through too much with you on this to back off. You know that."

Katrina found herself doubting that, but she couldn't let Gabrielle know it. Comforting her was important for the moment. She couldn't be allowed to get hysterical. They both had to remain as rational as possible. Freaking out wasn't going to help at all.

Katrina knew, if she hadn't seen Gabrielle's need for stability, she'd probably be going to pieces herself. Gab was holding up well considering Heaven was her daughter. Katrina couldn't picture what she might do if one of her babies had been snatched away by some lunatic.

"This guy must not be in any hurry to hurt Heaven," Katrina said. "He's had all the time in the world to do it with his Gnelfs and he hasn't. He's only toyed with her."

"True," Gab agreed. The thought seemed to soothe her a little, not much but enough to make her sit down and collect herself.

"Danube will be here," Katrina said. "If he was sent to do good like he said, whatever got him here before will get him here again. The old preachers would always say, trust in the Lord."

Gab took her hand, and they bowed their heads in unison, praying that this ordeal would end quickly, praying also for Heaven's safety.

They were still praying a few minutes later when a loud knock jarred the front door. Katrina answered it to find Danube standing before her, a disheveled and drawn-looking Danube who had strips of cloth tied around his hands. Was this the man they'd been hoping could come up with answers?

He rushed into the room when she told him Gabrielle was waiting for him, and his desperation seemed to match theirs when he was told what had happened.

"Into nothingness?" he asked.

"Totally," Gab said. "I saw it happen, and even with everything else that's gone on, I still can't believe it."

"We've looked everywhere," Katrina said. "We've tried to find where he might have slipped out, but there's nothing."

Danube sat down, resting his elbows on his knees and bending his head forward to rest it on his bandaged palms, his fingers entwining in red locks of hair.

"What did he say?"

"At the end?"

"Yes. What exactly did he say, about hell?"

"He said he was going to hell." She hesitated, thinking. "Then he corrected himself. Something about Hades. He said he wasn't going to hell but to Hades, or words to that effect."

"Then that's where he is. It makes sense of a sort."

"How so?"

"He's been dabbling with an amalgamation of spells drawn from a couple of ancient books. He's evidently devoted a lot of time to finding lost volumes, *The Book of Raziel* which was cast away by God, and *The Red Book* which was stolen from Satan. He's been crossing things up, summoning demons and building his own personal powers. With each spell he's learned more. He's been experimenting while assaulting Heaven."

"For what purpose?"

"To build his skills to this point. I do not know what he expects to gain, but I think I know where he is trying to go."

"Where, dammit?" Gabrielle demanded. "He's got my daughter. What do you think he's doing?"

"In the beyond, there is a place of hatred and suffering. It is a place separated from God, a place that has no loving kindness. It is a place born with the beginning of the world, a place where those angels in rebellion against God formed a kingdom. Hades is in those nether regions, beyond the outer darkness.

"Hell is beyond Hades, in the pits where the torture and the suffering of lost souls takes place. That is where Satan reigns. If he specified that he is going to Hades, then it is not Satan he plans to encounter. Suffering is not his purpose."

"I'm not following you. If he's not after the devil what does he want in hell?"

"He's going to a part of Hades, Tartarus. You understand, Satan and his angels rule in hell, and Satan has sway over forces on the Earth. But the old legends also tell of a more powerful demon-god who ruled in Hades and was an overseer. Satan and his lieutenants had one function, but the one called Hades was the ruler over them all. He was viewed one way in Greek myth, but the older legends know him as who he truly is. Simon is evidently going to the emperor of the nether regions, Samael, to see what powers he will bestow."

"And Heaven is his sacrifice. She's pure, innocent. That's the kind of sacrifice he would take. Right?"

Danube was silent, solemn for a moment before he nodded. "He mentioned he'd made promises."

"We have to go after them," Gabrielle said.

"That was the solution I was going to suggest. I will not ask you to come with me."

"I have to go," Gabrielle protested. "She's my daughter. I can't wait here while you chase them. Take me with you, Danube."

"It will be very dangerous."

"That doesn't matter. Don't argue."

He shook his head. "It would do little good. Show me where he stepped away. I think we can follow him from there."

He knelt beside Althea's body for a moment, then stepped around the room, his eyes fierce as he studied the area.

"The Gnelfs vanished when he did?"

"Just after that," Gabrielle answered.

Danube looked at the floor. "There are no markings, no symbols of a gate. He went through a rift that was opened for the passage of Althea's soul."

"She went to hell?"

"No. I don't think so. But the curtain to the beyond, the veil, was opened to let her through. The opening may be here still."

He reached out for Gab's hand. "We're going to have to step through and go from there. The opening won't take us to Hades. You cannot get there from here. But you can get there from there."

"Are you trying to be funny?"

"Simply trying to use phrases you can understand."

She gave him her hand, biting her lips as they moved past Althea's body. Her willingness to undertake this surprised her. It was so alien, so strange, so frightening. It went against her nature, but she had to do it—for Heaven.

They had survived the last few days together, and they would get through this some way. Heaven would want her to come; she would need to see her mother and not just a stranger.

Drawing a deep breath, Gab stepped when Danube stepped, following his commands. Just as she had seen the sorcerer disappear, she now saw the room vanish.

One moment they were peering at the wall. The next they were adrift in a void of blackness and stars. Were they flying? She thought so for a moment, but then realized that they were passing through some intangible veil. They were not walking exactly, because they were in a world where things were different, where substance had a different feel.

She listened for Rod Serling's voice.

Slowly, the blackness began to fade. This was no light-at-the-end-of-the-tunnel experience, however. It merely melted into a dark gray world. Looking up did not reveal a sky, only a great vastness of gray that seemed to stretch on forever.

She looked down and realized she was standing at last. At least it felt like she was standing, the ground beneath her feet a slick mass of oily gray clay. They were on the shore of what seemed to be a body of water. As her sight adjusted, she saw it stretched out to infinity, and she noticed small waves lapping against the clay.

"Where are we?" she asked.

She had never seen anything quite like the water, which was somehow like smoke, somehow like fog, yet also like liquid.

She looked up at Danube, who was squinting, staring out through the mist that rose above the water.

"Danube, where are we?" she repeated. "What are you looking for? Is this the way he brought Heaven?"

"It has to be. It has to be what he planned."

"Then where are they?"

"They've already traversed the gulf."

"This is the gulf?"

"You remember the parable of Lazarus and the rich man, do you not? The gulf that separated hell from heaven and Earth. Or you might recall your mythology. Gabrielle, you are on the banks of the River Styx."

"This is impossible."

He nodded toward the outline that was slowly fading through the fog. "Unreality has no meaning here, and what you perceive is not as tangible as you might hope. But we are here, and Heaven is here, and whatever is manifest here, or however our minds perceive it, that is the reality."

"I don't understand. This can't be."

"There are rules in the physical world. Our minds are designed to read the tangible things there and to react to them. This is a different realm; our minds cannot comprehend the things we see here. Thus, they are processed for us in terms that we can understand. This water is not water, but our minds cannot perceive it in its true spiritual form, so we perceive it as liquid, the closest thing we can understand to its actual makeup. It's much like a computer being given information in a different computer language. It will interpret the data as well as possible. The same will be true of beings we see. They may not have human form here, but our mind has no frame of reference so we see them as we must, as men or monsters. Remember also, this is not our realm. We are not dead, but we are not immune here either. We can be touched and killed in the same way we would on Earth."

The boat eased through the swirling mists, cruising through the murky liquid, a long, black gondola. The man who stood at the stern, guiding the craft, was clad in tattered robes, with rags wrapped around his face and head like bandages. His hands, too, were covered with tattered cloth, and his eyes were not eyes but glowing red orbs that seemed to float within empty cavernous sockets.

"Meet Charon," Danube said grimly.

The glowing eyes of the figure stared at her blankly, burning. She saw no opening for a mouth, but she had not expected him to speak.

"Danube, what can we do? The dead gave him coins in mythology."

"I think he will let us pass," Danube said. He reached into the pocket of his coat and drew out two pieces of silver. The coins were worn almost smooth, their original markings long unreadable.

A quivering, withered hand, swathed in gray tatters rose slowly and, twitching badly, reached out for the money. Danube dropped the silver into the palm, and quickly the being secreted it. Then the hand began to reach toward Gabrielle. She started to pull away, but she realized Charon was reaching out to help her aboard.

The craft rocked slightly as she eased her weight onto a seat. She gripped the sides as Danube also climbed aboard. She wanted to wake up, still not believing what was happening. This was myth, fairy tale, and yet she had been drawn into it; Heaven had been drawn into it.

Evil had reached out and dragged them into its realm. She had, in her way, always believed in hell, but it had never, in her mind, seemed quite so literal.

In a few moments the movement began, and Heaven saw the craft's bow begin to slice through the water. As she watched ripples break around the hull, she looked down into the gray liquid and gasped.

Decaying bodies floated there, ruined and fragmented. Severed limbs drifted past, and whole corpses. She recoiled, swallowing the coppery taste at the back of her throat.

"How broad is the gulf?"

"I have never had occasion to cross it before," Danube answered.

"So you don't know where we're going either?"

"Not exactly. I have heard stories and read volumes which had accounts of the beyond."

"Have others been here?"

"Some pages say that the Nazarene walked there in those three days after"—his voice broke, and he choked up for a moment—"after his death," he managed finally. "He moved through the corridors and set free those who were righteous."

"The Harrowing of Hell?"

"Precisely."

Something swept down just over their heads. Gabrielle felt her muscles tense, and she ducked down, rocking the boat with her movements as she raised her hands to shelter her head.

Danube was looking off in the distance toward the form of the reptilelike creature. Its leathery wings flapped in the mist, carrying it higher and higher.

Gab spun around to see another, its face hideous, its red and yellow eyes peering down at her as it fluttered onward. Sharp, horned ridges protruded over its brow, and a long tail that tapered to a sharp point trailed behind it.

Clutched in its talons was a ragged body which had been tortured and was now a mass of open wounds and lesions. It hung limply beneath the creature, but slight movements indicated it was yet alive.

"Dante and the artists weren't far wrong, were they?" she asked, trying to control her fear.

"I am sure the things we have heard only scratch the surface."

Danube was looking ahead now, trying to see through the mist. It was impossible to make out anything more than a few inches away, however, even though the boatman had ignited a glowing orange lantern and seemed to know where he was going.

The next assault on Gabrielle's senses came from the side of the boat, screams and the gurgling of throats filled with water. As they passed on through the mist, she looked off to where a cluster of people splashed about, clinging to each other and trying to keep their heads above the murk.

They seemed like passengers left by a sinking ship. She was reminded of the *Titanic* as the water sloshed around them or their attempts to swim failed.

Suddenly, a huge and greasy-looking tentacle shot up from the water's depths, wrapping around one of the figures and dragging it down.

"They were trying to escape," Danube said.

"The bodies in the water? Did all of them try to escape?"

"This is the land of the dead. The corpses were discarded when the souls were cast into the abyss where no one dies. They live in torment."

Finally, the craft pushed out of the mist, and they looked up at the rocky shore that became visible. Huge black buildings jutted up from the stone, and beyond them stood tall ebon towers, a palace of the damned.

As the boat glided to shore, Gabrielle began to make out the lumbering shapes of the dead. They shambled along the narrow streets, aimless and tortured by the nothingness.

"The City of the Dead," Danube repeated. The boatman eased the craft onto the rocky bank, and Danube took Gabrielle's hand to guide her onto the shore.

"Where do we go to look?" Gabrielle asked.

"He'll be headed toward the palace," Danube said.

They made their way across the jagged ground between the shore and the edge of town. In a few moments they were standing on one of the powdery streets. The dead figures moved around them as if they were not there, or if they bumped into them, the dead moved back a few steps and went around.

Gabrielle's flesh tingled, crawled as the saying goes. The faces were rotted masses of tattered flesh and open sores which oozed gray-black slime.

Eyes were missing from sockets, teeth from mouths; and chests were ripped open, revealing blackened organs that threatened to spill from the containment of skeletal frames.

Gab pulled back and grabbed Danube's arm when a figure passed her, the snaking ropes of its intestines dangling down its side and dragging along the ground.

"This is damnation," Danube said.

"Hell is worse?"

"This is torment. In hell there is torture. All of it is unrelenting."

They eased on through the narrow pathways, stepping over figures too badly damaged to do more than drag themselves along in the dirt.

"Where are they trying to go?" Gabrielle asked.

"Somewhere it doesn't hurt."

She was reminded of images she had seen, paintings and depictions of Europe during the plague. This was a thousand times worse, because waste and deterioration was all she could see.

The path that led toward the castle wound upward through a twisting rise of rock and debris. On an outcropping crouched the grimy Gnelf Master, a dark robe draped around his form, a sickle clutched in one hand. He was almost a parody, except that he was too hideous.

His leering face turned toward them as they approached, and his yellowed eyes raked over Gabrielle.

"You've come for your little one?"

Gab clenched her teeth. "What have you done with her?"

"The master took her up toward the castle."

"You mean Simon?" Danube asked.

The laugh was sickening. "The mage who first summoned us."

"What's he trying to do with my daughter?"

"He wants to offer her to our father."

She looked to Danube, who nodded in confirmation. It was as he had predicted.

"You filthy bastards have a father?" she asked Gnelf Master.

"We call him father. He has sat on his black throne for eternity."

"What does he want with my daughter?"

The Gnelf nodded toward the dead figures that picked their way aimlessly across the stones. "He is the ruler over all of them, but they are not fresh and pure."

"What does Simon expect to gain?"

"Knowledge," the Gnelf said. "Strength. More powerful magic. We slept here until he summoned us. Not many have learned to call on us in recent centuries."

"You welcomed a chance to get out of this place and tear things up."

He flexed the muscles of his arm. "I was given this form, your brain helped shape it for me. I can use this for a long, long time. And if you lived here, wouldn't you want to flee from time to time?"

"Take us to the girl," Danube said.

"Find her yourself. I have other tasks to perform."

Danube stepped toward him. "You will take us."

A snarl rasped from the creature's throat. "You seek to command me?"

"I will rebuke you to the depths of hell where all of the unrighteous belong."

Sullenly, the Gnelf eyed him for a moment before finally giving a slow nod. Hopping down from its stone perch, it began to move up the path, steadying itself with the shaft of the sickle.

Gabrielle and Danube supported each other as they climbed. The cracks and openings in the ground made each footstep a challenge, but they moved quickly up the ridge and finally to the broad canyon which encircled the palace.

The stone bridge which led across it was narrow, and looking down into the abyss, Gabrielle saw the glowing slime that coursed through the gorge far below. It was a bright magenta ooze, and slithering through it were reptiles, thousands upon thousands, small and giant.

She gripped Danube's arm tighter as they made their way across the bridge. Somehow she knew what a fall would mean. Sinking into the sickening slime would be bad enough, but to be trapped there with the snakes would be eternal terror.

The cries of the people mired below rose to her ears, and she tried to shut out their screams as she passed.

Finally the Gnelf opened a huge door and led them into a narrow black foyer. Torches blazed there, emitting a light that was almost green. Shadows flickered off the obsidian walls, and the smell of decay drifted to Gabrielle's nostrils.

The screams that came from somewhere far back in the palace were high pitched and filled with agony. The sounds of torture, of the searing of flesh and the breaking of bones mingled with the cries of agony.

"Welcome," said the Gnelf. "I am sure we will find your daughter here. Somewhere."

Chapter 23

The halls were narrow and twisting, jagging back and forth around corners stained with blood. Bones lined the corridors, and the hideous beings that crawled in and out of the crevices had glowing eyes and slimy bodies that gleamed in the dim light.

Heaven walked past them, wincing at the sight of them as Simon tugged her along. He held her hand the way a parent might lead a child, but he was far less gentle than her mother. She knew he held her hand not to insure her safety but to keep her from fleeing.

He showed no sympathy for her inability to keep up and paid little attention when she cried out upon seeing something frightening. Controlling her tears, she scurried along at his side, trying to keep up with his long strides.

The Gnelfs led the way down the long corridor, their small forms clad in dark brown robes much like the one Friar Tuck wore in her Robin Hood book. Their cackles echoed through the hallway, and they turned back occasionally to leer at her.

Simon ignored them, his eyes focused straight ahead. He was excited. Heaven could sense that. Like he was looking forward to opening a Christmas present.

She wondered why he was taking her along. She didn't feel fear exactly, but the thought that he might harm her did cross her mind. He had hurt others. She couldn't stop thinking about what he'd done to Althea, and she knew he was responsible for the Gnelfs bothering her all this time.

The Gnelfs were nasty, but they didn't seem as threatening anymore. They were concentrating on what was ahead also. She bit her lip, wondering if what awaited was worse than the Gnelfs.

She hoped Mommy would follow her somehow. If there was a way, she knew Mommy would find it. Mommy wouldn't let her be harmed without putting up a real struggle.

They rounded another corner and walked up a slick black slope which stretched up to a pair of tall black doors. The Gnelfs quickly swarmed around the doors, their hands scrambling for the latch.

Then, together, they pulled the doors back, holding them open for Simon. A broad smile crossed his face, and he walked forward with Heaven. They moved through the doors, into a broad, high-ceilinged room.

Heaven looked through the darkened room, the only illumination coming from purple stones that were set in the walls. Simon continued to smile, and dropped to one knee, his head bowed.

"I have come to you, Master," he whispered.

She closed her eyes. She did not want to look at what she saw.

Danube held Gabrielle's arm with his bandaged hand as they rushed through the narrow corridors, kicking aside the oozing things that moved beneath their feet. Gab's heartbeat quickened. She was not feeling exhaustion now, but confusion and the unreality of it all made her almost dizzy.

She kept thinking they were going to round one of the corners and find Heaven's body torn to shreds or in the jaws of one of those nightmare beings. Hell had always seemed a concept, a myth. Not that she hadn't believed it in a way, but she'd never expected to encounter it in this literal sense. This wasn't hell, she realized, but it was bad enough.

And whatever it was, she didn't want her daughter here. It was no place for a child. She wanted to claw to bits the man who'd brought her here. Who was this bastard that he thought he could use her daughter to get what he wanted? Whatever they found when they caught up with him, she would fight to save Heaven. Some way or other she would free her daughter.

There had to be a way to save Heaven. Nothing they had ever done could make them deserve this.

Gab had plans for Heaven, for her education, her life, and they—*dammit*—would be fulfilled. No devils or magicians would destroy that.

She was still thinking that as they moved through the final narrow passage behind the Gnelf and watched him climb up a slope toward some open doors.

They were about to pass inside, into what Gabrielle realized was a huge throne room illuminated with glowing stones, but their movements were quickly hindered when the Gnelf in front of them was joined by a dozen others. The Gnelfs swarmed forward, and before Gab could struggle, their hands closed on her, tugging her away from Danube and dragging her forward.

As she was hurried toward the center of the room, she could see Heaven standing beside the magician who crouched before the throne.

The child's face was turned away from the figure on the throne, and though her eyes were squinched shut, she had no visible marks of injury.

Gabrielle started to rush forward to her daughter, but the Gnelfs held her, their tiny hands closing on her forearms, gripping them so tightly that she could not move. She looked back toward Danube, but he, too, was in the grip of the small green monsters.

She jerked her head around toward Heaven, looking

past her at the figure on the throne. She had not yet focused on him, but now she braced herself to view something hideous.

He was.

Even in the eerie glow, she could see that his flesh was like yellowish leather and was reptilian in texture. Ridges ran in parallels across his skull, and his face was cracked and lined.

Dark robes covered this being's frame, but the hands which rested on the arms of the obsidian throne were like claws, their thick yellow nails protruding several inches.

These aspects of its appearance, though strange and alien to her, were not what made the thing so frightening, however. It was its eyes, or the mysterious absences of them in the sockets. These were not empty like the cavernous eyes of a skull. They were like voids which swallowed light and substance, and looking into them was chilling. It was like peering into eternity, and somehow Gabrielle knew she would never come any closer to eternity than this point.

As the creature's head turned toward her, she tried to look away, afraid of meeting its gaze. Then she realized it could not see her. It seemed to sense her presence, however, and its forehead tilted forward almost imperceptibly in a greeting.

The magician got to his feet now, one of his gaunt hands extended in her direction. "You see, Master?" he called to the figure on the throne. "I've delivered them to you. All of them. The mother and daughter, their love intact."

He turned toward Danube. "And him. The one who has walked the earth for so long, the wanderer, the vagabond. He has tortured your children. He has hampered the efforts of many adepts, and he is the son of him who brought sorrow to your land, the man who delivered the One to his enemies and changed the course of destiny for all of us."

"I know who he is as well as I sense the offerings you

have brought," the figure said, the voice deep and unearthly. "Why have you disturbed me, magician?"

"To bring you these gifts."

Slowly the being's hand rose, gesturing toward a shadow-covered wall. With that movement, the stones seemed to glow brighter, chasing back the darkness.

On the walls, figures were chained into place, pale, emaciated beings barely clinging to existence. When they realized they were in the light, they began to wail and beg for release. A couple of them even began to dance as much as their chains would allow, a futile effort to capture pleasure or at least escape the retribution of the creature on the throne.

"I already have gifts," the being said.

"But oh, great Samael, none has delivered you gifts such as these. The child is a gift so pure, and she is not a being plumbed from the depths. She and her mother alike are yet alive."

"I sense the aura of their living," Samael said. "I sensed it as they entered the negative. It sent ripples."

"They could serve you," the magician said. "I have worked my entire life to find the doorway to you, to draw back the veils in Ain, Ain Soph, and Ain Soph Aur."

"So you opened them with sacrifice and prayers?"

"I found the symbols that were the keys, and those symbols were planted in the mind of this child. They were in the storybooks, and they sank into her mind so that she became a bridge for me to reach you. I had sought for so long. I had learned to open the doors, but only she made it possible for me to pass the veils. I worked my magic on her, but her own purity and her absorption of the forbidden markings served so well."

"You summoned up my little ones and gave them form in your world?"

The Gnelfs began to bounce about at the mention of their existence.

"I needed them." Simon pulled the helm from the folds of his cloak and held it high. "I bought this to control concentration, to protect my thoughts as I summoned them."

"I let them come," Samael said. "I always let them go when they are called."

"They served me well," Simon whispered. Desperation was quivering through his voice, along with the excitement that tempered every word. He was realizing a dream and savoring it.

"They find joy in the life a summoning avails them," Samael said.

The Gnelfs laughed and jeered to show their appreciation of his remark.

"I have no such release," the demon king continued. "I live here, sitting in this nothingness. It is a pleasure when they bring someone to amuse me."

"I want to please you," the magician said.

The leathery hand at Samael's side lifted, and he gestured toward the wall. "Those sought to please me as well."

"They failed you?" Simon asked.

"All fail me."

"But I brought these people to you."

"For what? Sacrifice? I live in the city of the dead. Do you think more dead men will please me?"

Simon got to his feet, his growing concern becoming evident. "What can I do?"

"Let me out of here. Help me stop sitting here to see the tortures and hear the screams. That is my lot, because I was devoid of love for any living thing. Satan rebelled, but I was cast down because I cared for no one and showed no kindness."

Simon's voice wavered. "You must be very powerful if you control all of the demons."

"I watch over them, listen to their stories of their dances in your world and their games in the nether regions. My existence is filled only with nothingness."

Simon began to tremble. He was uncertain as to how to react to the revelation that this monster could not offer him what he had worked all his life to find.

"You thought you would please me and reign here beside me? Be the king of nothingness if you like. It will help fill up eternity."

"No," Simon shouted. "You are the king here. You should be able to grant all desires."

"This realm is different from yours, magician. You cannot expect to find things here as they are in some other existence. This is the absence of a place. Here light does not fall, the Creator does not walk. It is the brink of damnation, and its rewards are the great nothing."

Simon's head jerked from side to side as he tried to express his denial. Tears filled his eyes, and he clenched his fists at his sides.

"You can't say this to me. I've served the darkness. I've worked so hard to find you."

"You have found me. Now please me."

Simon's voice brightened. "How can I do that?"

Samael stood, his form shaking as he stepped down from the throne. His hand reached out toward Simon, and the magician reached up to grasp it. Before he could accept the demon's touch, however, the hand shot past his offered palm.

Gabrielle screamed and rushed to Heaven, grabbing her and covering her eyes. Heaven buried her face in her mother's shoulder as they heard Simon's screams.

The terror was drowned out by Samael's laughter as he plucked the eyes from Simon's sockets. They pulled free in a quick sound of suction, and as Gabrielle peered over Heaven's shoulder, she watched the demon fill his own empty sockets. Blood dripped down his cheeks like crimson tears as the pupils adjusted. The look of them set in his face was unnatural, a parody somehow, and a cloudy glaze covered the orbs.

He stood near his throne, turning his head slowly from one side of the room to the other, taking everything in.

"An eternity I wait, just to see what surrounds me in this room which is my prison," the demon said. "My greatest pleasure is to look at the corners and the shadows." He bowed his head. "What a thrill you have brought me."

He looked down at Simon who had fallen into a heap on the stone floor. Blood sprayed through his gaping eye sockets, and he fumbled about.

A moment later, however, his hands steadied on the stone, and he tilted his head backward. The cry that came from his lips was in a language Gab had never heard.

In the next heartbeat, electricity shot away from the glowing stones, and the bolts slammed into Samael's form, sparks dancing around his body. He was consumed for a moment in the interlocking fingers of energy, but as they subsided he was unharmed.

"You try now to oppose me. Using the power that you generated through calling on me? You have almost entertained me."

He reached down and took Simon's hair, then, dragging him across the room, flung him into the midst of the souls against the wall.

As Simon struck the wall he gasped loudly, and before he could orient himself with touch, Samael wrapped him in chains.

"This will be your home. Yes, reign with me. Rule this room with your amusements. You've earned your place here, magician."

Samael spun around and moved back to the center of the room where Gabrielle and Heaven crouched together. Danube moved toward them now, but the demon held up his hand, stopping the holy man's movement.

Then, reaching down, he cupped Gabrielle's chin. "You are very beautiful," he said. His hideous hand reached over and stroked her hair.

She jerked Heaven away before he could touch her child's hair as well. That made Samael laugh.

"You seek to deny me? You will not deny me anything, woman. You and your child were my gifts."

Gabrielle looked around at Danube, her eyes pleading

for help. He hesitated, watching the demon.

"You would try to help her? You are a gift as well," said Samael. "You followed through the veil. What did *you* expect to gain?"

"I came only to help the woman and the child."

"You cannot help them. This is my palace. You have no magic and no power here."

Danube moved forward despite the admonishment. "Take me and let them go free."

"I have all three of you. You came here willingly."

"The child did not come willingly. We followed only because we had to."

"Because of love? I am afraid you will find no sympathy in me. I have no feelings."

"Let us leave here," Gabrielle said. "We didn't come here by choice. We never wanted any part of you. We were dragged into this by sickness and hatred. And those things," she said pointing at the Gnelfs.

The demon's fingers closed on her hair and yanked her to her feet. Looking into her eyes with the bloodshot orbs he had stolen, he glared down into her soul.

"You could be my bride," he said. "And she could be my child. You could be my family. You could tell me stories, so that I would not have to wait for those who come before me to confess their sins and face my pronouncement of judgment to the abyss. I hear their wicked deeds and that is all I have, but you could talk to me of many things."

"I don't have anything to say to you," Gabrielle stated firmly. "You want nothingness? That's what you'll receive from me. And Heaven too."

The demon's head tilted back slightly, and his expression registered his assessment of her defiance. He was surprised but not amused.

He let go of her hair as if it had grown hot in his grasp, or as if it were dirty and he no longer wanted to touch it.

"Leave here then, if you think you can escape. But your daughter remains. She pleases me. I will watch her grow. I will nurture her, and it will be as if she were my own."

Gabrielle met his gaze now. "She's been through enough. Everybody wants to attack the child, but it's time for that to stop. It's time for her to be allowed to grow without interference, without everyone trying to use her or control her."

"You would attempt to take her back to some pristine chapel? She will be better off here than shaped by what would be offered in your world."

"She'll grow up with whatever protection I can provide, without the influences destroying her."

"A noble attempt. Yet is it enough?"

"It's all I can do, and it's better than you can offer."

"Perhaps."

"Then let us walk out of here."

"That would be entirely too easy."

She realized he was playing with her. Her presence was a diversion for him, and he would keep her for as long as she amused him.

She turned back to Danube, searching his eyes, looking for some indication of what should be done. She could find no answer in them, and she realized he had done what he could. He had brought her here. But the final battle for her daughter and for their freedom had to be hers.

But what was there to do? They had stumbled and struggled through the attacks by the spirits Simon had summoned. How could she now defeat the demons' leader?

Physical confrontation could not bring victory. This was his domain, and to oppose him was to wind up in chains as Simon had.

Samael had tired of Simon quickly. Simon had groveled. Gab realized it was because her defiance amused him that Samael had not quickly relegated her and Heaven to the wall.

She had opposed Samael, had stood up to him instead

of groveling. What must she now do? Further defy him, show him the ultimate in defiance.

A challenge.

She looked over to the wall where Simon's battered form dangled in chains. His head seemed about to fall from his neck, and his sockets still dripped blood and other fluids.

"You brag, Samael, that you feel nothing," she said.

He nodded, and she noticed the pupils of his borrowed eyes were beginning to cloud even more. A film was creeping across their surface. They would meet his needs only for a short time.

"You have no touch of loving-kindness," she stated calmly.

"None."

"I have none for Simon," she said. "He tortured my daughter, and he brought us here. But I challenge you. If I can show him compassion, if I can go over to him and treat his wounds and support him, then I challenge you to find the same capacity within you."

"What could I, Samael the Wicked, offer in confirmation?" he asked, his hand rising to his chin. Gently, one finger touched his lips in consideration of her proposal. She had intrigued him.

"Samael the Wicked could show his compassion by thinking not of himself but of my daughter. Let us leave this place. Let us walk from the doors and cross the gulf without harm."

"This is but a trick to gain your freedom."

"No. You can sense my anger and my hatred of the magician."

"So if you, a lowly human, can overcome them, I should be able to as well? Is that a challenge or a request for a magnanimous gesture on my part?"

"Take it as you will. It should at least be a diversion for you. That's what you're looking for, isn't it? That's why you have your Gnelfs, or whatever they are. Their deeds give you a vicarious thrill. When people come here for your pronouncements, you listen to their sins for the same reason."

He laughed. "You attempt to apply human rules of psychology to me. I am because I am. I seek not thrills as much as knowledge."

"Then expand your existence."

He continued to stroke his chin. "Let us see what happens," he said. He gestured toward the wall. "Go to him."

Slipping her hands from around Heaven, Gabrielle took a couple of steps toward the wall. Even upon seeing Simon's pitiful state, a part of her wanted to hurt the magician further for the harm he had caused.

But she took control of her anger before moving on, combating the revulsion she felt for the ravaged figures chained around him.

They grunted at her as she neared them, their tongues fluttering through tattered lips as they uttered lewd remarks in hissing voices. Their torment had not curtailed the lusts and desires which had won them eternity here.

Kneeling beside Simon, she grasped the shackles on his wrists. They were difficult to open, but she managed to pry them apart, freeing first his left hand then his right.

He slumped against her then, and she held his weight until she could ease him back to the wall. As his head rolled back, she found herself looking into the caverns where his eyes had been.

Stringy bloody matter still clung to his cheeks, like tentacles stretched across his drawn, white flesh. He groaned as she cradled his head and ran a hand across his forehead.

"Easy now," she whispered.

He mumbled something. Apparently pain and loss of blood had put him into a delirious state.

"Simon, can you hear me?"

He didn't respond, but his head shifted slightly as if he might have heard. Evidently he was somewhat disoriented.

"Simon, I'm going to help you," she said. "I know it hurts. I'm going to do something for your eyes."

She tugged the scarf from her throat and wrapped it around his face. She wasn't sure if it would do any good, but she hoped it would slow the flow of blood or at least absorb some of it.

He sat up on his own then, supporting his weight. She took his arm, and helped him to his feet.

She turned to Samael now. "Let me take him out of here too, he needs help."

The demon's eyes seemed even more clouded then before. He took a step toward her before he spoke. "You would take him home?"

"For my daughter mostly, but yes. Even with what he's done, I will help him."

"A good deed wins no grace from me, even though I find it interesting."

"What do I have to do to get out of here?" she asked.

The demon grinned. "There are possibilities."

He was about to reach out for her again, when Simon pushed her aside and dropped to his knees. His hands shot forward, aimed in the direction of Samael's voice.

At the top of his voice he screamed something, a word alien to Gabrielle's ears. He followed it with a string of other words from some odd language.

From the tips of his fingers a light began to tingle, and then in an instant the light turned into a blaze. In a cloud of orange and blue the light exploded forward toward the demon.

Gabrielle shielded her eyes against the heat that was produced, but she continued to watch as the cloud billowed through the air, reminding her of a nuclear explosion.

Samael did not move as the cloud enveloped him. He

stood still, the orange billow surrounding him before he could resist. He screamed, not in pain but in anger as the flame wrapped around him.

"Die, you bastard," Simon called as the flame continued to chew at the air. The portion of his face not covered by the cloth was twisted in anger.

"Bastard," he shouted again.

In the next instant, the flame was gone, and the demon stood there unharmed, wisps of white smoke dancing off his flesh. He lowered his head, and his jaw seemed to drop open.

His shout was in the same language Simon had used, just as coarse and guttural. Gabrielle jumped away from the magician just as swirling clouds of flame burst onto him.

He screamed in agony as his flesh burned away from his body, and as the flame continued, he began to writhe about inside the cloud.

Through the flame, Gabrielle could see him crumbling, flesh dropping away, then bone. She didn't bother to watch any longer. Rushing forward, she snatched Heaven into her arms and ran past the cluster of Gnelfs.

Seeing her movement, Danube, who had been crouched near the door, acted as well. For some reason, he dashed toward the smoldering form of the magician, but he paused only for a moment over the body which had turned to ashes. Then, meeting her at the doorway, he pushed her through, curling his injured hands around the edges of the huge panel.

As the Gnelfs rushed after them, he shoved the door forward into place. Then he was behind her, running with her along the hallway.

She heard the door burst open, but she didn't look back as she threaded her way through the narrow corridor. She felt the sickening things slithering beneath her shoes, but she ignored them. She had to concentrate on finding the exit.

Heaven was heavy in her arms, an almost unbearable

weight, as she tried to hurry through the darkened passages. Cries of torment came from the rooms on either side of her.

As they reached a point where the passage widened, Danube reached up and tugged a torch free of its holder. Then he put an arm around Gabrielle's shoulders and urged her forward.

One of the black things on the floor reared up at them, its mouth hanging open to expose fangs. Danube dipped the torch down, letting the flame force the thing backward.

Then they were moving again, racing down the jagged hallway. Gab almost slipped when one of the floor dwellers moved beneath her foot, but Danube steadied her.

Behind them now, the Gnelfs' footsteps were echoing, as was the cackling laughter. Samael might not follow, but he had dispatched his minions or at least had given them free reign.

"We can't outrun them," she said.

"We can try." He gave her a slight push, and they moved along the last stretch of the corridor. At the main door they moved together out onto the narrow walkway which stretched out across the canyon.

Easing Heaven to the ground, Gabrielle took her hand, unwilling to risk balancing her in her arms as they traversed the chasm. "Don't look down, baby," she warned. "This is just like walking on a fence or something. Understand?"

Heaven nodded.

"Be brave. You're a big girl."

"Yes, ma'am."

"Let's go then."

They started out onto the crossway. Ignoring her own advice, Gab looked down at the slithering masses beneath her.

They had covered half the distance across when the Gnelfs broke from the castle. Danube was waiting for them and drove the torch into the face of the first one that emerged from the doorway.

That sent the creature backward into his brethren. His green hands clutched at his face, and he screamed in agony.

Pushing him aside, two more Gnelfs came at Danube. Raising the torch, he touched it to the clothing of one of the demons. The cloth ignited immediately, and the Gnelf began to flail about.

Before the other one could move, Danube swung the torch like a baseball bat, striking the creature across its small rib cage. The force of the blow sent it sprawling. Before it could gain control of its movements, it went over the edge.

Screams rose up from the pit as it fell amid the serpents which quickly moved to entwine it. Like anything that fell into the pit, it was subject to the tortures.

Now Gabrielle understood the motivation of the demons in the biblical story. She could see that living amid the swine would be preferable to this place. Hell must be even worse.

Holding her breath, forcing herself to look straight ahead, she rushed Heaven on across the bridge.

Turning to hurl the torch, like a spear, into the remaining Gnelfs, Danube then ran across the bridge himself. Behind him, the creatures danced about, some of them enveloped in flames. They were susceptible to fire for some reason, and several more plunged over the edge, their screams rising as they fell.

Danube didn't look down as he ran, didn't worry about misplacing his steps. He just tried to keep his course straight, mustering as much speed as his weary muscles would allow. He was near collapse, and it showed in his movements. Still, he managed to cover the distance quickly, and he hoisted Heaven into his arms when he reached Gabrielle.

Gabrielle didn't argue. In spite of his wounds and exhaustion, Danube managed to carry the child. Who knew what power he might be calling on for support.

She followed him as they worked their way down the path which had brought them to this place. It seemed more treacherous now with its cracks and holes. She tried to ignore the voices of the Gnelfs that still pursued them, but she was unable to shut out the sounds. They were bent on destruction, and they swore and spat out curses, their weapons clanging, sending echoes of warning.

"We can't fight all of them," she said through gasps for air as she ran along at Danube's side.

"I am trying to think of something," he said.

"Even if we reach the shore, will the boatman take us back?"

"Crossing the gulf is not our immediate concern," Danube replied.

Chapter 24

The village was still a jumble of lumbering forms when they reached the base of the trail. The figures continued to shamble about, ignoring the humans in their midst as they continued their endless trek toward nothingness.

With Heaven still in his arms, Danube began to lead the way through the tangled mass of bodies. The beings bumped into each other, stumbled, and fell, only to pick themselves up and try again.

There seemed to be more of them now, thousands swarming the narrow pathways that zigzagged through the landscape. They were like a wall. Running was impossible here, but for a few moments Gabrielle was glad of that, even with the Gnelfs pursuing. Her lungs were begging for relief.

"We can make our way down to the shore," Danube said. "If they catch us there, we will have to stand and fight."

Dodging a rotting figure with long silver hair and a sunken face, Gabrielle voiced her agreement with one syllable and they began their attempt to break through the group.

The bodies did not part for them. They moved so determinedly on their course that they were almost impassable. Danube managed to step around one, and then another so that he and Heaven became something like a stone in the stream of minions flowing around them, but passage was slowed as he sought another opening to move forward.

Gabrielle moved with even more difficulty, finding it almost impossible to break into the group. When she pushed through in front of one form, she felt the fingers of panic crawl up her back. It was terrifying to be trapped in the midst of these things. They brushed against her, and the touch of their putrid flesh made her cringe.

She groped her way past the second row of them, struggling to keep Danube in sight. He had made it into the middle of the flow now and was weaving through a twisted tangle of walking corpses.

Heaven's head was lifted above the crowd, her eyes wide as she took it all in, terrified. Gabrielle wanted to shout to her, to tell her not to watch; but she had to concentrate on her own passage.

Behind her she could hear the horrible voices of the Gnelfs. She didn't dare look back over her shoulder because she feared becoming entangled among the moving bodies and being dragged away. She didn't have to look back anyway. She knew the Gnelfs would be making their way through the crowd also, and with their smaller bodies, they would have a better chance of moving quickly.

"Danube," she yelled above the crowd. "They're coming."

He looked back only briefly to acknowledge that he'd heard her. Then he continued forward. A large, gray figure bumped into him, but he put his shoulder into the figure's chest, diverting him.

Gabrielle felt as if she were smothering. Tilting her head back, she tried to keep her face aimed toward the gray sky. She could not shut out the foul smell that rose from the bodies, but she could at least see more than just the withered faces and cracked skin that surrounded her.

A scream tried to escape from her throat, but she stifled it. Danube might think it was caused by something other than fear and try to help her. He had to keep moving. Even if she couldn't make it out of this mass, perhaps he could break free and take Heaven to safety.

She saw that he was nearing the edge of the herd. Holding Heaven protectively, he nudged and elbowed his way through the bodies, making a path for himself.

Each time he pushed a few aside, others stumbled into their places. He was beginning to appear more and more exhausted. Only determination seemed to keep him going.

Gabrielle forced herself to exert the same determination. Using her hands, she pushed at the forms around her, lashing out at them, twisting and forcing herself through the spaces between them.

"Let me through, you bastards. Let me through."

The razzing voices of the Gnelfs followed her. They were weaving through the corpses' legs. That made her work even harder. In a few moments, they would be grabbing at her calves, perhaps tripping her so that she would be trampled by the lumbering monsters.

She looked ahead again and saw Danube breaking free of the moving bodies. He had made it, and Heaven was still clutched in his arms.

Ducking her head, Gabrielle followed, proceeding as quickly as the corpses would allow. They brushed past her and bumped into her continuously, making her carom about, but finally she was only a few feet behind Danube again.

Her breath was rasping now, her lungs dry and heavy. She steadied herself only for a moment before moving ahead, now at Danube's side.

They hadn't traveled far before she heard the Gnelfs breaking out of the crowd as well. Danube spun around, looking back at the line of creatures as they approached.

Gabrielle turned also, ready to claw at the monsters or do whatever was necessary to keep them away from Heaven. She clenched her fists. She had not had a physical confrontation since high school, but she was ready for whatever might happen.

Danube's hand fell against her arm, checking her movement. She realized he had set Heaven on her feet.

"We cannot stop them by force," he said. "There are too many."

"You were fighting them like a madman a few minutes ago."

"That was to hold them back. I thought we could get away."

She jerked her head around toward him, looking at his face for an instant before glancing back toward the approaching crowd. "What do we do then?"

"Heaven has to do it," Danube said.

Gab felt her heart flutter, and she glared at him. "What?"

"They were originally summoned through her. Her thoughts gave them the form they are still using. Only she can banish them."

Gabrielle dropped to her knees at her daughter's side, wrapping her arms around the child to protect her. "What can she do?"

Danube also knelt, dropping one hand onto Heaven's shoulders. The Gnelfs were moving faster, the blades of their weapons swishing in the air.

The one called Gnelf Master was at the forefront, a pitchfork clutched in his hands. The fangs in his mouth curled down through his lips as his grin twisted up his cheeks.

"So little one, you're still here. Didn't we tell you everyone would suffer?"

Grabbing Gabrielle's sleeve, Heaven buried her face against her mother's shoulder in fear.

"Do not be afraid," Danube said to her. "They have no power over you. They were summoned to torment you, but the spells are gone. Turn to them, rebuke them."

Hesitantly, Heaven eased her face away from Gabrielle's shoulder and looked at Danube. "Tell them you want them to go away," Danube said.

The Gnelfs were pausing but not retreating. They hovered at their leader's shoulder, their heads tilted forward. The anger in their eyes made them look like wild beasts eyeing prey.

"We will destroy you all," Gnelf Master said.

"No," Heaven screamed, anger and defiance in her voice. "Leave us alone. Quit hurting Mommy."

"Little one, you have no say," Gnelf Master warned. "None at all." He jagged the pitchfork in front of him as if to punctuate his remarks.

"Go away," Heaven shouted. "Go away and leave me alone."

The creature stabbed a finger toward Danube. "You have no sway here. This is our realm."

"Your realm, but you still hold the form you used to come into our world. The form you took from Heaven's thoughts. Enough. The summoning is over. She is not a conduit for you any longer. She has chosen to close the gate."

Nervously the Gnelfs began to grumble among themselves. They were not able to fight his words, and they began to shudder.

"Clear your thoughts of them," Danube commanded. "You too, Gabrielle."

Clutching Heaven against her, Gabrielle forced her mind to go blank. She created a black field and concentrated on keeping it oblique.

"Think of something else, baby," she urged. "Think of pretty things. Lace and flowers and bluebirds."

She was reminded of a Zen exercise she'd encountered while in college. They had been discussing something called a double bind, and the instructor had said, "Whatever you do, don't think of a green elephant."

Of course that was impossible. The first thing the motion-picture screen in the brain did was set off a reel of green elephants. It was the kind of thing radio advertising depended on. In her own head, she fought the images, holding them back from her black field, but how could she help a five-year-old control her thoughts?

The Gnelfs began to inch forward. She could hear their small feet scraping across the dry dust. They were losing steam but not giving up.

"Baby, listen to me," she said. "I want you to picture a big wide field, but whatever you do, don't think of any blue elephants grazing there. Don't think of that at all. You can think of birds or flowers, but not blue elephants."

"Mommy, I can't help it."

The Gnelfs' growls seemed to indicate pain now. They were frightened. They stomped the ground and rattled their weapons.

Danube placed himself between Heaven and the group. He would be able to provide some delay if they charged, but that would not be enough if Gabrielle was unsuccessful.

As she concentrated on maintaining the black field and continued making suggestions to Heaven, Gab realized she hated deceiving the child, even in this situation, but there was no choice.

"Mommy will have to spank you if you think of those blue elephants," Gabrielle scolded. "And I don't want you to picture pink monkeys on their backs."

"Mommy, I can't help it if you say it," Heaven shouted.

"You'd better. Don't think of those elephants. Don't look at them plucking orange sunflowers with their trunks."

"Mommieeeeeeeeeeeee."

The Gnelfs charged, Gnelf Master in the lead. He extended the pitchfork, aiming it at Danube's midsection.

Stepping slightly to the side, Danube grasped the weapon's handle and forced the shaft backward so that the tip struck the Gnelf in its midsection.

The Gnelf was forced backward into the others, and they all tangled around him, spilling backward.

Angry, the little monster got to his feet and ran toward Danube, preparing to rip at him with his bare hands. Danube caught him beneath his armpits and, lifting him, slammed him to the ground with a loud thud.

Blood showed on Danube's bandages now, and he staggered as he braced himself for the approach of the others. They didn't hurry, but they jangled their weapons and roared, a mob out for vengeance.

Heaven was on the verge of tears. With her eyes closed, she chewed her lower lip, her features twisted as she tried to obey her mother's command.

"Quit telling me," she said. "Every time you say something it comes into my mind before I can help it."

"Green birds aren't perched on the monkeys' shoulders, are they?"

Heaven stomped her feet, struggling to empty her mind. Before Gab could offer another suggestion, she screamed. The sound rose loudly, piercing the dry air, and in the same instant, the Gnelfs began to shudder.

Weapons slipped from their grasps, and their bodies seemed to quiver from within.

Gabrielle allowed herself to stare at them now, even as she continued whispering to Heaven, calling up every form she could imagine to keep her daughter's thoughts off the Gnelfs.

In the next instant, she saw Danube stepping toward her, pulling something from the folds of his coat. It was charred and black, and at first she wanted to keep him away. She thought he had been struck by some madness and was trying to harm Heaven after all.

He forced her hands aside without speaking and pushed the object he held down onto Heaven's head. It was the reason he had knelt beside Simon's ashes. He had pulled this small metal skullcap from the remains, and now Heaven wore it. It fit loosely, but he held it in place.

"It will protect her thoughts now," he said, brushing soot away from the twisted images on the helm's surface. They seemed to be Greek or Hebrew in origin, not evil symbols at all but those that might be found in biblical manuscripts.

"Sorcerers use signs of light to protect them," Danube explained. "This will do the same for her."

With the helm in place, the Gnelfs seemed to melt, their green flesh peeling away and dropping from them like wet clay. When they burst apart, the vision was not something Gabrielle could easily comprehend. They were not without form exactly, but their forms defied her frame of reference.

They were dark things, shadowlike with gleaming eyes; and deprived of their previous shells, they scrambled about wildly. Or were they floating, like thin black veils dropped toward the ground?

The sounds they made were filled with terror, and they seemed to be seeking cover. Some of them tried to dart back toward the crowd of corpses.

Others tried to sink into the gray powder, but from above the flutter of leathery wings sounded.

Danube looked up, and ducked abruptly as one of the winged things swept down. It was not after him, however. It swooped over him and dipped, snatching at one of the dark things in its claws before beating its wings to gain an upward lift.

Quickly, Danube peeled his coat off and held it in front of him the way a matador might hold a red cloth. Cautiously, he then crept back to Gabrielle's side.

She was hugging Heaven now, clutching her tightly against her breast and cooing to her.

"Everything's all right, baby," she said. "Everything's going to be all right."

More of the winged creatures came down, ear-piercing screeches raking from their beaks as they snatched even more of the veils.

"Makes sense that they wanted to venture to our realm," Danube said. "The torment for all beings is continuous here."

"Will they hurt us?" Gab shouted.

"We don't belong here. For a while they'll ignore us."

He draped an arm around Gab's shoulder and led her down to the shore.

The boatman waited there in front of the gondola. His ragged hand stretched slowly forward for Gabrielle's arm, and he helped her aboard.

The trip back across the gulf seemed to take an eternity, but gradually the agonizing cries from the shore faded. Gabrielle concentrated on comforting her daughter.

Heaven was crying, but she appeared relieved, and with each sob, more tension seemed to flow from her body.

When they reached the far shore, Danube helped Gab from the boat, then hoisted Heaven into his arms.

"Was that real?" Gab asked. "Or some nightmare from that bastard's conjuring. Did we imagine it?"

"Is anything real?" Danube responded.

"Is the path to reality still open?" Gabrielle was still tense.

Danube nodded, then eased Heaven into Gab's arms where she seemed to want to be.

They walked a short distance, moving to the edge of the infinite darkness. Gab looked past the entrance they were about to take. Another path diverged, curling upward toward a blanket of light.

"You could go there now?"

Danube paused, his shoulders sagging with weariness. He turned his face toward the golden glow, and a gentle breeze seemed to emanate from it, sweeping back his hair and ruffling his beard.

"I could," he agreed. For a moment, he continued to look toward the bright blaze, but then he took Gabrielle's arm and guided her into the void.

Chapter 25

Gab's head felt heavy as it lay on her pillow, her eyes peering through the darkness at the small digital clock on her night stand. It had been a gift from Dave one Christmas, its face always too bright, glowing like a college-football scoreboard.

At one time she had kept it turned face down so that the numerals didn't blaze into her consciousness if she inadvertently shifted her face in their direction in her sleep.

Now she watched them, watched the colon between the hours and minutes blink with each passing second, watched the minutes click past.

12:45
12:46
12:47
. . .
1:25
. . .
2:31
. . .
2:45

She always knew what was coming, and did not really need the clock. Watching it only occupied her thoughts as she waited. She never knew the exact moment, only that it was on its way. As the minutes clicked past, and that moment drew nearer, her heartbeat quickened. It was harder to draw breath, and nothing could quell her anticipation.

3:00

3:01

3:02

3:03

And Heaven screamed, the sound piercing the night. Gab always rushed up when she heard the sound, flipping back the covers and hurrying down the carpeted hall to her daughter's side.

Sitting on the edge of the bed, she held Heaven's hand and stroked her hair. She touched her shoulder, noticed the slope of her cheeks and the way the braces on her teeth made her lips protrude.

No matter how much she urged her daughter to relax, and no matter how much counseling they sought, the dreams always returned. And with them the fear.

Heaven could not stop dreaming about the Gnelfs. In sleep she was vulnerable to whatever her subconscious trotted out, and they both lived in fear that at some point the dreams would be enough to bring them back.